Mother

Amir Clayton Powell

Mother

by Amir Clayton Powell

Published by Praying Mantis Press, PO Box 868, Remsenburg, NY 11960 • publisher@oldschooljournal.com

Phone: (571) 210-5382

First Edition: 2026

International Standard Book Number: 979-8-9964152-0-5

Printed in the United States of America

Dedicated to:

Glenna, LaVerna, Nellie, Debbie, Betty Francis, Jeannie, Linda, Doris, Emma, Pearl, Kathy, Mildred, Jean, Joyce, Pam, and Vickie.

Thank you for teaching me how to love and respect women.

Acknowledgements

Over the years, I have been blessed with the opportunity to witness various relationships between sisters. I was in high school when I realized my mother and her sister, Betty Francis (whom I also call "Auntie" and "Mommy II"), shared a unique relationship. It became apparent to me from there that sisters possess a bond that, dare I say, transcends space and time. The story of *Mother* revolves around the special relationship shared by sisters. Whether they are born into the same family or become bonded together through a family of their own making, I have always appreciated the affinity women have for each other when they decide to be bound to one another through that special relationship called sisterhood. So, I would like to offer a heartfelt "Thank you" to Debbie and Betty Francis, Tracey and Candace, Doris and Emma, Kisha and Kindra, Linda and Diane, and of course, Maddy, Bia, and Osh. You may not have noticed me watching, but your love for each other has had a profound effect on me and this work.

Speaking of this work, *Mother* would not have been possible were it not for the inspiration I drew from the seminal work of the great Anthony T. Browder, founder and director of IKG Cultural Resources. One of the best things I have ever read remains to be *Nile Valley Contributions to Civilization: Exploding the Myths, Vol. 1*. I got a copy during my freshman year in college, and the force of Browder's research has continued to inspire me ever since. To be sure, the work of other authors helped shape the world of *Mother* and its characters. These works include *They Came Before Columbus: The African Presence in Ancient America* by Ivan Van Sertima; *The African Origin of Civilization: Myth or Reality* by Cheikh Anta Diop; *Stolen Legacy* by George G. M. James; and *The Strange Career of Jim Crow* by C. Vann Woodward.

And I would also be remiss if I did not acknowledge the initial idea that blossomed into the world of supernatural beings based on Kemetic deities, intergalactic empires, and star-crossed lovers. On 3 March 1993, along with six other young men, I crossed the burning sands to enter the oasis that is Alpha Phi Alpha Fraternity Inc. Alpha Phi Alpha, founded in 1906 at Cornell University, dubbed our seven founders as the "Jewels". Since there were seven of us, our line was acknowledged as a "Jewel Line". The Big Brothers named our line the Seven Sons of Chaos. Individually, we were named Batmyte, Godzuki, Rasta, Dr. Frank N' Boots, Scarecrow, Praying Mantis, and Crip.

When our chapter advisor, the late, great Kevin D. Williams, explained the name of our line to us, that was the first time I heard the story of Chaos, the primordial cosmic soup from which the universe itself came into being. As an avid comic book fan, I could think of only one thing from that point on: turn the Seven Sons of Chaos into a superhero team. Yeah, it took me more than thirty years to bring the science fiction version of the Seven Sons to life, but better late than never.

So, to my Sands, the real-life Seven Sons of Chaos, I say "Thank you" for being the true heroes you are to your families, colleagues, and communities. Individually and collectively, you have been an inspiration to me since 1993. There would be no World of Mother without you. Love y'all!

Hawwah Menewa

The One Who Lives: Mother of All Living

Table of Contents

CHAPTER 1
AFTER THE FALL

Heart pounding, breath heavy. Mind racing. H presses her back into the smooth, cold stone she found in the middle of the dimly lit cavern. She taps the back of her head against the tall, dark pillar.

"Stupid! Stupid!" H screams in her head, jamming her head more forcefully into the stone behind her. "This can't be real… can it?" H thinks hysterically to herself.

Concentrating on her fears so intensely, she does not notice that the stone has cracked from her head thumping against it. Her hands grip the sides of the column of stone as if she were holding onto it for dear life. The air is chilly and damp.

She pushes her back so hard against the column that her head and back make an impression on it. Again, she does not notice that the imposing, hard stone is giving way to her flesh. She peeks around the column to her left, then to her right. Fear grips her. She cannot seem to regain control of her emotions.

The column is tall and wide, reaching high into the darkness. Hiding behind this stone pillar, she wonders if it will serve as enough of a barrier to protect her from what approaches. Something truly terrifying has been hunting her since she entered this cave.

"Why did I do this?" she breathes in exhaustion.

Her breath remains heavy. Her mind is still racing. Her heart pounds so hard now that its beats ring in her ears. The constant drumming only heightens her anxiety. She feels like her heart might explode.

H begins to comb through her memories, thinking back to how she got here. She was wandering along the river basin when she saw a man. It was difficult to see him, except that on his back was a pair of beautiful, glowing wings. She had never seen anyone or anything like him before.

Before she realized it, she had followed the man over several miles. She even hiked up and over a hill to find the entrance to this cave. She did not imagine all this would have happened from a simple act of curiosity. *There is nothing wrong with being curious,* she thought. In this case, her curiosity might lead to her death.

H had left the surviving members of her family only a few days before. Her husband passed many years ago. Her oldest son moved across the sea and deep into the mountains. She has not heard from him in so long that she does not know if he is still alive. Her second son died tragically.

Mother

Things were already hard between her and her husband, and the death of their son only drove them further apart. She did her best to make her husband love her. She genuinely and truly desired him, his attention, his affection, his companionship, his lust, but he seemed more driven by ruling over her. Their relationship remained this way until he passed.

Her youngest has his own family now. His children grew up and created families of their own. In fact, he now looks older than H. Time stood still for her. While everyone around her grew older, she did not.

Wrinkles developed in the skin on her husband's face and hands. Her skin remains tight and smooth. She has not even been so much as sick in the last one hundred years. H left her family, hoping they would think she had died. Her son and grandchildren were beginning to ask her questions she could not answer. And not because she did not want to answer them. She simply has no answers to offer.

She has memories of the time before she was here with her husband. Images of her past glory circulate through the recesses of her mind. These absorbingly grand visions often cause H to wonder if they are real or just figments of her imagination.

Not to mention the strange dreams she has been having lately; she dreamed of herself flying, and not just through the sky with the birds, but among the stars. She has seen visions of herself expelling powerful beams of energy from her hands and eyes. She had another dream in which she lifted mountains and walked through fire without being burned.

She also saw herself wearing a crown, standing in front of throngs of cheering people. The dream she remembers most vividly dealt with her fighting a horrifying creature and defeating it with ease. H wishes someone would tell her what all this means.

The man with the glowing wings seemed like a connection between her dreams and the reality of her longevity and vitality. The other reason she followed him was that she believed that if she could get close enough to touch him, she could prove to herself that he was real, and maybe all the other things in her dreams were real, too. In other words, she needed confirmation that she was not losing her mind.

H followed the man for so long that the day turned into night, but the man was walking so fast that she lost sight of him. So, she could only follow the warm glow emanating from his wings.

At one point, she thought she caught up to the man and his glowing wings, but there was no man. There was no longer any glow, either. Instead, she found a monster.

H pondered for a very brief moment whether the beast had devoured the man. She prayed that she would not be next.

The column H clings to is but one natural pillar among a dozen or more littered across the center of this space. Strangely, the lack of light does not diminish her ability to see the details of the structures in the cavern. She can even see the depth and width of the chamber.

Over the last several years, she has noticed that her eyesight, especially in areas with little to no light, seemed to be much sharper than anyone else around her. She could also see things from afar when others could not. In fact, all her senses were more acute than those of her family and friends.

She could not only smell things from farther away, but she could also connect scents to people, places, and things. She had also grown much stronger than her son. Perhaps she was always stronger. That did not matter as much as the fact that she did not want anyone to know, which is the other reason why she left.

She felt like she was hiding so much from the people she loved. She was afraid they would no longer accept her if they discovered all the things she could do.

Rumors were beginning to circulate among her people about the giants who lived beyond the sea, in the lands where her oldest son made his home. The stories of the fierce might of the giants made people afraid. What if people became afraid of her because she possessed the same strength as the giants across the sea?

H felt like she could not shoulder any further rejection. Her husband had consistently rejected her since they were forced from their home, the land where they were born. He blamed her for their fall from grace, and she blamed herself, too.

She simply hoped her husband would eventually forgive her. She always believed his forgiveness would allow her to forgive herself. Now that he is gone, she doubts she will ever heal from the emotional wounds left open by their relationship.

She knows she will not ever get the chance to find out what healing feels like if the leviathan stalking her ends her life today. That sobering reality returns her focus to her present circumstances.

"Cave…" H breathes to herself. "Stop talking! Stop moving…" are her next thoughts.

As she regains control of her senses and slows her mind down, she can hear a reverberating trickle of water. Closing her eyes for an instant, she can hear the faster-moving water being fed by a creek streaming through the floor of the chamber.

This part of the cave looks expansive. And this brief moment of clarity seems like an eternity. The scent of moss fills her nostrils. And then, she suddenly catches a whiff of something else.

"Sulfur…" she whispers.

She lunges forward as an inescapable impulse to move overcomes her. As she travels through the air, the column explodes in a burst of flame and electricity, struck with tremendous force.

Everything surrounding H seems to move in slow motion as she lands hard on the cavern floor. She takes a deep breath, gathers herself, quickly scurries up onto her hands, and rolls over onto her back. The sudden leap carried her across the cavern, but not far enough away.

The beast is almost upon her.

H has finally come face-to-face with it now, a gigantic, fire-breathing dragon. Its large, dark form creeps across the chamber. She hears the clicking and scratching of its talons as it claws and slithers the length of the cavern toward her.

The stone floor beneath its feet cracks and crumbles under the pressure of its tremendous weight, its long tail dragging along the ground behind it. As the dragon continues to close in on her, it lifts its chest and spreads its massive wings like a cobra about to strike.

H can see the full view of its enormous frame. A warm glow emanates from the lingering flames falling from its mouth as it lowers its head to face her. She can see rows of sharp teeth lining its jaws. Its bottom jaw still gaping, a grin seems to form on its face.

H has previously encountered many dragons, but none has been this aggressive. Most dragons ignore humans so long as humans do not encroach upon their territory. Moreover, no other dragon she has ever seen has been this large and frightening.

Even more strange, H can perceive its thoughts; it seems to reason like a human. She can sense that killing her has nothing to do with hunger. It has not hunted her for food. It believes its "victory" to be imminent.

Its glowing eyes squint as it lunges forward with deadly potency.

"NNNOOOOO!" H exclaims with all her might.

Closing her eyes instinctively, H thrusts her hands forward as if she were throwing a vigorous shove to push the dragon back. When her hands stop in front of her body, a massive bolt of energy explodes from her palms.

The energy blast pounds the dragon's snout with such intensity that its head snaps downward into its chest, folding it over onto itself. The force of the blast lifts it off the ground; its wings lurch open wide as it is thrown backward.

The dragon goes crashing through several columns and lands on the opposite side of the cavern.

H does not open her eyes immediately. Although she hears the loud sounds of the stone pillars continuing to crumble, she was still expecting to feel excruciating pain as the dragon's teeth ripped through her flesh and crushed her bones.

The distant sounds of breaking rocks finally encourage her to open her eyes. She flutters her eyes open to find the dragon stumbling about, dazed and confused.

Despite the darkness of the cave, she can see it as clearly as she would be able to see anything in the light of day. Still lying on her back, H looks at her hands. They continue to glow with a warm light. Strings of energy sizzle and crackle as they leap from her hands and send sparks shooting into the air as they strike the floor close to her body.

"Well, I'll be…" she says softly, followed by a whispered final thought, "I guess the dreams I have been having were not just dreams after all."

Scrambling to her feet, a burst of confidence fills her. A primal cry erupts from her lungs. In a flash, H traverses the cavern and is upon the dragon.

It lunges forward, viciously snapping at her. H dodges its attacks with ease. She swings her right fist. The blow lands on the side of the dragon's head, knocking the beast to the cavern floor.

H looks down, only to notice that she is hovering off the ground. She's flying. Her head is near the shelf of the cavern ceiling. She does not give any thought to wonderment, however.

She dives toward her foe, who manages to sweep its tail with enough force to knock H off her path. She slams into the ground. Her body tumbles violently across the cavern floor.

Feeling no pain, H stands up and resumes her attack with blistering speed. She flies straight into the beast and pushes it forcefully against a wall. The dragon tries to claw at H, but its huge claws miss with each swift swipe.

The dragon whips its tail in another attempt to strike H. This time, she catches its tail, locks her hands and forearms onto it, and rises high into the air. She spins herself around with fantastic speed, generating enough lift to throw the dragon upward and back across the cavern. Its colossal body smashes through more columns as it hurtles haplessly through the air.

Before it can land on the ground, H rockets toward her foe and pounds it with an overhand right punch. She then whizzes downward at such speed that she reaches the cavern floor before the dragon's body does. She lands, crouches, and then propels herself upward, striking the dragon under its chin with a brutal uppercut. The blow drives the dragon upward with such power that its snout is nearly imprinted in the ceiling of the cavern.

The dragon comes crashing down to the cavern floor and lies still. For a moment, H feels safe.

"Well done," the dragon says, laughing. "Very well done."

The gigantic creature begins to melt away, expelling sulfurous clouds as it diminishes. It disappears, leaving behind a naked man with huge, feathered wings that illuminate the darkness and long, flowing hair.

His body is well-muscled; his frame is flawless. His skin radiates with a pale, luminous glow, as if there is a fire roiling beneath it. His chiseled face tilts down as he clasps his arms around his knees.

Sitting before H, he finally looks at her. The monster was the man with the beautifully glowing wings.

H begins to feel strangely betrayed by her own senses.

"I'm impressed," the winged man remarks in a genuine tone. "I did not think you had it in you," he continues. "What's it been? Almost…" he gasps momentarily, "more than 900 years?" he asks, pretending to be surprised.

The man stands and walks closer to H. She notices his sizable genitals swinging back and forth as he walks.

"I mean, I did not hear any talk of your… death," he says flippantly, putting his hands up to his throat. "I had to come back around to see if you croaked. I had to know if He would actually let you die. His sons, of course. I do not know if you have looked into the future at all," the man rambles.

The man pauses, as if he is shocked by H's nonresponse. He looks H up and down.

"No?" he asks.

Pausing again, he continues to trace his eyes across H's body. H begins to feel strangely uncomfortable.

"Anyway… I mean, He goes on and on about destroying me, even. But not you, huh? You're still here."

He continues his ogling of H's frame and pretends to look around her body so that he can view her backside. He chuckles to himself, then resumes his soliloquy.

"I am just saying. I thought you would have been the first to go. But no, your poor old husband received the punishment that was probably meant for you."

He stops for an instant to sneer and licks his lips lustfully.

"How's your oldest boy? Real winner, that one! Definitely my favorite," he inquires.

An evil grin spreads over the man's face before he answers his own question.

"Oh, that's right…" he quips.

H immediately throws a left hook into the man's right temple. He somersaults at high velocity into a wall on the opposite side of the cavern.

Other winged men rush into the cavern. That is when H realizes these are not men at all. The leader of the host steps forward.

"Stand down, Hawwah," he says in a soft voice. He reaches out his hand and places it on her shoulder. "It's over… for now."

****

Sitting at a console in the control room, the very nerve center at the headquarters of the famed fixers for the queen of Planet Chaos, Arisone Hotep, hacker extraordinaire, has been running a live stream projecting visions from H's meditative dream state onto a panoramic screen in the viewing room across the hall.

Sitting in the viewing room are the leaders of the major planets, territories, and law enforcement agencies of the Ant-Galaxo Devearous System.

Ant-Galaxo Devearous is the name used by the people who live therein to describe both the nine planets in a solar system approximately eighty light-years from Planet Earth and the wider galaxy in which that solar system resides.

"Wait," Arisone says quizzically. "Should we be showing this part?"

Pausing the stream being broadcast into the viewing room across the hall, Arisone directs that question to her employer and leader of the group of professional fixers known as The Gatekeepers, Princess Sarah Dahlia Amun.

Professionally, Princess Sarah is known as The Sphinx. She is the adopted daughter of Queen Hawwah Menewa I, leader of Planet Chaos, who is endearingly referred to as "H" by her family and friends.

Princess Sarah's birth father is a notorious space pirate, Captain LionMane, and her mother is Lady Biffu Djoser, the wife of the influential ambassador to Planet Chaos from Planet Memphis, Envoy Amun Djoser. While the queen has always publicly maintained that Princess Sarah is the biological daughter of such a prolific criminal, the identity of her biological mother has remained hidden from the public.

H agreed to adopt Sarah as a favor to her friend, Envoy Djoser, who agreed to not only remain married to Lady Biffu but also refrain from levying any form of punishment against his wife for her indiscretion, whether legal or socially acceptable.

The young princess grew up with the knowledge of her true parentage but was told by her adopted mother to keep her birth mother's identity a secret. Through the years, H made sure that Sarah and Biffu got ample opportunity to connect and know one another. And Sarah benefited greatly from H's undivided attention in the privacy of their home within the palace.

All throughout Princess Sarah's childhood, if H was not dealing with state affairs, H served as a very present and doting mother. In fact, the queen would not meet her current husband for 2,202 years after Sphinx's birth.

While Sphinx does not possess any of her adopted mother's phenomenal paranatural abilities, she is a Drākanashim, or Drāk, like her biological father.

The Drākanashim are an ethnic group of Eshanashim, the general term for the people inhabiting the Ant-Galaxo Devearous System, whose DNA has been combined with the genomes of various animal species.

Sphinx's particular physiology represents a mixture of human genomes combined with those of various genera of large cats, but predominantly *panthera tigris*, that is to say, the tiger. Microscopic hairs cover her body, giving her the appearance of having burnt orange skin with distinctive black stripes on her thighs and back.

The hair on her head blends the burnt orange and black motif into what looks like a tiger's tail when she wears her hair in a ponytail, which she often does. Like most Drāks, Princess Sarah is often referred to by the animal with which her genes are combined. People describe her as a "tigress" or simply a "tiger," as they might also refer to a human-elephant hybrid Drāk as an "elephant."

Physically, Sphinx is stronger than the strongest human on Earth. Her muscle and bone density match those of an adult female tiger, making her extremely agile and durable. She can run at speeds in excess of forty miles per hour and leap more than ten feet into the air on a vertical jump.

As a warrior, H had Sphinx trained by some of the best combat instructors on Planet Chaos. Sphinx achieved the rank of a 2nd Level Master in the predominant Kemetic system of martial arts. She is a master swordsman, an exceptional marksman as both an archer and a sharpshooter using firearms. In fact, her preferred weapon is her customized radiator.

Among the Eshanashim, a "radiator" is a type of laser blaster that can emit lethal and nonlethal laser beams. Colloquially, radiators are also referred to as "heaters."

Amazingly beautiful, the princess also ranks among the 100 most intelligent Eshanashim alive. She shares this distinction with several members of her family, including her younger sister, Princess Libby; her mother, Queen Hawwah; and her older brother, Prince Adisa, her nephew, the son of Prince Adisa, and Elder Wells, Prince Imhotep II.

Sphinx was given her *nom de guerre* by her enemies, based on the Greek legend of the winged creature with the head and breasts of a woman and the body of a lion that posed a riddle to travelers attempting to pass into Thebes, devouring them if they failed to answer correctly. "Sphinx" is a term that derives from a Greek word, which means "to strangle."

Sphinx became famous for carrying nanotech choker collars that deliver electroshocks to the wearer. She uses these "Chokers of Truth" to compel the suspects she interrogates to tell her the truth.

An avid admirer of Greek mythology, Princess Sarah accepted the moniker of the Sphinx, thinking it aptly described her both physically and professionally.

On this occasion, Sphinx presents a very pensive demeanor. She is very protective of her mother and will do anything to protect their family. After all, other than H's sister, Zilpha, also known as Lady Photon, and Zilpha's husband, Amen Hotep VI, better known as Starlyte, no one has been in H's inner circle longer than Princess Sarah.

Moreover, only a few people are as close to H as Zilpha, whom H affectionately refers to as "Z," and Sphinx. With so much at stake, Sphinx is determined to get everything right.

"This part is fine. What we want to screen are acts of questionable legality," Sphinx responds in an almost joking manner.

She is doing her best to keep her team loose while not showing any sign of how stressful this situation has become for her. As always, she leads by setting the example.

"You know, I have been meaning to ask you, Chief… do you worry that someone, even someone in the next room, might try to take a shot at the queen while she is in her dream state?" Arisone asks cautiously.

"They would have to get through us first. Besides, I do not think anyone will try anything with Colonel GiantStar and his team standing post," Sphinx says with a smirk, but firmly.

She points to the security monitors showing the team of Planet Chaos special forces operatives posted at strategic positions around the facility. In fact, soldiers stand post outside both the control room and the viewing rooms across the hall.

"I'm so glad they're here," Arisone replies with an exasperated exhale.

The two teammates share a nervous laugh. As soon as the moment of levity passes, Sphinx resumes her rumination on how this situation is no laughing matter.

Several hours ago, the horrifying news that thousands of children disappeared from schools around the globe on Planet Chaos came to light. In fact, throughout the day, further accounts have circulated that more than 33,000 children in total have been reported missing from schools throughout the Ant-Galaxo Devearous System.

C'mon, Mom... find these kids! Sphinx thinks to herself.

CHAPTER 2
THE MORNING OF

Hours before the alarming revelation that thousands of children suddenly disappeared from each of the major planets and moon colonies across the Eshanashim solar system, many of the planetary leaders now gathered in The Gatekeepers' viewing room were engaged in their daily routines.

Queen Hawwah and her husband, King-Consort Armacaust Menewa I, were making love in the moments before they would receive the announcement. As they do most mornings, even after being married for 215 years, Armacaust and H explore each other's naked bodies before undertaking their public duties.

Armacaust becomes almost uncontrollably aroused at catching the mere scent of his wife. For her part, H enjoys the attention she receives from her husband. The king is a very nice-looking man, but certainly not the most beautiful man the queen has ever seen.

But Armacaust dotes on H as if she were the most beautiful, interesting woman he has ever met. The funny thing is that Armacaust may sincerely see H that way. And that is more attractive and meaningful to H than anything any other man could ever offer her.

It is no secret that the future king held H as one of his idols when he was a young soldier in the Planet Chaos Planetary Defense Forces Joint Command, commonly referred to as the PDFJC. Now that he is married to her, he does not waste an opportunity to hold her close, consuming her warmth and gorging himself on the aroma of her natural musk by burying his nose in her hair or nestling his face between her breasts.

Both Armacaust and his brother, Idris, better known as CavalierStar, joined the PDFJC as soon as they graduated from the University of the Eshanashim's College of Military Sciences. Their younger sister, Neferure, received her legal letters from the university's College of Governance + Legal Studies.

Armacaust and CavalierStar also joined the PDFJC Special Forces Corps. Their courage and fighting skills allowed them to rise swiftly through the ranks. CavalierStar eventually accepted a commission in the Planet Chaos Naval Service, also referred to as "PNav."

Armacaust elected to remain in the PC Special Forces Corps. In Year 9066, he received an assignment to lead the security detail for a grieving Queen Hawwah, who requested to be in isolation for a period of not less than one year after returning from her 152-year sojourn on Planet Earth.

Armacaust leaped at the chance to be close to the queen. He was assigned six special forces operatives and sent to guard the queen at her private residence deep in the heart of the central region of New Kemet Province. For the next several months, he watched over H.

He was the only operative allowed inside her home. He strategically stationed the rest of his team around the grounds of the queen's complex.

He watched the queen as she ate her meals. He accompanied her as she went running and hiking through the lush rainforests of the region. Occasionally, he would even discuss subjects like paleontology with H if she came across a fossil discovery or other fascinating find.

H took a liking to Armacaust. She admired his dedication to the corps and the empathy he demonstrated for the needs of his soldiers. She also appreciated his genuinely curious mind. She loved the fact that he did not feel the need to try to impress her. She understood that he would not ever ask to take her out on a date, so she created opportunities for them to engage in private conversation. She even curated unique experiences they could share while he performed his duties of keeping watch over her.

One day, after H completed her daily workout, she returned to the main house to shower and change for dinner. As always, Armacaust followed her into the house. Instead of waiting until she got to her bedroom, she began undressing right as she walked through the door. Surprised, Armacaust turned his head. She knew that while she was in the common area, he would have to watch her undress.

"Mother, wouldn't you be more comfortable disrobing in your bed chamber?" Armacaust asks respectfully.

"Yes and no, I suppose," H replies playfully. "I just feel so sweaty and icky, I thought I would get these wet clothes off as soon as I could."

She had already stripped down to her sports bra and panties. She was still wearing ankle socks and sneakers as she walked to her sink to wash her hands. Armacaust could hardly contain himself as he watched the beautiful queen gracefully glide across the floor to the kitchen.

She slyly glanced over her shoulder to make sure Armacaust was watching. After washing her hands, she walked over to the refrigerator and opened the door to look for a cold drink. She purposefully hinged at her hips to give him a full view of her voluptuous, luxuriantly shaped glutes.

H smiled as she could hear the special forces officer swallow with nervous anxiety. She pulled a glass bottle containing a pre-prepared post-workout fruit puree beverage from the second shelf and closed the refrigerator door. She turned toward Armacaust while pressing the bottle to her lips flirtatiously, slowly sipping the elixir. She stopped for a moment.

"Would you like a sip?" she asks Armacaust, extending the bottle toward him with one hand.

"No, but thank you, Ma'am," Armacaust responds politely.

"Ok, suit yourself. It's really tasty, though," she replies with a smile.

"I think I am going to, uh, check the perimeter now, Ma'am. If you need me, do not hesitate to reach out to me on the comms," he says hastily.

"Oh, you're leaving?" she asks, acting surprised.

While holding the bottle with one hand, she reaches down with the other hand and slips off her sneakers. She then pulls off her socks and tosses them one at a time toward the door. Her socks land close to where Armacaust is standing. He looks down at the socks lying on the floor rather than at the queen's bare feet.

"It's a shame that you're leaving. I thought we might discuss the methods to achieve proper fitness," she says flirtatiously.

"I should really go, Mother," he says flatly.

Refusing to take the hint, H rises off the floor and floats wistfully over to Armacaust. She lowers her feet back onto the floor right in front of him. His acute sense of smell betrays him as H's pheromones fill his nasal cavities.

For the past several weeks, he has believed himself to be in love with the queen, and now, in this moment, he is sure of it. He stands frozen. His consummate professionalism will not allow him to break protocol even for a moment. Still, he knows he cannot resist H if she were to touch him.

Armacaust closes his eyes briefly as H leans closer to him. She takes one of his hands and places it on her chest.

"Do I make you uncomfortable, Armacaust?" she asks softly, her lips curled into a devious smirk. "I promise, I won't hurt you."

Armacaust closes his eyes again. H is sweaty. Her current scent should repel him. Instead, he finds himself almost uncontrollably attracted to her in this moment.

She rises onto the tips of her toes. He opens his eyes to see H's beaming face, her eyes locked onto his. He cannot resist it any longer.

He pulls his hand away from H's chest and wraps both arms around her waist, pulling her up so that her face meets his. He kisses her passionately, squeezing her tightly.

They stop kissing only momentarily to gaze into each other's eyes in a breathy intermission.

"Now, was that so hard?" H asks playfully, still breathing heavily.

"More than you will ever know," Armacaust replies.

H laughs.

Continuing to hold H in his arms, Armacaust begins to carry her toward the bedroom.

"Finally!" H exclaims.

Armacaust chuckles, then kisses H once again. She grips the sides of his head with both her hands. Instead of laying her on the bed, he walks into the shower.

"Oh, good choice," H says breathlessly.

She removes one of her hands from his face and fumbles around for the shower knob. She finally locates it and turns on the water. The couple barely reacts to the initially cold water streaming over their bodies.

Armacaust places H's feet back on the floor. She removes her sports bra and helps him get out of his gear. She becomes immediately excited by his muscular frame.

Once naked himself, he assists her in slipping off her panties. They begin to kiss again. He lifts her and pulls her close.

She wraps her legs around his waist.

"I know your powers include the ability to grow, like to the size of a small moon," H asks, staring directly into his eyes. "But it would stand to reason that you can also enlarge any part of your body at any given time, no?"

"You're about to find out," Armacaust replies playfully.

Armacaust gently slides one of his hands to the small of H's back and grips her upper back tightly as he thrusts himself into her.

She throws her head back in surprise. "Oh… oh… ooohhhh… oooohhhhhh… you can!" she exclaims delightedly.

After finishing in the shower, they continue to make love repeatedly throughout the night.

In the morning, Armacaust tells H, "I must report my violation of protocol and offer my resignation from this assignment."

H tells him, "I understand." She then asks him, "What time should I expect you for dinner?"

He laughs and offers her a time. She kisses him goodbye and runs into the bathroom.

Later that evening, when Armacaust returns to H's private residence, he tells her, "I have been placed on a mandatory ninety-day leave."

H does not react but begins setting the table for dinner.

"I know. I ordered it," she says, looking at the table while she arranges the eating utensils.

"You ordered me to be placed on leave?" he asks with an air of indignation in his voice.

"I may be in a self-imposed isolation, but I am still the queen," she replies, looking at him with a smile. "And if we are going to figure out how we are going to be in a relationship while maintaining a rigorous public life, I thought it might be helpful if we had some time alone to sort through the possibilities."

"I see," he replies in a soft voice.

A broad smile spreads across his face. He crosses his arms and stands still for a moment.

"So, you want to be in a relationship with me?" he asks playfully.

"Well, we'll see," she replies, her eyes open wide.

They laugh together. Over the course of the next several years, their bond grows steadily deeper. Finally, in Year 9089, H happily accepted Armacaust's marriage proposal. The couple married in Year 9100. They have remained blissfully wed ever since. And the present morning is no different.

The rich, deep chocolate hue of H's skin seems to glow even in the dark, ambient light, bouncing off each of her supple curves. Today, H awoke and immediately wrapped her soft lips sensually around one of Armacaust's nipples. Adding her tongue to this act of foreplay was too much for him to resist.

Once he raised his head, she smiled and rolled over onto her front into a child's pose, arching her back so that her buttocks reached toward the ceiling, with her exquisite feet elevated in a perfectly pointed position while she buried the side of her face into the mattress.

Taking the hint, Armacaust accepted H's invitation. Losing themselves in the synchronized rhythm of their motion, breathing, and moaning, they had blocked out everything else until H suddenly stopped moving and pulled away from him.

She rolls over onto her back, a look of concern and sorrow spreading across her face.

"What's wrong?" he asks, with a tone of great concern.

"I don't know. I can sense great sadness… across the entire solar system…" she responds.

He responds by pulling her close and holding her tightly. Just then, the palace's emergency signals begin to sound.

****

Over four astronomical units, that is, 4 AU's, away from Planet Chaos, in the royal palace located in the capital city of Nubt on Planet Ikw-n-tA, commonly referred to as the Ant Planet, Lord Abasi Horus has completed his morning constitutional.

Abasi, who prefers to be called by his *nom de guerre*, Monolith Ant, is the supreme leader of the oligarchy that rules the Ant Planet. Ikw-n-tA is the largest and most industrialized planet in the Ant-Galaxo Devearous System.

Monolith Ant himself ranks among the most powerful enhanced Eshanashim. To be *enhanced* among the Eshanashim is what humans on Earth refer to as possessing superhuman abilities or superpowers. Although less than 1% of all Eshanashim are born enhanced, being born Eshanashim provides certain physiological advantages that would make them all seem superhuman to the average person born on Planet Earth.

Most Eshanashim can produce sustenance from sunlight. Similarly, because their planets have a heavier gravitational pull than Earth, the average Eshanashim is stronger and more physically durable than the average person born on Earth. The skin and bones of the Eshanashim can resist tremendous amounts of pressure and temperature extremes.

Like their Earth-born counterparts, Eshanashim women are born with millions of eggs; however, atresia occurs much more slowly in Eshanashim women, allowing them to have children at virtually any point throughout their long lives. And because their core temperature is far higher than their Earth-bound cousins, the Eshanashim are immune to infection from most Earth-borne pathogens.

On average, the Eshanashim live between 1,600 and 4,500 years. Drākanashim typically have shorter lifespans, living between 2,500 and 3,500 years on average. Only the Pens, the colloquial name for the ethnic group of Eshanashim related to the people of Planet Pen-Meroe, have shorter lifespans than Drāks among the Eshanashim.

Pens, formerly referred to as Drones, live between 1,600 and 2,600 years. Upon their death, many Eshanashim spontaneously combust, or their bodies disintegrate into a pile of ash.

Like humans born on Earth, the Eshanashim are yet susceptible to various forms of cancer and genetic disorders like diabetes, albeit deaths related to cancer or diabetes among the Eshanashim are far less prevalent compared to the people of Earth.

Like people on Earth, Eshanashim also suffer from mental health disorders such as bipolar disorder, chronic depression, and schizophrenia. Even though their lives are marked by longevity, they continually watch for what they have come to refer to as "signs of aging," or "SoAs," in themselves or their loved ones.

SoAs begin to appear in the last millennium of an Eshanashim's life. It could be anything, as simple as wrinkles, gray hair, or reduced libido. As an Eshanashim person enters the last century of their life, they begin to age like "Earth-bound" humans.

The people of the Ant Planet and Planet Memphis share a common ethnicity referred to as "Ikwentashim." Like the Drākanashim, the Ikwentashim possess distinct physical features, the primary difference being the hardened yet flexible brain stems, described as antennas, protruding from their heads.

These antennas are external extensions of their brains and central nervous systems. The antennas of the Ikwentashim heighten their senses of sight, smell, and touch, and allow them to communicate with each other telepathically, although they are not able to read minds.

Monolith Ant and Aharon Mandrake, the President of Planet Memphis, were among the first Eshanashim to undergo the procedure to create the antennas of the Ikwentashim. Later generations of Ikwentashim developed thicker skin, similar to the exoskeleton of ants on Earth, which makes them nearly bulletproof.

Ikwentashim are also physically stronger and more durable, on average, than other Eshanashim.

Monolith Ant stands at a commanding six feet and seven inches tall. The same set of circumstances that produced the original group of enhanced Eshanashim replaced Monolith Ant's skin with organic stone. His eyes glow with the color of molten lava.

Monolith Ant possesses the equivalent strength and durability of ten million planets the size of Jupiter in Earth's solar system. He can fly at speeds beyond escape velocity and emit powerful beams of plasma energy. He is capable of massive energy outputs equivalent to the energy output of multiple supernovas occurring at the same time.

Lord Monolith, as he is referred to by his subjects and those who fear him, is also considered to be one of the greatest military leaders in the Ant-Galaxo Devearous System.

Monolith Ant's surviving wife, Mistress Kiya, has arrived in his bedchamber to offer her assistance in helping Monolith Ant prepare to face the public. Although he hears Kiya's footsteps as she enters the room, he remains motionless, staring intently out of the large windows in his bedchamber.

"Undress and lie down," Monolith Ant orders without even acknowledging Kiya's presence.Today happens to be the anniversary of the passing of Monolith Ant's wife, Liya. It has been seventy-two years since Liya's death. Many close to the supreme leader speak of Liya as having died of a "broken heart."

Monolith Ant took Liya to serve as the "Second Wife" in his household as a means to solidify his relationship with the strongman leader of Planet Pen-Meroe, the late President Menes Aharon Joseph Drone I, better known as "MAJ." Many suspected MAJ to be engaged in an illegal interplanetary grooming and trafficking operation that took young women like Liya from families facing financial distress.

MAJ's grooming targets were taken from the various planets and colonies across the galaxy. It was rumored that MAJ's own wife, Lady Nebula, was kidnapped from Planet Chaos when she was only twelve years old and forced into a subservient marriage to MAJ.

MAJ groomed Liya by subjecting her to repeated sexual assault committed by his wealthy friends. Liya endured this life until she was ultimately sold into service to Monolith Ant in exchange for promises of increased trade between the two planets, as well as cooperation between the two leaders in contesting the growing influence of Queen Hawwah.

When Monolith Ant discovered the truth about Liya's past, he grew indifferent to her. He remained that way toward her throughout their entire relationship, seemingly blaming Liya for the abuse to which she was subjected in her youth.

On many mornings just like this one, Monolith Ant would have Liya ushered away by his aides without so much as a pleasant word. Dismissing Liya in such a manner usually indicated that he intended to have sex with Kiya.

Liya not only paled in comparison to Kiya in terms of physical beauty, but Liya also did not give birth to any children. The sexual abuse she suffered as a child and young woman may have likely caused irreversible damage to her reproductive system, rendering her virtually infertile.

Kiya, who many Eshanashim consider to be one of the most attractive women in the entire System, is the mother of all three of Monolith Ant's sons. Unbeknownst to most, the supreme leader also sired three daughters with paramours living on the Giza Moon Colony. The existence of his daughters has been a very closely guarded secret that will be threatened by the current calamity besetting the System.

Cruelly, when Monolith Ant became dissatisfied with Liya, he would routinely force her to watch him, and Kiya have sex. But today, Monolith Ant feels compelled to bear a remembrance for Liya. He takes a deep breath, then, exhaling, walks away from the window toward the bed, where Kiya lies naked, already pleasuring herself by massaging her genitals in anticipation of Monolith Ant mounting her.

Stepping away from the floor-to-ceiling windows in the corner of his spacious bedchamber, he begins to disrobe in his deliberate march toward the bed. Suddenly, the palace alarm begins to sound. The alert is deafening.

Kiya stops touching herself and sits up.

"Who dares!" Monolith Ant bellows.

"My Lord!" an aide exclaims as he bursts into the room without knocking. "They're gone. Just vanished. Reports are coming in from schools across the region that hundreds of children just vanished. Many have said there was a flash of light, and they were gone. Just gone. What are your orders, My Lord?" the aide continues breathlessly.

Monolith Ant stands silently, motionless. He takes another deep breath, takes a step backward, and picks up his robe. Sliding the robe over his shoulders and tying a knot in the belt, he lets out an audible exhale as he tilts his head toward the ceiling.

"Put our forces on high alert. Tell Prince Abasi I would like an intelligence briefing in the next thirty minutes. And assemble the oligarchs," he orders.

He begins to walk toward his closet before stopping abruptly in his tracks. He turns and calls out to the aide, who is feverishly typing something into his handheld device.

"What of Giza? Were there children abducted from Giza?" Monolith Ant inquires.

"Yes, My Lord," the aide responds.

Monolith Ant lowers his head and walks into his closet. Kiya hops off the bed and quickly covers herself. She cannot help but wonder what is behind her husband's specific interest in children being taken from the Giza Moon Colony.

She leaves this curiosity for now as she slides her feet back into her slippers and scurries back to her own bedchamber to get dressed.

CHAPTER 3
THE BALLAD OF SHADOW ANT

Some 2.15 astronomical units away from the Ant Planet, on Planet Memphis, President Aharon Mandrake settles into bed with his wife, Lady Cindy Drone Mandrake.

After a long day of negotiating trade deals and putting out political fires, Aharon can think of only one thing: having his wife or one or more of his many concubines service him sexually.

Sensors begin to activate the lights inside the public spaces, as well as outside on the grounds surrounding the perimeter of the palatial presidential palace. Aharon's official residence lies in the heart of the capital city, Djanet. In fact, the presidential palace is the geographic center of the district. The outside lights make the palace look spectacular as the night descends.

Aharon is one of the original enhanced Eshanashim. And like his bitter rival Monolith Ant, Aharon, also known as Shadow Ant, is one of the original Ikwentashim.

Every one of the original Eshanashim was born on Planet Earth. Aharon was born in Kemet in the year modern historians on Earth list as 1147 BCE, that is to say, "before the common era." People of the so-called "Western World" on Planet Earth associate what would be considered the "common era" with any time following the birth of Jesus of Nazareth, also known as Jesus the Christ.

To the Eshanashim, 1147 BCE relates to the year 6053. Kemet is the name by which the people who lived in Northeast Africa at that time referred to what modern historians call "ancient Egypt." Kemet means "land of the black soil," or "black land," referring to the rich, fertile soil of the Nile River Valley.

For many historians and those who study Kemet and its culture, the name Kemet also relates to a description of the skin tone possessed by the vast majority of the people who lived in and around Kemet.

Kemites, the people of the region, were a mixture of people who lived in the lands known in modern times as Egypt, Eritrea, Ethiopia, Djibouti, and Sudan.

Aharon was a soldier and a spy in the armed forces of Kemet and served under three different pharaohs: Ramesses VII, Ramesses VIII, and Ramesses IX.

From childhood, Aharon had a talent for hand-to-hand combat. His combat skills were unmatched among his peers. In fact, he was considered the greatest swordsman in all of Kemet and

Kush. He parlayed his talents into becoming a master spy and the pharaoh's most trusted clandestine operative.

In 1127 BCE, Aharon met H and Zilpha while on a mission to extract the daughter of a wealthy member of the pharaoh's administration from a gang of traveling human traffickers. H and Z were attempting to bring down the entire trafficking ring.

Aharon joined forces with the sisters and helped them dismantle the traffickers' operation. He fell madly in love with the beautiful, charismatic, and fearless H almost overnight.

Over the course of the next several years, Aharon joined H and Z on many other adventures. For her part, H did not reciprocate Aharon's romantic gestures or overtures, as she was highly focused on her work.

While she admired his passion and fighting skills, H did not want to surrender to Aharon for fear that his need to protect her would cause him to interfere with her undertaking dangerous missions.

As best she could, H kept her phenomenal paranatural abilities a secret from everyone but Zilpha. H allowed Aharon to think she could be injured or even killed by conventional means, and he never missed an opportunity to keep the sisters out of harm's way.

H did, however, admit that she found Aharon very physically attractive. On many occasions, she would purposely look away from the handsome Aharon's well-chiseled body when his clothes would be ripped off in the throes of battle or when he would bathe in a river in between missions. But more than that, she was attracted to his spirit. So, she decided to keep him close. And though Aharon desired to be intimately tied to H, he contented himself with remaining a trusted associate of hers.

In 1123 BCE, H sent word to Aharon to meet her at their usual meeting location, a café in the market just outside the palace walls. In the weeks before receiving the request for this rendezvous, Aharon had been hinting to H that he intended to propose marriage to her.

While H had not indicated that she would simply decline such an offer, she did not seem enthusiastic about the prospect of marrying him either, so he was both extremely excited and unbelievably nervous regarding this meet-up.

He was hopeful that he could convince H to marry him by promising to give her the latitude to continue the work she loved so much. And that hope fueled him, motivating him to be the best version of himself.

Aharon arrived at the café early. He paced outside the entrance, rehearsing his lines in his head, ruminating over how to overcome what he anticipated to be H's objections.

The night air was crisp. The warm glow from the hundreds of lamps lining the streets calmed him just enough to quiet his mind and allowed him to focus. He had cheated death so many times before; *This encounter should be easy,* he thought to himself.

Yet this meeting with the woman he loves produced the same anxious feelings he experienced at the inflection point of a dangerous mission or in a fight against a bloodthirsty foe. In his mind, rejection by H of his marriage proposal would feel like his life was over, as the future he so desperately desired to create with her would be no more.

By the time H arrived, he was an emotional wreck. He flashed her a nervous smile and walked her into the café. The aroma of brewing tea leaves and other delights filled the air.

H walked slowly at Aharon's side, her eyes focused on the ground as if she had committed a shameful act.

His heart began to pound as he could sense that she was about to deliver some upsetting news. He began to fear the worst.

"What's wrong, my love?" he asked gently.

H sat down at a table and looked at him. Her eyes were sad. Aharon's heartbeat became so intense that he could hear its thumping in his own ears.

"I have been reunited with my former husband," H began slowly. "I know you have feelings for me, and I hope you know that it was never my intention to hurt you in any way, but… I love him, and we are going to pick up where we left off."

Aharon was instantly devastated. He mustered all the courage he could not to show it. He immediately became aware of the energetic atmosphere of the café. Before H delivered her news, he had blocked out everything in their immediate environment, focusing all his attention on her.

Now that reality had come back into clear focus, he was forced to adjust to the world surrounding him.

Taking a deep breath, he managed to contemplate an appropriate response. He steadied himself and continued what proved to be, for him, a very difficult conversation.

"I understand. Since you love him, I will not get in the way," Aharon replied.

"I hope we can continue to be friends," H offered, reaching out and caressing his hand firmly. "You have always been so good to me and Z," she continued. "Plus…" she pauses, looking down at the ground. "There is something else I want to ask of you. We want you to join us on a mission we are planning. We are planning to seek a new home world beyond the stars, and we want you to join us on this expedition," H says, staring intensely into his eyes.

"What? I… uh… oh, my…" Aharon mutters.

He struggles for a moment to focus his thoughts so that he can deliver a coherent response. His hurt feelings and confusion combine to hamper his usually brilliant elocution.

"We???" he finally manages, almost indignantly.

"Yes, my husband and I, plus Z and her fiancé, Amen," H explains.

"Wow…" Aharon replies.

"I am planning a wedding for Z and Amen. It would mean a lot to me and Z for you to be there," H says with a smile.

Unable to resist her smile, Aharon agreed to attend the wedding. One year later, he helped defend more than 250,000 people H and Z recruited to join them in leaving Planet Earth against Apep the Dragon and his hordes of unnatural marauders. It was also during that year that he first learned of H's unbelievable abilities.

Watching H give her love and adoration to another man had a profound effect on Aharon. He allowed himself to grow emotionally distant. He began engaging in sexual dalliances with random women. He purposely selected women with whom he knew there would be no chance of developing a prolonged, significant relationship. In many instances, he treated the women he entertained with an almost cruel indifference.

H and Z noticed the change in Aharon's demeanor. H attempted to talk to him, but he pushed her away, unable to suppress his resentment toward her enough to accept her genuine concern and kindness.

A few years after they arrived on Planet Chaos, Aharon and H rekindled their friendship. In the aftermath of Apep's assault during their exodus from Planet Earth, H had lost her husband, who sacrificed himself to ensure H could launch the spacecraft that would carry their company from Earth to their new home.

Her husband's sacrifice also, unfortunately, caused H to be separated from her newborn son, Adisa.

Aharon cautiously entertained H in the early stages of building a new society on Chaos.

H welcomed Aharon's support, having held him as a trusted partner for so long during their many years working together on Earth.

Aharon eventually fell in love with H all over again. This time, she reciprocated his affection. Aharon did not press his advantage. Instead, he positioned H to become the leader of the new government being negotiated.

He also resisted the urge to surrender to H's sexual advances, wanting to keep her free from the appearance of any undue influence on his part. Since there was no evidence that they were sleeping together, Aharon believed no one could claim that he was secretly steering H toward any particular decision.

Unfortunately, Abasi Horus held both Aharon and H in abject contempt. Abasi played spoiler to any positive proposals offered by either H or Aharon and ultimately accused them of attempting to become the first royal family of Planet Chaos.

In a moment of anger and frustration, Aharon publicly proposed to H during a meeting of the makeshift planetary council. Surprisingly, she accepted. It was at that moment that the other prominent figures gathered to negotiate the creation of a planetary system of government agreed that Aharon and H should lead their new planet as co-pharaohs.

Angered, Abasi left the council and vowed to form his own government.

Aharon and H began planning their wedding while continuing to negotiate the final details of their new governmental structure. At one point during the fast-moving developments in their lives, Aharon came to H with another proposal.

H had completely enveloped herself in the idea of being Aharon's wife. She had grown to love him very much and was very excited by the possibilities of sharing her life with him, even though she had to say goodbye to so many loved ones before Aharon, who met with the bitter reality of death, while her apparent immortality allowed her to persist into an unknown future.

Though they were not having sex, Aharon would visit H in her bedchamber every night before retiring himself. On this particular night, Aharon arrived a little earlier than usual.

When he entered the room, H was in the middle of brushing her hair. She sat naked on a stool in front of her mirror. As soon as she noticed her love, she leaped from the stool and raced across the room, jumping into his arms.

She wrapped her arms around his head and neck, kissing him enthusiastically all over his face and playfully biting his muscular shoulders.

"Look at me… I'm naked," H whispers teasingly in his ear.

Chuckling softly, Aharon delivers a soft kiss to H's lips. Continuing to hold her aloft, he stares intently into her face, smiling warmly.

"I need to talk to you about something," he says softly.

H slides down Aharon's torso until her feet touch the floor. She grabs his right hand with both of hers and walks him over to her bed. Once seated, they sit gazing into each other's eyes.

H reaches up and places her hand on the side of Aharon's face. He immediately closes his eyes and lets out a long exhale, placing his hand on top of hers. For a moment, he considers abandoning his plan and surrendering to his desire to fold himself into H's naked body. But instead, he decides to proceed with his proffer.

"I met a geneticist today," he begins.

"Are you seeking some sort of male enhancement for our wedding night, my love?" H asks playfully, reaching out her other hand and placing it on Aharon's crotch.

"No!" he replies with a surprised laugh.

Now, relaxing even further, he decides to continue. His words grow even more nervous as he continues.

"Abasi has been working with a team of scientists to create genetic enhancements that would allow us to possibly live on other planets in the solar system, in addition to Chaos," he explains.

H pulls back her hand from Aharon's crouch and lowers her head. Unbeknownst to him, she has already seen the aftermath of this experimentation in a premonition she experienced during one of her meditations.

H rarely discussed her visions of future events with anyone other than her sister Z. Although she loved Aharon intensely, she had not gotten around to providing him with full insight into all her powers. For one, she understood that her visions of the future were only one possibility among a seemingly infinite cascade of various possibilities of the same event.

Humans, acting in their capacity to exercise free will, could change the outcome of a possible future at a moment's notice.

"I… I… hmm… I cannot be a part of anything like that," she says cautiously.

H's eyes remain lowered. Fearing Aharon's disapproval of her rejection, she cannot bring herself to look into his eyes.

Having been in this position with H before, Aharon turns his face away from her. All the previous feelings of resentment toward her begin to flood his heart and mind once again. He fights becoming angry but succumbs to his baser impulses.

"Why can't you just follow my lead in this? Haven't I demonstrated all I need to prove to you for you to accept me as your husband? He convinced you to leave the planet. I am asking you to accept a few changes so that people feel comfortable undergoing a procedure that may help us expand our society and populate other worlds throughout this solar system. The people love you! They will follow you to the ends of the universe if need be. We have a chance to do something humans have not ever done before," he says forcefully.

Tears begin to stream from H's eyes. Her grip on his right hand tightens.

"We've already done something humans have not ever done before. And I almost died to help us get here. I lost my husband and my son. Isn't that enough?" H says softly.

Aharon does not react. He glares at her angrily.

Pulling away from Aharon completely, H stands and turns her back to him.

"I love you, Aharon. Please stay here with me. Please be my husband. Please be my partner on this new mission. Let's you and I be the example that people do not need to change who they are to claim the future they desire," she says in a breathy tone.

Aharon did not respond to H's plea. Instead, he stood, turned, and walked silently out of her bedchamber.

After Aharon departed, H collapsed onto her bed and sobbed uncontrollably for hours. In the morning, Z brought word from the other members of the leadership council that Aharon had resigned from his position and announced that he would no longer be seeking H's hand in marriage.

H erupts into tears once again at the news.

Z covers her sister's nakedness with a blanket and lies next to H, attempting to console her as best she can.

The next day, the remaining members of the leadership council waste no time in naming H as the head of their new government and giving her the title of "Queen" so that she can raise an army and prepare for a possible invasion by Abasi and his growing following.

H accepts her election and assumes the title Queen Hawwah of Planet Chaos. The council divides itself into two legislative bodies, the College of Elders and the Senate.

In the ensuing months, both Abasi and Aharon, along with thousands of other Eshanashim, underwent an intensive battery of procedures to enhance their bodies in anticipation of facing harsher environmental conditions on the other inhabitable planets in their new solar system.

These throngs became the first Ikwentashim, or "ant people," also colloquially referred to as the "Ants."

Abasi eventually convinced his newly formed leadership group to name him the supreme leader of the ruling class of citizens of their new national order. That is when he took on the moniker of Monolith Ant.

Heartbroken, H delivered a strong warning to Abasi and his followers to leave Chaos peacefully or face the consequences for their sedition.

Realizing that he had made a grave mistake, Aharon created a faction among Abasi's followers and developed expeditions to other planets, eventually establishing Planet Memphis.

Back in the present, Aharon often reminisces about his time with H and wonders what could have been if he had simply stayed the course and married her. He has secretly never stopped loving H.

In fact, Aharon has not ever truly committed to the idea of being with one woman since being engaged to H. He is the father of twenty children, none of whom he shares with Cindy, who serves as the First Wife in Aharon's household.

Aharon agreed to marry Fausta Drone to appease Cindy, who thought that Aharon having a Second Wife she could otherwise control would curb her husband's appetite for women outside their household. This arrangement did work for a time. Aharon shares four children with Fausta.

Cindy and Fausta were able to contain Aharon's lust for 131 years, until he met a twenty-six-year-old teacher by the name of Tawaret Amun. Aharon felt things for Tawaret that he had not felt since his relationship with H.

Tawaret and Aharon would have two children before her tragic death in the year 9220. Their children are Darius Amun, better known as Captain LionMane, and Lady Fukyana Aten, wife of the highly influential and widely respected royal ambassador from Planet Chaos to the Giza Moon Colony, Horemheb Aten.

Unbeknownst to Cindy, she is actually a clone of H, genetically engineered to resemble H and model H's behavioral traits. Cindy was among the first genetically engineered, cybernetic humanoids called "Drones" to be brought online.

In the early days of the technology that produced the first Drones, each of the Drones brought online would eventually experience a circulatory condition that gave their skin a rich purple hue. Drones were also used in missions to Planet Earth to retrieve animals, minerals, and plants.

In Earth's atmosphere, the purple hue of the Drones' skin would turn green, giving rise to rumors among government officials on Earth that "little green men from Mars" were planning an invasion of Earth.

Cindy suffers from this condition. Cybernetic enhancements to Cindy's brain allow her to mimic H's intellectual prowess, but her physical appearance and intellect are as close to being H as Cindy can come. Though grown from H's actual cells, Cindy does not possess any of H's paranatural abilities. But it is Cindy's face and eyes that give Aharon some semblance of peace at night.

On this night, he will need it as he hears the palace alarms sound.

CHAPTER 4
IT WASN'T HIM

Once dressed sufficiently to be among the public, H and Armacaust receive several briefings, from which they are able to piece together a fragmented picture of the situation.

Thousands of children have been reported missing from all over the Ant-Galaxo Devearous System.

With no clear evidence of a single perpetrator or motive, H begins to fear the worst, namely, an attack led by Apep. She realizes that if the children are not found quickly, Apep will kill them all.

Reports continue to pour into the palace situation room, where various military leaders and administration officials desperately scramble to gather more intel.

"Mother, you have a call from Speaker JaneStar," Shango Wepwawet, the queen's chief of staff, yells over the crowd.

Shango Wepwawet is the son of Bastet Filia Wepwawet and Judge Den Aten. Bastet and Den never married. In fact, Bastet Wepwawet, a former member of the famous "Bridge Team" that worked tirelessly around the clock to save H's life during the first Eshanashim's journey across the stars from Planet Earth to Planet Chaos, maintains romantic relationships with two men, Den and the father of her other two sons, Hannibal Seshperonch, Director of IT/IS for the Warp Star Authority, also referred to as the WSA.

While Bastet did not develop paranatural abilities as a result of her exposure to H's radioactive blood, she carries the genetic markers capable of producing enhanced, that is, *superhuman,* offspring.

Shango himself was not born enhanced; however, both his oldest and youngest sons are. His oldest son, Nasir I, better known as SunWolf, serves as the senator of New Andalusia Province. His youngest son, Set, better known as WolfSpider, serves as the Intergalactic Patrol's principal investigator on Planet Chaos.

Shango's middle son, Haile, aka The Wolf, moved to his mother's home planet to join the Memphis special forces corps. Haile's combat skills and effectiveness as a secret agent caught the eye of President Aharon Mandrake, who appointed Haile to serve as the Memphis envoy to Ant Planet.

Of Shango's three wives, his most intimate relationship rests with Haile's mother, Ketanji, the queen's personal physician. Knowing what the queen means to his own mother, Shango takes his responsibilities very seriously. Through meticulous attention to detail and unwavering dedication to improving the lives of all Chaosians, Shango has made himself indispensable to H's administration.

"On screen," H says.

Speaker Hajera Pen-Nekhbet Menelik's face appears on the situation room's 360-inch wall monitor. She leads the Chaosian Senate, the lower chamber of the Chaosian legislature. The Government of Planet Chaos has eight subdivisions, called provinces. The people of each province elect a senator who serves as both the provincial chief executive and representative of the province in the legislature.

The Chaosian Senate, in turn, elects a speaker to serve as both its chief executive and representative in official proceedings with the queen or the upper legislative chamber, the College of Elders.

Hajera, better known as JaneStar, is the daughter of Ahmose Pen-Nekhbet Callis, better known as Elder Tubman, and the elder's late boyfriend, Moses. Elder Tubman is also a former member of the "Bridge Team." A renowned author and public speaker, Elder Tubman developed several paranatural abilities as a result of her exposure to H's blood.

JaneStar was born with the ability to infuse every cell in her body with electromagnetic energy, giving her tremendous strength and making her virtually invulnerable to physical harm. In fact, in her energized form, she is the twelfth strongest Eshanashim in the entire System. She can also fly, but not at supersonic speeds.

JaneStar's current husband, Kevin Jeffrey Drone, better known as SkatterStar, killed her first husband, Ramesses, in a freak accident. She retained her late husband's surname as a way to honor him. Each of the six children she shares with SkatterStar also bears the Menelik surname, including Brigadier General

Ramesses Menelik II; the intergalactic marshal, Afework Menelik, better known as Constellation; and Captain Kevin J. Menelik, better known as Pulsar.

"Hotep, Mother!" JaneStar says.

Her usually pleasant voice sounds distant and cold. She waits for H to respond before speaking further. This demeanor indicates to H that JaneStar will be "all business" during this call.

"Hotep, Madame Speaker! How may I be of service?" H replies.

"What can you tell me about this thing that's happened?" JaneStar probes.

"I do not know much more than the reports we have received. There is no credible intelligence on the kidnappings that I can share. Unfortunately, I do not know who did it or why, as of yet," H answers.

"How soon will you be able to take action?" JaneStar probes further.

"I am gathering intel so that I can organize the proper response, Madame Speaker," H declares. "Before I put anyone in harm's way, I need to know what we're facing."

"My Queen, I know that, if anyone, you understand the importance of bringing those children back alive and 'in one piece.' On a personal note, my son Pulsar's children are among those missing. So, please, be the finder of lost children you have always been and bring them home," JaneStar says, with tears welling up in her eyes.

"I promise you that I will do everything I can, Hajera," H replies. "I am also sorry to hear about the captain's children. What are their names?"

"The oldest is Asenat. She's sixteen. Then, there is Shaka, fifteen; Sojourner, thirteen; and Solomon, eleven," JaneStar replies.

JaneStar begins to cry, as she can no longer hold back the emotion of the moment. Instead of releasing the full weight of her emotions, she gathers herself and wipes her eyes.

"Thank you for taking the time, Mother," JaneStar says.

H nods, and the screen goes dark.

Shango tells H that she has another call. The caller is another member of the Chaosian legislature, Senator Aha Meketaten III, better known as Nova, of New Kemet Province.

"On screen," H calls out.

The screen comes back to life, presenting the confident expression of Senator Nova. He pauses before tendering his greeting.

"Hotep, Mother!" Nova greets.

Nova's deep, melodic voice booms into the room. There are only a few men across the entire System who rival Aharon Mandrake in terms of physical appearance, and Nova happens to be one of them. His dark chocolate skin wraps around and encases his tall, muscular frame.

Always well-spoken and dressed impeccably, Nova possesses a commanding presence that never ceases to capture the attention of his colleagues and peers or the imagination of nearly any woman in close proximity.

More than just a pretty face, Nova owns the distinction of being second, in terms of paranatural ability and raw power, only to the queen herself. He possesses the equivalent strength and durability of thirteen million stars. He is capable of generating an energy output greater than the force of ten million supernovas. He can also fly three times faster than the speed of light.

Both Nova and his wife, Sekhmet Ankhesenamun, better known as Lady Twinkle, have a parent who was a member of the famed "Bridge Team." Nova is the grandson of Dr. Aha Meketaten, who served as a physician and medical researcher on the starship that carried the first Eshanashim from the Milky Way to Ant-Galaxo Devearous. Twinkle is the daughter of Baahir Ankhesenamun, the pharmacist who assisted in the medical treatment of H during the now infamously difficult journey.

Twinkle, who holds the current record for the second-fastest flight time among all Eshanashim, gets annoyed by the constant attention her husband receives, especially since Nova's torrid affair with Mehari Nubian Saba, the daughter of the highest-ranking officer in the Memphisonian military.

Nova shares a son with Mehari, named Jefferson Saba. A year before she gave birth to Jefferson, Mehari married one of her father's ex-special-forces operatives, Kato Saba. Kato agreed to raise the boy as his own son to spare Mehari's father any embarrassment.

Nova only agreed to the arrangement as a means to appease Twinkle. Mehari's beauty, combined with the way women fawn over Nova, causes Twinkle to feel self-conscious about her own appearance.

Although Twinkle recognizes her limitations in terms of physical attractiveness, she and Nova have been inseparable since their purely coincidental meeting one night in the dorm room of a mutual friend during their time at the university, her for her first degree and Nova for his second of three Master's degrees.

Twinkle's only child, DwarfStar, was born two years before H's youngest son, Prince Armacaust II. The two boys met at a sporting event and have been best friends ever since, and remain very close, even though DwarfStar has started university.

"Hotep, Senator! How may I be of service?" H asks.

"I'm sure you're in the midst of your investigation into this tragedy, so I'll be brief. I thought you might want to know, however, that my son, DwarfStar, is among the missing. I know how close our boys have become over the years. Twinkle would have called herself, but she is inconsolable right now. I won't delay you any longer, My Queen. I know you will do everything in your power to bring our kids home," Nova answers.

H puts her hands up to her mouth. She literally wants to fly to her friend so that she can be at Twinkle's side. H begins to think through all the late nights and travel dates to support the boys she and Twinkle have endured together. But she cannot. This moment demands that she be the queen first.

"I am so sorry for you both, Senator," H says, with a genuine note of concern in her voice. "Please give Twinkle my best."

Nova nods. The screen goes black. Shango raises his hand, as if to get the room quiet.

"Another call, Mother," Shango says.

H begins to feel the emotional fatigue brought on by the suffering this situation has already caused. She wants to walk away from the situation room and get started on solving the problem, but she also realizes that a huge part of her role as the leader involves ensuring that the other leaders who answer to her can draw both direction and strength from her actions. So, she must stand firm and exemplify the resolve she wishes them to communicate to the people they serve.

"Ok. I'm ready. On screen, please," H responds.

The image on the screen displays a distraught Senator Moses Garrett Garvey, leader of New Canaan Province. This time,

H does not await a greeting from Senator Garvey before she speaks.

"Hotep, Moses! What can I do to help?" H asks earnestly.

"I can't even cap right now, Sis. I'm hurtin', Yo! They … uhm … they took both my babies…" Senator Garvey offers, choking back the tears.

"It's ok, Moses. I understand. What are their names?" H asks.

"My daughter's name is Brooklyn Betty Francis. And, my boy is Malcolm," Senator Garvey says, sniffling. "I'm just so scared right now. My wife needs me; my constituents need me, but I just don't know what to do."

"We will do everything we can to bring all our kids back home! In the meantime, I am going to pray that all these children stay safe," H replies.

"I know," Senator Garvey says, breathing normally now.

"Good. Go hug Fannie Lu for me," H says with a smile.

Senator Garvey nods. The screen goes black. Shango raises a document above his head.

"People, I just received this report. According to our own intelligence, and corroborated by our partners across the System, the count is 33,300 children missing," Shango declares.

The situation room erupts in a combination of gasps, plus administrators and managers shouting directions to their respective staff members and frenetic movement throughout the space.

Finally, Shango yells over the energetic volume in the room to alert the queen that she has received a call from Monolith Ant.

"Quiet!" H commands.

The room instantly falls silent. H puts herself in the right frame of mind. Monolith would not be calling unless he desires to stir the pot or simply sling unfounded accusations against H or Aharon.

"On screen," she orders, using a hand to draw her robe further over her breasts and hold it tightly closed.

"Good morning, Hawwah. I am glad to see you are decent enough to receive my call," Monolith Ant says condescendingly.

"What do you want, Abasi? As you can see, I have a lot going on here," H responds firmly.

"'Monolith will suffice. I need intel. What do you know about this thing that's happened?" Monolith Ant asks more collegially.

"I don't think I know any more than you know at this point, Monolith," H responds sincerely.

"You know, I cannot think of a single person or group, even, powerful enough to pull something like this off so quickly and without leaving a trace. That is … except for you," Monolith Ant says, leaning forward toward his camera and glaring menacingly into the screen.

"If by accusing me, you want witnesses to hear that you did not do this, you have gotten what you want. Unfortunately, while I am flattered you would think of me, I had nothing to do with this. Then, again, do not sell yourself short, Monolith. You are quite powerful. How do I know you are not behind all this?" H retorts.

"Well, there are only three people in possession of the paranatural abilities and resources to accomplish such a feat, and that list includes you, me, and—"

"Aharon," H interjects, cutting Monolith Ant off.

"Yes, Aharon. Your former fiancé," Monolith Ant says with a smirk.

H only responds by looking at the floor and shaking her head. She folds her arms and looks back up at the screen.

"I propose a truce. The three of us can work together to find the missing children. After which, I want a full investigation into the perpetrators, regardless of where the evidence leads. And I demand that the ICoJ prosecute the wrongdoers to the fullest extent of the law! Agreed?" Monolith proposes, with a sneer.

"Fine, but I want all of us here, in the same room. And by all of us, I mean you, me, Aharon, Neith, and Sekhmet. Agreed?" H replies firmly.

Monolith Ant's face reflects both his disgust at being affronted by H's boldness and his genuine concern regarding the situation at hand. He shifts his position in his seat slightly.

"But not at your palace," Monolith Ant retorts gruffly. "We can convene at your daughter's headquarters. Do we have terms?" he asks sternly.

"Agreed." H sighs. "I will meet you there in four hours," she says, looking directly into the screen.

"Agreed," Monolith Ant replies in an even tone.

The screen goes black. Looking away from the screen, H sighs.

"He had nothing to do with this," H says, turning to face Armacaust.

"I tend to agree with that assessment," Armacaust replies, with something of surprise in his voice.

"Somebody wake Sarah up, please," H yells over the crowd.

Turning back to Armacaust, H asks, "You thinkin' what I'm thinkin'?"

Puzzled, Armacaust replies, "Maybe?"

"Babe, I need your best special forces operatives on post. Sarah's team will need security support. Could you also send requests to Aharon, Neith, and Sekhmet to meet us at The Gatekeepers' HQ? After that, please gather your troops and head to Sarah's. I need to make a few stops first," H responds.

"Absolutely, Luvie!" Armacaust replies with a broad smile.

"Someone get me Chief Solicitor Powell on the line. Thank you!" H shouts again.

Rubbing her temples with both hands, H stands in the middle of the situation room, awaiting Shango to join her. Shango gives his final instructions, then walks over to her.

"Where are we headed first, Mother?" Shango asks.

"Get the transport ready. I need to wash and get dressed, then we are off to the Intergalactic Court of Justice," H answers.

"ICoJ. Got it. I'll meet you on the transport," Shango replies.

CHAPTER 5
AGREED UNDER PROTEST

After returning to her chambers, H bathes thoroughly and dresses properly. First, H reapplies the pale blue polish to her nails on both her fingers and toes. Next, H adorns herself in a white linen dress that is mostly open below her upper thighs. A long sash extends from the sarong, giving the appearance of modesty to those who would expect as much of the queen.

A golden belt, featuring an ornate, bejeweled clasp, lies over her small waist, holding the folds of her sarong closed. The belt's long golden tassels move back and forth as the queen glides with elegant strides from her dressing room to the mirror, where she brushes her hair.

H makes a point to continue wearing traditional Kemetic fashion when she faces the public in her official capacity. For this reason, she clasps bejeweled bands over her upper arms, then slips several jade-encrusted bangles over each wrist. She also lays her official royal collar over her shoulders. Hanging from the collar is the Star of Chaos, the official symbol of the people of Planet Chaos.

The Star of Chaos is a six-point star, best described as a five-point star with a tail extending between the two points at the bottom of the star.

H carefully brushes her hair. Her hair is of even length and runs from the crown of her head to the small of her back. She brushes a section of her luxuriously shiny hair over each shoulder, then rests the headband that symbolizes the head of government over the top of her forehead. The emeralds and rubies in the headband glisten in the rising sun.

Finally, H slips on her favorite high-heeled sandals, a superb pair of open-toe pumps with golden ankle straps. Just then, H hears a knock at the door.

"Come in, Chief Solicitor. You're right on time," H says with a smile.

"I heard you wanted to see me, Queen Mother," Chief Solicitor Powell responds.

Chief Solicitor Marie-Cessette Paris Powell serves as the chief legal officer to the Chaosian government, representing both the College of Elders and the Senate in legal controversies and providing legal advice to the queen regarding matters of state. Chief Solicitor Powell is married to Brigadier General Chappie Powell, the head of the Intergalactic Intelligence Service, also referred to as the IIS.

Under General Powell's leadership, the IIS has become the most revered intelligence organization in the Ant-Galaxo Devearous System, the name used to refer to both the Eshanashim solar system and the wider galaxy in which it resides. Ant-Galaxo Devearous is also commonly referred to as "the System." For her part, Chief Solicitor Powell is considered by many legal scholars to be the best attorney on Planet Chaos and one of the greatest barristers across the System.

"I need your consultation, and we do not have much time to talk, as I need to be in front of the ICoJ in an hour," H responds.

"Anything, Mother," Chief Solicitor Powell responds. "What need do you have of the ICoJ?" Chief Solicitor Powell asks playfully.

H explains her thoughts to Chief Solicitor Powell, and the two women have a concise conversation on the potential pitfalls surrounding the situation and H's intended offer to the ICoJ.

"I can see why they would grant your request, but I can also see a very strong reason for denying it. It will all depend on who's in the room. If you get a friendly panel, you will walk out of there with what you want. Judges are people, too. As much as they do not want the rest of us to know it, their personal beliefs and feelings creep into their judicial decisions.

So long as you do not get too many 'wildcards,' like an overzealous prosecutor asked to participate as a guest of the Court, I'd say your chances for success are extremely high," Chief Solicitor Powell advises.

"Good to know! Thank you so much," H says with a sly smile.

A little more than fifty minutes later, H, Shango, along with key members of their administrative staff, arrive at the headquarters of the ICoJ in the capital city of Abdju on the Giza

Moon Colony. Shango negotiates H's clearance. Once cleared, the administrative aides escort H through security.

She and her entourage are conducted to a large conference room just outside the main courtroom, where the fully empaneled Court hears appeals. H tells Shango to have the rest of the aides wait outside as she enters the conference room. Once inside, she is greeted by Bisrat Moab Armana, senior solicitor and Clerk of Courts at the ICoJ. Shango takes a seat in the visitors' gallery.

"Hotep, Queen Mother! And, welcome. We are honored by your presence," Bisrat says with a warm smile.

"Hotep!" H responds, placing her right hand over her heart and bowing her head slightly.

Bisrat is the daughter of Elder DuBois. Born Thutmose Moab on Planet Chaos, Elder DuBois is a member of the Chaosian College of Elders, the upper legislative chamber of the Government of Planet Chaos. His wife, Semat, is a Drākanashim whose genetic makeup reflects the combination of human and zebra DNA.

Semat's body is covered in microscopic hairs that give her the appearance of having snow white skin with distinctive black stripes. A former track and field champion, Semat is also one of the fastest non-enhanced Eshanashim in the entire Ant-Galaxo Devearous System.

Bisrat inherited her milk chocolate skin tone from her father, but she also bears distinctive black stripes on her legs. Bisrat's younger sister, Alem, who looks like a carbon copy of their mother, is arguably the most famous pop music icon in the galaxy.

Though a loyal citizen of Planet Chaos from such a prominent family, Bisrat's impeccable reputation as an impartial jurist earned her the respect of the legal scholars, other attorneys, and the judges that make up the ICoJ.

"Allow me to make introductions, Mother," Bisrat continues. "I would like you to meet our Chief Justice, The Honorable Darius Aten. And, seated to his left are Associate Justices Malia Pen-Nekhbet Ma'at, Djoser Armana, Imhotep Ma'at, and Bennu Amun Hotep. Seated next to Justice Hotep are Marshal Constellation and Roba Ma'at Aries, chief solicitor and lead prosecutor for the Galactic Security Council. Chief Justice asked Roba to attend this meeting in the spirit of cooperation between us and the GSC," Bisrat says without missing a beat.

"That would be my 'wildcard,'" H thinks to herself.

The justices each take their turn standing and greeting H with a hand gesture as their names are called.

Bisrat knows her introductions are performative, as H already knows most of the members of the ICoJ.

Malia Pen-Nekhbet Ma'at is the sister of Elder Tubman, a leading member of the Chaosian College of Elders and one of the original Eshanashim recruited by H and Z before they left Earth to establish Planet Chaos.

Additionally, Elder Tubman is an enhanced Eshanashim with the ability to perceive thoughts and emotions. She is also an accomplished psychologist, author, and public speaker.

Justice Ma'at is married to Justice Imhotep Ma'at, a Pen born naturally on Planet Pen-Meroe as a result of the Pens figuring out how to translate their cybernetic coding into DNA sequences, allowing them to give birth to completely organic offspring. Roba Ma'at Aries is the daughter of Imhotep and Malia.

Roba is married to Neptune Aries, a Pen-Meroe special forces team leader and the son of the supreme commander of the Pen Planetary Defense Forces. Being married into the most prominent military family on Planet Pen-Meroe encourages Roba to be very loyal to her and her father's home world. Roba respects H but does not feel any particular sense of loyalty to the queen.

Marshal Constellation, whose given name is Afework Menelik, is the granddaughter of Elder Tubman and the daughter of JaneStar, who serves as the Speaker of the Chaosian Senate.

Justice Bennu Amun Hotep is married to H's sister Zilpha's great-grandson, Col. Taurus Hotep III of the Giza Planetary Defense Force (GPDF).

Over the last millennium, or longer, H has developed significant relationships with the people in this room or their families. In fact, H was counting on such warm feelings of familiarity among the people in this room, given what she was about to ask.

Other than Roba, the only two wildcards in this equation would be Chief Justice Aten, a loyal citizen of Planet Memphis, and Justice Armana, a staunchly loyal citizen of the Ant Planet.

"Esteemed Justices," H begins. "I have come before you today to request immunity from prosecution for certain acts I committed long before we established the Ant-Galaxo Devearous System."

H pauses for a split second when she notices Roba leaning forward in her seat in anticipation of what she will say next. Doing her best to make sure she hits every point, H continues without hesitation, "In approximately Year 5701, and if anyone is also counting Earth years, that would be around 1499 BCE, some 377 years before I led a group of people from the kingdoms of Kemet and Kush off Planet Earth, I accidentally destroyed a planet in this System.

"Again, this was an accident. I scanned the planet for life forms before I unleashed a beam of focused electromagnetic energy that penetrated the entire planet and ruptured its core. The planet exploded as a result. A split second before the planet exploded, I sensed a life force reaching the planet's surface, perhaps having traveled there using a wormhole. After the explosion, there was nothing left. The asteroid field beyond Planet Shu is the remnants of that world," H finishes, with a stoic expression.

"As you no doubt know by now, thousands of children from our System, including my own teenage son, Armacaust II, along with two of my grandchildren, and many more children connected to the families and loved ones of the people in this very room, have been abducted by an actor or actors yet to be determined.

"I can enter a meditative state that allows me to view the past, present, and future simultaneously. I will use this ability to determine not only who is behind this heinous act, but also the location of the missing children. As I cannot control the order, length, or duration of the visions that I see while meditating, I will not be able to selectively filter the content.

"The Gatekeepers have developed technology that allows them to project my visions onto a panoramic screen in a viewing room at their headquarters. I have invited the leaders of the other governmental organizations in our System to view these visions as I attempt to locate the missing children.

"I humbly request immunity from prosecution for any of my past actions, my visions reveal that applicable law enforcement entities may find legally questionable, much less criminal."

Roba and her father sit back in their seats at the same time. Justice Armana begins to chuckle as he shakes his head.

"Well, I think I speak for all of us, Queen Mother," Chief Justice Aten begins, "when I say that we are glad you came to us with this. I am afraid we would be creating quite a judicial precedent by providing a blanket immunity for acts we have not even determined are or, even, could be criminal."

"Chief Justice, I must say that this is an unprecedented situation. I believe we can carve out an exception for the Queen Mother in light of the galactic emergency the System is facing," Justice Malia Ma'at offers.

"I agree. This situation warrants such an exception. And the Queen Mother has proven herself to be a trustworthy defender of life and promoter of justice throughout her reign on Planet Chaos," Justice Hotep offers.

"Obviously, the decision belongs to you, esteemed Justices, but I see no legal issues in granting the Queen Mother such a blanket immunity," Bisrat offers.

"Unfortunately, I must agree with the Chief Justice," Roba chimes in. "I cannot agree that the GSC will not want to prosecute even someone who has been a 'champion of justice,' even someone like the great Queen Hawwah, without reviewing each of the acts in question for potential criminality, especially… since Queen Mother may have just confessed to murder."

H casts her gaze down and to the right as Roba finishes her statement. She looks up again when she hears Chief Justice Aten address her.

"Queen Mother, are you here to confess to murder?" Chief Justice Aten asks gently.

"I do not believe I murdered anyone. But I, too, am human, so absolutely flawed as anyone else," H says directly.

"Chief Justice," Roba asks respectfully, "may I ask Queen Mother a few questions on the record?"

"The floor is yours, Solicitor," Chief Justice Aten replies.

Roba stands and walks slowly toward the middle of the room.

"Queen Mother, I need to swear you in," Bisrat says.

"Certainly," H responds.

"Please raise your right hand."

H complies. Once she raises her right hand, Bisrat initiates the swearing-in process.

"Do you attest that the testimony you are about to give is true and accurate to the best of your knowledge?" Bisrat asks.

"I do," H replies.

"You may proceed, Solicitor," Bisrat says to Roba.

"Queen Mother, please state your name and official title for the record," Roba begins.

"My name is Hawwah Menewa I. I serve as Queen of Planet Chaos," H testifies.

"When and where were you born, Queen Hawwah?" Roba asks.

"The year I was born is indeterminate. Even I cannot say for certain. As far as where I was born… if we are limiting our discussion to me in my present state, let's just say somewhere on the African continent on Planet Earth," H testifies further.

"So, by your own admission, your origin is somewhat unknown, then?" Roba asks.

"That is not what I am saying at all. My origin is likely beyond your understanding, especially if you did not piece it together from the clues I just gave you," H answers, rather condescendingly.

Somewhat embarrassed, Roba drops that line of inquiry and moves to her next question.

H notices the change in Roba's demeanor.

"How did you come to possess the extraordinary paranatural abilities you exhibit?" Roba asks.

"I was born this way," H responds.

"Is it true that there are no real upper limits to your powers?" Roba asks.

"Oh, my powers have limits. I assure you. In flight, I can reach speeds that exponentially exceed the speed of light; however, I cannot fly as fast as my sister, Z, or Lady Twinkle, for that matter. Besides, since I was created, there is obviously something, more accurately someone, far greater in power than me out there. I cannot nor have I ever claimed to be 'all-powerful," H responds with a straight face.

"Is it true that there are those on Planet Earth who worship you?" Roba asks.

"Yes, there have been sheer, untold millions of, we will call them, 'uninformed' people throughout human history who have worshipped me and other beings possessed of extraordinary gifts. In fact, I believe in ancient Greece there were those who referred to me as 'Kaos,'" H replies. "On the Arabian Peninsula, some called me 'Khairunnisa.'"

"Is that why you destroyed entire planets? You wanted to test whether you were truly a god?" Roba asks.

"No, I have not ever intentionally destroyed a planet. But, in learning the extent of my powers, I have made mistakes," H testifies.

"Do you believe yourself to be above the law?" Roba asks, staring directly into H's eyes.

H leans forward in her seat to match Roba's gaze.

"No, which is exactly why I'm here," H answers.

"Solicitor, I think we have what we need," Chief Justice Aten interrupts.

"Thank you, Your Honor. No more questions," Roba replies and retakes her seat next to Marshal Constellation.

"If Queen Mother is not confessing to murder, then I do not see what we have to contest. Let's grant her the immunity she seeks and allow her to do what she does best, stand as our champion against the forces that seek to cause destruction and discord across the System," Justice Imhotep Ma'at offers.

Once Justice Ma'at completes his statement, the other justices nod in agreement, as they generally do each time he speaks. Roba crosses her arms and presses her back firmly into the back of her seat.

"Then, by the power vested in me by the authority of this tribunal, I declare Queen Hawwah Menewa I will be immune from prosecution for any of her past acts revealed by her attempts to discover the location of the missing children, in addition to the identity of the wrongdoers behind the current emergency faced by the governments across the Ant-Galaxo Devearous System we serve," Chief Justice Aten declares with an air of finality.

"Well, I urge the Clerk to reflect in the record that I agreed under protest," Roba says with a hint of indignation.

"So noted," Bisrat responds immediately.

"Chief Justice Aten, esteemed justices, I sincerely thank you for your candor and understanding. I will not fail you," H says before standing and exiting the room.

Bisrat rushes out behind H and calls to her as H and her entourage walk briskly toward the facility entrance. H and Shango smile broadly at each other as they walk down the long corridor.

"Mother!" Bisrat shouts.

H stops and smiles as she looks in Bisrat's direction.

Bisrat runs up to H and throws her arms around H's neck. Tears flow freely down Bisrat's face.

"Thank you, Mother, for all that you do! I know you will bring these kids home and restore order to this dark situation like you always have," Bisrat says.

H hugs Bisrat back. For a moment, H thinks back to the many conversations she had with the curious little girl who has grown into the powerful woman hugging her in the hallway today. The moment heightens H's resolve to find the missing children.

"Thank you, Bisrat. I will do my best! And, for the record, you are doing fantastic work here!" H says enthusiastically.

H releases Bisrat and leans back so that she can wipe the tears from Bisrat's face. H flashes a hearty smile at Bisrat, then continues to exit the building.

CHAPTER 6
ONE MORE STOP BEFORE SARAH'S PLACE

H and her entourage return to Planet Chaos. Traveling at the speed of light, the queen's transport arrives in the royal palace docking bay within forty-five minutes of leaving Giza's atmosphere.

Before she heads to The Gatekeepers' HQ, she returns to her bedchamber and changes into her battle suit. Her AI-enhanced, nanotech-equipped battle suit sports a sleek black and gold motif. The highly functional, rugged apparel accentuates the queen's voluptuous curves but also reflects the same homage to Kemetic style her royal apparel displays.

The collar bearing the Star of Chaos connects to the bodice and forms both a breastplate and protective guard around the queen's neck. A golden belt hugs her waist much like the one that adorned the dress H wore to her meeting with the ICoJ. The royal headband she wears with her battle suit sits lower on her forehead and under her hairline, rather than on top of it.

H wears this gear more for the fashion statement it makes rather than for the protection it can offer her. Her skin and bones are virtually unbreakable. As far as anyone knows, she is completely indestructible and invulnerable to all manner of injury, except for significant exposure to antimatter or an attack from a being possessing strength approaching her own power levels, such as Netcher, Senator Nova, her younger daughter Princess Libbyèré, Monolith Ant, or her mortal enemy, Apep.

Aside from her invulnerability, any injury H does sustain generally heals in seconds, if not instantly. And, unbeknownst to most, she loses her invulnerability to harm and her enhanced ability to heal from injury during childbirth. From the time she goes into labor until several hours after giving birth, H can be physically harmed or even killed by a powerful weapon or a being wielding incredible power.

Once dressed for the occasion, H floats up to the ceiling of her bedchamber. She presses her right thumb into the biometric scanner next to the skylight handle. The scan confirms her identity and unlocks the skylight. She opens the skylight hatch and streaks out of the palace.

H had the skylight installed in the bedchamber as a special exit for her to sneak out of the palace so that she could take night flights without her security detail. She flies furiously toward the headquarters of the Intergalactic Patrol, commonly referred to as the IGP, the preeminent law enforcement agency of the Ant-Galaxo Devearous System.

H soars high above the city, stretching her arms out wide and turning barrel rolls. She always feels a sense of pure freedom when she flies. She enjoys feeling the wind on her face and taking in a view of the landscape that can only be appreciated from the sky.

The lights of the various buildings below sparkle as she whizzes by. The streets are far quieter on this day than usual. H takes a moment to extend her empathic abilities around the globe. She winces from the immediate flood of pain she senses. People in thousands of households across the planet are reeling from the shock of their children being abducted.

H refocuses herself and rockets toward the IGP headquarters.

Instead of walking into the facility through the main entrance and taking a chance of being slowed down by the security screening, H decides to fly directly to Chief Inspector Charles Callis's office. She elevates to ten thousand feet off the ground. Even at that height, H triggers the IGP facility's defense systems as she approaches.

She remains at ten thousand feet so that the plasma cannons will not be fired directly into the city. She avoids the dozens of shots fired by the building's plasma cannons with ease and flies directly to Chief Inspector Callis's office on the 30th floor. H knocks on the window to get the Chief Inspector's attention.

The Chief Inspector is engaged in what seems like an intense discussion with his aides, including two faces H recognizes: Assistant Chief Inspector Eskender Djet Drone and Inspector Set Wepwawet, better known as WolfSpider.

WolfSpider notices the queen hovering outside the Chief Inspector's window and alerts his boss to her presence.

The Chief Inspector taps his badge and orders the window in his office to be opened. The golden badges worn by the officers of the Intergalactic Patrol are fashioned into the shape of the Star of Chaos. Together with the rich royal purple color, the uniforms and badges of the IGP pay homage to Queen Hawwah as the pioneer who led to the discovery and establishment of the Ant-Galaxo Devearous System.

These badges are also virtually indestructible and custom-fitted to each officer's uniform so that they cover the officer's heart. H floats into Chief Inspector Callis's office as the window opens. The Chief Inspector ushers his aides away as H enters. Each gives the Chief Inspector a snappy salute before exiting the office.

Charles Callis assumed the role of chief inspector in Year 9234, following the passing of the IGP's first chief inspector, Montu Menewa, the uncle of King-Consort Armacaust Menewa. Callis's mother is the niece of Baahir Ankhesenamun, the renowned pharmacist who served on the famed "Bridge Team" during the voyage from Earth to Planet Chaos.

Charles serves as both the principal investigator and the chief executive officer of the IGP. As only the second chief inspector in the IGP's nearly three-thousand-year history, the leadership Chief Inspector Callis provides has been instrumental in making the IGP mainstream.

In his private life, Charles married Elder Tubman of the Chaosian College of Elders in Year 9136. The couple shares three children: famed journalist Professor Ida Callis, and their twin sons, Lieutenant Charles Callis II, better known as Sword, and Lieutenant Vertner Callis, better known as Shield. Both of his sons followed him into service at the IGP.

A masterful detective in his own right, Charles Callis has yet to be met with a case he cannot solve. And he expects the current calamity facing the System to be no different. Still, having the assistance of an ally as powerful as H could be of great benefit in his agency's endeavors to find the missing children.

"Queen Mother, you honor me!" Charles says warmly. "What may I do for you?"

"I need your help, Charles," H says directly.

"Anything for you, Mother! Lay it on me," Charles replies.

H explains her plan to find the missing children. She even tells him about the immunity deal she secured from the ICoJ. She then asks Charles for logistic and combat support from the SS Long Arm, the premier starship in the IGP's fleet.

By all accounts, the SS Long Arm is the largest and most powerful starship in the System. The SS Long Arm is roughly the length of a 100-story-tall skyscraper. It is an entire city block wide and thirty-six-story tall. It is armed with twenty-five plasma cannons and twenty-four antimatter warheads. Its thirty torpedo bays make it the most well-armed starship ever developed by Eshanashim engineers.

Despite its gargantuan size, the SS Long Arm can achieve speeds beyond the speed of light. It also carries up to 150 combat spacecraft and thirty-nine shuttles. Its 7,500-person crew also performs a variety of services, from routine medical treatment to structural engineering. The Long Arm's medical bay can service 1,500 patients at a time, and many of the kidnapped children may require immediate medical attention. Further, the Long Arm's nuclear core can power an entire city for a month.

The Long Arm can also offer humanitarian services that other starships simply cannot, and the use of *soft power* may help them secure the support of the governments on Planet Earth.

H explains to Charles that she is neither sure what they will face once they arrive on Planet Earth nor how long this campaign will last. She does know that the SS Long Arm is equipped to deal with anything they will likely come across in the Milky Way.

"Not only do I need the Long Arm, but I also need its captain to pick up a few special guests," H says.

"Ok. Who are we talking about, Mother?" Charles asks, somewhat skeptically.

"Mostly, the parents of the children I know have been abducted. I would like to bring Krebret and Makeda Dawit," H begins.

"The heir to the East Solar System Trading Company? He's married to Gen. Powell and your chief solicitor's daughter?" Charles asks.

"That's right," H responds.

"No problem there. Who else?" Charles says.

"Ambassador Aberash Hotep and his wife, Lady Dani," H continues.

"A member of the GSC, huh?" Charles asks with a chuckle.

"Yes, but not for the political checkmark. As you probably already know, both of President Sekhmet Djet Drone's children were abducted. I want to make sure that we bring as many of the parents or close family members of the children as we can," H replies.

"Good point! Ok. I can live with them. Continue," Charles replies.

"Senator Moses Garvey and his wife, Lady Fannie Lu," H continues.

"I LOVE Moses! Of course. He's good to go," Charles replies.

"I know, right! Who doesn't love Moses?" H says enthusiastically. "I also want to bring Rear Admiral Torian Grey II and Deputy Ahaneith Grey."

"Admiral Grey and Satellite. I'm good with that, too," Charles replies.

"Dr. Addisu Hor-Den and Prof. Alpha Rho Hor-Den."

"I don't know them, but I'm sure they do not present any problems for me. Who else you got?" Charles replies.

"Dean Starlyte and my sister, Z."

"Absolutely," Charles replies.

"Elder Shadd and Prof. Kebede Hotep."

"Sure! I really respect Elder Shadd. Next?" Charless replies.

"Deputy Aha Jupiter and JJ."

"I know, Capt. Jupiter very well! Good man. Yeah. Who else?" Charles replies.

"Dr. Den and Admiral Ayana Powell."

"Sure! I heard that he was a naughty boy during The Gathering, though," Charles chuckles.

"Nothing gets past the greatest detective in the System, I guess," H remarks with a laugh. "Unfortunately, I heard the same thing. Still, you and I both know that The Leader and Racism send those girls around the galaxy to compromise men just like Den."

"Yes, but still …," Charles replies with a skeptical expression on his face.

"I am picking up what you're putting down," H replies with a giggle.

"Alright, who else you got?" Charles asks.

"Marshal Constellation."

"One of my favorite people! Absolutely. Anyone else?" Charles replies.

"My son, Adisa, and Elder Wells."

"Yes, of course," Charles replies.

"Chief Justice F.B. Shadd and his wife, Carla."

"No issues there, either. Who else?" Charles replies.

"A handful of politicos, to include Speaker Setepenre Djoser, Prince Wepwawet, Prince Montu, and Speaker JaneStar."

"I love it! And that is a good move on your part," Charles replies.

"And, last but not least, Prince Bekele and Captain Ayana PN Horus," H says, scrunching her face up as if she knows she will receive some pushback.

"Ok. Now, that one we need to talk about," Charles replies. "My intel suggests that he is the vigilante known as 'Jegina-U,' dispensing his own brand of 'justice' on Giza. If he is on our ship, it should probably be in cuffs, rather than us giving him a ride to Earth," Charles explains. "Also, aren't he and his father, Prince Wepwawet, at odds?" Charles asks.

"My intel suggests that he is likely Jegina-U, as well. However, it does not sound like anyone has proven that yet. And, at the risk of upsetting Abasi, I LOVE Ayana! Their kids were kidnapped. I think if we give Prince Bekele the chance to 'play nice,' he will. And, if he doesn't, your officers will be right there to arrest him," H says with a smile.

"Ugh… Ok. You got your guest list," Charles says, rubbing his forehead. "And, as far as the Long Arm, of course, you shall have it."

He taps his badge again to open a communication channel to his mission control unit. The comms crackle to life.

"Yes, Chief Inspector," the voice on the other end says.

"Have Captain Menes get his vessel ready for launch," Charles commands.

"Captain Menes arrived hours ago, Sir. He anticipated receiving this call from you," the voice on the other end of the line responds.

"Excellent!" Charles exclaims. "Let him know he will have several special guests on this voyage," Charles adds, winking at H.

"Yes, Sir!" the voice responds.

"Queen Mother, please do not worry about the guests. I will make the proper arrangements, and they will be aboard the Long Arm by the time the voyage is ready to get underway. You have my word," Charles says with a broad smile.

"Thank you, Charles!" H says, hugging him tightly. "Please tell Elder Tubman I bid her 'Hotep,'" H says before exiting the same window through which she entered his office.

Once outside, H rockets toward The Gatekeepers' HQ at Mach 7.

Charles watches her speed away. H disappears from view in a matter of seconds.

"Good hunting, My Queen." He exhales, gazing eastward.

CHAPTER 7
SARAH'S PLACE

The scene at The Gatekeepers' headquarters has become intense. The air inside the facility hangs heavily over the spaces in which final preparations are being made to receive their distinguished guests.

The king arrived with a team of special forces operatives from the PDFJC only a few hours ago. As the other planetary leaders arrive, their suspicion and caution can be seen in the expressions on their faces.

The circumstances surrounding such an impromptu gathering present an almost irresistible opportunity for nefarious parties to make an attempt on the life of Hawwah Menewa. And while most Eshanashim believe H to be indestructible, rumors have been circulating in recent years that certain planetary leaders have been entertaining experimental and theoretical methods to neutralize or even kill Hawwah, if doing so were to become necessary.

Before resigning herself to the mediation chamber, H gave Sphinx a pep talk in which H expressed her unwavering confidence in Sphinx's ability to maintain order. For her part, Sphinx is determined to prove that her mother's confidence in her has not been misplaced.

The Gatekeepers' HQ sits on a narrow strip of land on an island off the east coast of New Kemet Province. Planet Chaos is nearly a mirror image of Planet Earth. Its continents, other land masses, and oceans provide a near-perfect replica of the arrangement of the topography of Earth.

New Kemet Province is the same size and shape as the continent of Africa. The island that serves as the home of The Gatekeepers' HQ lies in the same place and is the same size and shape as the island nation of Madagascar.

The most noticeable difference between Planet Chaos and Planet Earth is the capital city of Planet Chaos, which lies on an island off the west coast of New Kemet Province. Meroe Island, also called "The MI," has neither a twin nor a parallel land mass on Earth. It stands as an independent jurisdiction that serves as the seat of government for Planet Chaos.

While each Chaosian province, which would be continents on Planet Earth, is led by a senator who acts as its chief executive, the administration of The MI is under the direct control of the queen. Meroe Island is also the home of the Galactic Security Council, also referred to as the GSC, and its primary law enforcement arm, the IGP.

Meroe Island, a circular land mass, is roughly one-sixth the size of a small continent. Layers of beaches, military bases, mountain ranges, and resorts form the perimeter of the island. Government installations form the outer ring. The inner ring is reserved for the residences of the royal family and key government officials, including the royal palace. The center of the island is a lush, massive wildlife reserve and national park.

Also, unlike Planet Earth, gargantuan reptiles that would be called dinosaurs on Earth still roam the forests, plains, oceans, and swamps of Planet Chaos. These animals are even more prevalent on planets Ikw-n-tA and Memphis, as well as the Giza Moon Colony.

Once a well-kept secret, the location of The Gatekeepers HQ, also referred to as TGHQ, has become common knowledge among the heads of state of the various planets in the System. As the renown of The Sphinx and her team grew across the System, planetary leaders commissioned espionage operations to gather as much intel as possible on the princess and her activities.

TGHQ is a marvelous facility that embodies sheer structural engineering wizardry. With nine levels above ground and four subterranean levels, the massive compound is part military installation and part R&D laboratory that features some of the most sophisticated scientific equipment on the planet. It is also a part training center and serves as the primary residence of The Sphinx herself.

Sphinx's best friend and teammate, Setepenre Saba, whose code name is "Vixen," along with The Gatekeepers' chief solicitor and the chief legal counsel to the Chaosian royal family, Nefertiti Djoser, both maintain apartments at TGHQ. Nefertiti is the youngest daughter of Sphinx's biological mother, Biffu.

TGHQ is home to an indoor, amphitheater-style briefing room with seating for up to 250 people. It also has thirteen conference rooms and three large ballrooms, which can be segmented into smaller event spaces. TGHQ has sleeping quarters with the capacity to house over 700 guests.

Plus, the eight commercial kitchens can serve several thousand people at a time. The infirmary features advanced diagnostic and surgical capabilities and also provides 400 licensed beds. The observation deck above the penthouse boasts one of the most powerful telescopes ever devised, designed and built by H herself.

The viewing room where the planetary leaders will be convening is part of the observation deck on the ninth floor. The chamber the queen uses for her meditative state sits between the control room and the telescope observatory. The walls surrounding the meditation chamber are reinforced with thick panels of black metal.

Black metal ore can be found on large planets that simply lack the size to produce the nuclear fusion that would allow them to become stars. Virtually unbreakable, black metal is the primary material used in weapons development across the System.

The control room sits across the hall from the viewing room. The hallway leading from the primary elevator bay to the observatory is a long corridor. Guests are free to walk out of the elevator and wander past the viewing room and into the observatory or veer off to the right or left to either enjoy refreshments and repose in the lounge area or connect to their workplace in the office space area, littered with hotel-style workstations.

The Gatekeepers' staff is comprised of 360 workers, including 160 kitchen and food preparation staff members, eighty security professionals, forty IT professionals, thirty-five housekeepers, twenty facilities engineers, fifteen groundskeepers, and ten administrative professionals.

Additionally, there are the twelve Gatekeepers themselves: 1) Princess Sarah Amun, also known as The Spinx, Team Leader and CEO, 2) Nefertiti Djoser, Chief Solicitor and Legal Counsel to the Royal Family, 3) Setepenre Saba, better known as Vixen, Lead Operator, 4) Mina Bona, Field Operative, 5) Dr. Heka Menes, Medical Examiner and Team Physician; 6) Cassius Carneas "CC" Drone, better known as Hammer, Field Operative, 7) Dr. Gbeto Hotep, Chief Technologist, 8) Arisone Hotep, Hacker and Tech Specialist, 9) Eman Menes, Executive Chef and Director of Facilities, 10) Berknesh Djoser, Administrator of the Memphis Safe House, 11) Latifah Wepwawet III, Administrator of the Pen Safe House, and 12) Kiya Armana, Travel Chef.

On this day, other than the safe house administrators, the entire team and staff are *in-house.*

While security is normally tight, the security today at TGHQ has been heightened exponentially. This occasion marks the first time Sphinx has hosted the full pantheon of planetary leaders all at once.

Hawwah's ability to see the past, present, and future through meditation requires her to separate her spiritual form from her physical body. Though H is practically indestructible, her body becomes vulnerable to attack when she enters such a meditative state, as she is unable to defend herself.

With the queen unable to defend herself while The Gatekeepers play host to so many of the queen's political rivals, King Armacaust and Sphinx are taking no chances.

Though King Armacaust serves as the supreme commander of the Chaos Planetary Defense Force Joint Command, he will convene with the other planetary leaders in the viewing room. Therefore, leading the PDFJC security detail is the king's younger brother and chair of the PDFJC, Admiral Idris Menewa, better known as CavalierStar.

CavalierStar, also known as CavStar or Cav, possesses the ability to generate force shields and regenerate damaged tissue almost instantly, allowing him to heal from most injuries. Cav can also teleport and run at speeds in excess of 100 mph. Because he can absorb tremendous amounts of energy, he does not ever become exhausted.

Like his older brother, King-Consort Armacaust, Cav is one of the best hand-to-hand combatants in the System. His incredible agility and mastery of weapons make him one of the most respected warriors across the System.

Along with Admiral CavalierStar is General Nasir Wepwawet II, better known as BioStar. General BioStar leads the Planet Chaos Ground Force. He possesses tremendous strength and durability. His power levels make him one of the most powerful enhanced Eshanashim. Only a handful of enhanced Eshanashim can heal from injury faster than BioStar. Like his twin sister, MoonStar, BioStar can mimic the paranatural abilities of other enhanced beings.

The rest of the PDFJC security detail features some of the most powerful enhanced Eshanashim on Planet Chaos, including Lieutenant General Thutmose Meketaten, better known as FireStarter; Brigadier General Ramesses Menelik II; Colonel Ptah Hotep, better known as GiantStar; Commander Jo-Molefi Menewa Meketaten; Colonel Taurus Hotep II; Captain Kevin J. Menelik, better known as Pulsar; and Lieutenant Serethor Menelik.

Capt. Menelik and Lt. Menelik are not only married, but this mission is also extremely personal for them, as all four of their children are among those missing.

The only non-enhanced Chaosian military officer assigned to the TGHQ security detail for this mission is Brigadier General Chappie Powell. Gen. Powell leads the IIS. His assignment is to conduct a threat assessment of each and every person admitted into TGHQ today.

As arguably the best clandestine operative in the Ant-Galaxo Devearous System, Gen. Powell serves as a walking encyclopedia of the enhanced and/or specially trained soldiers and spies among the Eshanashim.

As the planetary leaders and other officials begin the screening process to enter her facility, Sphinx feels prepared but realizes that it will take the combined skills and strengths of The Gatekeepers and the PDFJC to protect the queen.

CHAPTER 8
THE GANG'S ALL HERE

Leader Neith Ramses, also known as WingDrake, becomes the first planetary leader to arrive at The Gatekeepers HQ and begin the security screening process. Neith serves as the head of the Giza Authority Directorate, also referred to as the GAD. Established in Year 6260, the year that would be described as 940 BCE on Earth, by a joint resolution of Planets Chaos, Ikw-n-tA, and Memphis, the GAD provides some semblance of a representative government for the millions of Drākanashim living under the apartheid rule of Planet Ikw-n-tA.

Giza, named for the city in modern-day Egypt that serves as the home of the Heru-em-Akhet, the edifice mislabeled the Great Sphinx by European observers, together with the great pyramids, is the largest natural satellite of Planet Ikw-n-tA and the only one with an atmosphere capable of supporting life. Unlike other moons, Giza rotates on its axis as it orbits Ikw-n-tA, only at a much slower rate than the planet itself.

Neith was born a century before the GAD was established. The result of sophisticated genetic engineering, Neith is among the first Drākanashim to be born naturally. Her biological makeup represents a combination of human genomes and the recombinant DNA of multiple species of birds, but most prominently the Martial Eagle in her case.

As intellectually and physically formidable as she is beautiful, Neith stands at a modest five feet and four inches tall, but she is one of the fiercest warriors in the System. Her rich, dark chocolate-hued skin is smooth and even. Large black feathered wings adorn her back and perfectly complement her sculpted frame. She is one of the primary reasons Giza has any form of self-governance, having lobbied both Queen Hawwah and President Mandrake to intervene against the atrocities the Drāks faced at the hands of the Ant Planet settlers.

In fact, in the aftermath of Aharon Mandrake's split from H, Neith and Aharon found comfort in each other's arms for a time. The former lovers share three daughters. Their relationship, unfortunately, unraveled due to Aharon's reluctance to make Neith his wife. Feeling scorned, Neith allowed the anger she felt because of Aharon's apparent rejection to fuel her desire to set Giza free.

Neith both respects and resents H. Neith blames H for Aharon's inability to commit to any other woman, but she respects the queen for being an outstanding role model for young women across the System. The disappearance of five children who belong to close colleagues of hers at the GAD has motivated Neith to put her faith in H on this occasion.

Sphinx watches on camera as Neith and her aides move through the security screening with ease.

Next to arrive is President Sekhmet Djet Drone, leader of Planet Pen-Meroe. Sekhmet is the fifth child and youngest daughter of Ambassador Benerib Djet Drone. Amb. Djet Drone was appointed by Queen Hawwah to be the official envoy of Planet Chaos to the people of Pen-Meroe. She married a high-ranking officer of the Pen military and had six children.

Sekhmet was born with a birth defect that gave her an enlarged right arm and hand that looks like it belongs to a person twice her size. After her father's assassination in Year 9211, Sekhmet joined the resistance against the corrupt and repressive regime of the second president of Pen-Meroe, Menes Aharon Joseph Drone II, better known as MAJ II.

She even married the leader of the resistance, Marcus Douglas Drone. In the final conflict to depose MAJ II, Sekhmet's husband was killed. After the dust settled and the transitions began, the Pens elected Sekhmet as their new president. She then married MAJ II's younger brother, Adisa, as a means to unite the various factions vying for political power across Pen-Meroe. Sekhmet and Adisa share two children. Both of Sekhmet's children are among the missing.

The next guest to arrive is President Aharon Mandrake, also known as Shadow Ant. He is arguably the greatest warrior in human history. His skill with a sword is nearly unmatched. Only the Vindicator is Aharon's better with a sword in her hand. His prowess as a hand-to-hand combatant is almost untouchable.

Only a young warrior on Planet Earth, all but unknown to most Eshanashim, and his former pupil and lover, WingDrake, have ever even been rumored to come close to matching his fighting ability. These attributes, combined with his paranatural capabilities, make the Shadow Ant one of the most dangerous Eshanashim in the System.

His ability to envelop himself in shadows not only makes him virtually invisible, but it also allows him to move from one place to another almost instantly, almost like a form of teleportation. He can also change shape into anything he sees, mimicking the physical characteristics of animals, people, or things.

Aharon can also induce illusions in the minds of the unsuspecting and project his voice over several miles. His senses of sight and smell are extremely acute, and he can heal virtually any injury in a matter of minutes. In addition to his mental and physical capabilities, Aharon's intelligence ranks just below the level of a super genius.

Aharon takes inventory of everything he sees as his aides negotiate his security screening.

"Do you find anything interesting, Mr. President?" Gen. Powell asks, probing.

"General Powell," Aharon responds, extending his right hand.

The two men shake hands. Gen. Powell pauses momentarily, taking a second to look at his monitor displaying the data returned by the thermographic scanner. Seeing no weapons on Aharon's person, the general smiles.

"It is always a pleasure to see you," Aharon responds warmly.

His electric smile becomes disarming, even to men who are not physically attracted to him. But Gen. Powell resists the urge to become distracted.

"It's unfortunate we have to gather here under such circumstances," Gen. Powell replies in kind.

"Yes, certainly. How's the queen?" Aharon says.

"Focused," Gen. Powell says directly. "As we all should be."

Gen. Powell concludes the niceties by staring straight into Aharon's eyes. Aharon does not alter his expression. The two men nod approvingly at one another, and Gen. Powell ushers Aharon and his aides through security.

Gen. Powell then turns and speaks into his communicator. "He's clean."

"Copy that. Thank you, General," Sphinx responds.

Next to arrive is Grand Envoy Tutankhamun Armana, official ambassador of the Ant Planet to Planet Chaos and chair of the Galactic Security Council. Envoy Armana is a loyal follower of Monolith Ant and one of eighteen oligarchs who wield tremendous power in the regime that rules the Ant Planet.

Comprised of the fifteen ambassadors representing the major planets, plus Leader Neith Ramses, Viceroy Kato Ramses, and GSC Executive Director Oshun Grey, the GSC provides humanitarian aid, general intelligence, and law enforcement services to the planets, settlements, and territories that make up the Ant-Galaxo Devearous System.

The GSC oversees both the IGP and the WSA. Its charter also provides for the GSC to negotiate and settle territorial disputes between the planetary governments. In its law enforcement capacity, the GSC works with the ICoJ. The GSC investigates crimes and takes suspects into custody, and the ICoJ conducts criminal prosecutions.

Envoy Armana is followed by Director Merneith Mandrake, administrator of the WSA, the younger sister of

Shadow Ant. She resents H for breaking her brother's heart on Earth and not following his lead on Chaos.

She became the administrator of the WSA through skillful political maneuvering by her brother. The Warp Star itself is actually a very large planet that sits at the mouth of a nebula. Too small to be a star, but too massive to be pulled into orbit, the Warp Star lies beyond the Eshanashim solar system.

This planet serves as the nexus of millions of wormholes connecting various points of the known universe. Its rings are actually gateways across the galaxy, between galaxies, and to other dimensions. Its surface, too, is littered with wormhole entrances and exits.

The WSA monitors the activity of the various wormholes, logging the travel that occurs via them, and also conducts structural analyses on the gateways to ensure the paths remain open and free of piracy. Since the Eshanashim rely so heavily on the Warp Star, the WSA wields immense influence among the planetary governments.

Assistant Chief Inspector Eskender Djet Drone, second in command of the IGP and younger brother of President Djet Drone of Pen-Meroe, arrives next. He greets Gen. Powell with a crisp salute and is ushered into the facility.

Inspector Djet Drone is the most decorated and respected law enforcement officer among the Eshanashim. His exploits are legendary, and his integrity is unquestionable.

Finally, Monolith Ant arrives as if he were awaiting everyone else to be seated so that he could make a grand entrance. He attempts to walk past the security station, but his path is immediately blocked by Commander Jo-Molefi Meketaten.

"I understand you may be a formidable warrior, my dear, but you do not have the power to deny me," Monolith Ant says in a cold tone.

"We all have a job to do, sir," Jo-Molefi responds, without taking the bait.

"If you would, Lord Monolith," Gen. Powell says gently, stretching out his arm to show Monolith Ant back to the security station.

"See, it takes a man to show the proper respect. I suggest you learn some, girl," Monolith Ant says condescendingly to Jo-Molefi.

Jo-Molefi does not react. She simply turns her head to look in a different direction as she stands her ground. As Gen. Powell ushers Monolith Ant back toward the security station, Jo-Molefi notices a member of Monolith Ant's party lingering at the entrance of the facility.

"You, please step forward," she says sternly, pointing to the loitering aide.

The rather large figure begins to walk backward out of the entrance and attempts to turn, appearing to prepare to walk in the opposite direction. Jo-Molefi does not hesitate to spring into action. Capable of reaching supersonic speed in flight, Jo-Molefi streaks across the foyer of TGHQ and flies directly into the back of the aide, tackling him to the ground before he can take another step.

As Jo-Molefi flips him over onto his back, the aide takes a swing at her. She dodges the strike with ease, takes a step backward, and pulls her escrima sticks from the holster on her left hip. The aide uses an acrobatic move to hop onto his feet. But before the aide can initiate another attack, Jo-Molefi beats him unconscious with a series of strikes from her escrima sticks, with deft precision and astonishing speed.

Another aide begins to take a step toward Jo-Molefi. She extends her left arm so that the end of one of her escrima sticks comes within inches of his face. The aide stops cold in his tracks, throwing his hands up in surrender.

Gen. Powell walks over calmly. Tilting his head, he examines the unconscious aide. Lifting up the aide's cap, Gen. Powell smiles as he recognizes the familiar face.

"Major T. Horus," Gen. Powell says, shaking his head. "Never a dull moment with you, sir."

Gen. Powell then turns to Monolith Ant.

"Can you blame me? Your queen brought a special forces team and her chief intelligence officer. Should I not have a comparable security detail at my disposal?" Monolith Ant asks indignantly.

"Well, our host has rules that supersede even our military protocols," Gen. Powell replies.

"Princess Sarah has a vested interest in giving her mother every advantage," Monolith Ant bellows. "I insist that my men be allowed to accompany me."

"I want the names and ranks of each of the special forces operatives you are attempting to smuggle into this facility, and I want that information, now… Your Lordship," Gen. Powell replies just as assertively.

Monolith Ant reluctantly acquiesces. Even he understands that cooperation among the planetary leaders will be essential to bringing the missing children home alive.

Once Monolith Ant is ushered into the elevator, Gen. Powell hails Sphinx on the communicator.

"Did you get all of that?" he asks in a joking tone.

"Yeah, I'm tracking," Sphinx responds. "This is gonna be fun," she says sarcastically.

"Chief, all planetary leaders and aides are seated and ready for viewing," a voice interrupts over the comms.

"Copy," Sphinx replies. "So, it begins," she thinks out loud.

CHAPTER 9

AN UNSCHEDULED FIELD TRIP

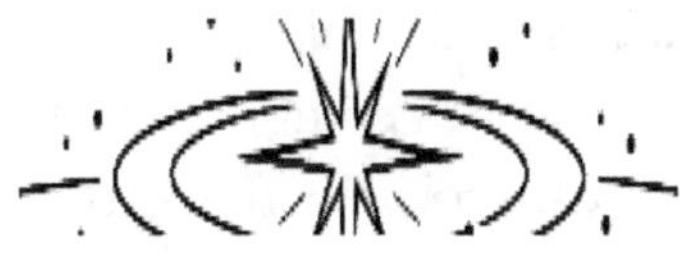

In a dimly lit cavern in an unknown corner of the universe, thousands of confused and terrified children huddle together. Their ages range from five to eighteen. Representing every planet in the System, most were abducted from their schools, either shortly after arriving to begin the day or while awaiting the final bell. Several hundred children were even taken from orphanages.

The darkness surrounding them, combined with the rising volume of children crying and speaking loudly, becomes disorienting as they look around in sheer bewilderment.

Steadying himself, sixteen-year-old Prince Armacaust II, the youngest child of Queen Hawwah and King Armacaust I, rises into the air to address the massive group. His best friend, eighteen-year-old Aha Meketaten IV, better known as DwarfStar, joins Prince Armacaust in hovering over the throngs of Eshanashim children.

DwarfStar's nom de guerre has nothing to do with his stature. In fact, he, like his father, is rather tall. He possesses the ability to control the force of gravity. His mastery over gravitational forces is great enough to collapse small stars, turning them into black holes.

Hovering twenty feet off the ground gives the young prince and DwarfStar a startling revelation of the sheer magnitude of the number of children taken from their homes and brought to this place. Prince Armacaust gasps at the sight. DwarfStar has a similar reaction but expresses it in a slightly different manner.

"Holy sh—" DwarfStar begins.

Prince Armacaust places his hand on DwarfStar's shoulder to interrupt him before he can complete the statement. The young prince takes a deep breath to prepare himself, as he realizes what must be done.

"HOTEP! Please, listen to me," Prince Armacaust yells, attempting to get the attention of enough of the kids in the crowd to begin calming the entire group.

DwarfStar follows the prince's lead, attempting to yell over the growing chorus of verbalized anguish. Older children begin to join in with Prince Armacaust and DwarfStar until, eventually, the cavern is as quiet as it can be, given the circumstances.

"Hotep! I am Prince Armacaust Menewa II of Planet Chaos," he begins, speaking as loudly as he can.

The younger of the queen's two sons, Prince Armacaust, shuns the spotlight. His older brother, Prince Adisa, will likely succeed their mother as king when H abdicates her rule. Pursuant to Chaosian law, queens and kings must be elected by the people and confirmed by the College of Elders.

If the people reject the ruling leader's firstborn child, the Senate may offer each of the ruler's additional children for election. If the people reject all the ruling leader's offspring, the Chaosian Senate may then select another candidate.

Even if the people did not accept Prince Adisa as their king, Prince Armacaust still stands behind his sisters, Princess Sarah and Princess Libbyèré, in the line for H's throne. Even though Princess Sarah has made it clear that she intends to retire from public life when their mother decides to conclude her reign, Princess Libbyèré, commonly referred to as Libby, is a natural leader and already serves as the senator of New Frangistan Province.

Having no clear path to the throne, Prince Armacaust prefers to pursue his athletic endeavors and other interests. Needless to say, he does not undertake many opportunities to practice his public speaking.

"You're the prince!" a young voice squeals in excitement.

"Yes, I am one of the princes of Planet Chaos," Prince Armacaust continues. "My older brother Adisa is Al-Amir. He's the one whom the College of Elders will likely select to be king someday. I'm the younger one."

"Yeah, you're the gorgeous one!" a young lady yells.

The outburst makes the young prince blush. He smiles and clears his throat before continuing.

"Uhm… this is DwarfStar. His parents are Senator Nova and Lady Twinkle of New Kemet," he says, pointing to DwarfStar. "Look, I know many of you are scared. I am, too. But if we work together, we can make it out of here."

Prince Armacaust uses both his telescopic and night vision abilities to scan the multitude of children to identify the older members of the group. He, however, does not recognize any of the faces he initially sees.

"DwarfStar and I could use some help getting organized. Please raise your hand if you are sixteen or older," he says.

Hundreds of young gentlemen and young ladies raise their hands. DwarfStar slaps his hand to his face.

"Oh… ok…" he says, surprised at the number.

"I got this, bro. I have an idea," DwarfStar says to Prince Armacaust with a confident smirk on his face. "If you're sixteen and like talking to people, step forward," he yells.

A handful of young people heed the direction. Prince Armacaust and DwarfStar exchange an enthusiastic high-five.

"Awesome! Everybody else, hold tight while we talk to these guys," Armacaust yells over the crowd.

He and DwarfStar float down to join the other teens who stepped forward on the ground. Leading the group of teens to a quieter corner of the cavern, Armacaust commences with introductions.

"Let's introduce ourselves. Give your name, where you are from, and who your parents are," Prince Armacaust directs.

"Ok, I'll start," a very lovely young lady says, stepping forward. "My name is Addis Hor-Den. My brother, Imhotep, and I are from Giza. Our parents are Dr. Addisu and Professor Alpha Rho Hor-Den," she says.

"I will go next," another young lady declares.

She locks eyes with Prince Armacaust as she steps forward. He wants to look away, but cannot seem to resist the temptation to remain focused on her as well.

"My name is Addis Hor-Khufu. Twinzees, girl!" she says excitedly, high-fiving Addis Hor-Den. "I'm from the Ant Planet. My mom is Cleopatra Hor-Khufu."

"Wow! My name is also Addis," another young lady says, walking out of the shadows. "I'm Addis Horus. My sister Nekhbet, my brother Bekele, and I are from Giza. Our parents are Prince Bekele Horus of Planet Ikw-n-tA and Captain Ayanna Pen-Nekhbet Horus of the Giza Planetary Defense Force," she says proudly.

"Ok, to make it simple, let's call you guys Addis HD, Addis HK, and Addis H," Prince Armacaust says, pointing to each of the young ladies in turn and sounding as if he is questioning the logic of his own suggestion.

"Prince Bekele?" DwarfStar blurts out quizzically. "That makes you the great-granddaughter of Monolith Ant," he says, with a tone of alarm.

"Yeah, but my dad does not believe the same things as his grandfather, which is the reason why we live on Giza," Addis H replies defiantly.

"We are not here to judge," Prince Armacaust interjects. "Right, DwarfStar?" he says, staring directly at his friend.

DwarfStar shrugs his shoulders and looks in the opposite direction. The other two Addises begin to giggle. The teens continue to introduce themselves.

"I'll go next!" says a young lady in an energetic tone. "My name is Seraphina Hotep. I am from Planet Chaos. Go PC, baby!

My parents are Elder Shadd and Professor Kebede Hotep," she says, rolling her neck and snapping her fingers on both hands.

"Looks like we're next," a pair of young ladies says in perfect unison.

"I'm Kamia Jupiter," the first says.

"And I am Nkenge," the second offers.

"We're the Jupiter twins, and we're from Giza," they say as their voices, again, blend perfectly. Our parents are Captain Aha Jupiter and Jenna Mandrake Jupiter."

"Do you queens always talk like that?" Seraphina asks quizzically.

"Wait, your mom is Jenna Mandrake?" Prince Armacaust asks.

"Not always," the twins reply, turning to Seraphina first. "And yes, Prince, our grandfather is President Aharon Mandrake," they say, turning back to Prince Armacaust.

"That's spooky," DwarfStar chimes in, unsolicited. "I am going to start tweaking if you girls keep talkin' like that."

DwarfStar slinks back into the periphery when he feels Prince Armacaust glaring at him. Addis HD walks over and places a hand on DwarfStar's shoulder.

"It's not weird," a young lady says, stepping forward confidently. "Looks like I am next. My name is Asenat Menelik. My sister Sojourner, whom we call SoJo, and our brothers Shaka and Solomon are from PC. Our parents are Captain Pulsar and Lieutenant Serethor Hotep of the PDFJC," she says with a smile.

"Well, I guess I will go last. I'm Prince Imhotep II. I'm the son of Prince Adisa and Elder Wells of PC. That's my sister over there, Princess Zilpha. Armacaust here is our uncle, even though me and him are the same age," Prince Imhotep declares.

"Anybody else notice how all of our parents are pretty important people?" DwarfStar asks the group.

"I did notice that, too," Addis HD replies with a grin.

"I wonder what that means," Prince Armacaust says.

"Could they be holding us for ransom?" Prince Imhotep asks.

The teens pause for a moment until Addis HK perks back up. The teens give her their undivided attention.

"So, what do we do now, Prince? Armacaust, I mean. But no disrespect, Prince Imhotep," Addis HK says with a smile.

"Let's get the rest of us organized and calmed down. Whatever happens next, we need to be prepared," Prince Armacaust replies in an even tone.

"We really should also discuss what we do about food," Addis HD adds. "It seems to me that quite a few of us are Drākanashim, which means not all of us can live off sunlight."

"You got that right, queen," Seraphina chimes in.

"That also means we should probably take a count of how many of us are enhanced. Knowing who can do what may also be helpful," the Jupiter twins say in perfect unison.

DwarfStar stands, looking up into a high corner of the cavern, trying his best not to react. Addis HD starts to rub the back of his shoulder, trying to keep from laughing.

"That's a good point," Prince Armacaust replies. "I'll start. I'm really strong. I can fly pretty fast. I absorb energy, and I can also create an electromagnetic pulse effect that temporarily shuts down any paranatural abilities in close proximity."

"Whoa, bruh! That's crazy wicked!" Seraphina says enthusiastically.

"I can control gravity," DwarfStar chimes in. "I can also fly, not at light speed yet, but I am working on it."

"I grow and control magnetism," Prince Imhotep declares. "My sister, Zilpha, can fly really, really fast. She's also very strong. Oh, yeah, she can open warp gates, too."

"Oh, then she can just take us home," Addis HK exclaims.

"Well, it's not that simple. Zilpha can only open gateways to places she has seen, which means we would all have to go to the same place. And since we are from all over the System, Zilpha could only take us to a place she's familiar with. Whoever brought us here on this little unscheduled field trip may be aware of that and could be waiting for us on the other side," Prince Imhotep explains.

"Theoretically speaking, of course," the Jupiter twins add.

DwarfStar clenches his teeth. Addis HD can no longer contain herself. She giggles softly at the expression on DwarfStar's face.

"Let's think about that some more. If we're trapped here for too long, it may be worth the risk," Prince Armacaust advises. "Who's next?"

"I can fly and create exploding orbs of light, and I also have vortex breath," Asenat says. "My brother, Shaka, is strong and nearly invulnerable. SoJo can fly. She's really strong. She can radiate focused beams of electromagnetic energy and can also change shapes. Yeah, SoJo can do a lot. She's a lot like our Aunt Connie. And my brother, Solomon, can fly and travel between space and time, something like that, I guess."

"Ok. My younger brother, Bekele, can run pretty fast. He is also super strong and a very good fighter. I mean, like, really good," Addis H says proudly.

"Alright, it sounds like we can defend ourselves pretty well, should the people who brought us here come looking for trouble. Let's focus on keeping the group safe. That should be our first priority. We should also split up into teams. We will need to find out if any of the other kids have powers. Finding someone who can turn invisible would be very helpful," Prince Armacaust declares.

The teens nod their agreement, then huddle together to discuss their next steps.

DwarfStar continues to bite his bottom lip each time the Jupiter twins speak.

CHAPTER 10

WHAT DID WE JUST SEE?

As the stream continues from what seems to be H's first encounter with Apep in a cave, Sphinx begins to notice common themes. She decides to keep her observations to herself as the stream continues.

Right before her team began the stream, Sphinx addressed the planetary leaders gathered in her viewing room. After welcoming her distinguished guests, she explained that The Gatekeepers' tech would allow them to see a slightly delayed stream of H's visions.

She hesitates now because, as she collects more data, she wonders if it would be beneficial to review earlier parts of the stream and compare what she has already seen to her developing theory. More importantly, she wonders who in the viewing room may have picked up on the same themes she has.

Of the people seated in the viewing room next door, only two of them would possess the same contextual knowledge Sphinx has about H. The only two who were born on Planet Earth and actually traveled to Chaos with H are Abasi Horus, known across the System as Monolith Ant, and Aharon Mandrake, known to the intelligence community as the Shadow Ant.

Hours pass. Sphinx steps into the viewing room through a side door and personally offers the planetary leaders and their aides a "bio break," followed by lunch in the dining hall on the fourth floor.

As Gen. Menelik and Col. GiantStar escort the guests to the elevator, Aharon Mandrake lingers behind and approaches Sphinx. It is out of sheer curiosity that Sphinx even entertains a conversation with Aharon.

Though Aharon is her paternal grandfather, Sphinx has had very limited contact with him. Not to mention Aharon's rocky relationship with the queen, he did not even admit to being the father of Sphinx's father, Captain LionMane, or his sister, Lady Fukyana Aten, for most of their lives.

It was not until their mother was violently murdered that Aharon publicly acknowledged the children of slain educator Tawaret Amun to be his. Most of what Sphinx knows about her grandfather she gathered from the numerous stories circulating about him from political rivals, scorned lovers, or people claiming to be his children.

"How is she, your mother? How's H?" Aharon asks in a soft voice.

"That sounds more like a question for her husband than me, Mr. President," Sphinx replies flatly.

"Hrmph." Aharon chuckles. "You are a lot like her, you know," he says with a smile.

"What is it that you really want to ask me, Mr. President?" Sphinx asks directly.

"Yup, just like her. Straight to the point, I see. Ok, fine. You saw what I saw. If we were to connect the dots, it seems like H's subconscious is pointing us to Apep and Earth, and not just any place on Earth, but back to Kemet and/or Kush. My question becomes, then, what is the connection between H, Apep, and Kemet?" he asks in a straightforward manner. "Once we know the answer to that question, we will know the whole story of Hawwah Menewa. But I surmise that the last thing you want is for anyone to know the 'whole story' of Hawwah Menewa," he says with a smile.

Stunned, Sphinx pauses for a moment as she tries to figure out a response. At most, she finally manages a tepid quip.

"You're right. But all I can think about right now is finding these missing kids. I will worry about my mother's impending PR nightmare later," she retorts.

She then nods respectfully as she begins to walk out of the room, the same way she entered. She pauses for a moment. She turns to Aharon as if she might open up more concerning his observations. Instead, she simply places her right hand over her heart and bows slightly.

"Mr. President," she says respectfully.

Aharon nods in kind. Sphinx then turns and exits the viewing room.

"Mr. President," Col. GiantStar beckons.

"Be right there," Aharon replies.

He pauses for a moment, then turns and follows Col. GiantStar to the elevator. Back in the control room, Sphinx begins combing through the recorded streaming footage.

"Where is this place on Earth?" Sphinx asks aloud in a demanding tone.

The techs in the control room perk up so that they can be ready to respond with speed to the boss's next inquiry. With no one able to provide an immediate answer, the techs begin feverishly typing inquiries into their keyboards.

"The backgrounds change, but it's all the same place, the same region. Oh, schiid! He's luring her back to Kemet, but why is the question," Sphinx thinks out loud.

As he walks off the elevator and into the entrance of the main dining hall, Aharon is greeted by his sister, Merneith, Director of the WSA. The two share a long, endearing embrace.

"How are you, brother?" Merneith asks with a warm smile.

"I'm well. How is Rhakotis this time of year?" Aharon asks.

Rhakotis Base, the headquarters of the WSA, serves as a fully functioning military compound combined with a highly sophisticated IT and software engineering laboratory. Other than the barracks housing various military personnel from the Ant Planet, Chaos, and Memphis, the main Rhakotis Base complex and its staff housing are the only structures on the surface of the Warp Star. The Warp Star itself is slightly larger than Jupiter in the Earth's solar system.

"Busy as ever. In fact, I have some leave coming up. I was thinking about coming home," Merneith says, awaiting Aharon's response.

"Yes, of course, you are always welcome at the palace, sis. Just let Cindy know when you will be arriving, and we will roll out the red carpet for you," Aharon replies with a huge smile.

Looking over his sister's shoulder, Aharon notices the other planetary leaders sitting at a table looking in his direction. Taking his cue, Aharon kisses Merneith on her forehead as a signal that he is about to make a move.

"Let's catch up before we leave here. It looks like those folks over there are waiting for me," Aharon says.

Merneith turns to look in the direction of Aharon's gaze. She notices the collective gaze of the other planetary leaders fixed on them.

"Yeah… sure. You better go," she says nervously.

"You good?" Aharon asks, noticing the change in Merneith's demeanor.

"Yeah… I'm good, brother," she says, squeezing his hand tightly, then kissing it. "Go," she says, ushering him off.

As Aharon walks toward the table where the other planetary leaders are seated, two of Monolith Ant's men approach him menacingly. Aharon pauses momentarily.

"Which one of you got beaten up by Jo-Molefi downstairs? You know, she was one of my students," Aharon says with a smile.

The Ikwentashim special forces operatives immediately step back. Major T. Horus walks over to a table and takes a seat without even looking back in Aharon's direction.

"Aharon, everyone knows you are the best fighter that ever lived," Monolith Ant says in a half-sarcastic tone.

"Well, I've heard rumors of a young man on Earth who could actually be a contender for the title," Aharon says with a huge smile.

"He needs to get in line," Neith Ramses chimes in. "I'm always game for another shot at the title," she says flirtatiously.

Aharon smiles. He notices President Sekhmet Djet Drone shaking her head with a sly smile on her face.

"The only thing he has ever loved more than fighting is women," Monolith Ant bellows with a laugh. "But wait. You've heard stories of an 'Earth-bound' that might be able to defeat you in combat?" Monolith Ant asks curiously.

"This kid may be from Earth, but if the rumors are true, he is no 'Earth-bound.' That part is for certain," Aharon replies.

"Interesting," Monolith Ant says slyly.

"My friends, not to break up this class reunion, but my children are still missing," Sekhmet says assertively. "Did anyone see anything in that stream that would lead us to solving the dual mysteries of 'who done it' and 'where they be'?" she asks insistently as tears begin to well up in her eyes.

"I don't recognize any of the places in the streams we saw," King Armacaust offers.

"That's because those places are on Planet Earth," Monolith Ant says with a grin. "Aharon noticed. Did you not, my old friend?" Monolith Ant asks, looking directly at Aharon.

Returning Monolith Ant's gaze, Aharon replies, "Yes, Abasi, I noticed. But it is still unclear that Earth is our target location. Besides, I do not think we want to send an invasion force to Earth prematurely. Not only will our Earth-bound cousins defend themselves, but they will also know that we exist, and that has been a well-guarded secret for several thousand years now.

"Furthermore, while I do not think they could ever devise the technology to reach us here, we should not incentivize them, either. Lord knows the greed of the wealthiest among their people undermines the greatness they could achieve as a society.

"If they would only put aside their petty differences and work together as a unified global community, they could solve all the world's problems and, perhaps, bring healing to the only racial identity that truly matters, the human race."

"Earth?!" Sekhmet shouts in exasperation. "Who would take our children to Earth?" she demands.

"Apep!" Aharon, King Armacaust, and Monolith Ant reply in unison.

"This isn't just about H. He's taking his revenge on all of us," Monolith Ant says dryly.

Seeing the distress remaining on her face, Neith wraps her wings around Sekhmet and steps in closer so that she can wipe Sekhmet's tears. Neith further attempts to console Sekhmet by walking her over to the lunch counter and helping her select a meal.

The five leaders break bread together and enjoy a brief repose before heading back to the viewing room.

Once back in the viewing room, the hours continue to roll on as fresh images stream through the panoramic monitors. The scene starting to develop is dark. The sky above a lush mountain valley displays the brilliant yet waning colors of sunset.

The perspective of the picture begins to focus on a mound in the middle of a thicket of tall trees. What sunlight remains trickles in through the leaves on the trees, tickling the ground and casting ominous shadows around the mound.

Suddenly, men with large, luminous wings appear, as if they are materializing from thin air. The planetary leaders rouse in their seats as one of the winged men starts to raise a ruckus. He passionately demands that the body of Moses be handed over to him.

"The… body… of Moses?!? He wants Moses' dead body?" Sekhmet asks, turning to Neith.

Neith responds by shrugging her shoulders and giving Sekhmet a confused look. Neith then looks to Aharon, who also shrugs his shoulders in confusion.

An additional figure suddenly enters the frame. It appears to be a woman wearing a brilliantly glowing, hooded cloak. Monolith Ant and Aharon stand when the mysterious woman removes her hood, revealing a face familiar to everyone in the viewing room. The familiar face belongs to H.

The winged men make a pathway for her to approach the winged man attempting to claim the body of Moses. H says something inaudible to the man. Suddenly, his flesh erupts, leaving behind the monstrous form of Apep the Dragon, a gigantic beast with seven heads.

Neith gasps as if she were startled by a thrilling scene in a horror movie. Now, Sekhmet stands, watching in amazement.

H completely removes her cloak and launches herself straight into Apep's chest. The Dragon's jaws snap violently as its heads lunge at her, one after the other. H moves much too swiftly for the Dragon to catch.

H lands blow after blow, pummeling the Dragon's heads. The beast finally lands a strike of his own by whipping his tail into H's back. As she crashes to the ground, the Dragon smashes her into the dirt with one of its paws, its massive talons cutting into H's skin.

Unfazed, H retaliates by blasting the Dragon with a massive bolt of energy. Then, flying over the Dragon's back, she unleashes a double-fisted strike that hammers the Dragon into the Earth, causing shockwaves that uproot many of the surrounding trees.

Apep tries to stand, but H grabs his tail with both arms. She rises off the ground and, with a powerful whipping motion, lifts the Dragon off his feet and slams him back to the ground as if she is straightening a towel she just removed from the dryer.

Apep lies on the ground, struggling to move. He finally rolls onto his back. H flies over the beast and then drops like a missile into its torso, ramming her feet into its chest, driving Apep deeper into the dirt.

Her hands radiate with smoldering energy. But before she can strike a final blow, one of the winged men pulls her back. He yells something at the beast. Upon hearing the man's command, the Dragon retreats immediately.

"You see, Hawwah. That is all you had to do. You still have much to learn," the man says to H.

"Yeah, looks that way," H replies, wiping blood from the corner of her mouth as she stares in the direction of the Dragon's exit.

A hush falls over the viewing room. Monolith Ant breaks the silence.

"Who or what is Hawwah Menewa?" he demands.

"I… I just assumed… I mean… I always thought she was from here, an alien on Earth," Sekhmet stammers.

"That could still be true," Neith replies. "The question now becomes how long she was on Earth before the Great Exodus.

The body of Moses, my God. It would have had to have been thousands of years."

All look toward King Armacaust. He remains seated and simply shakes his head in bewilderment.

Watching these reactions unfold from the control room, Sphinx decides to end the viewing session for the night.

"Cut the feed. Open comms to the viewing room," Sphinx orders.

"You're live, Chief," Arisone replies.

"Ladies and gentlemen, I think that is enough for today. My suggestion is that we all bunk here tonight and resume this investigation in the morning. I will make the recording from today's stream available to each of you for review in private. The dining hall on the fourth floor will also be available to you all night, as well as in the morning for breakfast. I only ask that you arrange for an escort by hailing the security desk before leaving your quarters. Col. GiantStar and his team will begin showing you to your quarters in about ten minutes," Sphinx says respectfully but insistently.

Sphinx stands over her console, closes her eyes, and inhales deeply. After taking a long, cleansing exhale, she presses a button on her console.

"Eman?" she calls out.

"Yes, Chief. Go ahead," Eman responds without hesitation.

"We need accommodations for seventy-five," Sphinx says.

"I have rooms available and ready for occupancy on five," Eman responds quickly.

"Outstanding. Coordinate with Admiral Menewa. Assign rooms and arrange for escorts. Thank you," Sphinx says, exhaling again in relief.

"Copy that, Chief. Over," Eman replies before closing her comms.

****

Back in the viewing room, the atmosphere remains hushed. This time, Sekhmet breaks the silence.

"I'm fine with that. I am not leaving here until I get answers," Sekhmet says to her aides.

"I can think of worse things," Aharon says, glancing over at Neith.

Neith smiles.

In less than ten minutes, Col. GiantStar and the Chaosian special forces operatives begin escorting the guests to their assigned quarters. Once all are settled into their rooms, an abnormal quiet settles over the fifth floor of TGHQ. Even the grounds outside, usually teeming with nocturnal hunters, seem unusually still.

After about an hour of nothing stirring, a security camera flickers to life as a motion sensor on the fifth floor picks up a figure moving about the hallway between the guest quarters. Security personnel are alerted and sent to the door where the mysterious figure seems to be headed.

A TGHQ security officer knocks on the door.

"Hotep," Neith says, greeting the security officers as she opens the door.

She notices a strange shadow spilling into her room, strange because it has no discernible origin. She does not give the security officers any indication that she has noticed anything out of the ordinary.

"Sorry to bother you, ma'am. Is everything ok here?" the security officer asks politely.

"Yes, I'm fine," Neith replies calmly.

"Ok. Call if you need anything, ma'am," the officer says.

Once the officers leave her door, Neith shuts the door and enters the locking sequence on the security pad. Once she hears the lock slide into place, she turns away from the door to find Aharon standing behind her.

"You're getting sloppy. Someone saw you," Neith says, looking directly into Aharon's eyes.

"Well, shadows cannot knock on doors. Someone had to get your attention so you could let me in," Aharon says with a smile.

Neith walks closer to him. They stand facing each other for a moment. Neith's hair has been loosened from the bun that held it in place hours earlier. She draws her hair back from her face with one hand and continues to gaze longingly into Aharon's eyes.

Perceiving this action to be an invitation, Aharon wraps one arm around Neith's waist and the other across her upper back, gently caressing her wing but pulling her closer with intention. Once she is close enough to feel Aharon's body against hers, Neith rises onto the tips of her toes and gently bites Aharon's bottom lip.

From there, the former lovers lock lips in a passionate kiss. Neith impatiently works to loosen Aharon's pants from around his waist. Aharon's hands do not move from Neith's waist and back immediately. However, once he feels Neith draw his pants down off his hips, he slips her tunic up over her head.

Neith lifts her arms to assist Aharon in removing her covering. As her breasts settle against her frame, Aharon recalls just how much he enjoys the sight of Neith's naked body. When he lifts her off the ground, Neith spreads her wings in excitement.

They continue to kiss as Aharon carries Neith to the bedroom. Her arms wrapped around his neck, she grips the back of Aharon's head with both hands, kissing his face and nibbling on his ear. As he walks, Neith wraps her legs firmly around Aharon's lean waist. She can feel his arousal intensify as they move closer to the bedroom.

Aharon lays Neith gently on the bed and moves over her. Time passes as Neith and Aharon lose themselves in the intensity of their reunion, exploring each other and sharing a deeply intimate connection.

* * * * * * * *

On the seventh floor, in a supply closet, Hammer and Dr. Heka Menes find themselves in a heated embrace, kissing passionately as their hands explore forbidden areas on each other's bodies. Suddenly, Heka pushes Hammer away with enough force to convey her intention. Although Hammer's muscles are cartoonishly large, he does not possess superhuman strength. Heka, on the other hand, does.

"We've talked about this, Cassius," Heka says while breathing heavily. "We're teammates. We should not ever compromise the mission because of momentary flights of passion."

"Who said this is 'momentary'?" Hammer replies. "Besides, we are not compromising anything at this hour. The PDJFC is on post for a few more hours. So, I am tantalizingly all yours, my sweet."

He reapproaches her cautiously, and when Heka does not resist his approach, he begins planting kisses on Heka's chest. His hands roam softly around Heka's midriff and hips until slipping between her legs. Heka's genitals are warm, soft, and wet. The area of her skirt where Hammer's fingers are applying tender pressure becomes soaked.

Heka reaches down and removes her heels. Hammer stops his actions briefly to catch a glimpse of Heka's bare feet. The sight throws him into an almost uncontrollable fit of desire. At six feet and seven inches, Heka is ostensibly taller than Hammer. Her Drākanashim physiology reflects an elegant blend of an elephant's strength and a bird's sleekness. Her gray skin provides a pleasingly aesthetic contrast against the royal purple hue of Hammer's skin.

His muscular frame presses against Heka as she lifts her skirt to allow Hammer complete access to her lower body. Hammer kicks off his boots and removes his pants and underwear. In one quick motion, he rips Heka's panties from her body.

"Oh!" Heka blurts out in surprise.

"Ahuhhuhhuh." Hammer chuckles weirdly while hiking his eyebrows up and down rapidly.

Heka lets out a loud, genuine laugh. It is in that moment that she realizes that Hammer is the only man who has ever made her laugh, at least, on purpose.

Hammer lifts Heka off the ground and settles her onto his rapidly hardening erection. They begin moving roughly at first, then more synchronized.

Heka is tall and flexible. She spreads her legs wide and wraps her wings around Hammer to pull him even closer.

Hammer grips Heka all the more tightly as he continues to hold her aloft. Their sexual ballet continues until they climax at the same time.

****

In her private quarters, a few miles to the north of TGHQ, Eman and Gen. Ramesses Menelik have been engaged in sexual congress for the past thirty minutes. Gen. Menelik thrusts energetically into Eman, who throws her head back in sheer ecstasy. Sweat drips from both their bodies as they pant, moan, and grind. They roll around Eman's bed, exploring various positions.

"Harder… harder!" Eman screams.

"Yes… Eman…" Gen. Menelik replies between labored breaths.

Eman finally rolls on top of Gen. Menelik and pins him to the bed by pushing her hands into his muscular chest. She begins to roll her hips in a circular pattern that incites Gen. Menelik to drive the back of his head into the mattress. The motion of Eman's hips is hypnotic, and she knows it.

Eman continues to ride like hydraulics.

"Oh, Eman!" Gen. Menelik cries out.

Eman grabs her headboard and begins to ride even more forcefully. Gen. Menelik places his hands loosely on the sides of Eman's torso, but not enough to impede her motion. He soon cannot hold back any longer and lets out a loud moan as he climaxes.

Eman, too, reaches her climax but continues to grind.

"Oh, my… I… I can't take it, baby," Gen. Menelik declares breathlessly.

"Yes, you can. You're enhanced, baby. You got this," Eman replies in a breathy tone.

She continues to grind, lifting her hands up and caressing the back of her own head. Eman's perfectly manicured fingers slide effortlessly through her finely braided locs. Gen. Menelik grimaces, overwhelmed by the pleasure, coupled with an intense tingling in almost every part of his lower body.

Eman works her hips until she reaches a second climax. Exhaling loudly, she slows her motion, eventually coming to a stop. She looks down at her lover with her face beaming. Gen. Menelik chuckles as he places a hand over his face in embarrassment. He parts his fingers so that Eman can see one of his eyes. The couple shares a brief laugh.

"Do you think the princess knows about us?" he asks.

"Probably," Eman answers right away. "Nothing gets past the chief."

****

Back in her penthouse, Sphinx steps out of her shower and picks up a tablet connected wirelessly to the facility's security feed. She reviews the report of a false alarm on the fifth floor involving Leader Neith Ramses.

She also notices that there are no logs indicating the whereabouts of Dr. Heka Menes or Hammer. It is not lost on Sphinx, however, that their security badges are pinging in the same location. She also sees that Eman used her badge to exit the facility ninety minutes ago. She then notices an alert advising her that Gen. Menelik was granted a two-hour break ahead of his next post assignment.

"Everyone in this place seems to be having sex except for me," she says to herself. "Lovely," she says, sighing. "Well, Geisha

Nine-Thousand, how would you like to help me take my mind off things?" she says, turning to the seven-foot automaton that serves as her personal AI assistant and bedchamber mate.

"Your wish is my command, Chief," it replies.

"Then get over here and do me hard. I would like to scream this day away," she orders, dropping her robe to the floor and stretching herself out across her bed.

CHAPTER 11
YOU LIKE HIM

Having done their best to calm the massive group of tired, hungry children throughout the night, the makeshift leadership group once again huddles to talk strategy. Prince Armacaust goes about assigning responsibilities to the other teens.

Overnight, they identified and recruited a new addition to their leadership group, fifteen-year-old Merneith Grey, the daughter of Rear Admiral Torian Grey II and Deputy Galactic Marshal Ahaneith Hotep Grey, better known as Satellite.

Merneith and her younger brothers, twins Gbeto and Abrax, are Drākanashim like their father. Their DNA reflects a mixture of human genomes with those of the water buffalo. Unlike their father, Merneith and her brothers possess features that are predominantly human, other than the horns atop their heads.

RADM Grey's body is covered in microscopic hairs that give his skin a dark gray hue. His ears are also shaped like those of a water buffalo. Merneith and her brothers are also enhanced like their mother.

Merneith can fly faster than the speed of light and bend light into hard constructs, even force fields. Gbeto and Abrax can grow to the size of a small moon, increasing their strength and durability proportionately, an ability that mirrors their mother's. The twins can also run at speeds in excess of Mach 3.

Prince Armacaust assigns them to stand guard and act as the last line of defense against anyone attempting to attack this section of the cavern. Addis HD and her younger brother, along with Addis HK and Addis H, plus her younger sister and brother, are assigned to organizing the thousands of children into smaller groups so that their needs can be identified and assessed.

Seraphina, together with Asenat, plus her sister and brothers, is assigned to scouting a possible exit on the west side of the cavern. Armacaust selects DwarfStar, Prince Imhotep, and Princess Zilpha to join him in scouting the east side of the cavern for an exit.

Feeling responsible for the younger Meketaten children, DwarfStar pulls fourteen-year-old Ahmose, along with her sister Amunet, better known as "Fusion," and their brother, ten-year-old Den II, into the group as well.

"Ok, now that we all have our responsibilities, let's execute," Armacaust says with a smile. "Remember, come back here to report if you encounter hostiles. And most of all, stay safe," he orders.

Throughout the night, Addis HK had become more and more infatuated with Prince Armacaust. She marvels at his courage and ability to lead. She finds herself genuinely wanting to help the young prince be successful.

Prince Armacaust appreciates her attention and advice. He finds that Addis HK's energy and willingness to engage wholeheartedly with the task at hand have a calming effect on him.

Just before the teams take off to undertake their responsibilities, Addis HK walks over to Prince Armacaust and places a hand on his chest.

"You be careful, too, Prince," she says, looking directly into his eyes.

Prince Armacaust places his hand on top of hers for a moment before rising into the air.

"Let's go!" Prince Armacaust commands.

"Copy!" DwarfStar replies enthusiastically.

DwarfStar joins Prince Armacaust in the air, and they begin to fly away. Prince Imhotep grows to an impressive size and begins to follow them on the ground. Princess Zilpha takes the hands of Fusion and Den II and walks behind Ahmose, who scampers quickly behind Prince Imhotep.

Addis HK watches the team leave until they fade from sight.

"You've got a crrr-rrrrruuuuuussssssh on him, queen," Seraphina sings loudly, wrapping her arms around Addis HK's shoulders playfully.

"Noooooo! I don't… I just… I just think he's kinda cute," Addis HK says with a wide grin on her face.

Asenat and Sojourner run over and join the two girls in a hearty laugh. Addis HD and Addis H look up when they hear the commotion.

"What's happening over there?" Addis HD asks, smiling.

"We'll tell you later, queen," Seraphina shouts back.

Seraphina, Asenat, SoJo, Shaka, and Solomon scamper off into the darkness in the opposite direction. Addis HK and Addis HD walk toward each other, looking in the direction Seraphina, Asenat, and the others had headed.

"I hope we find a way out of here soon." Addis HD says, sighing.

The two girls hold hands as they walk back toward the larger group.

****

In a corner of the cavern, a pair of winged siblings sit alone. They cling to each other, each with their wings wrapped around the other. Rajaa Dawit and her brother, Horo, are the children of Kebret Dawit II and Makeda Powell Dawit.

Kebret's father is the wealthiest Eshanashim in the entire System. His wife, Makeda, one of the most famous actors in the System, is the daughter of the man who leads the most revered, but also the most feared, intelligence agency in the galaxy. His mother is the sister of Leader Neith Ramses.

Kebret has been in constant fear that someone would attempt to apply pressure to either his father, his father-in-law, or his aunt by kidnapping him, his wife, or his children. Every day of his children's lives, he has unwittingly imprinted that anxiety onto their young psyches.

Even though thousands of children surround them, Rajaa and Horo cannot help but think this entire situation has everything to do with them. They fear what will happen if the other children discover this secret.

Another young Drākanashim named Anippe Boateng notices Rajaa and Horo sitting alone and decides to walk over and introduce herself. Like her mother, Anippe is a human-crocodile hybrid. Her mother, Kimboti, is the daughter of Abrafo Boateng, leader of the Sea Tribe of the Giza Moon Colony.

Abrafo has been rumored to be involved with several illegal activities, from smuggling to human trafficking. Most notably, he serves as a lieutenant in the Edwesu Crime Family. The Edwesus wield enormous influence on Giza.

The boss and family patriarch, Goliath, serves as the chairman of the powerful Giza River Authority Council (GARC). The GRAC oversees the shipping lanes across the various waterways on Giza and regulates border and territorial disputes on all of Giza's oceans, rivers, and lakes.

Goliath accepts bribes from any corporation, pirate, or planetary government seeking to "pay to play" for access to Giza's shipping lanes. Abrafo oversees the regulation of border disputes on the oceans and seas. Because evidence has been hard to come by for investigators, neither Goliath nor Abrafo has faced any serious legal peril.

Anippe is very connected to her mother and grandfather, but she does not know her father. The most Anippe hears about her father involves his work as a high-ranking government official with the power to change the lives of every person on the Giza Moon Colony.

Anippe desires nothing more than to simply meet her father. She often rehearses her introduction for the day she and her father will meet. So, when she sees other children in pain, she does everything she can to comfort them as a means of coping with her own anguish.

"Are you two ok?" Anippe asks softly.

Rajaa and Horo look up at Anippe over their outstretched wings, each with watery eyes. Anippe begins to feel all the more sorry for them.

"My name is Anippe, but people also call me 'Wavelength,' because I can stretch and change my shape into just about anything. What're your names?" she says.

"I'm Rajaa. And this is Horo," Rajaa replies cautiously.

Rajaa and Horo relax their wings for a moment. Anippe steps a little closer.

"Do you mind if I sit with you guys? Some of the other kids are not that friendly," Anippe asks with a warm smile.

"We don't mind," Horo replies.

"Why are you guys sitting over here by yourselves?" Anippe asks.

"We think this may be all our fault," Horo responds.

Rajaa gives Horo a sharp elbow. Her face becomes stern as she glares at her brother.

"You talk too much," she snaps.

"This can't be your fault," Anippe assures. "We don't even know where we are."

"Our dad says this was bound to happen someday," Horo says sadly.

"We just didn't think it would happen in a way that got other people caught up in our drama," Rajaa adds.

"What drama?" Anippe inquires.

"Our father works for his dad, Kebret Dawit. Grandad owns the East Solar System Trading Company. Dad says people might try to hurt us to get back at Grandad," Horo explains.

"And our aunt is Leader Ramses. There are a lot of people who would like to hurt her by kidnapping us," Rajaa adds.

"Your aunt is WingDrake?" Anippe says excitedly. "Wow! That's so cool! She's like my hero!"

"Well, Dad says that Auntie Neith and both of our grandfathers have a lot of enemies," Rajaa retorts.

"Do you think that's why all of us are here?" Horo asks Anippe with genuine concern.

"Nope!" Anippe replies confidently. "My father is a big deal on Giza, too, and my granddad is the leader of the Sea Tribe. Whoever did this probably just wanted to kidnap a bunch of kids of important people. The kid who spoke to us earlier is the prince of PC. I recognize him from pictures of him with Queen Hawwah."

"Mom says the queen is a really nice person," Horo says.

"I think Queen Hawwah is awesome!" Rajaa says, beaming.

Anippe grabs both Rajaa and Horo by the hand. She flashes them a wide smile. The siblings finally settle into a sense of calm.

"You'll see. Our parents are too important not to find us. Everything will be fine!" Anippe declares.

Anippe scoots in closer to Rajaa and Horo. The siblings stretch their wings out to cover Anippe.

"It's so nice to make new friends," Anippe says.

CHAPTER 12
SURROUNDED

Seraphina and her team, the Menelik kids, crawl, climb, and fly their way across the dark expanse of the cavern. Seraphina and Shaka, neither of whom can fly like Shaka's siblings, find themselves helping each other traverse the rocky terrain.

Seraphina is a Drākanashim like her father, and like Sphinx, Seraphina's skin is given a burnt orange hue by the microscopic hairs covering her body. But unlike the princess, Seraphina's distinctive bands of striping cover her arms and legs. Her tiger-like strength and agility allow her to leap and climb much more efficiently than Shaka.

Shaka, however, is an enhanced Eshanashim, possessed of superhuman strength and invulnerability. He also has a genius-level intellect, making him a fantastic inventor and mechanic. Even at fifteen, he is already surprisingly handsome. Seraphina thinks so, but she is far too proud to let Shaka know that.

They almost instinctively take turns pushing and pulling each other over the various obstacles along the path, instantly developing a mutual bond.

Seraphina uses her acute senses of hearing and smell to follow the stream of water running along the cavern floor and, at times, beneath it. The Menelik kids follow excitedly. The stream finally leads the team to an opening in the cavern wall.

The small window looks to be less than 100 feet off the ground. Hoping to finally see the sky again, Seraphina scampers excitedly up the wall, about fifty feet off the ground, and peeks through the small hole, peering into the chilly night. She suddenly smells a foul odor, a scent that she does not recognize.

Sensing trouble, she decides to ask one of the other members of her party to fly out through the window and provide a scouting report. As she turns her head to call to the others, a large red hand crashes through the opening in the stone and grabs the back of Seraphina's head.

"Hello, pretty cat!" a rough voice connected to the hand blurts out.

"Seraphina!" Shaka shouts, somewhat panicked.

Seraphina begins to squirm in panic and pain as she struggles to get free. The hand begins to apply crushing pressure to her head.

Seeing Seraphina in trouble, Asenat, Sojourner, and Solomon rush into action.

Asenat sets off a powerful flash bomb that temporarily blinds the assailant, while Sojourner sends a tremendous bolt of energy through the crack in the wall, driving the monstrous figure backward.

Seraphina begins to fall to the ground as the monstrous hand releases her head.

Solomon catches Seraphina before she hits the ground and places her gently in Shaka's arms.

Letting out a bloodcurdling roar, another monstrous figure with fiery red skin explodes through the stone wall and drops down to the cavern floor, landing as easily as if he simply hopped out of his bed. The creature is followed by another, then another.

"They must be really, really strong if they can jump down from that height so easily," Solomon declares.

"So am I," SoJo declares, clenching her fists.

The last red-skinned figure entering the cavern through the breach rises slowly. His neck cracks and pops as he leans his head hard to one side, then the other.

"Do what we do, boys," he calls out to the others.

"Certainly," one of the others replies roughly.

The four figures are the notorious Hyksos brothers. They are known throughout the System as the "Wiles of the Devil." Their brilliantly red skin and glowing eyes make them look like demons arising straight from "the Pit" itself, but in reality, they are the result of genetic experiments conducted by their adopted father and financier, the Grand Reverend, an avowed Satanist and antagonist to Queen Hawwah.

The oldest of the five brothers, also their leader, is Sobek, better known as Despair. The other four brothers are two sets of twins: Haile and K'Esiti, better known as Jealousy and Envy, respectively, plus Nganga and Hannibal, better known as Hatred and Animosity. Each of the brothers is very strong, capable of deadlifting over 100 tons.

They are also extremely durable. They have the further ability to burst into flames and burn their opponents with a touch, and to project powerful, even crippling emotions into the minds of the anxious, fearful, or brokenhearted.

Once on the ground, the Wiles of the Devil spontaneously burst into flames and begin a deliberate march toward Shaka and Seraphina. Anticipating being burned, Seraphina closes her eyes and buries her head in Shaka's shoulder.

But before the brothers can reach Shaka and Seraphina, Asenat, Sojourner, and Solomon swoop in between the Wiles of the Devil and their brother. Without hesitation, Asenat draws a deep breath and exhales a gust of wind powerful enough to extinguish the flames emanating from the brothers' bodies.

Surprised, Despair stops his advance and looks over his hands and arms in disbelief. But before he can resume his advance, Sojourner surges forward and lands a punch that launches him backward. Despair crashes through the now larger hole in the cavern wall.

"Oh!" exclaims Jealousy.

Hatred, the strongest of this band of brothers, and his twin, Animosity, lunge forward but are stopped in their tracks by exploding orbs of light set off by Asenat.

Seraphina leaps from Shaka's arms to join the fight, but Solomon grabs her and swings her back toward his brother. She snarls until she realizes she is back with Shaka. They share an endearing smile at one another until Shaka suddenly whirls Seraphina around to remove her from the path of a punch by Hatred.

The monster drops a thunderous blow into Shaka's head and chest, throwing him across the room. Seraphina punches back, but her attack has no effect. Before Hatred can throw another punch at Seraphina, Sojourner drills him into the ground with a powerful energy bolt.

Asenat rains exploding orbs onto the brothers, driving them back. Accepting their defeat, Hatred, Animosity, and Jealousy climb back up the wall and exit the cavern through the window.

Solomon flies over to the breach and watches the monsters scurry down the side of the mountain, disappearing into the distance and the mist.

"Well, I guess we're not going out this way," he says matter-of-factly.

The sound of sizzling and popping accompanies Asenat as she descends toward Shaka, who is gathering himself on the cavern floor, the remnants of her energy orbs dissipating. Without even looking at each other, Asenat and Sojourner share a triumphant fist bump as they arrive at adjoining spots next to their brother and a kneeling Seraphina.

Solomon also gently floats down to join the crew.

"So, what's next?" Solomon asks Asenat.

"We need to find Armacaust and let him know what happened here," she replies.

****

On the other side of the cave, Prince Armacaust and DwarfStar lead their team to what looks like it may be the entrance to the cavern.

"I see a light up ahead!" Prince Armacaust shouts excitedly.

As Prince Armacaust and DwarfStar fly faster, Imhotep and Ahmose break into a sprint. Princess Zilpha, still holding hands with Fusion and Den, begins to pick up the pace. The children's hearts begin to lift until they see Prince Armacaust stop abruptly.

Momentarily distracted by burning flint bouncing off the cavern wall, DwarfStar crashes into Prince Armacaust.

"Yo!" DwarfStar shouts.

They hover, frozen, as a disturbing voice breaks through the darkness. Ahmose, previously sprinting behind Prince Imhotep, slides to a stop. She stands cautiously behind Prince Imhotep's leg.

"You reek of her stench," Apep says coldly as he emerges from the shadows in his dragon form.

Apep's ten heads snake in different directions, searching out the cavern until all his eyes fix on the group of Eshanashim children standing before him. Prince Armacaust flies in closer as DwarfStar joins Imhotep, Princess Zilpha, Fusion, and Den on the ground, spreading out his arms in front of them.

"Yes, I think I'll kill you first," the Dragon's heads say in unison, squarely focused on the young prince.

The massive form of the beast leaves Prince Armacaust speechless. Two of the Dragon's heads draw breath and unleash a powerful blast of flame and lightning. The cavern grows almost unbearably hot, and the children on the ground scream in terror as they watch Prince Armacaust's body engulfed by the flames.

When the Dragon's onslaught concludes, Prince Armacaust is still alive. Although his clothing is completely burned off, he remains hovering in the same spot, steam streaming from his glistening skin. While not invulnerable to harm like his mother,

Prince Armacaust's paranatural capabilities include enhanced durability, enabling him to survive a nuclear explosion, combined with the ability to absorb tremendous amounts of energy.

At this stage in his life, the limits of his powers have not been tested in a real fight; notwithstanding, he gets an eerie feeling that he will not survive too many more blasts like that from Apep.

On the ground, Prince Armacaust's compatriots remain fixed on him. Though Armacaust's back is to the children on the ground, Princess Zilpha releases Den's hand to cover Fusion's eyes.

Shaking off his bewilderment, Prince Armacaust turns his head to the others and yells, "Run!"

Apep tries to blast the children on the ground, but Prince Armacaust raises a force field that deflects the blast. Again, the cavern grows swelteringly hot. The previously cool, moist air has been transformed into an extreme sauna.

The kids on Prince Armacaust's team begin to move more slowly, as if they will soon succumb to the overpowering heat. Prince Armacaust turns and courageously charges the beast, bashing one of Apep's heads with an overhand right and pushing another head into the cavern wall.

Though he may not be invulnerable like H, Prince Armacaust is incredibly strong. Even at this tender age, the young prince is capable of deadlifting an object with a mass equal to that of Earth's moon.

Apep uses still another head to grab Prince Armacaust by the leg, his jaws clamping down hard on the prince's lower leg. The vicious bite rips through Prince Armacaust's skin. Gnawing on the prince's shinbone, Apep whips his head around violently, slamming Prince Armacaust to the ground, then against a wall.

Seeing the prince is dazed, Apep uses three more heads to clamp down on Prince Armacaust's remaining limbs. Though he is in excruciating pain, the young prince refuses to give Apep the satisfaction of showing how much he hurts.

"So brave," Apep says with a sly grin, pulling the young prince closer. "Your mother is also brave, boy. But courage won't save her either." The beast sneers.

Apep opens another mouth wide, as if he plans to literally bite off Armacaust's head.

Watching this unfold, Princess Zilpha decides to join the fight. She releases Fusion altogether and flies furiously into action. She begins blasting Apep's heads with powerful bolts of energy, causing Apep to release his grip on Prince Armacaust and reel backward.

Freed from the Dragon's jaws, Prince Armacaust launches himself into the Dragon's chest, knocking the beast onto the cavern floor. Reacting with blinding speed, Apep whips his tail and delivers a massive strike to both Prince Armacaust and Princess Zilpha with one blow.

Prince Armacaust somersaults into an adjoining wall, bouncing off the wall and falling immediately to the ground. Princess Zilpha crashes violently to the cavern floor.

Seeing the older kids knocked down, Fusion springs into action. She streaks through the air and right into Apep's chest, punching and screaming wildly. To the surprise of all, each blow she lands knocks Apep back, until she finally lands a punch that lifts Apep off his feet.

Once in the air, Fusion continues her attack by flying straight into Apep's torso and pushing him out of the cave's entrance and driving him into the valley below, crashing through trees, frightening a flock of flamingos, and sending other wildlife scattering.

"Whoa…" DwarfStar mutters in disbelief.

"We need to go get her!" Prince Armacaust exclaims.

"Right!" DwarfStar shouts.

Prince Armacaust, DwarfStar, and Princess Zilpha propel themselves into the air and streak out of the cave's entrance. By the time the teens catch up to her, Fusion has pushed Apep to the shore of a large body of water.

Princess Zilpha grabs Fusion around her waist and pulls her away from the beast, barely avoiding Apep's jaws as several of his heads snap at her. Prince Armacaust delivers one final blow that throws Apep hundreds of feet offshore and into the midst of the water.

DwarfStar uses his mastery over gravitational forces to increase Apep's weight, causing the beast to sink beneath the water and out of sight.

"That will hold him for a minute," DwarfStar says excitedly, feeling quite pleased with himself.

The three teens zip back to the cave, with Princess Zilpha carrying Fusion in tow. Once back on the ground in the cave, the teens slump over with their hands on their knees, breathing heavily.

Still stark naked, Armacaust turns to DwarfStar with a puzzled look on his face.

"Dude?!?" he exclaims in a quizzical manner.

"I didn't know she could do that," DwarfStar replies, shrugging his shoulders.

"You never asked, silly," Fusion replies with a sly smile.

Princess Zilpha giggles and hugs Fusion tightly. Den and Ahmose walk over and wrap their arms around both the princess and their sister.

"Let's get back to the others," Prince Armacaust commands.

The team hurries back to the section of the cavern where the kidnapped Eshanashim children have been encamped. As soon as Addis HK lays eyes on Prince Armacaust, she runs over to him and hugs him tightly.

It is not until she pulls him close that she realizes the prince is completely naked.

"Oh… stand behind me," she says to him politely.

Armacaust steps behind Addis HK, and she reaches back and pulls him closer. After a minute, she feels a poke in her back. Trying to conceal her smile, Addis HK leans her head over her shoulder toward Prince Armacaust.

"That may come in handy when we get a little older, but for now, take a step back, Prince," Addis HK whispers.

Prince Armacaust blushes and steps back.

DwarfStar runs to his backpack and grabs his gym clothes. He walks over and hands the clothing to Prince Armacaust.

DwarfStar and Addis HK then stand in front of Prince Armacaust as he puts on DwarfStar's gym shorts and T-shirt.

Addis HD and Addis H walk up to Prince Armacaust and tell him they counted over 33,300 children in the lower cavern.

"33,300?!?" Prince Armacaust repeats in astonishment.

"Yeah… it's wild," Addis HD replies.

Addis H nods in agreement. The Jupiter twins each cross their arms, placing one hand on their chin.

"They even move at the same time? This is too much," says DwarfStar.

"How could anyone move that many people all at once?" Prince Imhotep thinks out loud. "Not even Dean Starlyte can do that… not without the Warp Star."

"This is getting weirder and weirder by the second," Prince Armacaust adds.

Just then, Asenat, Seraphina, and their crew burst back onto the scene. Seraphina doubles over and rests her hands on her knees, as if she has been sprinting over a long distance.

While Sojourner and Solomon tend to Seraphina, Asenat and Shaka step forward to report on their encounter with the "monsters" at the other end of the cave.

"We're… surrounded…" DwarfStar says with a very concerned look on his face.

"We need a plan," Addis HD offers.

"I second that emotion, queen!" Seraphina shouts between breaths.

"Ok, team! Let's put our heads together," Prince Armacaust says.

"What about up?" Kamia asks, pointing to the ceiling of the cave.

"Nothing?" DwarfStar asks offhandedly, looking in Nkenge's direction.

"How about up?" Nkenge replies with a giggle.

"I give up!" DwarfStar exclaims, walking off into a corner.

"You're not wrong," Armacaust replies to Kamia. "Their plan seems to be to keep us in the middle of the cave. 'Up' may be our best option."

CHAPTER 13
TEAM OF RIVALS

Several hundred miles from the cave, the sea begins to roil. Suddenly, a man with large, illuminated wings erupts from the water. He is Apep the Challenger. Apep lets out a primal cry and flies furiously back toward the cave.

He looks in the direction of the cave but turns north. Letting out another roar, the Challenger erupts back into Apep the Dragon. As his shadow moves over the top of the cave, the Dragon continues north.

At a campsite six miles northwest of the mountain peak, The Leader, together with his loyal subordinate and adopted son, Sobek Anubis, better known as Racism, waits along with a shadowy figure known only to them as the Grand Reverend.

Born Set Defiance in Year 6118, which would be 1082 BCE on Earth, The Leader is a first-generation Drākanashim, naturally born as opposed to being the result of genetic engineering like his parents. Though his body is covered with microscopic hairs, he appears to be a Caucasian male from one of the European nations along the Mediterranean coast on Planet Earth.

Notwithstanding, he possesses the same strength, speed, durability, and stamina as a fully grown male lion.

The Leader leads a cult of devil-worshipers who call themselves "The Takeover." Because they believe themselves to be superior to the humans on Earth, the members of The Takeover blend in among the people of Earth and work to sow discord and hatred, concentrating their efforts on pushing humankind on Earth ever closer to the brink of destroying itself.

Members of their cult have infiltrated the highest levels of Earth societies in every corner of the globe. They control governmental entities, lead major corporations, and run academic institutions. After operating on Earth for a couple of millennia, there is no facet of human society that they do not influence.

The Leader created his alter ego, Dr. Guillermo Elon Lynch, a billionaire philanthropist from Spain, to be his cover as he advances his mission on Earth. He hates Hawwah with every fiber of his being. His most ardent desires include H's destruction and for all of humanity to perish with her.

The Leader maintains homes and safe houses across the System but identifies as a citizen of Planet Memphis. His wife, Esha, even serves in the Memphisonian Senate.

While the primary focus of The Takeover is the destruction of human life on Earth, it was The Leader who planned, financed, and orchestrated the kidnapping of 33,300 Eshanashim children from schools and orphanages across the System.

"When was the last report you received from your 'men'?" The Leader asks the Grand Reverend rather condescendingly.

"I've already told you, Defiance; they will report when they have something relevant to share," the Grand Reverend replies, barely concealing his annoyance.

The men approach each other and stand face to face. Racism slides in between them with his back to his father, facing the Grand Reverend.

"Gentlemen, the sooner we get this over with, the sooner we can be rid of each other," Racism says glibly.

Racism has lived on Planet Earth for the better part of the last two thousand years. He serves as the public face of The Takeover. And like his adopted father, Racism poses as a wealthy European media mogul to conceal his Drākanashim origin. He uses the name G. Elon Lynch Jr. as his primary cover.

Racism believes Drākanashim and enhanced Eshanashim are the living embodiments of Satan's justification for feeling superior to humans, based on immutable characteristics like the fact that humans can be consumed by fire. Sobek Anubis adopted the moniker "Racism" to further champion this type of hatred, first perpetuated by the devil himself against all humankind, but refined in modern human history to be directed primarily toward so-called "Black" people.

He even playfully reminds his followers that if they identify as a "racist," they share the same mentality as his god, Lucifer, that is, the devil himself.

Sobek's wife, better known as Annie Cult, serves as the chief priestess of The Takeover. Annie Cult, like her husband, is also a Drākanashim, a human-tiger hybrid. On Earth, she has become a globally known conservative commentator and internet celebrity.

Racism and Annie Cult have four daughters: Bathsheba, Jezebel, Gomer, and Helen. Racism uses his daughters as props, directing them to seek sexual liaisons with influential men on Earth and back home in the System. He uses the existence of such relationships to exercise influence over powerful men and further his objectives.

Today, his assignment is to support his father in this most wide-ranging and complex caper. Racism is no fan of the Grand Reverend but realizes The Takeover requires the Grand Reverend's assistance to deliver for their master.

While The Leader and the Grand Reverend continue their staring contest, the super-assassin WarHorse enters the command center to let The Leader know that Despair and his brothers have returned.

The Leader does not break eye contact with the Grand Reverend, however. "Let them in," he commands.

The Grand Reverend walks toward the entrance to the command center. Upon entering, Despair recounts the defeat they suffered in the encounter with the enhanced Eshanashim children in the cave.

"So, if I am hearing you correctly, a little girl beat you up, my friend? Is that your report?" Racism asks condescendingly.

"I can show you better than I can tell you," Despair responds.

Racism begins to walk toward Despair before being stopped by his father. He looks Despair up and down. Racism, a former IGP officer, may not look it, but he is highly skilled in hand-to-hand combat and a master sniper. He shares the same fearlessness as an adult male tiger roaming the rainforests of Asia. Racism does not generally back down from a fight, regardless of the odds.

"Control your men," The Leader commands, turning to the Grand Reverend.

The Grand Reverend takes a seat and begins fidgeting with something on the desk in front of him. He pretends not to hear The Leader.

"I said, NOW!" The Leader commands, raising his voice.

"My son is far more capable of killing your son than yours is of even harming mine," the Grand Reverend says without even looking up from the desk.

He fashions a paper football out of a piece of paper on the desk and flicks it at The Leader. Taking his father's cue, Despair begins advancing menacingly toward Racism and The Leader.

WarHorse removes his bow from its holster, and drawing an arrow, he steps between the massive Despair and The Leader.

"Last chance to call your man back, Grand Reverend," WarHorse says coldly, aiming his shot at Despair's head.

"Stand down, Despair!" the Grand Reverend says, sighing in a playful manner.

Despair stops his advance and stands completely still. WarHorse does not lower his bow. Instead, he pulls the bowstring back even further. The sound of the increasing tension can be heard by everyone watching the situation unfold.

"These people are no fun," the Grand Reverend says.

While he continues staring in The Leader's direction, the Grand Reverend rises from his seat slowly, slams his hands on the desk, walks slowly over to The Leader, and stands face to face with him.

"Tell your son to hold his tongue, or I will have one of my boys pull it out," the Grand Reverend says directly to The Leader.

"I'm aware of your little genetic experiments, Grand Reverend. You would be making a tragic mistake thinking I didn't come prepared to neutralize every threat. How else do you think my organization and I've survived for centuries, contending against beings with god-like powers?" The Leader replies.

WarHorse, maintaining the tension on his bow, has not lowered his aim. It is not until the Grand Reverend looks past The Leader that he notices WarHorse's son and partner, K'Esiti Seshperonch, aiming an arrow at the back of Despair's head.

"Has he been in here this whole time?" the Grand Reverend asks with great surprise.

The Leader simply smiles in response.

While the standoff continues inside the command tent, screams begin to arise outside from the surrounding tents. The Leader and the Grand Reverend burst through the entrance of their command center to see Apep in his dragon form, hovering above the camp and randomly murdering their soldiers.

The Leader and the Grand Reverend drop to one knee to kneel before Apep as he lands. The Dragon dissolves to reveal the Challenger.

"I'm vexed," Apep the Challenger says with a sigh. "How many of these wretched children have your men captured or killed so far?" the Challenger bellows.

"None, my lord," The Leader replies in a lowered tone.

"I was promised 700 *untouched* girls," a voice declares from behind the Challenger.

"And who are you?" inquires the Challenger, turning his head in the direction of the voice.

"They call me 'Rings.' I represent the Syndicate. My employer sends his regards," Rings answers as she walks toward the Challenger.

Born Gomer Lukaku on the Giza Moon Colony, Rings serves as the primary lieutenant of the Buyer, the frontman for the Syndicate, the most powerful organized crime ring in the System. The leader of the Syndicate, Seth Hyksos, better known as Partyman, is the second-wealthiest person in the System. He uses his legitimate business concerns to launder money earned through the Syndicate's criminal enterprises.

The Syndicate traffics in drugs, prostitution, and slave labor. They hire pirates and other mercenaries to intimidate or even assassinate political leaders and law enforcement officials who stand in their way.

For her part, Rings is a human-gorilla hybrid Drākanashim. She grew up orphaned and impoverished on Giza. Her parents were murdered by the Giza Garrison in one of their bogus raids following the robbery of an Ant Planet settler.

Rings found herself fostered by a member of the Edwesu Crime Family, who groomed her to be a sex worker. She eventually "earned" her way out of the sex trade by developing a talent for luring other young women into the Edwesu's web. She eventually caught the eye of the Buyer, who had become annoyed with the Edwesu's pricing structure.

The Buyer offered Rings a position in the Syndicate. She accepted and never looked back. She derives her nom de guerre from her expertise with throwing knives. She wears two nanotech-powered bands on her thighs that reshape to form razor-sharp throwing discs.

In addition to her deadly proficiency with throwing knives, Rings is an exceptional archer.

"Hmmmph, the sex trafficker," snorts the Challenger. "Understand this: you may have your claim, but I couldn't care less if they all die," growls the Challenger in the Dragon's voice.

"Understood," Rings replies calmly, backing away.

Standing, the Grand Reverend asks, "Master, what's the significance of Emba Soira? Why here? Eritrea seems random. Isn't Hawwah a Kemite? Why not a site in what the Earth-bounds call 'Egypt'? Or perhaps a site in Europe would have been a better location."

"Alkebulan… or 'Africa,' as it is known today… is where it all started. This is where Hawwah and I first met. She does not remember our first encounter. But it was in that cave where she revealed herself to me, her true self. I helped her unlock the version of herself we all know today," Apep the Challenger retorts.

Apep then turns to Racism and wags his finger approvingly. His lips curl into an evil grin.

"You know, I started the whole 'racism' thing," the Challenger continues. "Humans and my kind are of decidedly different 'races.' I love what you have done with the concept, though, namely, convincing a particular group of people that they are somehow superior to every other group of people on this planet based on the color of their skin. Well, in their case, it's actually the lack of color. And to think, everything you've taught them to prize, from blond hair to blue eyes, represents recessive traits in the human genetic scheme. Chef's kiss. Simply brilliant." Pointing to the Grand Reverend, he says, "Hawwah is a liar! She plays at being human. She is not! She is no more human than you are, my green-skinned minion."

As a Pen, especially a first-generation Drone, the Grand Reverend's skin turned floral green in the Earth's atmosphere. Even with his mastery of genetic engineering, he has not figured out a means to counteract this genetic deficiency.

"But HE prefers her to me, like the rest of you. She represents something special to Him that simply must be corrupted. Well… I corrupted her, but she's still here," the Challenger pauses momentarily. "So, I intend to bury her here, next to her husband," he growls, gazing to the southwest.

CHAPTER 14
WHERE ON EARTH?

Right before the kids bunk down for the night, Addis H brings a younger member of the massive group of kidnappees to Prince Armacaust with a revelation that he needs to hear.

"We're somewhere on Planet Earth," the young lady says confidently. "I conducted both chemical and isotopic analyses on the various materials lining the floor of the cavern and its walls. The rocks that compose the structures in this cave bear mineral content, grain size, and texture very similar to those found on Chaos, Ikw-n-tA, and Memphis; however, the fossils indicate that we're no longer on a planet in our solar system. But, given the similar physical characteristics and chemical composition of the rocks here, we must be on a planet very similar, if not identical, to the planets in our solar system. And that leaves only one conclusion… Earth."

Prince Imhotep speaks up before Armacaust can respond. The young lady seems ready to engage in a debate to defend her thesis. And Prince Imhotep seems poised to oblige her.

"How did you achieve the pyrolysis necessary to separate the isotopes?" Prince Imhotep asks.

The shocked and impressed teens spend time turning their attention back and forth between Prince Imhotep and the young lady as they debate her scientific conclusion on their location. After several minutes of exchanging antithesis for thesis, the pair of debaters reaches a synthesis.

"I think I agree, Unc. We are on Planet Earth," Prince Imhotep says, turning to Prince Armacaust. "And she may be even smarter than me."

"You go, queen!" Seraphina shouts, walking over to the young lady and giving her an energetic high-five.

"If that's true, we're about eighty light-years away from home," Addis HD says, with great concern in her voice. "This whole thing just seems impossible."

Satisfied with the conclusion, Prince Armacaust asks the young lady for her name.

"Brooklyn Betty Francis Garvey," she responds proudly. "And that's my brother, Malcolm," she adds, pointing to her younger brother standing in a group of boys.

"Your father is Senator Garvey," Addis HK says to Brooklyn.

"That's right. Daddy is senator of New Canaan Province," Brooklyn replies excitedly.

"How old are you?" Addis H asks.

"I'm nine," Brooklyn says with a giggle.

"Earth…" the Jupiter twins mutter in unison, shaking their heads.

DwarfStar makes a weird face at them, then looks away almost immediately when he notices Asenat and Sojourner looking at him with disapproving expressions on their faces.

"Another prominent family with missing children," Kamia says.

"The evidence would suggest our kidnappings were not random but made to look that way, perhaps to conceal the perpetrator's true intent," Nkenge adds.

"That makes sense," Shaka chimes in. "The question is, what do all of these families have in common?"

"If we are on Earth, that means this isn't about us, Unc," Imhotep says, turning toward Prince Armacaust.

"Yeah, this is about Mom and the people who traveled with her from Earth to PC," Armacaust replies.

"It also means that we're not being held for ransom. We're the bait!" the Jupiter twins exclaim.

"And things never work out so well for the bait any time I go fishing, Bro," DwarfStar says, placing a hand on Prince Armacaust's shoulder.

"I think I know how we can get out of here," Princess Zilpha interjects. "And now that we know where we are, let's talk about getting something to eat."

"Agreed!" Prince Armacaust declares. "Brooklyn, can you help us identify plants around this cave that would be safe for us to eat?"

“Sure. I’d just need to see them and run a few quick tests,” Brooklyn replies.

“Outstanding!” Prince Armacaust replies. “Django!” he calls out loudly.

Prince Armacaust’s younger cousin, Django Hotep, runs up to the prince from among a crowd of other boys. Fourteen-year-old Django is the youngest child of Starlyte, dean of the Chaosian College of Elders, and H’s sister Z.

Seeing Django emerge from the crowd, Prince Imhotep and Princess Zilpha run over to him and hug him. Like Prince Armacaust, Django is another uncle of theirs who is their age. Such relationships are the common family dynamics among the Eshanashim. Their long lives and ability to have children, even after being centuries old, produce situations in which adult Eshanashim can have aunts and uncles who are infants.

“Django and I found each other earlier in the day. He can not only ‘energize’ his skin, but he can also turn himself invisible. Which means—” Prince Armacaust begins before he is cut off by the Jupiter twins.

“He can go outside without being detected,” the Jupiter twins declare with blended voices.

“Can you get me some samples?” Brooklyn asks, walking closer to Django.

“Sure,” Django says.

“Let’s split up again. Asenat, Seraphina, take your team back to the other end of the cave and see if you can find any mushrooms growing there. I’ll take Addis HK and Django outside to the valley we flew over. We’ll cover Django as he collects samples,” Prince Armacaust offers.

“You’re taking Addis?” Seraphina asks with a sly smile.

"Well… yeah… I guess," Prince Armacaust stammers. "I mean… that is, if you want to go," he says, looking at Addis HK.

"I'd love to," Addis HK answers enthusiastically, grabbing Prince Armacaust's arm with both hands and pressing her head into his shoulder.

"Ok. Let's go!" Prince Armacaust commands. "DwarfStar, if Addis and I don't make it back, don't come looking for us. It will be your job to keep everyone safe at that point," he says, turning to his best friend.

"I got you, Bro!" DwarfStar declares.

Prince Armacaust wraps one arm around Addis HK's waist and the other around Django. He rises off the ground and flies toward the entrance to the cave.

Seraphina and Asenat look at each other and smile. SoJo and Solomon rise into the air and fly in the opposite direction. Shaka begins to run after them. Asenat and Seraphina follow close behind.

Once outside, at the entrance to the cave, Armacaust sets down behind a large rock adjacent to the mouth of the cave. Addis HK and Django crouch next to him.

"You see anything, Cuz?" Django whispers.

"You can see in the dark?" Addis HK asks quietly.

"Yes, and in infrared and telescopically," Prince Armacaust answers just as quietly. "I don't see anything, Cuz. Do your thing."

Django renders himself invisible and scampers down the side of the incline to a small landing, then scurries into a patch of trees. Although most people would not be able to see Django, Prince Armacaust remains fixed on his cousin's heat signature.

"So, what would you be doing if we weren't here trying to survive in a cave?" Prince Armacaust asks Addis HK politely.

"I don't know. I spend a lot of time with my mom," she says, giggling slightly. "We like to play games and watch movies. She doesn't hang out with friends or go on many dates. She keeps saying how much she can't trust people since my dad chose his job over her."

"Oh, wow. What does your dad do?"

"He's a crew member on the SS Superlative. He's deployed a lot, so I hardly ever see him."

"I'm sorry. That sounds tough."

"Don't be. My mom's AWESOME!" Addis HK replies excitedly. "She had me while she was still attending university. Though she became a mom, she still graduated on time, went on to earn her law degree, and got a job as a diplomatic liaison, working for the most chauvinistic planetary leader in the System. So, you know she's the bomb! Plus, she does it all while being GOOORE-G-EOUS! I know I'm biased, but my momma is F-I-N-E! She gets a lot of attention from men. She just doesn't trust anyone. She says she doesn't mind being alone. I don't always believe her, though. But we're happy! I just worry what will happen when I start university in a few years."

Suddenly, a bunch of plants dances their way up to the stone behind which Prince Armacaust and Addis HK are hiding. A startled Addis begins to scream, but Prince Armacaust places a hand over her mouth before she can make a sound.

Django reappears and apologizes for scaring her.

Addis HK playfully punches his shoulder.

"There are a bunch more just like this down there. I wonder which ones are edible," Django declares.

"Let's get these back to Brooklyn and find out," Prince Armacaust replies.

He once again scoops Addis HK and Django up into his arms and flies back into the cave.

****

On the opposite side of the cave, Seraphina uses her acute sense of smell to ferret out mushrooms or other fungi that may be suitable for human consumption. While most Drākanashim are not capable of photosynthesis, their digestive systems feature enzymes capable of effectively processing raw meat and botanical elements that the digestive systems of other humans cannot. While she does not readily detect any mushrooms, she does find something with which she is very familiar.

"Shea nuts," Seraphina exclaims excitedly.

"No! Where?" Shaka asks.

"Right here, under the hole in the wall where we fought those monsters earlier," Seraphina replies.

Solomon and SoJo fly up to the window and look out cautiously. Not seeing anyone, SoJo decides to fly outside the cave to investigate further. About 100 feet from the window, SoJo sees a grove of shea trees.

"Solomon, come with me!" SoJo shouts.

"Incoming," Solomon shouts back.

"I'd better go and keep an eye on those two," Asenat says to Seraphina, grinning ear to ear.

As Asenat soars up and out through the hole in the cavern wall, Shaka and Seraphina smile at each other and continue to follow the path of the water streaming through the cavern floor.

They stop and explore the various plants and rock formations they see along the way.

At one point, their hands accidentally touch. When neither of them pulls back immediately, they decide to hold hands and continue walking.

"So, do you have, like, a boyfriend back home?" Shaka finally builds up the courage to ask.

"No!" Seraphina blurts out full-throatedly.

"Why do you say it like that? I mean, you're really pretty. I just thought maybe you liked someone, or they maybe liked you," Shaka asks, fumbling around his mind for the right words to say in the right order.

Seraphina blushes and does not make eye contact with Shaka. She grips his hand tighter and begins to swing her arm back and forth.

"So, you think I'm pretty, huh?" Seraphina asks playfully.

"Well, yeah… I guess. Is that okay?" Shaka asks very shyly.

Seraphina stops walking briefly. She turns to face Shaka and holds his hand with both of hers.

"Yes, that is alright with me," she says softly, looking directly into his eyes. "And I think you're pretty, too."

Both teens break into hysterical laughter. Seraphina suddenly perks up.

"I can hear Asenat calling for us," she says. "We'd better get back."

"I'll race you," Shaka says playfully.

"Your funeral," Seraphina says with a broad smile.

Seraphina removes her sandals and sprints back along the path at full speed. Shaka's enhanced strength allows him to keep pace, but he is simply not fast enough to overtake Seraphina.

When they rejoin Shaka's siblings, they both fall to the ground and roll around laughing boisterously.

"Where have you two been?" Asenat asks sternly.

"Have you been eating whacky weeds or something?" SoJo asks.

"I think maybe they found the good mushrooms," Solomon adds.

Asenat simply shakes her head, then breaks into a smile. SoJo and Solomon help Seraphina and Shaka off the ground.

"Let's head back," Asenat says gently.

The crew starts off back toward their camp inside the cavern. Shaka and Seraphina hold hands the entire way.

CHAPTER 15
REVELATIONS TAKE SHAPE

As daylight begins to spill into the guest quarters through the partially open blinds around the fifth floor of TGHQ, Neith rouses awake. She smiles with sheer delight as she notices Aharon is still lying next to her. He hardly moves as she sits up in the bed.

A painful reality begins to weigh heavily on her heart and mind. She takes a deep breath, slips out of bed, and walks toward the bathroom. She stares at her naked body in the mirror and sighs deeply. Her subconscious will not allow her to forget that Aharon does not belong to her.

A wave of anxiety rushes over her as she thinks that, as soon as this present situation ends, the only man she has ever loved will go back to his wife and their magnificent palace on Planet Memphis, and she will return to Giza alone. Saddened, she begins to brush her teeth.

Well, he's mine right now, she thinks to herself as she spits the toothpaste into the sink.

Neith looks back up at her reflection in the mirror and smiles. When she returns to the bedroom, Aharon is awake and sitting up in bed. His naked body is just as she remembers it.

"Grand rising," she says.

Aharon smiles and turns his body so that he faces Neith. He raises one knee and wraps an arm around it, as if he is posing for a photographer.

"Grand rising to you, dear Neith," he replies.

"You have always been so beautiful," Neith says in a soft voice.

"I'm sure I pale in comparison to you, my dear," Aharon replies with a smile.

Neith sits next to Aharon on the bed, catching a whiff of Aharon's natural musk. She recalls that she has always loved the way he smells. She nestles herself next to Aharon, burying her head into his shoulder and chest, and plants a hand on his chest.

Why can't I resist him? she thinks to herself.

Aharon does not move, allowing Neith to rest against his body. When she tilts her head up to look at him, Aharon leans in and kisses her passionately. He lifts Neith into his arms as they stare longingly into each other's eyes.

Aharon very smoothly lies Neith on the bed and enters her. Neith gasps and tilts her head back in ecstasy. She digs her nails into Aharon's back as he thrusts into her energetically, her wings stretching out to their full span.

Neith's heavy breathing turns into screams as she loses her self-control. Aharon does not let up in his motion. He slides one of his hands down her back so that he can grip Neith's buttocks. Neith wraps her legs tightly around Aharon's thighs.

What seems like an eternity passes before Aharon finally gasps.

"Oh, Neith!" he exclaims, quivering.

Neith continues to breathe heavily as she caresses the back of Aharon's head and shoulders, pulling him closer. Aharon all but collapses onto Neith. They fold themselves into one another and simply lie still.

****

In the dining hall on the fourth floor of TGHQ, the atmosphere is electric. Aides from across the major planets and intergalactic organizations walk swiftly past each other, gathering food for their respective leaders and conducting calls. Eman Menes' staff handles the bustling activity flawlessly.

Eman is a tall, shapely, very attractive woman. She was born on Planet Chaos to military parents. She married early, hoping to experience the happiness her parents seemed to enjoy, but ended her marriage after only a few years when she discovered her husband was having an affair with one of her sorority sisters.

Eman had offered him the option of having more than one wife, but he refused, telling her that she would be all the woman he needed for the rest of his life. The betrayal proved to be more than she could stand.

Cooking had always been an outlet for her creativity, as well as a remedy for loneliness throughout her life. She left Planet Chaos and moved to Planet Memphis, where she found work in the resort industry. Eman quickly became a sought-after chef.

She was even invited to cater for a gala hosted by First Lady Cindy Drone at the presidential palace. It was at this event that she met Sphinx, and the two became fast friends. When TGHQ opened, the princess invited Eman to become the executive chef for the Gatekeepers. Eman accepted without hesitation.

Over the years, Eman has proven to be a valuable asset to the team. She operates and leads with military precision. Eman not only leads the kitchen staff, but she also leads the entire facilities management operation for the Gatekeepers.

In addition to TGHQ, the Gatekeepers maintain safe houses on Planet Memphis and Planet Pen-Meroe. During intense situations like the one the team faces today, Eman is always prepared. And no matter the circumstances, the team never worries if their facilities will be secure or well-provisioned.

Eman receives several smiles and nods of approval as the various aides and staffers grab coffee and pre-packaged meals to take back to their leaders' quarters.

As the planetary leaders begin filing back into the viewing room, Sphinx and Vixen plop down in chairs at their respective consoles in the control room. Vixen looks Sphinx up and down, noticing a glow the princess is projecting.

"Did your sex bot work those kinks out of your spine?" Vixen asks playfully.

"Oh, yeah, it worked all the kinks, knots, and stiffness out of me all over," Sphinx replies with a laugh.

The two friends clasp hands and try to contain themselves. Vixen tries to resume her professional demeanor when she notices techs watching the exchange between her and Sphinx.

"You know… you should really try the real thing once in a while," Vixen says, smiling while looking directly into her monitor.

Sphinx smiles and focuses straight ahead. She hates discussing her love life, or the lack thereof, with anybody, especially her mother and Vixen. The only person from whom Sphinx even tolerates such intrusions, in the form of inquiries into her dating adventures, is her Auntie Z.

"What's it been, thirty years since your last date?" Vixen says, turning her head toward Sphinx to catch a glimpse of her reaction.

Sphinx types something into her keypad, then stops abruptly. She pushes herself away from her console and turns her chair so that her entire body faces Vixen.

"Has it been that long?" Sphinx asks quizzically.

Vixen leans in with a broad smile. Sphinx does everything she can not to break into hysterical laughter.

"Yes, girl, it has!" Vixen says quietly.

The techs in the control room make veiled expressions, pretending not to listen to the two friends' exchange. Sphinx lifts her head to make sure the other people in the room are not obviously eavesdropping.

"The last guy you dated was that soldier from the Ant Planet," Vixen whispers.

"Yeah… General Aharon Kebede… He was a creep," Sphinx replies in her lowest tone. "Didn't I go out with that guy… the detective from the IGP… what was his name?"

"If you don't remember his name, sis, he obviously doesn't exist," Vixen replies with a laugh.

"Do you remember those twins we dated, Sword and Shield?" Sphinx asks with a smile.

"I try not to," Vixen replies.

Both women break out into animated laughter. For a moment, they forget they are working.

"Chief, we're ready to begin the stream," a voice interrupts.

"Proceed," Sphinx orders. "Start with what we recorded overnight at 3x speed and then play at normal rate once we catch up to Mom's visions from this morning."

****

Over the next few hours, the planetary leaders view several segments recorded from H's visions the previous night.

In one segment, H walks toward a man with a sword in her hand. Her face and upper body are heavily splattered with blood. The expression on her face is intense as she approaches and steps toe to toe with the man. They stare directly into each other's eyes.

After a few tense moments, H and the man embrace. He takes her by the hand and leads her to an opening overlooking a massive gathering of people. They are standing on a landing atop a set of stairs outside a temple.

The man raises H's hand in the air excitedly. They both raise their opposite hands high, each lifting a bloody sword above their heads as they stand before the cheering crowds.

"That's Menes," Monolith Ant offers.

"The founder of Kemet. He also established Memphis as its capital," Aharon adds.

In the next segment, H sits alone in a room with a man wearing the headdress of the high priest of Ra. They read together from various texts. H seems to make various sexual advances toward the man that he ignores.

At one point, the man shoves H away angrily and walks away from her. H slumps down to the floor, sobbing. Instead of exiting the room, he turns, walks back over to H, and lifts her off the floor. They embrace and share a passionate kiss. The man lifts her off her feet, holding her tightly, and twirls her around. As he turns, his face comes into full view.

"I know you recognize that face, Aharon," Monolith Ant remarks slyly.

"H's husband. What's the timeline here?" Aharon shouts out, as if he expects to hear an answer from the control room.

Arisone looks to Sphinx to nod her approval before answering. Sphinx nods her approval.

"As best we can determine, this vision seems to be dated sometime between Year 4503 and Year 4552, or 2697 BCE to 2648 BCE on Earth."

"That would make that man her husband, Master Imhotep himself," Inspector Djet Drone offers.

"C'mon, baby boy. That can't be Imhotep. You don't know everything," Sekhmet teases.

"No, Sis… that's him," Insp. Djet Drone insists.

King Armacaust remains silent. The king sits forward in his seat.

"Yes, H was married to Imhotep. Only I know of her being married to a man she identified as Imhotep, the man who is Prince Adisa's biological father… in Year 6077," he continues.

"Wait… are you suggesting THE Imhotep, Master Imhotep, is Prince Adisa's father?" Aharon asks in disbelief. "You know, that entire year before we left the planet, she never called her husband by his name, at least not in front of us. Oh, my God!"

"Which also means our queen was once Renpetneferet, the young woman who is believed to have been Imhotep's wife… and former student," Inspector Djet Drone posits.

"But there is no record of Imhotep living that long. There would be 1,500 years between when they met and when Adisa was born. It should also be noted that there is a period of time for which Imhotep would have been unaccounted," Monolith Ant offers. "It seems we're being fed more mystery than resolution."

The room falls silent. Monolith Ant stands for a moment, grimaces, then retakes his seat.

The next segment shows H flying close to a planet in deep space. She stops briefly, then stretches out her right hand. She unleashes a massive bolt of energy that slices right through the planet's surface. But just before her blast, a tiny light can be seen making its way to the planet's surface. H reacts by pulling her hands to her face in shock. She begins to fly closer to the planet, but stops after a series of eruptions on the planet's surface causes the planet to explode.

Sekhmet stands as she notices something in the background of the scene. She waves her hands rapidly, trying to get the attention of the control room.

"Yes, Madame President?" Arisone asks.

"Could you rewind the stream about fifteen seconds and isolate the upper left corner of that last frame?" Sekhmet asks.

"Yes, ma'am. Doing it now," Arisone replies.

"Freeze frame," Sekhmet shouts.

As the stream pauses, Sekhmet walks over to the wall of huge panoramic monitors and stares intently at the image on the screen.

"Do you all see what I see?" she asks the room.

Emotionally spent, no one replies verbally, but all shake their heads no. Insp. Djet Drone stands and walks over to the monitor to get a better look.

"This happened in the System. You see this?" she says, pointing to a bright light against a multicolored backdrop. "That's the Warp Star. I was an astronomy geek as a child. I would know the pattern of its nebula anywhere."

"Now, who's acting like they know 'everything'?" Insp. Djet Drone teases, returning his sister's previous jab.

"Shut up, you!" Sekhmet retorts, playfully punching the inspector on his shoulder.

King Armacaust immediately lowers his head into his hands and rubs his face. Insp. Djet Drone puts a hand over his mouth, as if reeling from shock, when he realizes his sister's assertion is absolutely correct.

"H destroyed a planet in our System?" Aharon asks, with a tone of concern in his voice.

"Looks that way." Neith sighs.

"How long ago was this?" Envoy Armana asks.

"Sometime between Year 5702 and Year 5703," Arisone replies.

Sekhmet walks away from the screen, shaking her head. Insp. Djet Drone, following his sister's lead, retakes his seat.

"This would have been long before the Great Exodus, then," Insp. Djet Drone offers.

No one responds. Merneith shakes her head.

"Does that matter in a legal context?" Neith asks.

"That would be a question for the ICoJ," Envoy Armana answers.

"Hmmmm…" Monolith Ant grumbles disapprovingly.

"Let's see the next frame," Merneith prods.

CHAPTER 16
THE WOMAN WHO DARED TO BE KING

The stream resumes. H sits alone, legs crossed, posture perfect, in the magnificent throne room in the pharaoh's palace at Djeser-Djeseru.

The detail in the hieroglyphics etched into the throne upon which she sits belies the fact that the sculptors who crafted it hewed it from a single piece of limestone. H wears a golden-laden bodysuit that fits snugly around her curves. A royal collar lies elegantly over her shoulders. Bejeweled bangles adorn both her wrists. Beautiful earrings, accentuating the colors in her collar, hang from her ears.

A king cobra, with its hood spread wide open, stands proudly atop her headdress. The cobra represents the goddess Wadjet, the protector of Lower Kemet, and symbolizes sovereignty. H is not the wife of the pharaoh. She is the pharaoh.

A man enters the throne room. His name is Kandake Mandrake, and he is the pharaoh's closest and most trusted royal advisor. He walks at a quick pace across the great hall. He stops at the base of the platform upon which H's throne sits. He rests one foot on the first step leading up to the platform and bows, leaning on his raised knee.

"Majesty," Kandake speaks in an even tone.

He looks up at H. She raises her right hand, palm up, signaling to Kandake that he has permission to address her further.

"The building at both Pakhet and Ipet-isut proceeds according to Her Majesty's wishes."

H's mouth spreads into a broad smile. She leans her head forward without moving her back or shoulders.

"Tell me about the trade negotiations with Punt," she orders with a smile.

"The leaders in the Land of the Gods have agreed to terms, Majesty, just as you predicted," the man answers.

"Fantastic. I would like to survey the progress on the restoration of the Ipet-isut Temple Complex. Prepare a convoy. I want to leave as soon as possible."

"It will be done, Majesty."

He bows again, then hurries back across the expansive hall, making his exit.

H stands once Kandake is out of her sight. She takes a long yawn and descends the steps to the granite floor of the great hall, exiting the throne room through a side entrance reserved solely for her use.

She walks the long corridor that leads to her bedchamber. She reaches out her right hand and allows her index finger to drag along the wall as she glides wistfully up the hallway to the entrance of her bedchamber.

H walks past her bed and onto the balcony overlooking the west bank of the Nile Valley below. She places her hands on the stone banister and leans forward, taking a deep breath.

Eighteen long years have passed since the death of her husband. She initially served as the regent to her two-year-old stepson but seized the title of pharaoh through deft political maneuvering.

Now, under her leadership, the kingdom is once again thriving. She has worked diligently to restore the previous luster all but erased by the Hyksos occupation.

She sometimes lies awake at night, contemplating how long she will be able to sustain her reign without the traditionalists around her attempting to reinstall her stepson or some other male to the throne.

While the thought weighs heavily on her mind, she has not allowed her concerns to paralyze her from taking the actions she believes to be in the best interests of her people.

"Mother!" H's teenage daughter, Neferure, calls to her from the entrance of the bedchamber.

"Yes, my love?" H replies.

Neferure runs into the room and wraps her arms around H's torso. H hugs Neferure tightly, rocking back and forth.

"What did you learn today, my dear?" H asks softly.

"Ahmose taught me how to calculate the relative speed of an arrow shot from a bow in high winds," Neferure replies with a smile. "It was all very interesting, but I cannot think of a single reason why I would have any use for such knowledge, Mother."

H squeezes Neferure tighter, plants a kiss on the top of her forehead, and smiles as she shakes her head.

"Oh, my sweet daughter, trust me. You never know when a woman will be forced to defend the people she loves. Knowing how the wind affects the flight of an arrow may prove to be useful information in the right situation."

"Have you ever, Mother? Have you ever fought in a war?"

H laughs. She thinks back for a brief moment to the very founding of Kemet, when she fought beside Menes in many bloody conflicts.

"Let's just say, I have seen my fair share of battles, my dear." H replies with a laugh.

"Majesty," a man's voice calls out from the entrance of the bedchamber.

"What is it, Senenmut?" H responds with a tone that suggests she is annoyed by the intrusion.

"Her Majesty's transport awaits," Senenmut replies more respectfully.

"Very well," H replies.

H pulls back from Neferure so that she can see her face and plants another kiss on her daughter's forehead.

"I have some work to do, love. Return to your studies and eat well tonight. I will see you in the morning. We will go riding along the west bank."

"Yes, Mother," Neferure replies, gazing lovingly into H's eyes.

Just then, a chill runs down H's back. She pauses for a moment, then ignores the sensation. She watches Neferure exit the bedchamber, giving Senenmut a high-five as she scurries past him. H shakes her head.

In her mind's eye, she sees an image of herself holding the lifeless body of her precious daughter.

"Majesty, shall I tell the driver you no longer wish to travel?" Senenmut asks.

H tries hard to shrug off her concerns. She is unsure whether the vision she saw represents an actual premonition or an extension of the greater concerns escaping her subconscious. She clenches her fists and turns toward the entrance of her bedchamber.

"No," she says sternly. "I'm coming," she adds as she begins to take steps toward the entrance.

She exits the bedchamber and follows Senenmut down the private stairwell to the back of the palace. H strides quickly to the back entrance of the palace, where her carriage awaits.

Several soldiers rush over to assist her as she steps up into the carriage. She settles in her seat and focuses her gaze forward. Senenmut sits across from her. H lifts and lowers her right hand. The carriage takes off slowly at first, then gradually picks up speed.

Approximately an hour into the ride, Senenmut rises and takes a seat next to H. H flashes him a harsh look for his sheer insolence.

"I trust you have a good reason for violating my personal space," H says indignantly.

"You must understand that I never wanted any harm to come to either you or the girl," Senenmut begins. "Unfortunately, the others do not feel the same way. They demand blood. You will die. And the girl will be married to her half-brother. I promise that you will not suffer, but your reign ends here today," Senenmut says, with an air of satisfaction in his voice.

H can feel the carriage slowing to a stop. When the carriage pulls to a full stop, the soldiers driving it hop down and begin walking toward her and Senenmut. She turns her attention back to Senenmut, who has drawn a long dagger from behind his back.

"I'm sorry, Majesty. For what it's worth, you have done a magnificent job bringing the empire back from the brink. You were simply too good at doing what you did. You, unfortunately, left no room for the man who will assume the throne after you to ascend to his own greatness. It was not meant to be," Senenmut says coldly, before grabbing the back of H's head and jamming the blade into her midsection.

H does not break eye contact with Senenmut.

The smug expression on Senenmut's face quickly fades to grave concern as he notices that H does not seem to be in any pain.

H looks down at his hand holding the dagger, as if to direct Senenmut's gaze to the blade. Senenmut looks down to see that the blade has completely bent, being unable to pierce the pharaoh's skin.

H, again, locks eyes with Senenmut. Her mouth curls into a devious smirk.

"Your plan had one flaw. I am far beyond anything for which you could have prepared," H says coldly.

H notices that the soldiers have not moved any further. She surmises that they are likely waiting for Senenmut to complete the murder so that they can collect her body. H grabs Senenmut by the neck in a crushing grip. She stands to her feet, holding the treacherous Senenmut aloft.

The soldiers react by drawing their swords. H snaps Senenmut's neck and drops his body to the floor of the carriage. Before the soldiers can even make another move, H zips from the carriage, circling it so that she can grab them both, one in each hand.

She flies swiftly into the sky, soaring higher and higher until the air grows thin. When the men begin gasping for air, H simply opens her hands. The two soldiers plummet back to the earth. H does not bother watching them fall.

She instead rockets back to the palace, maintaining her altitude so as not to attract any onlookers. H renders herself invisible and dives from the sky straight into the armory. Once inside, she removes her headdress and collar, pulls off the leggings of her bodysuit, and removes the slippers from her feet.

H grabs a bow, a loaded quiver, and two swords. She straps the quiver to her back and secures the sheathed swords to her hips with a belt. H runs back toward her residence as fast as she can without using her powers.

As she approaches the residence, the courtyard seems eerily empty. H decelerates from a full sprint to a brisk walk, then to cautious steps. She pulls the bow from her shoulder and draws an arrow from the quiver.

She looks up toward the balcony of her bedchamber and sees Kandake standing behind Neferure, his left hand holding the back of Neferure's neck.

"Stop right there, Majesty!" the Kandake commands.

H stands still. Kandake steps to the side of Neferure, brandishing a long needle in his right hand. The needle glimmers in the waning sunlight.

"Majesty, throw down your weapons. I will not harm the girl if you surrender now," Kandake shouts.

H does not respond. She whips an arrow from the quiver on her back and takes aim.

"I would prefer if you surrender," H shouts back.

Kandake shakes Neferure roughly in response. H tracks the movements of the Kandake's head with her bow.

"This needle is tipped in asp venom. If it punctures the girl's skin, she will surely die. Throw down your weapons and surrender," Kandake shouts.

Two other men join Kandake on the balcony, each of them holding a similar needle.

H does not lower her bow. Seeing her mother's resolve gives Neferure a boost of courage.

"Mother, you need to adjust the angle of your arm. At this elevation, you will need to aim higher so that the arrow strikes the target in the desired spot," Neferure says calmly, choking back tears.

"Thanks, my love," H says, adjusting her elbow without releasing the tension on the bowstring.

Seeing H's continued defiance, Kandake angrily passes Neferure off to the other two men and turns back to H. As soon as his face moves back into position to face H again, his forehead is split by an arrow.

As Kandake drops, the other two men turn back toward the balcony to find H standing before them. They stand frozen in their astonishment. H snatches the swords from their sheaths and begins to slice the men into trembling, bloody husks.

She drops the swords to the ground and grabs the two men, one in each hand. She flings them behind her. The two men soar off the balcony and crash to the ground hundreds of feet away.

Neferure stands shuddering before her mother. The fear breaks, and Neferure runs to H, falling into her mother's arms. H clutches Neferure and holds her tightly.

"Mother… how… how did…?" Neferure struggles to say, but finds herself interrupted by H.

"Sssshhhhhhh… Calm yourself, my love," H says gently. "I promise that I will explain all to you later."

H lifts Neferure, cradling the young woman in her arms. H walks over to the bed and lays Neferure onto a long pillow. Neferure rolls over and clutches the pillow.

H removes the quiver and belt, securing the swords to her waist. She then curls up in the bed next to Neferure and quietly strokes the back of her daughter's head. H listens as Neferure's breath and heartbeat slow to their normal rates. H closes her eyes and lets out a long exhale.

In the morning, H opens her eyes and sits up. The sun is pouring into the bedchamber from the east-facing balcony. H gently rocks Neferure's hip. She notices that Neferure is cold to the touch. She begins to shake Neferure more briskly. Neferure still does not move.

H scoops Neferure into her arms. The young woman is not breathing. The men attempting to conduct the coup must have poisoned Neferure with a slow-acting toxin earlier in the day, long before they followed through on their assassination plot.

H surmises that they probably were going to use the poisoning as a means to coerce Neferure into marriage to her half-brother. They would have given her the antidote had she agreed to be her half-brother's wife and turn a blind eye to her mother's murder.

In a moment of self-regret, H realizes that she killed the conspirators before interrogating them. Had she questioned them first, she might have uncovered the full details of their scheme.

"Nnnnooooooooooooo!" H wails.

She begins to sob hysterically, rocking back and forth with the lifeless Neferure in her arms. The sounds of H's mourning become deafening. Her chamber maids rush into the room and fall at her side. They surround H and do their best to comfort her.

H oversees the mummification of Neferure herself, continually kissing and stroking the top of her daughter's head. She orders Neferure to be entombed in the grand burial chamber recently constructed to house the next several pharaohs and their households.

As H watches the final preparations for the afterlife being applied to her beloved daughter, she gets a thought. She departs the morgue, running back to her bedchamber. She finds a chambermaid she trusts and pulls her close.

H gives the chambermaid a set of instructions for the morning. The chambermaid begins to shake and pleads with H to change her mind, but H insists until the maid agrees.

That night, as people from across the empire gather to mourn the death of the young princess, H watches the memorial with an expressionless gaze. At one point, she pretends to swoon. Aides rush to H and carry her back to her bedchamber.

H lies still on her bed and immediately slips into a trance. H knows that by the next morning her body will feel cold, like she has died.

In the morning, the chambermaid she enlisted to help with this plan tells the other maids and aides that the pharaoh has died in the night. Physicians inspect H's body and determine that the pharaoh has, in fact, passed from this life.

The chambermaid tells the palace administrator that H has provided strict instructions that she is not to be mummified upon her death. The administrator orders H's body to be carried into the burial chamber and laid next to Neferure.

Once the burial chamber is resealed, H awakens from her deep meditation. She sits up and looks at Neferure's sarcophagus. Tears begin to stream from H's eyes.

She hops off the slab and walks over to her daughter's resting place. H kisses the fingertips of her right hand and presses them against the face of the sarcophagus. H then walks over to the entrance to the chamber and moves the large stone.

She exits the burial chamber, carefully puts the stone back in place, and ascends skyward, disappearing from sight.

Back in the viewing room at TGHQ, the planetary leaders watch with rapt attention. Many of their aides dab their eyes clear of tears.

"She's dealt with so much loss," Sekhmet says softly, wiping tears from her own eyes.

"It's amazing her experiences haven't driven her mad," Insp. Djet Drone replies softly. "Also, it would seem that 'H' does not merely stand for 'Hawwah.'"

"Certainly, my favorite pharaoh of the old empire," Neith declares.

"Indeed," Sekhmet adds.

CHAPTER 17
WALKING THROUGH THE SEA

The stream progresses onto the next segment. The picture displays a somewhat chaotic scene. A massive assembly of people moves across a sandy plain toward the shore of a large body of water. The sounds of cattle, sheep, camels, and people speaking loudly blend at a robust volume. H pulls on the reins of two large bulls hitched to a wagon by a yoke. The wagon is loaded with several large crates and loose household items.

"Lifting this wagon and carrying it the rest of the way would be easier than getting these unruly cows to pull it," H says to herself, thinking out loud.

H resists the temptation to exercise her tremendous strength. She has successfully concealed her paranatural abilities from these people, the neighbors for whom she has come to care so deeply, for many years. The myriad strange occurrences over the past several weeks have culminated in this exodus from Kemet. H cannot blame these people for seeking their freedom.

Two centuries have passed since H ruled Kemet. Each successive pharaoh following her reign seems to be even less compassionate than the one before. The leader of this caravan organized the people in a rushed fashion. To H, this feels more like fleeing than a willful migration to a better situation. The motivation that keeps them moving forward matters not to her. She continues to focus on assisting them in any way she can.

"Hawwah, help me with the young ones," a woman's voice cries out.

H looks in the direction from which it came. She sees her friend Miriam struggling to corral several children. H laughs, releases the reins to the yoke, and runs over to Miriam. H joyfully scoops up two children and whirls them around. She and Miriam smile at each other.

The journey ahead will be tough. The way will only grow more dangerous. From what H understands, their leader intends to take these people to the land across the sea. H wonders if he knows that giants occupy the lands across the sea. She found community among these people after more than a century of self-imposed isolation following the death of her beloved Neferure. Still, their safety means more to her than maintaining her secrets.

She determines she will protect her friends and their loved ones using all means available to her, should the need arise. Still, she gets the feeling the need will not arise. Something inside her tells H that the providence of these people has already been secured. The pace at which the caravan has moved from the capital city of Kemet to the shores of the sea has been nothing less than frenetic.

After hours of pushing, pulling, and trudging, the group finally reaches the water. That is when she hears it. The sound of horse-drawn chariots in the distance. Pharaoh's army approaches from the west. He intends to recapture the people or push them into the sea.

The people do not yet hear the sound. Even if any among them possessed hearing more sensitive than a normal human's, the sounds of the lowing cattle and clanking of personal possessions would likely drown out the thunderous clatter of hoofbeats from the chariots carrying armed soldiers. Since H can hear a pin drop across the cosmos, filtering the sounds of the approaching army is easy for her.

H tells Miriam that trouble approaches. Miriam has come to trust H's instincts, so she pushes her way through a crowd of men gathered around the group's leader, her younger brother, to bring him word of the impending peril. The leader remains focused on the task at hand. The body of water before them seems like an impassable obstacle.

As the leader stands looking out over the water, the people begin to despair. H can hear the sounds of groaning and some of the men among the people asking if they should go back and beg for Pharaoh's forgiveness. She wants to help but does not know how.

Then, suddenly, the leader lifts his hands to the sky. The water parts. The people look terrified at first, but begin to cross between two colossal walls of water. The land beneath their feet does not cause their livestock or the wheels on their carts to sink. They are walking on dry land.

The path descends to the depth of the seabed, making the walls more than 800 feet on either side at certain points.

H remains among the people until night descends. As the darkness falls, she works her way to the back of the group. When it seems like she is alone, she turns herself invisible and leaps into the sky. H shoots herself high above the throngs of people. The lowing of their cattle and sheep can be heard, even at the height she flies above them.

As the sun continues to set, H bursts into a pillar of flame and renders herself visible again. She remains flying high above the people, spreading her flame further and wider, lighting their way.

H remains in the sky above the people. She looks back to see Pharaoh and his army approaching the banks of the Red Sea. They pause. His men stand frozen in fright at the sight before them. Pharaoh commands them to follow.

H pauses. She rises higher and intensifies her flame to provide more light. She looks back at Pharaoh and his army. They have finally started to cross the seabed. The people are a little more than three hours ahead of the pursuing force.

H flies ahead. She suddenly hears screaming. She turns to see Pharaoh and his army being swallowed by the sea. H stops and places her hands over her mouth as she realizes what just happened. The closer Pharaoh's army comes to the people, the more the walls of water begin to collapse, barricading the distance between Pharaoh and the people he pursues.

As the people reach the shores of the Red Sea on the opposite side, H looks back. Pharaoh and his army have been consumed by the waters.

The next day, H can hear Miriam calling her name. H wants to join her friend on the ground, but she realizes that, if she does, she will not be able to perform the service she is currently providing. H hears Miriam ask several people if they have seen her.

Not being able to reveal herself to her friend saddens her; however, she comforts herself with the knowledge that she is being of service. For the next four decades, H continues to fly over the people each night, lighting their way.

****

Before the stream advances to a new segment, Monolith Ant begins to stir in his seat. He turns his head toward Aharon as if he had discovered a revelation.

"The body of Moses," Monolith Ant says with a chuckle. "She helped them. Moses was her friend's brother. Apep probably blames Hawwah for the Israelites' exodus from Egypt. In Apep's mind, Hawwah is the reason they escaped Pharaoh's clutches," Monolith Ant offers further.

"Why? H didn't part the Red Sea," Sekhmet replies.

"Since when have facts ever mattered to the devil?" Monolith Ant responds, turning to Sekhmet.

CHAPTER 18
YOUR PEOPLE WILL BECOME MY PEOPLE

The stream continues onto the next segment. H stands next to a young man. They clasp hands. A man dressed as a priest binds their hands with a piece of yarn. They kiss and turn to the people gathered in their midst. The people raise their own hands in celebration. H and the young man walk among them, exchanging hugs.

These happy images fade.

H kneels at a gravesite. The next frame reveals H hugging two other women. One looks to be older, and the other woman seems to be the age H feigns to be. Each of them wipes tears from their eyes. They kiss their goodbyes. One of the women departs. H waves as she leaves. She remains standing next to the older woman, the mother of her late husband, Naomi.

"My daughter," Naomi says softly. "You should return to the home of your father, just as Orpah is doing," she says.

H thinks of all the loss she has suffered, all the loved ones to whom she had to say goodbye. She knows she should leave and start over yet again, but she does not. Instead, H clings to her mother-in-law.

"Entreat me not to leave you!" H cries. "Wherever you go, I go! Wherever you choose to live, I will make my home there also! Your people will become my people! Your God will become my God! And where you die is where I will be buried," H proclaims passionately.

Naomi only responds by letting out a long sigh. Then they begin their journey together.

Time passes. H and Naomi finally arrive in Naomi's home country. They continue until they reach Naomi's hometown. The women of the town greet them. The reception is not necessarily welcoming, but H feels at ease that they were not shunned.

H asks Naomi for permission to work the barley harvest. Naomi tells her to go.

While she works, H catches the eye of a wealthy relative of her late father-in-law. The man asks his workers questions about H's identity. The workers tell the man that H arrived with her mother-in-law from the land of Moab. The man approaches H and offers her a place among a group of women from his own household, in a spot in the barley fields he owns, separated from the male workers who might treat her harshly.

"I am Boaz," the man says to H. "How did you come to be here in Bethlehem?"

"I came here with my mother-in-law, Naomi, from the land of Moab," H replies.

"Very well. I hope you will accept my offer, then," Boaz says.

H accepts and stays close to the women from Boaz's household over the course of the next several days.

Even though the harvest proves to be plentiful, Naomi begins to notice how much excess H brings home each night. So, she decides to ask H where she has been working. H tells Naomi of the handsome relative of Naomi's late husband who found favor with her and gave her a prime location to glean.

Naomi explains to H that this man could take her as his wife, according to the laws of her country. She then gives H instructions on how to move that conversation forward. Naomi tells H to bathe and anoint herself with sweet-smelling fragrances. Next, she instructs H to dress in her best garment and return to the threshing room. She is to wait for Boaz to finish eating and drinking, but take note of where he lies down for the night.

Naomi tells H the final step will be to undress Boaz and lie down next to him, and in the morning, he will tell her what will happen next. H promises to do everything Naomi has instructed her to do.

H prepares herself just as Naomi instructed and returns to the threshing room. She finds Boaz. His presence commands attention. H watches as he finishes his meal. He stumbles into a corner of the threshing room and falls fast asleep on a mat. He appears to have drunk too much.

H quietly walks over to where Boaz is lying. She stands over him silently. She snaps her fingers, and a small but brilliantly burning flame appears. H flicks the flame onto Boaz's clothes. His garments burn away rapidly. H removes her outer cloak and uses it as a blanket. She loosens the belt from around her waist and lies next to Boaz. She then lifts his arm and places it around her lower back.

When Boaz awakes the next morning, he sees his own naked body with H lying next to him. He grabs her and shakes her awake.

"Who are you?" Boaz asks H in a state of panic.

H looks directly into Boaz's eyes with a longing expression on her face. She tilts her head slightly and speaks softly to him.

"I am your maidservant you took under your wing several days ago. I was told you are a close relative of my late husband and his father, who also passed," she responds.

Boaz pauses. He looks intently at H. He is almost overwhelmed by her beauty.

"I understand what you must want of me; however, there is another relative who may be closer in relation than me. It would be his right to marry you under our laws and customs. I will make an inquiry with him. If he does not accept you as his own, I will take you myself," Boaz says softly.

H nods that she understands. Boaz helps H to her feet. He borrows a robe from one of his workers and makes his way to the other relative.

A day later, Boaz returns and asks H to marry him. H accepts enthusiastically.

A year later, H gives birth to a son. H and her husband name the boy Obed.

Time passes. H's mother-in-law transitions from this life. Decades later, Boaz also dies. While her son grows strong, he continues to advance in years. Try as she might, H cannot seem to pretend to grow old.

So, she does what she has become accustomed to doing. H fakes her own death and departs the land. The screen fades to black.

****

The planetary leaders in the viewing room begin their commentary. Monolith Ant leans forward in his seat and tries to get the attention of King Armacaust.

"I bet you had no idea that your wife was so cunning, did you, Armacaust?" Monolith Ant asks King Armacaust slyly.

"Unlike you, Lord Monolith, I don't ever underestimate my wife," King Armacaust replies dryly.

His lips lift into a smirk as he returns his focus to the viewing room's large panoramic screen. Aharon cannot contain himself as he laughs at the king's response.

"I would agree with that position," Aharon says, displaying a hint of satisfaction.

"Cunning or not, it is clear the queen is not who any of us imagined her to be. I wonder if this entire exercise, the kidnapping of the children, holding them on Earth, is all a part of a larger gambit," Envoy Armana posits. "What if the perpetrator or perpetrators desire also to expose what they believe to be the queen's hidden nature or flaws? What if their additional goal lies in diminishing Hawwah's ability to lead and hold influence throughout the System?"

"I was wondering that myself," Merneith adds.

"How would the perpetrators of this scheme even conceive that H would reveal herself in this way? She certainly did not have to invite us to view the stream we've been watching," Aharon argues.

"True that! And I have not seen anything that would make me trust her any less," Sekhmet adds.

CHAPTER 19
A SISTER'S LOVE

The next segment starts with H standing in the middle of the desert. The sun beats down on her, but she does not move. Every single cell in her body absorbs ambient energy. She can even absorb energy from sound waves. And exposure to direct sunlight makes her stronger and more resilient. H can also process sunlight into sustenance the same way plants conduct photosynthesis.

She awaits a caravan heading in her direction. Her incredibly acute hearing picks up the grunting of the camels in the distance. H received word that a company of traffickers, transporting slaves from Upper Kemet to Lower Kemet, would be traveling along this route. This particular cartel specializes in enslaving women and children.

Mother

For the last twenty years, H has dedicated herself to rescuing women from the clutches of the sex trade. She has been tracking this caravan for months. Today will be the day she finally comes face-to-face with her target.

H squints her eyes to get a better picture of the approaching caravan. Like a finely tuned telescope, her eyes magnify the image of the large party that includes six-wheeled cages, thirty men on horseback, another fifteen on camels, and a dozen or so boys pulling donkeys carrying supplies. Each of the cages contains ten or more women and young girls.

H shakes her head.

"Light work," she says to herself.

H removes her belt. Knives tucked securely in sleeves on either side of the back of the belt click together as she folds the belt in half and places it neatly next to her on the ground. She slips her bow over her shoulder and head. Setting the bow aside, she loosens the strap holding her arrow quiver and two swords to her back. Her swords and quiver fall to the ground.

She takes a seat on the hot sand. She sits up straight, legs crossed, her spine is long with a deliberate posture extending through the crown of her head. She touches each index finger to the thumb on each hand, placing her hands gently atop her thighs. Taking deep breaths, she waits.

In this meditative state, she can see the past, present, and future simultaneously. Visions begin to flood into her mind's eye as if on a tri-split screen, until finally she sees a man dismounting from a horse. He draws a sword and walks over to her, as the large contingent behind him slows to a stop.

"You there! What are you doing out here?" the man shouts in a Mesopotamian dialect. "Answer me, woman!" the man shouts angrily, pointing his sword directly at H's face.

H returns to her body and flutters her eyes open. She looks up at the man, tilting her head to the side.

"Tell your friends to release the women and children, and I won't harm you," H replies calmly.

The man reels back. Without removing his sword, he looks over his shoulder to receive direction from his compatriots. One of the men sitting atop a camel makes a motion with his hands that seems to indicate the man standing in front of H should slit her throat.

The man remains standing in front of H with his sword extended directly at her face. He nods.

"How dare you, witch?" he says, drawing back his sword to strike a fatal blow.

Many of the women and girls in the cages let out cries and gasps at the sight. The man swings his blade at H's neck. She stops the blade with the palm of her hand. Her lips spread into a broad smile.

As she slowly stands, her hand slides down the edge of the blade. The man watches in astonished disbelief. Once fully standing, H delivers an upward open-hand strike to the middle of the man's chest. The force of the blow throws him high into the air. As the man falls swiftly back down to the Earth, he crashes violently into two of the camel riders.

One of the other men on horseback draws his sword and motions for the others to charge. H whirls around and snatches her quiver, swords, and bow. With unimaginable speed and dexterity, she straps her weapons across her body and secures them to her back. She draws an arrow and fires directly into the lead horseback rider. He lurches from his mount and falls to the ground several feet away.

She fires twelve more arrows, emptying her quiver, before the other riders reach her. All twelve of the arrows find their targets. Each of the men struck by these shots falls from his horse.

H ducks a sword being swung at her head. She reaches up and snatches the man attacking her from his horse and throws him into another, charging toward her. Both men land forcefully on the ground and lie unconscious.

H rises off the ground and flies swiftly into the crowd of riders, punching or pulling the riders from their horses. She propels herself skyward and disappears. The terrified men look to the heavens, probing the sky for any sight of her.

H reappears suddenly. Before any of the men can react, she flies between the camels, delivering hand strikes and spinning kicks. Bodies begin flying in every direction as H continues her ferocious assault.

H pauses to survey the scene. She sees a man about 100 feet from her crawling toward a sword that appears to have landed vertically in the sand. H retrieves an arrow and fires it at the sword. The blade flips out of the sand, landing far from the man's reach.

The man stops moving and rolls over onto his back. He looks back at H.

"Khairunnisa…" the man mutters before dropping his head onto the sand and passing out from pure exhaustion.

H turns and walks toward the cages. She rips the cage doors from each wagon and helps the captives dismount. As the women huddle, crying and thanking her, H walks over to one of the more mature-looking women.

"Where do you come from?" H asks gently.

"My daughters, sisters, cousin, and I were taken from a village just outside of Ineb-Hedj," the woman replies.

"My sisters and I were taken from a village along the river delta," another woman says excitedly.

Other women begin calling out locations along the Nile. H begins plotting a course in her mind along the river that will allow her to return each of these women to their homes.

"Ok, we will get each of you back home," H says with a smile.

H notices a girl standing off to the side by herself. She walks over to the young lady, who begins to shrink away from H as she approaches.

"I won't hurt you, little one," H says softly. "What's your name, child?"

"I am called Zilpha," the child replies.

Each of the ladies in the viewing room at The Gatekeeper's HQ places their hands over their mouths at the same time, as if they were following the flow of a scripted piece of dance choreography. Monolith Ant sits forward in his seat.

"You have a pretty name, Zilpha. A pretty name for a pretty girl," H replies. "Where are you from?" H asks with a warm smile.

Zilpha walks straight into H, wrapping her arms around H's waist. Zilpha buries the side of her face into H's midsection. Tears begin streaming from the child's face.

"They killed my family," Zilpha sobs. "I have no one left," she says between heavy breaths.

H begins to cry, too. She lifts Zilpha into the air and pulls the child's head to the side of her own, holding her tightly.

"Well, you have me now, little one," H says softly.

Tears begin to flow in the viewing room. The sound of onlookers blowing their noses can be heard throughout.

H gathers the horses and camels, then goes about reclaiming her arrows. She tells the boys pulling the pack mules to help her, and she will return them to their homes as well. Most of the boys agree. A few of them run off into the desert.

After loading the women and girls onto the camels, horses, and wagons, H leads the caravan south, back along the Nile toward Upper Kemet. At every stop they make along the river, H takes the time to train Zilpha to use a bow. H also teaches Zilpha the finer points of sword fighting, as well as the basics of hand-to-hand combat.

H decides to treat Zilpha more like a sister than a daughter. Zilpha reminds H of the mother-in-law she followed from the land of Moab to Bethlehem all those years ago. Zilpha comes to cherish her relationship with H, and the two become an inseparable pair.

As Zilpha's skill grows, they do not miss any opportunity to rescue women and girls from the hands of traffickers. The grateful women returning to their families always offer H and Zilpha clothing and food for their ongoing travels.

Throughout the Nile Valley, stories spread far and wide of the "Great Khairunnisa," who is more than simply the "goodness of women," but the goddess protector of women. The legends include tales of a woman who can soar like a bird and possesses the strength of a hundred men.

H and Zilpha, upon whom H bestows the nickname "Z," delight themselves in regaling the women and girls they meet with stories of their adventures. Though she can sense that Z feels a sense of security, H can also tell that Z has questions about what this all means.

Z has been cautiously building up the courage to ask H about the fantastic feats of strength and other wonders she has witnessed H perform over the last few years. So, at their camp near the Ipet-isut Temple Complex, H decides to answer all of Z's questions.

"Is it true that nothing can hurt you?" Z asks.

"I am, uh, pretty much incapable of being physically harmed… I think. But I can be 'hurt,' because I do have feelings," H replies with a smile.

"Are you really as strong as a hundred men?" Z asks with a giggle.

With an exuberant expression in her voice, H replies, "No, I am much, much stronger than that. I once picked up a beast as tall as the highest treetops you have ever seen and threw it across a chamber in a cave. And you should have seen the look on his face."

The sisters share a hearty laugh at the visual. After a lengthy, intense conversation, H and Z finally begin to relax. Z, however, grows serious again, as she has one more question.

"Will you ever die?" Z asks.

H can detect the great concern in Z's voice. Z, experiencing the loss of her family, continues to have a traumatizing effect on Z's young mind. H realizes that, if Z were to lose her, it would be so shattering that Z might not recover. H wants to reassure Z but opts for a more practical approach to her answer.

"I will die one day. It's just going to take a long, long, very long time… unless one of our enemies figures out how to kill me first," H says with a wry smile.

Z's eyes begin to water, and her lips start quivering. Z looks directly into H's eyes. Her lips part.

"So, I will die one day, and you will still be here?" Z asks.

H realizes the question is meant to follow up on the earlier question regarding whether H can feel pain or not. H feels herself being overwhelmed by emotion. Over the course of her long life, H has been a wife, a mother, a friend, and even a daughter. But she has never been a sister or felt the genuine concern of a sister's love.

H leans in and locks eyes with Z.

"I hope the world ends before you and I have to part!" H replies softly but intently.

Upon hearing this, Z leaps forward and wraps her arms around H's neck and shoulders. The tears flowing from Z's eyes wet H's hair and shoulder. Experiencing feelings she has never felt before, H wraps her arms around Z, too.

****

The panoramic screen in the viewing room once again fades to black.

"She found her…" Neith says, with a tone of surprise in her voice. "She trained her," she continues, her lips shaking, fighting back the tears. "I didn't understand their story before. I just assumed H inherited Z through a marriage that ended on Earth."

"It's so beautiful," Merneith offers.

The stream restarts with images depicting Aharon and his partnership with the sisters during their adventures across Kemet and throughout the land of Kush.

Sekhmet leans forward in her seat. She tries to get Aharon's attention but opts to shout playfully across the room instead.

"So, you have always been this handsome, Mr. President?" Sekhmet asks flirtatiously.

Aharon smiles but does not look in Sekhmet's direction. Neith throws Sekhmet a very noticeable side-eye.

"Oooooo, somebody did not like that comment," Merneith shouts.

Merneith and Sekhmet break out into hysterical laughter. King Armacaust sighs and sinks into his seat.

The following images show the horrific battles with Apep, now a ten-headed dragon, leading hordes of giants and other very unnatural-looking warriors against H and a group of warriors that includes both Aharon and Monolith Ant.

"Is that what you looked like before…" Neith begins to ask.

"Yes," Monolith Ant replies sternly, cutting her off.

"This walk through the queen's past is all very interesting, but unless we are going to see how these visions connect to the present, I think it is obvious that Apep is the perpetrator behind the dastardly deed that has befallen us," Envoy Armana says assertively.

"It is also curious that the screen continues to go dark at certain points. This portion of the stream clearly demonstrates that Hawwah can see the past, the present, and the future all at once. So, what is the princess not showing us?" Monolith Ant asks the room.

"What, indeed?" Aharon asks.

CHAPTER 20
IT WAS ALL GOOD BACK THEN

When the stream continues, the images on the screen depict the bridge of a starship hurtling through space at mind-bending speed.

H sits in a captain's chair with myriad controls on the armrests and a large panel in front of her. The chair and control panel are on an elevated platform, about four feet high. The adjoining control panels are aligned in a concentric half-circle configuration in front of the captain's chair. All the consoles face the large, windowed aperture that provides line-of-sight visibility for navigating the ship.

H is dying. The battle against Apep the Dragon and his hordes has left her body battered and broken. And she gave birth mere hours ago. Open wounds spill her blood onto the floor. The starship draws its power from H herself. If she dies, the entire mission will be lost, and the more than 225,000 people aboard the ship will perish in deep space.

The planned crew of the starship included Amen, Z, Aharon, Abasi, a physician named Abrax Menewa, Imhotep, and H. Amen, originally intended to serve as the navigator, takes over the responsibility of piloting the ship. Z, intended to serve as the ship's communications officer, leaves her station to find a ladder or other device that will allow her to stand next to H.

Before they launched, Imhotep expressed to Z the importance of H remaining in the captain's chair. The specially designed captain's chair serves as the connection between H, as the power source, and the starship's engine and life support systems.

Because Apep blocked his path to board the ship, Imhotep initiated the launch sequence but remained behind with the baby. Shortly following the launch of the starship, H joined Imhotep on the astral plane to share a moment with him and their newborn son. H could not, however, sustain her astral projection for very long due to her injuries, compounded by the dual exertions of childbirth and supplying enough power to the massive vessel for it to achieve escape velocity.

H's power must supply the starship's thrust while providing the artificial atmosphere and gravity required for the people, plants, and animals onboard to survive.

Watching H slip away, Imhotep telepathically summons a team of people with specialized training and skills to assist the crew and attend to H. He calls a nurse named Bastet filia Wepwawet, a midwife named Anippe Lassiteeri Akhet, a pharmacist named

Baahir Callis Ankhesenamun, an additional physician named Aha Meketaten II, and a psychologist named Ahmose Pen-Nekhebet.

All rush onto the bridge.

Abasi and Aharon dismantle the chairs connected to the other control panels and fashion stepladders, which Aha, Abrax, Bastet, and Anippe can use to reach H more comfortably and effectively. While the makeshift emergency medicine and surgical team works feverishly to save H, Baahir gathers supplies to mix into medicines and ointments to fight any possible infections and speed up H's recovery. Aharon and Abasi stand guard at the door to the bridge to prevent any unnecessary intrusions.

King Armacaust watches with an expression of great pride on his face as the images on the screen show his grandfather, Abrax, working feverishly on H. Others in the viewing room express their awe at how poised the young Anippe Akhet is, known to them as both Senator Wepwawet and the Vindicator, who is undoubtedly the greatest sword fighter in the entire Ant-Galaxo Devearous System. In fact, the best sword fighters in the System have learned under her.

Several hours pass aboard the starship. The fight to keep H alive starts to seem hopeless. She has been nonresponsive since the ship left Earth's atmosphere. The starship's power remaining constant serves as the only indication that H endures.

Ahmose attempts several psychologically sound methods to revive H. Everyone on the bridge has come into contact with a significant amount of H's blood, which, after careful study by Abrax, is determined to be radioactive. In fact, the badly injured H seems to be leaking nuclear radiation.

Aha also discovers a strange phenomenon. His skin seems to be absorbing H's blood. When Z mentions that she has experienced the same reaction to H's blood, Aha delves deeper into his research and begins conducting more tests.

A week passes. H remains unconscious but firmly connected to the captain's chair. Amen and Z provide daily updates to ensure that everyone on board the ship remains steady on course.

When Ahmose and Z begin to exhibit symptoms of radiation poisoning, it is determined that the people on the bridge will begin working in rotating shifts. Z, of course, refuses to leave her sister regardless of the cost to her own personal safety. Her faithful husband, Amen, decides he will stand by his wife's side. Aharon also decides he will stay on the bridge. He and Abasi agree to take shifts.

Aha suggests the newly dubbed "Bridge Team" submit to frequent radiation testing. All agree. Abrax and Aha begin to work together to determine the possible long-term effects that exposure to H's blood and radiation could have on normal humans.

After copious research and testing, the two doctors convene a briefing with the Bridge Team.

"We have determined that the radioactive isotopes in H's blood, if activated by the right stimulus, could trigger a transmutation event," Abrax begins.

"What does that mean?" Aharon asks in a worried tone.

"In other words, anyone who has been subjected to significant exposure to H's blood and radiation could experience a series of mutations if also exposed to the proper stimulus. These mutations could result in becoming more like H, exhibiting a series of paranatural abilities, or spontaneous combustion," Aha explains.

"And that group would include any of us," Abrax adds.

"What is this 'stimulus' you are referring to?" Amen asks.

"We don't know yet," Aha begins. "It could be exposure to additional bodily fluids H may secrete, such as saliva or urine. It could be exposure to a similar form of radiation, like electromagnetic radiation from a star larger or otherwise more powerful than Earth's sun.

"I think the point we want to make is twofold: 1) Be careful and always wear protective gear when rendering medical care or other services to H; and 2) Everyone onboard this ship should be tested for radiation exposure or poisoning," Abrax suggests. "Our skin seems to be absorbing her blood rather than repelling it, as human skin would do with any other liquid."

"Amen, with Em unavailable and H out of commission, you are the closest thing we have to a captain. Would you feel comfortable giving such an order to the passengers?" Aha asks.

Amen sighs. He did not want this responsibility, but he understands the need for competent leadership at a time like this.

"Let it be done," he says assertively.

"Aye, Captain," Aharon says enthusiastically.

He stands and gives Amen a snappy salute. The rest of the Bridge Team laughs at Aharon's attempt at levity. No one questions Amen's leadership. Having a captain proves to be a comforting thought to many of the passengers on board.

Two months pass. The rate of speed at which the ship has been traveling has gotten noticeably slower to everyone on board. The members of the Bridge Team begin to wonder if all their efforts to save H's life have failed and if the reduced speed means she will soon expire.

Members of the Bridge Team begin taking turns expressing their goodbyes to H. Each time one of them enters the bridge, Z and Amen pretend not to listen. When Aharon makes his way to the captain's chair, Z and Amen perk up and pay attention.

"Oh, you two are just going to listen to mine, huh?" Aharon asks.

Neither Amen nor Z responds. Z giggles as she watches Aharon shake his head with a smirk on his face. He takes a deep breath, then lets out a big sigh. He steps forward and begins to offer his words to the still unconscious H.

"You and I have been friends for some time now. But I am still in love with you… No matter how much I fight it. And it hurts me to see you in this state. But I want you to know how proud of you I am for what you have accomplished. No matter what happens here, you showed us all how to reach for the stars, quite literally, as it were. But right now, that legacy is very much in doubt. If you let go now, all of us will perish. We need you. Come back to us, Hawwah. You have had a long enough break. It's time to get back to work. Do you hear me?" Aharon pronounces.

"Yes, I hear you, Aharon," H replies.

She lifts her head and opens her eyes. She shifts her shoulders back and forth a bit before scooting up in the captain's chair.

"Where's Z?" H asks, blinking uncontrollably.

"I'm right here!" Z yells.

Z's eyes immediately burst into tears. H begins laughing nervously. Z climbs up into the captain's chair and throws her arms around H.

"Am I strapped into this thing?" H asks sarcastically, noticing that her arm movements are restricted.

"We had to," Z replies with a laugh.

"Doctors Menewa and Meketaten, please report to the bridge," Amen calls out over the ship's communication system.

"Amen!" H calls out, hearing her brother-in-law's voice.

"I'm here, Sis! It's good to have you back!" Amen calls back.

The two physicians rush onto the bridge, followed closely by Bastet and Anippe. H turns her neck as far as it will go in an attempt to see behind the captain's chair. Abrax steps forward and puts his hands over his mouth. Bastet and Anippe begin hugging each other and jumping up and down in excitement.

"Doc, can you get me out of these restraints? I do not want to break them in case these things are important," H asks Abrax.

"Right away, H," Abrax says.

Aha walks over to the captain's chair and begins taking measurements of H's vitals. He also measures the levels of radioactivity that H is currently releasing. Returning to consciousness seems to have resolved the leak.

"How long was I out?" H asks.

"Too long," Z responds with a huge smile.

"Two months," Ahmose answers from the back of the room, walking onto the bridge.

"Two months. Wow…" H says in an exasperated tone.

H rubs her wrists and makes circles with her fists as Abrax removes the restraints from her arms. He also releases the strap from around her waist. H steps up in the captain's chair and places her palms onto the raised half-orbs at the end of the armrests.

Moving her arms forward causes her to catch a whiff of her own armpits.

"Oh, wow! I need to bathe," H exclaims. "Ok. Time for that later. Everybody hold on to something!"

She provides a jolt of power that restores the starship to its full capacity. The ship responds by accelerating to a rate of speed the passengers have not felt since takeoff. The ship speeds toward an asteroid field.

"Aharon, raise the shields. Amen, prepare for evasive maneuvering. Z, tell everyone to hold on to something," H orders calmly.

The starship lurches forward. Bastet, Abrax, and Aha leave the bridge to help secure the passengers. Abasi walks onto the bridge to see what the sudden acceleration has already revealed. Hawwah lives.

"Amen, open the observation panel. I need actual visuals for this next part," H orders.

She deftly pilots the ship through the asteroid field, narrowly avoiding collisions with large floating stones. Just as the ship passes through the field, a focused beam of light pours into the bridge as a result of the seven suns of the solar system aligning in a perfect line.

Everyone on the bridge experiences immediate changes.

Aharon disappears from view, then reappears with a very confused look on his face. Abasi's skin begins to crack and sizzle. He screams in pain. His muscles seem to double in size as he grows visibly taller. Amen and Z begin to float off the ground. Z somehow immediately understands what is happening and flies over to Abasi to check on him.

Abasi stands silently, shaking. He looks over his hands in disbelief. His skin continues to smolder.

"What's happening?" Ahmose asks H without opening her mouth.

"Ahmose, are you speaking to me?" H asks.

"You could hear that?" Ahmose asks aloud this time.

"Yes, you spoke to me in my mind," H says, raising her eyebrows.

"I did?" Ahmose asks.

"Look what I can do," Anippe shouts, as she manipulates the shape of the platforms previously used by Abrax and Aha to treat H.

Anippe stretches out her right hand and concentrates intensely. One of the platforms rises off the ground. Closing her eyes and concentrating, the hunk of metal slowly transforms into a sword.

"Whoa," Anippe says in amazement.

"Oh, boy," H says.

Z continues to squeal in sheer delight, flying loops in the air above the bridge floor. Aha and Abrax run back onto the bridge.

"What did we miss?" Aha asks in amazement, watching Z fly around the bridge.

"A focused beam of sunlight hit us," Amen says dryly.

"The sunlight, solar energy, which is primarily comprised of electromagnetic radiation, provided the stimulation event we projected," Aha explains.

"Well, too bad we missed it," Abrax laughs.

"Well, the radiation levels to which we were exposed will likely result in both of us having children who possess *enhanced* abilities like our friends are now exhibiting," Aha replies.

"Seriously, we could have children with powers like H's?" Abrax asks.

"Yeah, some may have abilities even greater than hers. The intensity of those abilities will depend on various factors, but it is highly likely that our offspring will be among the enhanced in a generation or two," Aha explains.

"Wow. I would love to continue to conduct some research on your theories in that regard," Abrax suggests.

"A partnership, then?" Aha asks.

"Absolutely!" Abrax responds.

The two doctors exchange a hearty handshake. Bastet returns to the bridge and nearly faints at the sight of Z flying. Abrax and Aha catch her. The three medical professionals share a laugh.

****

The stream continues to display images from the Great Exodus from Planet Earth to Planet Chaos. The viewing room remains silent until both Monolith Ant and Aharon begin stirring in their seats. Aharon sighs. Monolith Ant looks away from the screen.

"You all really took care of each other once," Sekhmet offers.

"That was long ago," Monolith Ant replies dryly.

CHAPTER 21
THE GIZA CONNECTION

The next segment begins with Aharon storming out of H's bedchamber, leaving a naked Hawwah sobbing uncontrollably on her bed. Z rushes to H's side to comfort her.

Aharon stirs in his seat in reaction to the visuals on the screen and only further reacts by letting out an audible sigh. Neith folds her arms and looks in the opposite direction.

Scene after scene flows into the next. An image develops on the screen portraying H sitting at a round table along with Aharon and Monolith Ant, several aides, and other dignitaries such as Ambassador Horemheb Aten, Royal Ambassador to Giza, and Amen Hotep, better known as Starlyte, Dean of the Planet Chaos College of Elders.

Seated immediately to the queen's right sits a young woman held in high renown across the System for her advocacy on behalf of the Drākanashim living on Giza. Her name is Neith Ramses. On the other side of the queen sits another well-known native daughter of the Giza Moon Colony, Professor Sebayt Loemba Menes, known in her professional capacity as the Convener.

"Monolith Ant, the atrocities occurring throughout the Giza Moon Colony against the indigenous inhabitants simply cannot continue. You say you recognize the need to preserve life and allow the Drākanashim some semblance of self-determination, then do something. We've been in this room going round and round without you advancing one actionable proposal. Planets Chaos and Memphis are prepared to assume administration of Giza and restore order. As it stands now, Giza has become a known hub for pirates and traffickers. Cannibals kill with impunity, as do the members of your Giza Garrison. Your settlers are forcing Drākanashim families from their homes, leaving women and children to sleep on the streets. I do whatever I can to avoid war, but I will not continue to stand by and watch people get slaughtered," H declares forcefully.

"I want to echo the words of Queen Hawwah. Monolith Ant, either you will ensure the people of Giza, all the people of Giza, receive the benefits of justice, peace, and tranquility, or we will," Aharon adds.

"You both come here and accuse me of turning a blind eye to human suffering. You claim to present evidence of atrocities occurring throughout a lawful territory of Planet Ikw-n-tA, a sovereign planetary entity recognized by the Galactic Security Council. How was this evidence gathered if not by espionage? Moreover, you make demands of me, feigning to claim some moral high ground. The girl sitting next to the queen of Planet Chaos is engaged in an illicit affair with the president of Planet Memphis. No, neither of you possesses the right or moral clarity to judge me. I will, nonetheless, offer concessions to the Drākanashim. The settlements and land annexed by Ikw-n-tA for those settlements shall remain in our possession. However, no new settlements will be developed. But the Giza Garrison shall remain in place to protect my people. The Drāks may create their own government to establish home rule. But any military they raise shall be mobilized solely for the defense of their homeland against interplanetary invaders or pirates. Their military shall be strictly prohibited from engaging in any form of law enforcement activities. Do we have terms?" Monolith Ant declares dryly.

H looks to Neith. Neith stands, placing her hand on the table.

"We will need the settlers to pay taxes on the real estate and personal property they've seized. Add that provision to your offer, and we have terms," Neith declares assertively.

"Agreed," Monolith Ant says without another thought.

H and Neith walk out of the conference room and onto the steps of the Ant Planet State Capitol complex. They are immediately swarmed by reporters. The two women clasp hands and raise their arms in jubilation. H addresses the crowds gathered to hear the news.

"Today marks the establishment of the Giza Authority Directorate!" H shouts triumphantly. "And perhaps this measure will provide a small token of hope to the people of Giza for a future free from fear and oppression."

H and Neith find themselves separated momentarily. They receive congratulations from multitudes of supporters and well-wishers. Neith takes a break from shaking hands and makes her way back to H. The two women hug each other tightly, hopping up and down.

****

The screen once again fades to black. When this portion of the stream continues, the planetary leaders view with rapt attention.

"I must admit, she has always supported me," Neith says, wiping a tear away from her eye.

"She has been there for all of us, if we were to be honest about it," Sekhmet adds. "Even the two of you," Sekhmet says, pointing at both Monolith Ant and Aharon, then tilting her head indignantly.

"I think I am starting to see a pattern here," Insp. Djet Drone declares. "Each of these visions draws a line pointing to either the perpetrators or the location of the missing children. For example, take the scenes we reviewed from H's time on Earth. Most of those experiences took place on the African continent. It is doubtful the perpetrators live on Earth, so I bet the kids are likely being held somewhere in Africa," he explains.

"Sounds logical, Inspector, but you also think you see a connection to the perpetrators? Please elaborate," Envoy Armana interjects.

"We all know that Queen Mother will move heaven and earth to rescue women or children from traffickers. Which planet in the System has the highest rate of human trafficking?" Insp. Djet Drone asks.

"Giza," Neith replies, sighing, with a frustrated gaze fixed on Monolith Ant.

"I have nothing to do with the pirates or traffickers plaguing your home world, and any notion to the contrary is simply absurd!" Monolith Ant retorts in a calm but indignant tone. "You have your own army. Get rid of the 'bad apples' from among your society."

"You refuse to allow us to enforce the law without your approval. It almost seems like your oligarchs are allowed to engage in all manner of lawlessness… so long as they do it on Giza, that is," Neith replies passionately.

"Then running a nation-state may not be a job for a woman after all," Monolith Ant replies, staring directly at Neith.

"Alright, let's remain civil," King Armacaust declares in an attempt to defuse the situation. "I think the Inspector is on to something. Unfortunately, it makes sense if the perpetrators are using Giza as their base of operations. Leader Ramses, do you have any idea who might have an organization large enough, or even sophisticated enough, to pull this off?"

Neith replies, "As you say, unfortunately, I can think of three possible entities: #1 The Takeover, i.e., The Leader and his bunch; #2 Captain LionMane and his fleet; and #3 the Grand Reverend. The Takeover primarily focuses its attention on the destabilization of governments on Planet Earth. And they do have a large footprint on Earth. Captain LionMane has the resources but not the sophistication to pull this off. He is more of a 'gun for hire' than a general contractor. The Grand Reverend, however, is probably the most dangerous operator of the three. He has resources, a small fortune he has earned from selling his technology and genetic engineering services to parties throughout the System. He also possesses the sophistication. He even has the muscle. Those genetically engineered, enhanced thugs he calls "sons" terrorize anyone who gets in his way."

"I wouldn't be surprised if they are all working together for an operation this large. Kidnapping 33,300 children, by all the reports we have been receiving over the past twenty-four hours, would require more capacity to plan and the ability to execute than any one of those groups could muster alone," Insp. Djet Drone adds.

"Well, we just need to confirm the location of the children, then go make arrests, yes?" Sekhmet asks.

Everyone in the viewing room pauses, casting judgmental looks in Monolith Ant's direction. Monolith Ant simply stands and walks into the restroom.

CHAPTER 22
DUMAS, L'OUVETURE + DESSALINES

As the panoramic screen comes back to life, H can be seen returning to Planet Earth. She enters Earth's atmosphere and lands on a large island between two continents in the Western Hemisphere.

"Arisone, on which island did she land?" Insp. Djet Drone shouts.

Arisone pauses the stream to respond. She types a search inquiry into her keyboard.

"Ayiti. During this period on Earth, the colonizers refer to it as 'Haiti,'" Arisone responds.

"What's the time period?" Aharon asks.

"As far as we can tell, this takes place in Year 8971, the year that would be referred to as 1771 on Earth."

"Thank you," Aharon replies.

Arisone resumes the stream.

H returns to the sky and flies over the island several times before landing on the grounds of a plantation. H looks around the expansive farm. She sees an enslaved African woman walking toward the slave quarters. H follows the woman closely.

The woman walks behind a row of connected shacks and begins to remove a few tattered articles of clothing hanging on a line between two trees. By the time the woman places the articles in a basket, H walks right up behind her and places a hand over her mouth. The woman trembles with fear.

Keeping her hand over the woman's mouth, H renders herself invisible and hurries the woman back around to the front of the row of shacks.

"Which one is yours?" H whispers to the woman.

The woman lifts a shaky hand and points to the shack at the end. H hurries the woman into the shack. H renders herself visible and slowly removes her hand from the woman's mouth.

"Can you tell me your name?" H asks the woman in French. "Do you understand? I think I am speaking the right language."

"They call me Marie-Cessette. What do you want with me?" the woman responds in Creole.

H recognizes the vocabulary as a combination of words borrowed from French, blended with fragments of words used by people from Central and West Africa. The unique grammar and syntax make H smile.

"I am going to try to speak your language," H says. "Forgive me if I get some works couched."

Marie-Cessette laughs at H's misspoken vocabulary. She quickly gathers herself well enough to muster a response.

"I also speak French," Marie-Cessette says, continuing to chuckle.

H responds with a nervous laugh of her own. H hesitates for a moment, trying to figure out how to proceed in a manner that will allow Marie-Cessette to continue to relax.

"You are not from here. What do you seek?" Marie-Cessette asks.

"I'm looking for someone," H replies. "I've been searching plantations across these islands for more than fifty years now."

"Who do you seek?" Marie-Cessette asks.

"My son," H says intently. "He would appear to be a young man, not much older than you. Only, we have been separated for so long, I may not be able to describe him to you very well. His name is Adisa," H states, taking Marie-Cessette by the hands.

"There are many young men here. Take your pick," Marie-Cessette replies in her Caribbean accent.

"I have an idea," H says.

While still holding on to Marie-Cessette's hands, H's features begin to change, moving and shifting until H becomes an exact replica of Marie-Cessette.

Marie-Cessette snatches her hands away from H.

"Oh, my God!" Marie-Cessette exclaims. "Are you some kind of Mambo?" she asks, with a tone of shock and contempt in her voice.

"No, I'm you, just for a little while. I'll be you whenever you want to take a break. I will perform our chores and bring you all the food you want. I just need to walk around the plantation without anyone asking questions," H replies in Marie-Cessette's exact voice and accent.

"You want to perform my chores? You look a bit too skinny for that. You want to bed down Monsieur Davy, too? He uses me for that whenever he gets the notion, or his wife can't or won't. All four of my children are his. Speaking of which, you'll need to bring enough food for my children, too," Marie-Cessette replies with a skeptical expression on her face. "Alright, then. Get going. They'll be handing out cornmeal in a few minutes over at the big house," Marie-Cessette says insistently.

"Which way?" H asks with a smile on her face.

"Not to worry. You'll see it when you get out there," Marie-Cessette says, scooting H out through the door of the shack. "And don't come back until everyone's bedded down for the night. Lord knows you'll scare my children half to death looking like that," Marie-Cessette scolds.

H ventures out onto the plantation grounds. The setting sun paints a picturesque portrait against the backdrop of the well-tended fields of the plantation. H follows a group of enslaved field hands walking toward a large, manicured lawn. She looks up and sees the plantation house not far off.

Men carrying large bundles of sugarcane and women holding the hands of children line up to exchange their bundles for bags of cornmeal. The enslaved receive only cornmeal for food. During the holidays or after a large party, the plantation owner,

Marquis Alexandre Antoine Davy de la Pailleterie, may spare them scraps from the leftover meats and other delights their fellow enslaved have prepared for Monsieur Davy and his guests.

On every other day throughout the year, however, the only thing Monsieur Davy provides for the enslaved to eat is a single bag of cornmeal. Most of the enslaved people use the cornmeal to make cakes that they heat in the fireplace in their shacks. The cakes are placed on a gardening hoe and cooked one by one in the fireplace. These "hoecakes" have become a staple and the primary source of nourishment for enslaved African people throughout North America and the Caribbean.

As H gets closer to the storehouse, she remembers that she does not have a bundle to exchange. She steps out of line and looks around frantically, trying to think up a solution. She notices an open side door to the big house. She runs over and peeks inside. She steps very quietly inside.

A large-breasted woman wearing an apron spots her.

"Marie-Cessette, what are you doing in here? Did Monsieur Davy call you over tonight? His wife is here, you know," the lady says insistently.

"I just forgot my bundle. I was nervous and got out of line. I didn't know what else to do," H says.

The lady looks H up and down with a skeptical expression on her face. She then walks over to the pantry and gathers an armful of smoked meats, cheeses, and bread.

"Here, take these, child. Now get!" the lady shoos H out of the door.

H smiles and leaps from the door. She finds a sack near the storehouse. H carefully bags the food and slings the sack over her shoulder.

H begins walking around the slave quarters, looking over the young men, hoping to catch a glimpse of anyone resembling the image of Adisa she has seen in her meditative visions. A young man notices her conspicuous gaze and begins to follow her. H begins to wonder if he might be Marie-Cessette's lover. H slows her pace until she finally stops.

"If you are going to follow me, you could be a little less obvious about it," H says without turning to face the man.

He stops a few feet behind her. H can hear his heart beating slow and steady. She then scans his emotional intent. She soon realizes that her stalker means her no harm.

"I didn't know if you would take my introduction well," the man replies.

H turns to face the man. Atop his short, athletic frame sits a round face. His appearance reminds H of many of the people she met along the west coast of the African continent.

"I might accept you better if you tell me your name," H responds cautiously.

"I am Toussaint L'Ouverture," the man says with a smile on his face. "You look like you are seeking someone, no?"

"Yes, a young man. He would be about your age. He's my son," H replies.

"Wouldn't he be among the field hands? You look like you work in the house. I would imagine that most of the men around here are washing for supper, but you could likely find him in the morning," L'Ouverture replies.

"You're not from this plantation. What are you doing here?" H asks with a hint of skepticism.

"I was making a delivery and was about to be on my way before I saw you," L'Ouverture answers.

"Why did seeing me stop you?" H probes.

"Just thought I could be helpful," L'Ouverture returns.

"Well, I don't need any help. You should stay focused on your tasks, mon ami," H suggests.

L'Ouverture flashes H a wide smile. His face is beaming as he bows respectfully.

"Bonswa, bèl fi." He gestures with a tip of his cap.

"Bonswa," H responds.

H hurries away. The sun has fully set. The stars shine brightly in the sky high above the plantation. H can feel the Earth moving beneath her feet. She has almost forgotten how much she loves the sensation created by the rhythm of the rivers of molten rock shifting and moving far below the Earth's crust.

She rushes back to Marie-Cessette's shack. H carefully places the sack on the stoop, knocks on the door, then turns herself invisible. H can hear footsteps walking toward the door. Marie-Cessette's nine-year-old son opens the door and looks out into the night. Just before he closes the door, he looks down and notices the sack. Lifting the sack and holding it open, he examines the contents. His eyes light up.

"Thomas-Alexandre!" Marie-Cessette hollers.

Hearing his mother calling for him, the boy shuts the door briskly and runs excitedly back inside. H beams with delight. Remaining invisible, she flies high into a mountain. H returns to her normal form and makes a camp for the night.

H returns to the plantation in the morning. Marie-Cessette is already hard at work sweeping the front porch of the big house. She makes eye contact with Marie-Cessette, who shakes her head and chuckles at seeing H.

H transforms into Marie-Cessette once again. She picks up a basket she finds close to the storehouse and makes her way to the field. H pretends to be bringing the field workers binds for their bundles. She inspects each of the young men she crosses. None of them looks like Adisa.

She has seen Adisa in her meditations, but has not been able to get a read on his location from the background scenery. H freezes when she hears horses approaching. She adjusts her eyes so that she can telescopically magnify the approaching convoy.

Two roughly dressed men on horseback ride in front of a carriage pulled by two more horses. A well-dressed man sits in the carriage alone. Six other men ride behind the carriage. The men behind the carriage are prodding a dozen or more Black men and boys to walk faster.

H clenches her teeth. It takes everything in her to fight the urge to fly over and set the captives free. As she continues to monitor the approaching convoy, she recognizes the face of the man riding in the carriage.

It's Sobek Anubis, also known as "G. Elon Lynch Jr.," but better known as "Racism."

H hurries toward the road leading up to the plantation house. She pretends to be tending to the bushes on either side of the gate at the entrance to the plantation. As the horsemen pass her, she walks alongside the carriage. She finally catches Racism's attention. He reaches his hand out toward her. She takes his hand, and he helps her into the carriage.

"Bonswa, ma chère," Racism says with a lustful expression on his face. "How fortunate that I would come across you here. May I have the pleasure of your name?"

"Here, I am called Marie-Cessette," H starts in Marie-Cessette's voice. "But where we're from, people refer to me as Queen Mother!" H says sharply in her own voice.

Racism reels back at hearing H's voice. One of his henchmen notices his discomfort and begins to ride closer to the carriage to investigate. H notices the henchman approaching and scoots closer to Racism. She puts her hand on his crotch and begins to apply excruciating pressure to his genitals. H leans in closer to the side of Racism's head, placing her lips next to his ear.

"Pretend like you are enjoying this, or I will squeeze harder," H whispers.

Racism obliges. He motions his hand, indicating to the henchman to ride ahead.

"Very good, Sobek," H says. "You're not quite as dumb as you look. Now tell me, what business do you have here?"

"I realize I do not possess the power to kill you myself, Queen… Mother… But have you considered the carnage I could unleash on the people lawfully being enslaved here just by exposing you for the fraud you are?" Racism retorts softly.

"I've considered that. But I know how much you would rather not die yourself. So, I'll resist the urge to send you to hell, as long as you give me the information I want. Agreed?" H responds.

"Fine. What can I answer for you?" Racism snaps.

"Again, why are you here?" H asks insistently.

"Isn't it obvious? I'm a slaver. I own a plantation in the British Colonies. Actually, I own several plantations in the Colonies. But the real money these days is not in selling sugarcane or textiles. It's actually in selling flesh. So, I trade your people for money. I trade slaves all over this part of the world," Racism answers glibly.

"They're your people, too, Sobek. Never forget that you are a descendant of the very Africans you reduce to ordinary household items," H replies indignantly.

"No! You, of all people, should know that my kind is the result of cruel experimentation your former lover performed on misled and trusting people he saw fit to treat as less than human in his attempts to recreate you," Racism argues sharply. "So, you are in no position to lecture me about the evils of the slave trade."

"I stopped the drone program. I could not contemplate that Aharon would continue his experimentation on actual people. But some of the people I love most in this world are Drākanashim," H replies in a lowered tone.

"Yes, your beautiful, extremely sexy daughter, Sarah, is a Drāk," Racism replies with an evil grin on his face. "I'd love to violate her one day."

Racism looks directly into H's eyes as if he is daring her to react. H does not change her expression. She applies more pressure to Racism's genitals. Racism lets out a small gasp.

"Careful, big boy. Don't give away the game yet. You'll have plenty of time to scream from the pain later. That I promise you," H says glibly.

Just then, one of Racism's henchmen begins yelling and cursing loudly. H looks up to see the man riding toward a teenage boy who has fallen and is slow to stand. The other chained men attempt to help the boy back to his feet, but the situation has attracted the attention of the overseers, who begin walking over with their whips in hand.

"Ok, I need you to park this carriage. We will finish this little conversation in private. Also, please bring the boy," H demands.

"Fine," Racism grunts.

"Stop here," Racism commands in a faux accent reminiscent of a gentleman farmer of the American South. "I need to repose myself before discussing business," Racism says, placing a hand on the back of H's head.

Racism's men begin to sneer and laugh. H releases her grip on Racism's crotch so that he can stand. Racism stands and hops down from the carriage. He points to the exhausted teen.

"You there! Come over here and get yourself together. Lord knows I won't get five pence for you in your current condition," Racism declares.

Racism turns back to H. He extends a hand and helps her down from the carriage.

"Lead the way, chère," he says seductively.

H flashes a fake smile. The teenage boy runs toward the carriage and stumbles as he passes H. She catches him and holds him up. She genuflects while holding onto the boy's shoulders and raises her left hand, as if showing Racism to a private spot where she can service him. Racism straightens his clothing and proceeds to walk in the direction of a hut among a thicket of trees. H follows close behind, holding onto the boy. Racism's men close ranks and stand in front of the thicket to keep any onlookers from viewing the happenings behind them.

Once H feels like they are out of the hearing range of Racism's men, she turns the boy around so that he can face her. She looks him up and down. She motions her hand toward his ankle shackles. The boy looks down. H sends a bolt of electromagnetic energy into the back of the shackle on the boy's right ankle, slicing it in half. The boy looks up at H in disbelief. She does the same on the other side.

"What's your name, boy?" H asks in Creole.

"I am Jean-Jacque… Jean Jacques Dessalines," the boy replies.

"It's a pleasure to meet you, Jean-Jacques," H replies. "Go sit over there. I need to speak with this man."

The boy hesitates. He looks up at Racism, who waves him off. The boy turns and runs toward a bench on the opposite side of the hut.

H returns to her normal form. She stares intently at Racism.

"Now, tell me, Sobek. Have you seen my son?" H inquires.

Racism's lips curl into a mischievous grin. He realizes he has a bargaining chip that he can leverage and perhaps use to survive this encounter.

"I know where you can find your son, Hawwah. But that is, obviously, extremely valuable information. What are you prepared to offer me in exchange for something so very important to you?" Racism replies.

H tilts her head down and laughs. She then grabs Racism by his throat and lifts him off his feet.

"How about I let you live? Good enough?" H replies.

H relaxes her grip. Racism falls roughly to the ground. Rubbing his neck, he looks up at H.

"I trapped and sold Adisa myself," he says with a smirk. "Only an Eshanashim would have been able to capture him. Like you, he pretends to be a normal human, but he is fantastically strong. I'm guessing he gets that from you… At any rate, I sold him to a vessel owned by a Jewish slave trader by the name of Aaron Lopez. The irony is almost too delicious. Didn't you help the Israelites escape slavery in Kemet? Then again, you also helped to establish Kemet, so like always, you played on both sides of the fence."

Racism pauses for a moment to chuckle, as if he is very pleased with himself. He dares not look directly at H. He can, however, feel her glaring at him. So, in the interest of self-preservation, Racism continues, "Mr. Lopez lives in Newport, Rhode Island. I cannot be sure where Adisa ended up after I sold him, but I know the ship carrying Adisa as cargo was headed here. So, you're in the right place, at least."

"Not quite," H replies. "Where did you say your plantation lies?"

"I didn't," Racism says cautiously.

The ominous-looking energy building up in H's eyes changes his mind. Racism raises his hands as if he is trying to shield himself from an imminent attack.

"Ok… ok. My main plantation is in Louisiana. My land lies just to the east of the Laurel Grove plantation," Racism exclaims breathlessly.

"Thank you. Now, I know where to find you should I not locate Adisa," H says calmly. "And by the way, Sobek, you're not the result of any genetic experiment. Aharon Mandrake is your father. Honestly, I don't think even he knows that. So, you see, you're the direct descendant of an African man born on the African continent. As you said, the irony is almost too delicious."

Racism stares at H as if he is about to burst into tears. H reaches down and hoists Racism off the ground, standing him on his feet. She then rips Racism's shirt open and bites his cheek so hard that she leaves a mark. She places her right hand on Racism's chest and digs her nails into his flesh. Racism grimaces as H scratches marks into his chest.

"Alright. Go pretend like you had a good time. Tell your men that the boy ran off and that you don't care to find him."

Racism nods and walks back toward his carriage. H shakes her head as she watches Racism leave. After Racism boards his carriage and resumes his business, H walks behind the hut to check on Jean-Jacques. She finds the boy still seated on the bench. H sits next to him. She begins to rub the back of his head. The boy rocks back and forth, trembling.

"I know, young one. None of this makes any sense," H says softly. "I would take you with me, but something tells me you need to remain here. You have a great destiny. I can sense it. In fact, there's someone I would like you to meet."

H takes the boy by the hand. They begin to walk back toward the plantation house. As they walk, H transforms back into Marie-Cessette. She scans the grounds using her telescopic vision until she sees a face she recognizes.

"Bonjou, L'Ouverture!" H calls out across the grounds.

L'Ouverture stops as he hears the familiar voice. He begins to jog toward H and Jean-Jacques.

"Bonjou, bèl fi," L'Ouverture replies with a bow. "Is this your son?"

"No, but he needs someone to look after him," H says. "Can we talk?"

"Natirèlman," L'Ouverture says.

He steps to the side of H and takes her by the arm. Looking around, he guides H to a secluded area on the plantation grounds where they can talk in private.

The scene abruptly switches to H sweeping the floor in a one-room house. She stops when she hears horses galloping up the trail leading to the house. She walks out onto the front step and waits for the riders to approach.

The riders appear to be wearing military uniforms. One of the riders gets off his horse and walks over to H. He removes his hat and hands H an envelope. The envelope is addressed to "Mrs. Huru-Nala Powell." She opens the envelope and reads the document inside.

She immediately collapses onto the ground, sobbing uncontrollably. The man tries to help her up, but H will not budge. She gets down on all fours and digs her fingers into the ground beneath her. Seeing that they cannot offer her any consolation, the two men get back on their horses and ride back up the path.

Once the men leave, H unleashes an energy pulse that decimates the house and many of the surrounding trees. She stands, still crying, and launches herself into outer space. H streaks through the cosmos at a ridiculous speed and does not stop flying until she reaches PC.

****

Once again, a hush falls over the viewing room. Feeling eyes focused on him, Aharon decides to speak first.

> "I think I can add some context to what we just witnessed. As we all saw, H was searching for Prince Adisa," Aharon begins with a tone of satisfaction in his voice, "in about Year 8913, I passed a note on to her that I received from an anonymous source. The note said that her son, Adisa, the son she had to leave behind during our exodus from Planet Earth, was being held in slavery on the Island of Ayiti. It turned out that the note was from Apep or, at least, one of his surrogates. Anyway, Adisa was being

used as bait to draw H away from this solar system and back to Earth. Which means…" Aharon pauses.

"Her powers are greater in our solar system. Apep could not defeat her on Earth, so he will not even take the chance of fighting her here," Insp. Djet Drone offers.

"He's using our kids as bait," Sekhmet declares. "He knows that protecting women and children will always draw H out into the open. But that also means…" she pauses.

Sekhmet's face grows white with fear. An aide reaches over and places his hand on her shoulder.

"He will not hesitate to kill the children once he has Hawwah back on Earth," Envoy Armana offers.

"This situation could be a poison pill. Recall the situation we viewed earlier, the one in which Queen Mother reigned as pharaoh. The men who plotted the coup had already poisoned her daughter. A gospel singer, popular on Earth about a century ago, by the name of Jonathan McReynolds, once said, 'the devil learns from our mistakes, even if we don't,'" Insp. Djet Drone adds.

"Speaking of mistakes," Monolith Ant interjects, "are we to simply ignore the suggestion that President Aharon Mandrake is the biological father of Sobek Anubis, known in two separate galaxies as the physical manifestation of 'racism'?"

"I was not going to say anything, but since you brought it up…" Sekhmet chimes in, staring down at the floor.

"I just… I just… I honestly just learned that myself," Aharon stammers. "H kept that nugget of information to herself for… wow… 344 years. No, wait, longer than that, because we have no idea how long she's known that," Aharon explains.

"Aharon, Aharon, I just cannot say enough about how much you surprise me. Your exploits as a swordsman are nothing less than legendary. But your penchant for fathering problematic sons is equally legendary. First Captain LionMane and now Racism himself. I cannot imagine what it's like to be you," Monolith Ant says condescendingly.

CHAPTER 23

THAT'S THE KID

The planetary leaders continue to ridicule Aharon as the next segment comes into focus. A tall, muscular Black man stands at a whiteboard. His bald head shines underneath the overhead LED light fixtures. He moves back and forth, highlighting strategic points on the diagram of their objective. Sitting in a half circle, listening intently, are seven young Sphinxmen, the title given to candidates who have elevated to the third and final stage of the journey toward full membership in The Mystic Order. The man speaking is Minister Charles G.K. Dessalines, better known as Mose Chaos, the renowned Minister of Defense of The Mystic Order.

In 2034, Year 9234 by the Ant-Galaxo Devearous calendar, a powerful AI froze the global monetary system on Planet Earth and seized control of the nuclear arsenals of several of the Earth's most powerful nations. The AI eventually launched nuclear strikes against China, Russia, the United Kingdom, and the United States. Not only did these four nations suffer heavy losses, but the entire existing world order unraveled because of the resulting carnage that ensued. Governments across the globe collapsed. With a third of the U.S. population killed in the attack and many of its major cities decimated, several states officially adopted secession measures, and the United States devolved into a second civil war.

The surviving members of the Divine Nine, the collective of the Black Greek-letter organizations, established The Mystic Order to identify, locate, and rescue African Americans being forced into involuntary servitude by parties attempting to revive American chattel slavery, as well as the segregationist policies of the Jim Crow Era that followed in the aftermath of the first American Civil War. The Mystic Order, also referred to as the Order, is led by a president and a Council of Elders. Administrators called "ministers" manage broad operational divisions of the organization. The Order generates revenue by performing the governmental functions of the states that comprise the territory known as "the Realm."

Minister Chaos commands the respect of most of his peers and many of the Elders. Under his leadership, the Order has expanded the borders of the Realm, the independent district encompassing the former U.S. states of Delaware, Maryland, New York, Pennsylvania, Virginia, and West Virginia, plus the District of Columbia. The United States has been reduced to Alabama, Florida, Georgia, Illinois, Indiana, Iowa, Kentucky, Louisiana, Michigan, Minnesota, Mississippi, Missouri, North Carolina, Ohio, South Carolina, Tennessee, and Wisconsin. The rest of the states fell under the control of large corporations or unaffiliated militias.

Minister Chaos's success has, unfortunately, bred jealousy among a group of officers and other administrators within the Order, including Minister Derrick W. B. Schuyler, JD. Minister Schuyler, who serves as the general counsel of the Order and Attorney General of the Realm, sees Minister Chaos' growing influence as a hindrance to his own ambitions to succeed Elder Darryl J. Almond as president of the Order. Minister Chaos generally remains focused on the mission rather than involving himself in organizational politics. Minister Schuyler, meanwhile, has been able to block the promotions of this particular group of Sphinxmen seated before Minister Chaos today.

Because Minister Chaos sees these seven Sphinxmen as the future of the Order, he is willing to undertake a big risk to erode the barriers Minister Schuyler has erected to impede their progress. Minister Chaos has assembled these young men today to discuss his audacious plan for them to permanently seize control of the Citadel Heru in Milot, Haiti. The Citadel Heru, commonly referred to as the Citadel, lies in a mountainous region in the northern portion of Haiti. The fort itself has an elevation of more than three thousand feet.

"Gad, you and Batmyte will approach from the southeast. Crypto, your team will include RahStar, Step, Bird, and Mantis. Crypto and his team will approach from the northwest. There is an exhaust port at the base of the armory. That's our entrance.

"Once inside, Crypto and his team will make their way to the server room. The server room controls the power and communications arrays for the entire facility. At the point we secure control of the server room, RahStar and the twins will head to the south wall. Bird and Mantis will set charges at points along the base of the Southwest Tower. Rah, you cover them.

Minister Chaos explains, "Once the charges are set, we sync up. The charges will detonate in exactly three minutes. Crypto, turn out the lights on Broadway when you hear the explosions. Gad, you and Batmyte will enter through the Southeast Tower and proceed to the engineering room in the East Wing. The garrison will be directed to neutralize the threat at the south wall.

"Step will monitor comms and signal Gad and Batmyte when the garrison reaches the Southwest and Southeast Towers. That's when Gad and Batmyte will trigger the blast doors, trapping the responding soldiers there. Crypto will put the entire facility into full lockdown mode. Rah and the twins will make their way back to the server room.

"Gad and Batmyte will release sleeping gas into the ventilation system, then make their way to the command suite in the Northeast Tower. You will take positions in the corridor leading to the server room and wait for the cavalry. Strictly nonlethals on this mission, Gentlemen. We believe most of the young men being held at the Citadel can be converted to Sphinxmen.

"Any questions?"

"What do we do about Hera? If he's there, he'll be posted up in the command suite," Mantis asks.

"Yes, your old partner will likely be on post. You're not to engage," Minister Chaos instructs, looking directly at Mantis. "Do you understand?"

Mantis vacillates. His jaw tightens. He knows this is not an argument he will win. So, he relents and replies, "Copy."

"What about reinforcements? Shouldn't we expect the Company to send reinforcements once the security feeds go dark?" Gad asks.

"That's a great question," Minister Chaos replies. "That's why Crypto isn't taking the security feed offline. He'll be creating a loop that makes it look like the facility is operating normally."

"What's our evac plan if stuff goes sideways?" RahStar inquires.

"If we meet any resistance for which we didn't account, Gad should call 'no joy.' At which point, Rah, you, and the twins will commandeer a transport and get the entire team out of there," Minister Chaos instructs.

"Any other questions?"

"How many men will we be facing?" Dr. Step asks.

"Our intel says three hundred, but we believe that most of the garrison is comprised of recruits, young men no older than yourselves. Remember, this installation is primarily used as a training facility and weapons depot more than anything else. Mantis was held and trained there before we found him," Minister Chaos answers matter-of-factly.

The Sphinxmen remain silent. Minister Chaos smiles.

"Alright, Gentlemen. If we succeed, the Citadel Heru will become our new base of operations, and you, my sons, will earn the right to face the Neophyte trials. Let's do it!" Minister Chaos declares. "One head!"

The Sphinxmen promptly stand out of their seats. They align in a single-file line from the shortest to the tallest. Batmyte stands at the head of the line, followed by Gad, then RahStar, then Dr. Step, then Bird, then Mantis, and then Crypto, each with their heads tilted upward toward the ceiling.

"Collect your gear. You're wheels up in twenty. Fall out," Minister Chaos orders.

The Sphinxmen file out of the briefing room. They relax only slightly as they walk down the long corridor toward the hangar.

"I'm so glad he thinks the seven of us are enough to handle a garrison of three hundred," Bird says jokingly.

"He knows we can. 'We' have me," Mantis retorts, increasing his pace to walk past Bird and Dr. Step.

"Was it something I said?" Bird asks flippantly. "And we're supposed to be twins. Aren't we supposed to be, like … inseparable … like have each other's backs and stuff like that? I mean, he looks like me. He just doesn't have any of my manners, I guess."

"Cut him some slack. This must be pretty hard for him. We're sending him back to the place where he was tortured and taught to do horrible things to people. He wakes up screaming in the middle of the night sometimes. I cannot imagine what he's seen," Dr. Step responds.

"What's the deal between him and, I guess, Hera?" Crypto asks.

"Hera Q. Lees was Mantis's partner at the Citadel. Hera, codename: Hercules, is also the reason Mantis is with us now. Hera left Mantis behind enemy lines after a mission that went sideways. That's when Dad found him," Dr. Step explains.

"Mantis was doing the teams at thirteen?" Crypto asks in a shocked tone.

"Yeah, he and Hera and a few others were subjected to a battery of steroid injections and psychological conditioning. They trained nonstop in combat, tactics, and weapons. The Company was trying to raise them to be some type of psychotic super mercs," Dr. Step replies.

"He still doesn't have to take everything so personally," Bird grumbles.

The Sphinxmen finally reach the hangar. A section leader shows each of them to their specific gear. They collect their materials and board the transport. The pilot flies them from the Order's New York headquarters to Puerto Rico. The Sphinxmen board a ship that carries them across the Caribbean Sea from Rincón to Punta Cana in the Dominican Republic. From there, they board a helicopter that flies them across the island and into Haiti. The helicopter sets down in Barriere Batant, and the Sphinxmen hike the rest of the way to the Citadel. Once the Sphinxmen take their positions on opposite sides of the Citadel, Gad gives the signal to commence the operation.

Crypto, Dr. Step, RahStar, and the twins use a torch to cut the chain securing the gate to the ventilation shaft and enter the Citadel. Gad and Batmyte position themselves in a thicket of trees just below the southeast wall and wait. Once inside, Crypto, Dr. Step, RahStar, and the twins make their way to the server room. The server room is guarded by two sentries. Crypto uses hand signals to direct the twins to subdue the guards. Bird and Mantis wait for an opening, then attack, each wrestling their target to the ground and rendering them unconscious with the famous Sphinxmen's grip, a nonlethal chokehold that renders most subjects unconscious in a matter of seconds. The twins slide the unconscious sentries out of view. Crypto hacks into the electronic locking mechanism and enters the server room.

Encountering no resistance inside the server room, Crypto types a code into his wristband that sends a signal to Gad that phase one of the mission is complete. The twins and RahStar make their way to the Southwest Tower. Dr. Step begins to take control of the Citadel's communication systems. RahStar and the twins make it to the south wall without encountering any resistance and begin setting the explosives. Bird types a code into his wristband that signals to Gad that phase two is complete. Gad returns the "go" signal to the team. The Sphinxmen sync their timers to three minutes. Gad and Batmyte scale the southeast wall to take positions on the landing outside the east wall of the Citadel. RahStar and the twins begin to make their way back to the server room.

The explosives detonate. Crypto cuts the power. Dr. Step disconnects the Citadel's communications. Alarms blare. Dozens of armed soldiers begin to fill the corridors of the East and West Wings of the Citadel. Gad and Batmyte reach the engineering room. Batmyte triggers the blast doors, sealing the soldiers in the corridors of the West and East Wings of the Citadel. Gad takes the sleeping gas canisters from his backpack and walks to the primary ventilation duct. Just as he gets close to the duct, a soldier steps from behind a boiler and puts a weapon to the back of Gad's head. Gad hears the click of the hammer being pulled back and puts his hands into the air.

Seeing Gad being held at gunpoint, Batmyte types a quick code into his wristband. Two additional soldiers enter the engineering room and point their rifles at Batmyte. The Sphinxmen in the server room receive the message that their brothers have encountered hostiles. Crypto restores power to the interior security cameras. He tracks the soldiers leading Gad and Batmyte to the Northeast Tower, navigating around the corridors sealed by the blast doors. Mantis immediately recognizes the team leader.

"Hera!" Mantis exclaims, shaking his head.

"Dad said not to engage," Crypto declares.

"Well, we can't just leave them," Bird retorts.

"Our orders were to commandeer a transport and return to base should we encounter opposition we didn't expect," RahStar interjects.

"Yes, but that was if Gad called 'no joy,'" Bird argues.

The Sphinxmen look down at their wristbands. Seeing no additional codes, they look back at each other. Mantis unstraps his backpack and removes the mic and headset. Connecting his audio communications, Mantis begins to walk to the door.

"Wait!" Bird calls out. "I'm coming with you."

Mantis nods. Bird removes his pack and connects his audio communications. The twins rush out into the corridor. Dr. Step and Crypto look at each other. Crypto restores power to the Northeast Tower. Dr. Step retakes his seat at the comms station.

"The hallways are clear all the way to the command center," Dr. Step calls out.

"Copy!" Bird responds.

The twins begin to sprint toward the Northeast Tower. Mantis leads the way. They arrive just as Hera and his team reach the command center. Hera directs Gad and Batmyte to put their backs up against a wall just outside the entrance to the command center. He types in an access code and directs the Sphinxmen to enter the command center.

Mantis springs into action. Running across the corridor, he grabs the rifle of a very surprised soldier and uses it to deliver a sharp uppercut to the soldier's chin. The other soldier reacts by turning his weapon on Mantis. Mantis spins while continuing to hold onto the other soldier's rifle. Once the soldier's body is between him and the rifle that was pointed at him, Mantis delivers a front kick that throws the first soldier into his partner. Both soldiers fall violently to the ground and drop their weapons.

Bird runs in and grabs the barrel of one of the rifles. Two quick swings by Bird render both soldiers unconscious. To their surprise, the door to the command center opens. Mantis and Bird enter the command center cautiously. Hera fires a single shot that strikes Bird in his left leg. Bird falls against a wall and tosses the rifle to Mantis.

"Up here, Menes!" Hera shouts. "I knew it was you. Somehow, I just knew."

Mantis does not respond; he simply aims the rifle at Hera.

"I'll tell you what. You throw down your weapon, and I'll only kill you. I'll let your friends leave. That's a fair trade, yeah?" Hera offers.

Again, Mantis does not answer. He continues to track Hera's movements with the rifle in his hands.

"Nothing to say. You're still mad at me, huh?" Hera says with a grin on his face. "Tell you what, put your gun down right now, or I will blow this cocksucker's head clean off!" Hera shouts, with spit flying from his mouth.

Gad and Batmyte kneel before Hera with their hands clasped behind their heads. Hera motions to Batmyte to stand. Batmyte stands slowly. Hera wraps an arm around Batmyte's neck and shoves his firearm into the side of Batmyte's head. Hera begins walking Batmyte toward the stairway leading from the upper deck of the command center to the main floor. A small room with thin walls encloses the stairway.

Mantis throws the rifle back to Bird and sprints toward the bottom of the stairwell. Bird catches the rifle and aims it in the direction Mantis is running.

As soon as Hera walks through the door with Batmyte, Mantis launches himself at Hera.

Surprised, Hera tries to release Batmyte so that he can take a shot at Mantis. Hera's reaction comes much too late. Mantis tackles Hera, and the two crash through the door.

Mantis scrambles back to his feet, wraps his arms around Hera's waist, and wastes no time going on the attack, driving Hera through a wall adjacent to the stairway. Both remain on their feet but wobble slightly after crashing through the wall.

Hera swings wildly, narrowly missing the side of Mantis's head. Hera's fist collides aggressively with a solid wall outside the small room encasing the stairwell. Hera pulls his hand back in pain.

Mantis takes a step and delivers a vicious spinning kick to Hera's upper torso that sends Hera flying several feet across the room. Mantis tilts his head and watches Hera land hard and tumble across the floor.

"You never could beat me," Mantis declares.

Hera staggers to his feet. He walks over to a console and opens one of the large windows lining the east wall of the command suite. The command center sits on the top floor of the Northeast Tower. The drop from the window would be more than 150 feet into a thicket of trees.

"One of us is going out that window, Menes," Hera says, motioning his head toward the open window.

"I don't know about you, but I've always liked the view from up here," Mantis retorts jokingly.

"Well, we'll see if you still like it on the way down," Hera replies.

Hera runs toward Mantis, who reacts in kind. The two foes meet in the middle of the room. Hera throws a bevy of kickboxing combinations at Mantis. Crisp jabs, hooks, and front kicks either narrowly miss Mantis's face or get blocked. Mantis responds with a sharp kick to Hera's left leg. Hera bends down slightly, and Mantis smashes him with an overhand right.

Hera shoots himself into Mantis's legs and tackles Mantis to the ground. They grapple for several seconds until Mantis manages to create an opening and delivers a sharp kick to Hera's upper body. Once again, Hera is thrown across the room.

As Hera slides to a stop, he sees Batmyte standing close to the window. Hera scrambles to his feet. Mantis handsprings himself back to his feet. Seeing Hera make a move toward Batmyte, Mantis begins sprinting toward the window. Hera rushes Batmyte and slams him against the wall.

Gad reacts by jumping over the railing and dropping onto the main floor of the command center from the upper deck. Hera snatches Batmyte, lifting the Sphinxman over his head. Seeing Mantis approach, Hera grins evilly and turns toward the window. Mantis dives toward the window just as Hera tosses Batmyte through the aperture.

Mantis twists into a barrel roll so that he can pass through the window horizontally. Extending his left hand, he catches Batmyte's outstretched hands and immediately clamps his right hand onto the window seal. The two Sphinxmen swing forcefully into the side of the Northeast Tower. Hera stands in front of the window, clapping and laughing.

"Oh, I know you too well!" Hera exclaims gleefully. "You never miss a chance to be the hero. That's how you got left behind. I just wish the enemy had finished the job."

Hearing Gad running up behind him, Hera turns and staggers Gad with a right cross. He then lifts Gad onto his shoulders and slams Gad hard to the ground. Hera then delivers a hard kick to Gad's midsection, sending Gad sliding across the floor in pain. Hera turns back to the window.

"I told you that I would piss on your grave, Menes," Hera says, stepping up onto the window seal.

Hera stomps a foot onto Mantis's hand. Mantis grimaces in pain as blood begins to trickle down his palm and drip down his wrist. Hera unzips his pants, pulls out his penis, and begins to urinate on Mantis's head and neck.

"He's peeing on you! Oh, that's groooossssss!" Batmyte exclaims.

"Yes, yes, he's peeing on me," Mantis shouts back. "You don't think I can feel that?!?"

Laughing, Hera finishes urinating and begins to shake his penis. He looks down at Mantis and Batmyte.

"Now that I've had the pleasure of pissin' on your head, I'm going to send you to hell so that I can piss…" Hera says before stopping abruptly.

Mantis looks up just in time to see Hera's eyes roll up into the top of his head. Hera leans forward and falls out of the window. His body plummets the ten stories of the Northeast Tower and disappears into the trees below. Mantis's eyes follow Hera all the way to the ground. He then looks back up to the window. Bird is standing at the window, holding a fire extinguisher.

"Dad said nonlethals only," Bird says dryly.

"You still killed him," Mantis replies glibly.

"Can we come back inside now?" Batmyte calls out.

Gad struggles to his feet. He stumbles over to the window and helps Bird pull Mantis and Batmyte back inside.

"Bird," Dr. Step calls over the comms. "We've got a lot of company over here. About thirty contacts are standing in the hallway. We apparently never got to the sleeping gas phase of this mission, so it looks like we will have to fight our way out of here."

"I'm on a bad leg. Gad is hurt. Mantis is down to one hand. We may be in trouble. Over," Bird responds.

"Thirty is light work," Mantis asserts.

Bird and Gad look at each other and shrug. Batmyte smiles.

"Never mind what I just said. Incoming," Bird exhales.

Bird removes his tactical gloves. Mantis had left his outside as they were setting the charges.

"Bandage that wound on your hand up and put these on," Bird says to Mantis, handing his twin the gloves.

Mantis looks at Bird with a grin on his face as he ties a piece of cloth torn from his undershirt around his injured hand. A broad smile breaks across Bird's face.

"What?" Bird asks quizzically.

"Nothing. I just knew you liked me deep down in there somewhere," Mantis replies.

"The jury's still out," Bird responds jokingly.

Mantis pulls the gloves onto his hands. He and Batmyte look at each other and nod. As they sprint back toward the server room, Bird hands the rifle to Gad. Gad helps Bird limp out of the command suite and into the North Wing corridor.

"Are we really sure we want to do this?" Gad asks Bird jokingly.

"It's been a blast so far," Bird counters.

Batmyte and Mantis arrive at the server room to see two soldiers attempting to hack the electronic lock. Batmyte uses hand signals to direct Mantis to the soldiers for which he will be responsible. Mantis nods and attacks. He runs directly at the group of soldiers. He stops abruptly and goes into a slide across the floor as if he is stealing second base in a baseball game, easily beating the throw from the catcher.

Mantis slides into the soldier working the locking mechanism. The force of his slide smashes the soldier against the door. Mantis delivers a hard headbutt with the back of his head, bashing the soldier's face into the door. The unsuspecting soldier drops unconscious. Mantis stands quickly and dodges a rifle butt as it crashes through the glass on the server room door. Mantis rams a body shot into the attacker's midsection and then delivers a sharp knee to his face.

Another soldier points his rifle at Mantis. Mantis grabs the barrel and spins, delivering an elbow shot with his opposite arm into the back of the soldier's head. As the soldier falls, Mantis takes the rifle and aims it at the rest of the group. The other soldiers stand, aiming their weapons at Mantis, seemingly paralyzed by indecision. Many of them turn momentarily as two more of their number fall to the ground unconscious. Batmyte whistles as he aims a rifle at the group's flank.

"Throw down your weapons. No one else needs to get hurt," Mantis orders.

The soldiers hesitate. Then, one by one, they drop their weapons to the floor. Batmyte walks closer to Mantis, his weapon remaining trained on the group of surrendering soldiers. Dr. Step peeks through the shattered door glass.

"Drop to your knees and put your hands behind your heads," Dr. Step snaps.

"What he said," Batmyte shouts.

"Nice work, guys!" Gad shouts from further down the corridor.

Dr. Step returns to the comms station and removes the encrypted satellite phone from his pack. He places a call back to New York. He waits until he hears the voice of Minister Chaos.

"We're 'Code Seven' here, Dad!" Dr. Step declares.

"Excellent!" Minister Chaos replies proudly. "I'm on my way."

****

The viewing room remains silent as the guests at TGHQ watch with absorbed attention. A smile breaks across Aharon's face as he has a revelation.

"That's the kid," Aharon declares. "I mean, that's got to be the Earth kid I've heard so much about recently."

"His skills are certainly impressive, but he absolutely looks Earth-bound to me, My Friend," Monolith Ant retorts.

"How long ago did this occur?" Aharon calls out.

"Two years ago, Mr. President," Arisone replies from the control room.

"They're members of The Mystic Order," Aharon argues.

"So?" Monolith Ant retorts.

"There are members of The Mystic Order who claim to know the location of the Waters of Kaos. And, as you know, those who bathe in the Waters of Kaos are said to arise from its waters," Aharon explains.

"Enhanced," Neith interrupts.

"Enhanced," Aharon repeats. "I'd bet my presidency that if we were to ask Gen. Powell who on Earth is among the enhanced, Minister Chaos and his seven sons would be on that list."

"Perhaps, but what does that mean for this investigation?" Monolith Ant inquires.

"It means a lot," Insp. Djet Drone interjects. "Consider what the queen's subconscious has revealed so far. We have our perpetrators. We have a motive. We have narrowed the scope of the possible location. And now, we have possible allies on Earth to assist in the extraction."

"Ok, but why is this all taking so long to piece together, then?" Sekhmet asks.

"I see why, now, I was put on the guest list. It takes the IGP weeks, sometimes months, to get this far in a criminal investigation. Even the supercomputers we use cannot help us connect all the relevant dots, sifting through the terabytes of data we receive at times, any faster. Now, imagine being connected to a database as large as the entire Known Universe. The queen has been able to connect all the 'relevant dots' over the last day or so. She's taken the universal database and distilled it to relevant data points faster than any AI ever could," Insp. Djet Drone explains.

"Agreed," Aharon adds. "The only thing we need now is a heading."

As the stream and the day roll on, the planetary leaders and their aides break for lunch and then dinner. Seeing worn-down faces in the viewing room, The Sphinx tells Arisone and her techs to stop the stream for the night. Eman arranges for Admiral CavalierStar to have the guests escorted back to their quarters.

CHAPTER 24
NO REPEAT PERFORMANCE

Before exiting the viewing room, Neith sends Aharon a message on his handheld, inviting him to come visit her tonight. Aharon responds with a sexually explicit note accepting her invitation. But when he returns to his quarters to freshen up, an unexpected guest has been awaiting his arrival.

"Hotep, Husband!" a woman with H's voice calls from the bedroom.

Aharon freezes in his tracks as if someone has drawn a weapon on him. He only knows two women whose voices match that pattern.

"Did you miss me?" Cindy asks, emerging from the bedroom dressed in a see-through nightgown and wearing open-toe high-heel slippers.

Cindy Drone Mandrake was genetically engineered to be as close to a physical replica of Hawwah as possible, even beyond what cloning technology could produce. Her voice was even modulated to sound exactly like Hawwah's. Cindy's brain was cybernetically augmented to replicate Hawwah's intellect. But even though Cindy shares H's beauty and brains, her richly colored, royal purple skin serves as a constant reminder that she is not the original.

"How did the viewing go today?" Cindy asks softly. "Princess Sarah told me that you and the other planetary leaders were watching a live stream of H's visions, trying to determine where the missing children may be," Cindy asks, desperately hoping to spark a positive interaction with her husband.

"It went well," Aharon responds. "In fact, we just wrapped. A lot of things came to light today," he continues, drawing a breath, then exhaling in exacerbation.

"Come; let me relax you," Cindy says, stretching out her hand.

Aharon looks at Cindy in a moment of awkward silence that seems like an eternity. He does not take her hand. He continues to hesitate, frozen in his own indecision. He does not want to lie to Cindy, but he does not want to spend the night with her either.

"In a minute, Luvie," he says clumsily. "I should probably take a shower first," he manages.

Aharon walks past Cindy on his way to the bathroom. He stops when he realizes he has neither hugged nor kissed her. He turns toward Cindy and gives her a perfunctory peck on the cheek. Cindy notices that Aharon does not even bother to remove any of his clothing before entering the bathroom, supposedly to take a shower. She drops her head as Aharon disappears from her sight and walks over to the bed. She pulls the covers back and slips off her shoes. She slides herself in between the sheets and begins to cry.

In the bathroom, Aharon frantically sends Neith a message from his handheld device. He does not indicate that Cindy has arrived. Instead, he tells Neith that he will need to take a rain check, as his head is pounding. Neith throws her device against the wall after reading Aharon's message. She had already prepared herself by bathing, brushing her teeth, spraying herself with her sweetest fragrance, and wearing nothing but a loose-fitting spaghetti-strap top and her high heels.

She kicks her heels off and grabs a pair of panties from the bag her aides brought her earlier in the day. She pulls on a pair of sweatpants and covers her feet with athletic-cut ankle socks. After sliding a long-sleeved tee over her top, she spreads her wings, collects her handheld, and asks the TGHQ AI to hail President Sekhmet.

"Dialing now, Leader Ramses," the AI responds.

"Hotep," one of Sekhmet's aides says, answering the call.

"Hotep! This is Leader Neith Ramses of the Giza Authority Directorate. May I speak to President Djet Drone, please?" Neith says assertively.

In less than a minute, Neith hears Sekhmet's voice. Neith exhales.

"Leader Ramses, what can I do for you?" Sekhmet asks.

"Girl, it's Neith tonight. I need a friendly hang. Can I come sit with you for a while?" Neith asks.

Sekhmet pauses momentarily, then responds with a tone of enthusiasm in her voice.

"Absolutely, girl! Come on over. I will send my people out for snacks!" Sekhmet declares.

Neith smiles and ends the call. She then calls out to the TGHQ AI again.

"Please arrange for the PDFJC to escort me to President Sekhmet's quarters," Neith requests.

"Calling Admiral Menewa now, Ma'am," the AI responds.

Neith begins to sob. She drops to her knees momentarily. After a few minutes, she hears the doorbell chime. She walks over to the security panel and opens the door.

"Hotep, Ma'am! I am Brigadier General Ramesses Menelik. I'm here to escort you to President Djet Drone's quarters," Gen. Menelik says softly.

"Thank you, General. Let's go," Neith replies, wiping her eyes.

Neith's aides walk slowly behind Neith and the general as they walk the hallway to Sekhmet's quarters. Neith notices the Memphisonian soldiers posted outside one of the guest rooms. She surmises that could only mean one thing.

"General, before we get to President Djet Drone's room, would you mind if we stopped at President Mandrake's quarters really quickly? I forgot to ask him something earlier today."

Gen. Menelik stops and speaks something inaudibly into his communicator. He awaits an answer before turning his attention back to Neith.

"Sure thing, Ma'am," he replies politely.

He turns and directs Neith back down the hall toward Aharon's room. Once in front of the door, Gen. Menelik presses the doorbell. Neith takes out her handheld and types a quick message to Aharon, telling him that she felt bad and wanted to bring him something to make him feel better. The Memphisonian soldiers glare at Neith menacingly until she puts the handheld behind her back.

Aharon responds to Neith's message, saying that he really just wants to be alone at the moment. He has apparently not heard the doorbell or simply ignored it. Gen. Menelik turns back to Neith, who calls Aharon on her handheld. Aharon answers.

"Hotep," he says.

"It's too late. I'm at the door," Neith responds.

"Who's at the door?" Cindy asks.

Neith grips her device in disgust. She pauses, then collects herself, suppressing her rage.

"It's ok, General. Let's go," Neith says loudly, hoping Cindy hears her voice.

Gen. Menelik tilts his head and follows Neith's direction, walking her back down the hallway. Hearing Neith's voice causes Cindy to become naturally suspicious.

"Who was that, Aharon?" Cindy asks softly but assertively.

Aharon does not answer. Instead, he simply sighs and rolls over onto his side. He reaches his hand up and stretches it out behind his body. Cindy stifles tears and takes Aharon's hand. Aharon pulls Cindy close. As Cindy nestles next to her husband, she whispers gently in his ear.

"Will I ever be enough for you, Dear Husband?" Cindy asks.

Aharon grips Cindy's hand, then switches the hand holding hers so that he can reposition himself on his back. He looks up at Cindy with a look of shameful remorse.

"I truly don't know, Luvie," Aharon replies gently.

Cindy pulls away. Aharon rolls back over onto his side. Cindy slips out of bed and walks into the bathroom. Once in the bathroom, she spills herself onto the floor and sobs. Aharon does not move. He feels terrible but does not do anything to comfort his wife.

In Sekhmet's room, Neith opens up about her former relationship with Aharon. Though it is common knowledge that Aharon and Neith share three daughters, many do not know why their relationship ended. Neith shares that she pleaded with Aharon to marry her and that she would have settled for being Second Wife, allowing Cindy to play the role of First Wife.

Neith recounts Aharon telling her that Cindy would never allow him to have more than one wife, but shortly after Cindy discovered Aharon's relationship with Neith, Cindy convinced him to marry a much younger woman, Aharon's Second Wife, Fausta. Fausta is a Pen, but unlike Cindy, Fausta was born naturally. While Fausta's natural hair color is a dark royal purple, Fausta's skin has a very smooth light brown tone. Fausta is the mother of four of Aharon's children.

Neith also tells Sekhmet that Aharon is the only man she has ever loved and that she has had trouble moving on from him. Even after all this time, she still cannot get herself to "quit" Aharon. Sekhmet hugs Neith and tells Neith she can bunk with her tonight. Neith gladly accepts. The two new friends laugh and talk the night away until they both collapse from exhaustion.

CHAPTER 25
THE PLAN

Back on Earth, as the third day dawns, the mood of the kids in the cave has devolved into restlessness. The smell from "trips to the bathroom" begins to overwhelm the natural ventilation offered by the cavern. Without sunlight or adequate food, the children begin to enter a state of abject panic.

"We cannot stay here," Prince Armacaust tells his leadership group. "We need a lot more food and fresh air. Whoever put us here wanted to cut us off from the sunlight. Without the sun and fresh water, they can begin to starve us," he says in a moment of realization.

"Apep wants to lure Nana into this cave," Prince Imhotep declares.

"Thousands of us could be hurt or killed if an attack comes from both sides," DwarfStar adds.

"They're waiting until they know that Mom is on her way to make their move," Prince Armacaust says, thinking out loud.

The teens agree that they will split the larger group up by age. They devise a plan to lure Apep and his minions to the back of the cave and distract them while the others flee to safety. All children between the ages of one and five, numbering roughly ten thousand, are assigned to Addis HD, her brother Imhotep, Addis HK, Merneith Grey and her brothers, plus Addis H and her siblings.

All children between the ages of six and thirteen, numbering approximately thirteen thousand, are assigned to Asenat, her siblings, and Seraphina. Asenat tees up winged siblings Raja and Horo Dawit to assist by serving as scouts in the air. All children over the age of thirteen are assigned to the Jupiter twins, their brother Aha, and Princess Zilpha. Prince Armacaust, DwarfStar, and Prince Imhotep will act as "the bait" for the bad guys.

The plan is relatively simple. While her uncle, her brother, and DwarfStar create a diversion, Princess Zilpha will use her ability to bridge two points in the known universe and create a wormhole from the cave to a safe place. The teens determine that they should have at least four locations selected just in case Apep and his minions can somehow follow them through the wormhole. If need be, the group will split into its divisions, sorted by age, and escape in four different directions in the hopes that some of them can avoid recapture.

One caveat exists with the plan. Unlike other Eshanashim who can bend space and time to create wormholes, Princess Zilpha must establish a connection with the endpoint in her mind's eye before she can create the bridge. In other words, she must have seen the place on the other side of the bridge.

With that being the case, Prince Armacaust proposes that he, DwarfStar, and Asenat accompany Zilpha on a trip around the Earth as a scout team to select the four locations. The teens agree. Prince Imhotep, Shaka, Merneith, Sojourner, Django, Bekele, Gbeto, Abrax, Solomon, and Fusion are tasked with providing security for the group. The three Addises and the Jupiter twins will lead the group while the scout team does its job.

Asenat takes a moment to hug each of her siblings as she prepares to take off with the scout team. DwarfStar, in like fashion, gathers his younger cousins together. He exchanges hugs with nine-year-old Abebe, whom he had only discovered was among the massive group of kidnapped children the night before, plus Ahmose and Fusion. DwarfStar then gives an enthusiastic fist bump to Den II.

"Let's go, Team," Prince Armacaust orders.

"Let's do this!" DwarfStar echoes.

The scout team lines up next to each other as if they are about to run a race. They share approving looks with one another as they prepare to launch.

"We will follow the same rules here that we follow at home. No flying at light speed inside a planet's atmosphere, and we will also maintain a high altitude until we are close to the target. We will get above the clouds. I can maintain visuals on the ground from that height. That said, we need to go fast but not too fast. We do not want to attract any unwanted attention," Prince Armacaust declares.

"How about we just follow your lead, Bro?" DwarfStar offers.

The other members of the scout team nod in agreement. Prince Armacaust propels himself into the air and zips toward the entrance of the cave. One by one, DwarfStar, Asenat, and Princess Zilpha streak through the cave, following close behind Prince Armacaust. To their surprise, there are no guards posted at the entrance of the cave, the place where they previously encountered Apep.

Once outside the cave, Prince Armacaust pauses for a moment to allow the others to reach his side. He points upward, waits for the others to acknowledge his signal, then rockets into the upper atmosphere at supersonic speed. As the scout team breaches the clouds, Prince Armacaust turns east and continues to travel at supersonic speed. He slows just enough to allow the others to catch up to him.

They fly over the Arabian Peninsula until a possible location catches Prince Armacaust's eye. He begins to descend through the clouds and hovers above a sports complex in Dubai. The teens follow Prince Armacaust down onto the field through the open roof. Princess Zilpha takes a quick look around and gives the rest of the group a hearty thumbs up. Prince Armacaust nods in acknowledgement, then launches back into the sky.

The scout team resumes its journey at supersonic speed.

After traveling thousands of miles north, the scout team reaches another large body of water. Prince Armacaust pivots over the water and swings wide to the southwest and spots what he thinks can be the next location, a high-rise hotel in Oslo. The scout team lands and enters the hotel through the lobby. Again, Princess Zilpha takes inventory of the sights, committing the space to memory. Once she feels comfortable, she signals that she is ready to move on to the next location.

* * * * * * *

From the Citadel Heru, a young Sphinxman alerts his section chief of some strange activity in the skies over the Middle East and Northern Europe. The Sphinxmen serve as the paramilitary arm of The Mystic Order. The Order holds a single mantra as its guiding principle and mission: The Order exists to set the captives free. The members of the Order advance this mission by bringing freedom to the enslaved, as well as providing capacity-building and security services to free-thinking people across the globe, regardless of race, region, or religion.

Initiates into the Order matriculate from trainees, commonly referred to as 'apes', to Greeks to Sphinxmen to Neophytes to Prophytes by passing mental and physical qualifying trials. Prophytes can be promoted to Deacons and eventually appointed to be Ministers. Though neither the founders nor the current leaders of the Order possess any empirical evidence that Hawwah exists, they nonetheless dedicate themselves to serving H as their queen. Historians within the Order believe they have tracked her various identities throughout history and can prove her existence. One of the most prominent ministers in the Order, the venerable Minister of Global Defense, Mose Chaos, claims to have found the Garden of Eden and points to its discovery as the most credible evidence of Hawwah's existence.

"I picked up four contacts traveling in excess of supersonic speed," the young Sphinxman reports.

He walks over to the section chief and hands her a printout. The section chief analyzes the data on the sheet and turns to her primary aide with an astonished look on her face.

"Wake Minister Chaos," she orders.

By the time Mose Chaos arrives in the control room in the Northeast Tower, the Sphinxman reports that he is tracking the same four contacts over North America. Minister Chaos reviews the data and notices a pattern. He summons Gad Sextantis and orders him to gather the group of enhanced Order operatives known as the Seven Sons of Chaos.

The Seven Sons of Chaos, also referred to as the Seven Sons or simply as the Sons, are not simply a contingent of superhuman military operators; they are the adopted sons of Minister Chaos. The Seven Sons completed their trial like all other Neophytes of the Order by literally crossing the Sahara Desert. However, they received their paranatural abilities by bathing in the Waters of Kaos, a pool that is believed to be the remnants of the primordial waters from which the world was formed.

Becoming enhanced allowed the Sons to cruise not only through their way to becoming Prophytes, as well as the deacon promotion trial, but also through the North American education system. The Seven Sons include Deacon Oyauma LaShawn Dessalines, DBA, codename: Gad Sextantis, better known as "Gad"; Deacon Adrian Miguel Dessalines, DVM, codename: Batmyte; Deacon Gregory Cox, codename: RahStar, also known as "Rah"; Jerrell Dwayne Dessalines, PhD, codename: Dr. FrankenStep, also known as "Dr. Step" or "Step"; Deacon Aharon Fatin Dessalines, JD, PE, codename: BlackBird, also known as "Bird"; Deacon Menes Asadullah Dessalines, MD, codename: Praying Mantis, also known as "Mantis"; and Dennis Kevin Dessalines, D.Eng, PE, codename: Crypto.

Once assembled, the Sons receive a briefing on the situation. Minister Chaos orders them to investigate.

"As far as we can determine, these contacts birthed from Emba Soira in Eritrea. If I'm right, this could be our first contact with the Eshanashim," Minister Chaos explains.

"Whoa! Actual people from Planet Chaos?" Gad asks.

"That's my thought," Minister Chaos responds. "Well, get going. I'm eager to learn what you find. And, as always, take care of each other."

* * * * * * *

The scout team, led by Prince Armacaust, stops at a football stadium in Indianapolis. Again, the team is able to descend onto the field through the open roof. Crossing the Atlantic at supersonic speed has proved problematic in only one instance, as night has fallen over much of North America. Princess Zilpha quickly takes mental images of the space and gives the signal. The team takes off back into the sky.

Prince Armacaust streaks back toward the southeast. They make their final stop at a resort in Montego Bay. Once the princess is satisfied with the location, the team launches skyward and rockets back across the Atlantic Ocean at speeds approaching Mach 7. By the time they reach the African continent, the trip has lasted roughly 4.5 hours.

Unfortunately, the Order is not the only group to track Prince Armacaust and the scout team. From their camp, Circe Defiance reports to her father, The Leader, that one of their LiDAR technicians has detected four contacts traveling beyond hypersonic speeds over the Atlantic and now bearing a heading straight for their location.

Apep orders the Grand Reverend to send the Wiles of the Devil back to the cave. Rings, Seth Zomibi, and Sphinx Genet decide to take a small incursion force to the entrance of the cave and capture any Eshanashim children they find. Apep tells Rings that she may keep any girls she deems valuable and bids her to kill the rest.

Circe taps Set Aha, Abanoub Boateng, and Ptah Mercury to accompany her as she tags along with Rings. Rings requests

Mina Seshperonch and her crew from the SS Dread Crescent to accompany her and provide additional security support to their small force.

CHAPTER 26
FIRST CONTACT

By the time the fourth hour rolls around, the children become very restless. Concern for the safety of their comrades begins to devolve into hopelessness. Brooklyn attempts to ease fears by assuring the worried kids that this recon mission will take approximately five and a quarter hours to complete if the recon team travels at an average speed of Mach 5, but will take considerably less time if they travel at Mach 6 or Mach 7.

Prince Imhotep lends a hand by leading a game in which the children are challenged to attempt to calculate the time it will take Prince Armacaust and crew to circle the globe traveling at hypersonic speed. They make a fun competition out of it. And just as the Eshanashim children begin to feel calm and settled, the fun is suddenly interrupted by the sound of a warp gate opening.

It starts as a low hum, then builds as the gateway grows. Sparks fly. Lights jump and dance as the gateway manifests in the same spot that the scout team launched into action several hours ago. At first, the children gather in excited anticipation, thinking that perhaps Princess Zilpha opened a portal to bring the scout team back to the cave. Instead of their comrades, the Eshanashim children step back in fear at the sight of the seven hooded figures stepping through the portal.

The seven hooded figures walk through the portal and stand shoulder to shoulder in a line, portions of their long black capes dragging the floor. Their relative stature is staggering. Their silence is unsettling. As one of them steps forward, he throws open his cape. The others follow suit. They raise their arms to part their capes, revealing black body armor similar to the uniforms worn by the soldiers on their home planets. Their battle suits are black with gold accents. And a large ankh, the Kemetic symbol for life, is emblazoned on each of their chests.

The figure walking toward the massive group of children removes his hood. The teens calm somewhat when they notice that he is a young man who looks to be no older than Prince Armacaust. The young man continues to walk slowly but deliberately over to the group of teens, looking at him in silent bewilderment. He speaks evenly but confidently as he introduces himself.

“Hotep! My name is Gad Sextantis. And we’re the Seven Sons of Chaos.”

Once they hear Gad introduce them, the six others with him remove their hoods. The Eshanashim children continue to settle, as the Seven Sons of Chaos appear a lot less menacing without their hoods.

"We were investigating the area and saw a massive group of people in this cave. Are you alright? Judging by the massive military encampment about twelve klicks from here, I'd say you need assistance," Gad adds.

The Seven Sons of Chaos also appear to the Eshanashim children as young men who do not seem much older than the teens who have been leading the group. Minister Chaos appointed twenty-year-old Gad to lead the Seven Sons because of his poise under pressure, together with his nearly unparalleled ability to communicate. Batmyte, the 194-year-old survivor of the 1921 Tulsa race riot commonly referred to as the Black Wall Street Massacre, blessed with immortality long before he bathed in the Waters of Kaos, and twenty-one-year-old Crypto are older than Gad. Minister Chaos's uncompromising faith in Gad's leadership encourages the Seven Sons to follow their brother through the various dangerous situations they encounter. And no one on Earth holds the collective loyalty and trust of the Seven Sons more than their father.

Each of the Sons carries an ancient weapon Minister Chaos claims was passed to him by Master Imhotep.

Gad wears golden boots that allow him to fly, levitate, and walk on air. Batmyte wears a belt that supplies acupuncture needles that heal injuries, temporarily immobilize opponents, and compel any person touched by one to tell the truth. RahStar formerly wore an impenetrable golden breastplate that endows the wearer with invulnerability.

Dr. FrankenStep, commonly referred to by family and friends as "Dr. Step" or "Step," wears an indestructible helmet that endows the wearer with the power of "allsight." One possessed with the power of allsight can see in infrared vision, microscopic vision, scotopic vision, otherwise known as *night vision,* telescopic vision, and x-ray vision. Allsight also allows anyone who possesses this ability to see through illusions.

BlackBird, also called "Bird" by family and friends, wields an impenetrable shield that can grow, allow its bearer to levitate, glide on the wind, and produce force fields. The Praying Mantis, commonly referred to by friends and family as "Mantis" and by his enemies as "The Sun-Toucher," wields an unbreakable sword that can slice through virtually any substance and bursts into flames the longer it is exposed to oxygen. The blade also inhibits the ability of enhanced beings to heal rapidly.

And Crypto now wears the same breastplate relinquished by RahStar. Each of the Sons can summon his weapon telepathically, making it hard for their enemies to dispossess them of their fantastic weaponry.

For his part, Gad is as charming as he is handsome. His charm and calm demeanor coax the teens leading the group of kidnapped Eshanashim children into a cautious peace. Prince Imhotep, Addis HD, Addis HK, the Jupiter twins, and Seraphina step forward and cautiously offer their own introduction by speaking in Amharic. They do this as a means to test whether these young men can decipher their native tongue, just in case they need to share communications that these young men cannot understand.

"Oh, I should have led with that. I'm sorry. I'm so used to speaking English, I forget that not everyone speaks it," Gad replies with a smile.

He repeats his previous introduction in Amharic. He pauses for a moment to gauge the reaction from the Eshanashim teens.

"Some of us, probably a lot of us, speak English," Addis HD replies. "We tend to watch a lot of content created on Earth."

"Oh, my apologies. You must think we're all a little weird," Gad replies with a smirk.

Brooklyn steps forward with an intense curiosity on her face. She squints as she peers directly into Gad's eyes.

"How is it that you can understand us?" she asks intently.

"Well, my brothers and I can communicate in every language known to humankind," he says, twisting to his backside with an open palm pointed toward the rest of the Sons. "If we couldn't understand you, it would mean that you weren't people," Gad says with a chuckle.

"It isn't obvious to you that we're not from your planet?" Brooklyn asks firmly.

"That thought had crossed my mind. But we actually came here expecting to run into Eshanashim visitors," Gad explains. "Besides, the very lovely young lady over there with the orange skin and stripes on her legs and arms is kinda giving 'I'm not from around here,'" he says, looking in Seraphina's direction.

Addis HK immediately leans in toward Seraphina's face and whispers, "He said you're cute, queen."

Seraphina playfully bumps Addis HK away with her elbow. She then tries to hide the smile creeping slowly onto her face.

"Now that we are all acquainted, how may we be of service?" Gad asks with a smile.

Gad stops talking briefly when he notices Praying Mantis lift his head. Gad casts his gaze in the same direction Mantis is staring. Mantis floats off the ground, his fists clenched as if he is about to respond to an imminent threat.

"Uh, oh!" Gad blurts out as he sees Mantis move quickly toward him.

Just as he reaches Gad, Mantis is tackled by Prince Armacaust, who flies into him at an incredible speed. Prince Armacaust pivots as if he is traveling along a rail and flies Mantis straight up into the rafters of the cave's ceiling. Mantis releases a massive bolt of energy from his eyes, pummeling the young prince and dislodging his grip on Mantis's battlesuit.

Mantis gathers himself and flies straight at Prince Armacaust, who begins throwing punches with great precision. Mantis evades each strike with shocking ease. Mantis again hits Armacaust with a bolt of tremendous energy from his eyes, throwing Prince Armacaust into the wall across the ceiling.

Prince Imhotep grows to an astounding height and swats at Mantis to protect his uncle. Only intending to shoo Mantis away, Prince Imhotep's actions are taken as aggression by the other Sons. Dr. Step enlarges himself also and snatches Prince Imhotep off his feet and hurls him across the cavern in the opposite direction.

Furious, Princess Zilpha flies into action. She blasts Dr. Step with a tremendous bolt of energy. Dr. Step does not even flinch. Gad reaches out his hand and increases Princess Zilpha's density until she can no longer fly or even stand from the weight. DwarfStar attempts to reverse the effect but soon realizes that Gad's mastery over gravitational forces far exceeds his own.

Batmyte transforms into a lion and lets out a bloodcurdling roar. Most of the Eshanashim teens step back. Merneith and her brothers spring into action. They are Drāks whose human DNA is combined with that of the water buffalo. Even at their tender ages, they possess amazing physical strength and durability. They also have large horns on their heads. Merneith tackles Batmyte and wrestles him to the ground. Batmyte immediately transforms himself into an African bull elephant and uses his superior size and weight to pin Merneith, immobilizing her momentarily.

While neither Gbeto nor Abrax can budge or harm Dr. Step, Dr. Step finds it difficult to control the energetic twins. They take turns attacking and running away from Dr. Step. Crypto stretches out a hand and causes ice blocks to form around the twins' legs, slowing them down just enough for Dr. Step to grab them both by the collar. The twins struggle but soon tire and give up, seeing that they are simply not strong enough to free themselves from Dr. Step's grip.

Django turns his skin into pure energy and runs toward RahStar. Django throws a punch at RahStar but realizes he is punching the air, as RahStar has teleported out of the line of the attack. RahStar reappears behind DwarfStar and shoves him into Django. Django catches DwarfStar.

Suddenly, Django and DwarfStar are outside. RahStar has teleported them out of the cave. Django releases DwarfStar, who immediately wraps his arms around Django and begins to fly back toward the entrance of the cave when RahStar opens a warp gate. DwarfStar is unable to stop before he flies into the gateway. The portal takes him and Django back into the cave, but points them directly into a wall. DwarfStar crashes into the wall, and both fall hard onto the cavern floor.

Realizing that the teens in the cave are simply traumatized, Gad releases Princess Zilpha. He looks at the various scrimmages taking place around the cavern and determines to restore order.

"Enough!" Gad cries. "Let's try and start over," he says rather firmly.

Almost everyone freezes in their tracks. However, high above the ground, a battle continues to rage between Prince Armacaust and Praying Mantis. And although Prince Armacaust is far superior to Mantis in sheer physical strength and durability, he cannot lay a finger on Mantis.

By contrast, Mantis's superior fighting skills and reflexes are blunted by his inability to cause any damage to Armacaust by throwing punches. Mantis can deadlift ten tons; however, his level of superhuman strength is simply not enough to hurt or even slow Prince Armacaust down. Mantis does not ever shy away from a fight. Moreover, the concept of living to fight another day does not ever occur to him.

On the ground, BlackBird searches Prince Armacaust's mind for a possible method to defeat him. BlackBird scans both Prince Armacaust's thoughts and emotions. BlackBird senses great anxiety within the young prince, but also a hesitation to use his primary ability. BlackBird uncovers thoughts that reveal Prince Armacaust does not want to hurt Mantis but cannot see any way to defend the Eshanashim children without unleashing what will be a devastating attack against Mantis and the rest of the Seven Sons.

Sensing that Prince Armacaust has decided to use this ability, BlackBird calls out to Mantis telepathically.

"Yo! Stand down! Fight's over," BlackBird yells in his twin brother's head.

"Are you sure?" Mantis responds telepathically. "He seems pretty intent on bashing my head in."

"Now, Mantis! Trust me on this," BlackBird insists.

Mantis immediately ceases to fight and throws up his hands. Confused, Prince Armacaust ends his aggression. The two combatants stare each other down as they slowly descend back to the cavern floor.

Gad extends a hand to DwarfStar. Rubbing the right side of his ribcage with his left hand, DwarfStar extends his right to exchange a handshake with Gad.

"Apparently, you are who we came to find," Gad says glibly.

"Do you guys beat up everyone you meet for the first time?" DwarfStar asks sarcastically.

"Most of us, no. But Mantis does, pretty much every time," Gad replies with a smile.

Mantis raises his left eyebrow as if indicating he is mildly amused by his brother's taunt. Gad resumes the introductions.

"Ok. Where were we? Yes, for the benefit of our new friends, I'm Gad Sextantis. We are the Seven Sons of Chaos. These are my brothers: Batmyte, RahStar, Dr. FrankenStep, BlackBird, Praying Mantis, and Crypto," Gad says calmly, pointing at each of the Sons in turn.

Each of the Sons takes turns pressing their palms and fingers together, slightly bowing and raising their connected thumbs to the middle of their foreheads as their names are called. Gad sits in a yoga easy pose, and the other Seven Sons follow suit. However, instead of sitting on the floor, Mantis levitates a few feet off the ground.

Prince Armacaust matches Mantis' posture until he hears Addis HK clear her throat. He sits directly across from Gad and begins to exchange intel. Prince Armacaust and his leadership team begin to detail their escape plan.

Dr. Step asks clarifying questions concerning the use of an Einstein-Rosen bridge large enough to transport thousands of people at once. Brooklyn and Prince Imhotep tag-team answering Dr. Step's questions. He offers to assist Princess Zilpha in practicing creating and sustaining the gateway. She enthusiastically accepts Dr. Step's offer.

Dr. Step, Princess Zilpha, Prince Imhotep, and Brooklyn walk to a corner of the cavern to begin their test runs. Pleased with the cooperation he sees, Gad pledges to do all the Seven Sons can to help the Eshanashim children remain safe until Queen Hawwah arrives.

As the Eshanashim teens and Seven Sons continue to make preparations, RahStar senses that the group is being watched. He leaves his physical form and enters the astral plane. As he surveys the area around the cave for onlookers, he sees a strange figure.

The being of towering height seems to be lurking around the cave. It looks like the entire universe in human form. RahStar recognizes the patterns of galaxies and nebulae against the dark canvas of the being's nebulous form. Though it has no face or other discernible features, RahStar can tell it has become aware of his presence. It turns its head in his direction and begins to move toward him.

"Whoa!" RahStar exclaims. He stumbles and falls backward and back into his body, exiting the astral plane. As he exits, he makes the mistake of allowing the figure's gaze to follow him back to the cavern where the Sons and the Eshanashim children are working together to make their next move.

RahStar tries to shut the strange being out but cannot resist the being's tremendous surge of energy. RahStar teleports out of the cave to the place where he and the Seven Sons first landed in Eritrea a few hours earlier. Leaving the cave seems to sever the strange being's connection.

Back at The Gatekeepers' HQ, H opens her eyes.

"Found you," she declares.

CHAPTER 27
YOU FORGET YOURSELF

The third day at TGHQ has not started as energetically as the day before. Aides and other staffers have descended on the fourth-floor dining hall to gather food for their respective leaders, but the air is much heavier. Fears that the children may not be found "in one piece" have begun to circulate among the various contingents.

As the planetary leaders gather to resume their viewing, tensions rise. During the first scheduled break of the day, Monolith Ant finally breaks the silence.

"I'm just going to say what many may already be thinking. This is all a ruse! Hawwah has devised this entire elaborate scheme to convince us that she is some sort of goddess. She wants to scare us all into believing threats exist from which only she can save us. Furthermore, I believe the goal of this plot is to get all of us to abdicate our governments and appoint her as the ruler of the entire System," Monolith Ant declares, standing to his feet.

"I don't know where this intolerable hatred for H comes from, but you and I were there when she nearly gave her life to defend us against Apep on Earth," Aharon begins, before he is abruptly interrupted by Monolith Ant.

"In service to a mission she invited us to join. This entire odyssey has been about her and her desire for power!" Monolith Ant bellows.

"Power? You think she wants power? With no evidence to the contrary, she already possesses world-shattering power. She already rules over what's arguably the most influential planetary government in the System. Many of our own people, and I mean yours on Ikw-n-tA and mine on Memphis, already consider her THEIR queen. Hawwah doesn't need us to acknowledge her power. She wakes up to that reality every day."

"You forget yourself, Aharon. Her real husband is sitting not ten feet from you. You walked out on her; remember?" Monolith Ant retorts.

"He still loves her," Neith blurts out, staring in the opposite direction.

Aharon hesitates for an instant to look in Neith's direction, then refocuses himself and begins to address the entire room.

"Look, all I am saying is that this scenario Monolith Ant seems to be painting rings untrue to me. If he's right, this would be a clumsy gambit at best. H would have had to allow her mortal enemy to launch an attack she could have possibly prevented, just so that she could convince the rest of us she's the only one capable of solving a problem she otherwise allowed to take shape. I'm sorry. I just don't buy it," Aharon argues.

Monolith Ant walks over to Aharon. The two men stand toe-to-toe. Monolith Ant's massive frame and ominous eyes would intimidate most others. But as he suggested on their first day together here, Aharon Mandrake, the Shadow Ant, might be the greatest warrior in human history.

"You know the woman for whom you continue to swoon isn't the only being in this galaxy possessed of immense power," Monolith Ant says coldly, staring into Aharon's eyes.

Aharon chuckles and tilts his head in abject defiance.

"Your wife or any number of concubines must have visited you last night. You seem to have a lot of courage this morning," Aharon retorts, with a glib smirk.

King Armacaust finally steps alongside the two rivals. Sphinx and Vixen watch intently from the control room.

"Gentlemen, we'll get nowhere if we fight one another," King Armacaust offers. "Besides, H agreed to advocate for the prosecution of all parties involved in this crime."

"Yes, but how convenient it was that she secured an immunity deal with the ICoJ before entering the trance by which we're viewing these very visions," Envoy Armana adds from across the room.

"You see, Aharon, your lost love isn't so altruistic after all," Monolith Ant snarls at Aharon. "And you, boy, I'd suggest keeping better tabs on your wife. There seems to be much that she neglects to share with you," Monolith Ant says to King Armacaust, without breaking focus on Aharon.

"Esteemed guests," Sphinx calls out from the main entrance to the viewing room.

She is flanked by two of her associates, Hammer and Mina. Vixen has entered the viewing room through another entrance on the opposite side of the room.

Sphinx continues in a warm tone, "I think this is the perfect opportunity to break for lunch."

Monolith Ant and Aharon separate and walk in opposite directions. The King walks over to Sphinx and places his hand on her shoulder before exiting the viewing room. Sphinx and Vixen walk toward each other, shaking their heads.

"Wow," Vixen says.

The two friends laugh nervously, then trail behind the last of the planetary leaders and their aides as everyone is ushered from the viewing room.

In the dining hall, very few words are spoken. The guests of TGHQ eat quickly and return to the viewing room. Just as they are seated, an image of a cave appears.

"We've seen this before, haven't we?" Envoy Armana shouts.

Merneith Mandrake, who was not paying attention before Envoy Armana's comment, looks up and sees the entrance to the cave. This time, she recognizes it. She begins to type something into her handheld device feverishly. Sphinx notices this activity immediately.

"Something is happening with Director Mandrake," Sphinx says, leaning toward Vixen. "Keep an eye on her for me," Sphinx orders.

"Copy!" Vixen replies.

Just then, Merneith rises from her seat and quickly exits the viewing room. Vixen and Sphinx look at each other and nod. Sphinx radios Admiral Menewa to have his people stand down so that Director Mandrake can be observed from a distance. Vixen leaves the control room to follow Merneith.

Vixen follows Director Mandrake past the elevator to the lounge area. She watches Merneith enter the restroom. Whatever has caught Merneith's attention has distracted her to the point that she does not notice that the Chaosian special forces unit did not react to her leaving the viewing room.

Vixen hangs back for a moment, then enters the restroom. Like Sphinx, Vixen is a Drāk possessing both human and large cat DNA. Vixen's acute sense of hearing allows her to overhear Merneith speaking angrily to someone on a second device she brought with her, rather than her primary handheld.

"She found you! And, now, I'm exposed!" Merneith declares angrily.

> "Get out of there, and I'll have a transport ready to take you to a secure location," the voice on the other end says flatly.

When Vixen moves closer to Merneith to question her, Merneith draws a weapon she has smuggled past the security checkpoint and points it at Vixen's midsection.

"Don't take another step. I have the emitter switch set to lethal," Merneith says coldly. "You and I will be leaving this place… together."

Merneith steps closer to Vixen so that she can press the barrel of the radiator into Vixen's ribs. Vixen raises her hands as if to surrender. As the two women turn to walk out of the restroom, Vixen sees an opening and attacks.

Vixen disarms Merneith with little effort, then launches a barrage of kicks, knees, and punches. To Vixen's surprise, Merneith is able to block or evade most of Vixen's strikes.

Merneith attempts to return the favor, but Vixen's defense is too strong.

Realizing Merneith cannot break through her defense, Vixen begins to use her superior strength to her advantage. Vixen employs a series of joint locks and throws until the painful stress on her joints, combined with the collisions with walls and furniture, takes its toll on Merneith. She eventually passes out from the punishment.

"The soundproofing in these walls is a-maz-ing! No one heard all of that?" Vixen thinks out loud. "Yeah, you're going to feel this tomorrow," she says, crouching over the unconscious Merneith.

Vixen takes Merneith's additional handheld device and calls the most recent number in the call log. A surprisingly distinguished voice answers.

"Have you escaped the facility?" the voice asks.

"No," Vixen replies.

"Code in," the voice responds.

Vixen's silence causes the person on the other end to terminate the call. Vixen radios Mina and Hammer. When Mina and Hammer arrive, they take Merneith into custody.

Vixen briefs Sphinx. Sphinx immediately gets Admiral CavalierStar involved. Merneith is brought to a secure interrogation room on the second sublevel of TGHQ.

Gen. Powell and Jo-Molefi start the interrogation while Sphinx and Vixen observe via a live feed to the control room. Sphinx and Vixen wear over-the-ear headphones so that no one else can listen in on the interrogation.

But just as it seems Jo-Molefi and the general are beginning to collect actionable intelligence, the muffled sounds of wailing and expressions of jubilation erupt from the viewing room. Vixen stands and covers her face. Sphinx snatches off her headphones. The scene streaming into the viewing room reveals that the missing children have been found.

CHAPTER 28

SENDING THE CAVALRY

H leaves her meditation and yawns, stretching her arms wide. Sphinx opens the meditation chamber door and runs to H. Sphinx throws her arms around H's shoulders and neck.

"You did it, Mom."

Tears stream from Sphinx's eyes as she squeezes H tightly. H, who has been levitating in a meditative state for the better part of three days, sets her feet on the floor, one at a time, smiles, and hugs Sphinx tenderly. She strokes the back of Sphinx's head and kisses her on the forehead.

"We did it," H says softly.

H pulls Sphinx back and looks into her daughter's eyes with a huge smile. Sphinx cannot contain her joy at having her mother back among the living, so to speak.

"Soooooo... what did I miss?" H asks sarcastically.

"You don't want to know," Sphinx says with a laugh.

"That bad, huh?" H responds with a chuckle.

"Yup!" Sphinx replies slyly.

"Okay. Help Armie handle the politics. I'm going to rendezvous with the IGP. Unless I'm mistaken, the SS Long Arm should be waiting in low orbit," H says with a smile.

"Copy!" Sphinx replies, her face beaming.

H wipes Sphinx's face. The two women exchange another long hug, then turn and walk into the control room. H is greeted with thunderous applause from the technicians gathered inside. Vixen runs up to H and gives her a big hug. H reciprocates.

H then gives high fives and shakes hands with everyone in the room. She stops when she sees King Armacaust enter. H runs over to him and jumps into his arms. The king kisses H fervently. He pauses for a moment and pulls back ever so slightly. H places her feet back on the floor.

Staring into H's eyes, King Armacaust places his hands on H's upper arms and begins to rub her arms and shoulders, as if he has something he desperately wants to say to her. H uses her ability to perceive the emotions and intentions of others to discern that the king is dealing with great inner turmoil regarding the images he has seen over the past few days.

"I probably have some explaining to do," H says playfully.

"Yeah, I would say so," King Armacaust replies. "Right now, I just need you to do what you do," he says with a smile.

"Okay. Can we talk when I get back?" H asks earnestly. "Hey, Love, please don't give up on me," H says softly.

She tilts her head down to avoid eye contact. King Armacaust takes a deep breath and exhales. He gently places a finger under H's chin to lift her face back up toward him so that he can see her eyes.

"Never!" he says emphatically.

The lovers resume kissing passionately. Vixen steps in front of them and gestures for the technical staff to get back to work. Sphinx hails Lt. Inspector Djer Menes, captain of the SS Long Arm.

"Inspector Menes!" she calls out into the communicator.

"Go ahead, Princess. I'm here," Insp. Menes replies.

"We have a heading. Sending coordinates now," Sphinx replies.

"Reading. Okay. Got it!" Insp. Menes replies. "My special guests embarked yesterday. We're ready to get underway. Just awaiting your signal."

Sphinx glances at the queen. Although H's lips are still locked with the king's, she lifts one hand off King Armacaust's arm and points skyward. Sphinx nods.

"Launch, Captain! You are cleared for takeoff. The queen will rendezvous with you en route. Over," Sphinx declares.

"Copy that!" Insp. Menes replies.

Sphinx can hear the inspector give the order to launch before the comms close. H kisses King Armacaust one final time, then takes a step back and launches herself through the ceiling of the control room, removing a section of the stone roof, plus a large solar panel from the top of TGHQ. Sphinx looks on in utter disbelief. High above the facility, H carefully lets the solar panel and other materials slide off her hands and fall more than nine stories to the ground.

"Wow! Thanks, Mom!"

"You're welcome, Dearie," H replies playfully, projecting her voice back to the control room.

H picks up her pace and reaches escape velocity in a matter of seconds. She uses her telescopic vision to locate the massive starship. H sees that the SS Long Arm has already exited Planet Chaos's orbit. She streaks toward the vessel at the speed of light.

As she reaches the vessel, an airlock opens and allows her to board. Once aboard, H is greeted by Z and Dean Starlyte. Z gives her sister an enthusiastic hug. Starlyte wraps his arms around them both and squeezes them tightly, lifting the two women off their feet. H and Z giggle with delight.

"Just like old times. All we're missing is Aharon," Starlyte says jokingly.

The sisters throw Starlyte a quick side-eye. Starlyte laughs heartily. He sets H and Z back on the floor and walks toward the airlock.

"Dean Starlyte, this is Commander Ramses. You are all set to go, sir!" a voice breaks in over the comms.

The airlock opens, and Starlyte flies outside the ship. Starlyte makes his way to the stern of the SS Long Arm. He waits for the full caravan to appear.

Two other starships pull close to the Long Arm, having decelerated from light speed. The first starship bears the symbol of the Ant Planet. The second ship bears the standard of Planet Memphis.

Amen Hotep VI, better known as Starlyte, dean of the Planet Chaos College of Elders, possesses the power of a warp star. He can bridge any two points in the known universe and allow for almost instantaneous travel between the starting location and the destination. He is so powerful that there does not seem to be any upper limit to his capacity to transport people or objects through space and time. He once removed a moon of Planet Memphis from the path of a comet.

In addition to his ability to move objects through space and time, Starlyte also possesses superhuman strength and durability. He can lift well over 250 tons and survive a nuclear explosion. He can also expel powerful bolts of electromagnetic energy. Moreover, the Eshanashim transmit both physical and mental capabilities through sexual contact. This is especially true among the enhanced.

Eshanashim scientists discovered that, after about a century of consistent sexual contact, enhanced Eshanashim couples will start to exhibit each other's powers. The partner who originally possessed the ability will usually hold a greater power level in wielding whatever the paranatural ability may be.

After having shared a marital bed with Z for more than three thousand and three hundred years, Starlyte has also mastered the ability to energize his cells, making him virtually invulnerable to harm. He has also gained considerable speed in flight, as his wife is the fastest flying Eshanashim on record. Z flies faster than even her sister, H.

At this moment, Starlyte will serve as the warp star to take the extraction party to Earth. Starlyte throws open his star-shaped cape. It grows and expands until it is wide enough for all three of the starships to pass through. Once the three starships pass through to a position a few miles outside of Earth's atmosphere, Starlyte closes the gateway.

H and Z make their way to the Long Arm's bridge. There, they are greeted by Lt. Insp. Menes and his executive officer, Commander Setepenre Ramses, also known as CDR Set Ramses. Lt. Insp. Menes briefs H and Z on the capabilities of his ship and crew. H and Z nod in acknowledgment.

CDR Ramses then ushers the sisters to a briefing room just off the bridge and unites them with other special guests. Princess Libbyèré jumps out of her seat and runs over to her mother and aunt. She hugs them both tightly.

Libby, as her friends and family call her, is often also referred to as "Little H," as Libby is arguably the third most powerful enhanced Eshanashim in the system. In fact, her power levels exceed Monolith Ant's in strength, durability, energy projection, and vortex breath.

"It's about time you two showed up," Libby says enthusiastically.

"You know we love to make an entrance," Z responds playfully.

Senator Nova and Lady Twinkle both stand and make their way over to H and Z. Aha Meketaten III, better known as Nova, is the senator of New Kemet Province, the largest province of Planet Chaos by both landmass and population. And despite what Monolith Ant may think, Eshanashim scientists who study the phenomenon of the enhanced and their abilities tend to agree that Nova is second only to H in terms of raw power.

According to relevant tests, Nova possesses the equivalent power of thirteen million stars in terms of strength, durability, and energy projection.

"My queen," Nova says warmly, bowing as he reaches H.

"Senator," H replies with a warm smile.

"Queen Mother," Lady Twinkle says with a bow.

"Twinkle," H replies. "How are you, gorgeous?" she says playfully, reaching her arms out to give Twinkle a friendly hug.

As their sons have grown so close, H and Lady Twinkle have spent countless hours together over the last decade. Lady Twinkle is the daughter of Baahir Ankhesenamun, the pharmacist who helped save H's life during the voyage from Planet Earth to Planet Chaos in Year 6078, also described as 1122 BCE by historians on Earth.

Unlike Starlyte, Z, Monolith Ant, and Aharon, Baahir was not on the bridge of the starship when the others were exposed to a focused beam of electromagnetic radiation caused by a rare alignment of the seven suns of the Ant-Galaxo Devearous System.

The injuries H sustained as a result of her battles with Apep and his minions during their exodus from Earth turned H into something similar to a severely damaged nuclear reactor. Exposure to her electromagnetic radiation caused the mutations that allowed the first generation of Eshanashim to draw sustenance from sunlight, as well as the increases in bone and muscle density that help them thrive on Planet Chaos and the other planets across their solar system.

The others who worked tirelessly on the bridge to save H also carry genetic markers that allow them to produce enhanced offspring. Nova and Sekhmet Ankhesenamun Meketaten, better known as Twinkle, represent the first generation of Eshanashim to be born enhanced.

Twinkle possesses the ability of superspeed. She is able to lift three tons and is completely bulletproof. In fact, Twinkle is the fastest Eshanashim on the ground, and only Z is faster than her in flight.

Other dignitaries make their way over to greet H. Intergalactic Marshal Constellation walks over and greets H with a hearty hug. She steps back and bows respectfully.

"Queen Mother. Long time no see," Constellation says jokingly.

"I hope Roba isn't too mad," H responds with a smile.

Prince Montu and his brother, Prince Wepwawet, of the Ant Planet, stand and walk at a deliberate pace toward the queen. They bow respectfully when they reach her.

"Queen Hawwah, I know you have had your differences with my father over the years, but Prince Wepwawet and I wanted to express our sincere gratitude to you for putting those differences aside for the greater good. We are pleased to be a part of this mission," Prince Montu declares.

"Thank you for accepting the invitation," H replies.

"Queen Mother," CDR Ramses's voice interrupts through the comms. "You asked to be alerted when we reached the first position."

"Very good! I'm on my way," H responds.

Then, turning back to the people in the briefing room, H says, "Well, shall we go say hello?"

H and the dignitaries from the briefing room are escorted to the bridge of the SS Long Arm. On the ship's monitors, they can see military aircraft converging on the position of the three starships.

"Captain, please tell the other ships not to engage," H directs.

"Open a channel," Lt. Insp. Menes orders.

"Comms open, sir!" a young ensign named Haile-Aset Amun responds.

"Rescue Clowder, this is Pack Leader. Raise shields and don't engage hostiles. Repeat. Raise shields and don't engage. Over," Lt. Insp. Menes orders.

"Copy!" the communications officer aboard the Memphis starship replies.

"Copy that!" the Ant Planet starship communications officer replies.

"Ma'am? What are your orders?" Lt. Insp. Menes asks, turning back to H.

"Let's go say, 'Hotep,'" H replies with a smile.

"Tell Detective Bolingoli she and her team are up," Lt. Insp. Menes commands.

"Sir!" CDR Ramses responds.

She presses her badge. The communication channel opens.

"Detective Bolingoli, have your team meet Queen Hawwah and her delegation in shuttle bay four," she orders.

"Copy that!" DSG Bolingoli replies.

H and her party are escorted to the shuttle bay. Once they arrive on the deck of the shuttle bay, DSG Bolingoli greets them with a snappy salute. Detective 2nd Grade Zuri Bolingoli serves as the team leader for the elite Intergalactic Patrol tactical unit known as the Diplomatic Security Service, also referred to as the DSS.

The DSS is comprised of some of the best operators in the entire IGP. They are equipped with advanced weapons and battle suits. And one of the team members, DSG Angola Tshisekedi, is an extraction expert.

"How would you like to proceed, ma'am?" DSG Bolingoli asks H.

"Detective, I think a few of us are going to fly down. Please board the remaining guests and follow us in the shuttle," H says to DSG Bolingoli.

"Copy that! Mavoungou, get behind the wheel. Tshisekedi, Massamba, and Kongo, the three of you are on standby. Antetokounmpo, you're with me," she orders.

The DSS team springs into action. And once the DSS makes sure everyone who is meant to be in the landing party is aboard the shuttle, DSG Bolingoli orders the shuttle bay doors to open. H, Z, Starlyte, JaneStar, Constellation, Libby, Satellite, Prince Montu, and Prince Wepwawet float out into the air.

As they descend, they can see military aircraft circling the starships, while heavily armored vehicles amass on the ground beneath them. Off in the distance, H can see media aircraft attempting to breach the airspace but being turned away by the various military agents. Z looks around and floats closer to H.

"Why are we over the Sahara?" Z whispers to H.

"I didn't want to give away the location of the cave," H whispers back.

Z nods her acknowledgment and agreement without changing her expression. H lets the IGP shuttle land before she comes to a stop, hovering approximately ten feet off the ground. A man wearing an Egyptian military officer's uniform steps out of one of the vehicles.

Heavily armed helicopters surround H and the landing party. Soldiers wearing the uniforms of various countries point their weapons at the Eshanashim landing party.

The Egyptian officer walks closer to H and the hovering Eshanashim dignitaries. Even though he is wearing sunglasses, he uses one of his hands to cover his eyes as he looks up at the hovering Eshanashim delegation. He looks sternly at the IGP shuttle and then back up at H and the group of flying people hovering above him.

"I am Minister of Defense, General Mohamed Sobhi. Who are you? And what do you want here?" the Egyptian officer yells in Arabic.

"I am Queen Hawwah Menewa. And we mean you no harm," H replies in Arabic.

H descends closer to Gen. Sobhi but does not touch her feet to the ground. Z follows close behind.

"You speak Arabic?" Gen. Sobhi asks in a confused tone.

"Yes, and a few other languages, in fact," H says with a smile.

"Okay. What is it that you want here?" Gen. Sobhi asks firmly.

H gives the general a playful smile and rises back into the sky. She looks out over the landscape and begins to speak. Without raising her voice to a volume any louder than it was when she was speaking with Gen. Sobhi, H projects her voice to every corner of the globe. Every person on Earth hears her speaking without the use of any listening device.

In a clear, calm voice, H introduces herself to every person on the planet.

"People of Earth, I am Hawwah Menewa, Queen of the Eshanashim, an ancient people who live in a solar system very similar to yours but nearly 100 light-years from here. We mean you no harm. Our people, some 33,300 children to be exact, are being held captive somewhere on your planet. We have merely come to retrieve them. Help us, and we will return to our home in peace," H declares in English.

H repeats this introduction three more times, reciting it in Arabic, Mandarin, and Spanish.

People around the world stop what they are doing to listen intently to the voice. Many stand frozen in terror, staring at the sky. Others walk outside to look at the sky. More turn on the nearest television to find a news report that may explain this unexpected phenomenon.

At the Citadel Heru, Minister Chaos orders his aides to get his jet ready for takeoff. He walks deliberately off the observation deck with his hands clasped behind his back. A broad smile creeps across his face.

Inside her castle in Ireland, Maeve Turner, also known as Miss Witch, sinks into her makeshift throne. Maeve feels a wave of terror suddenly rush over her. Realizing the severity of her situation, she decides to take a trip to Africa to confront The Leader.

At The Leader's campsite, hundreds of mercenaries and support staff scurry about, grabbing weapons and equipment. The Leader and the Grand Reverend stand patiently, awaiting their master's command.

"Go back to the cave and kill them all," the Challenger snarls.

As The Leader and the Grand Reverend walk away barking orders, Apep the Challenger grins evilly. The moment he has been awaiting has finally arrived. He will once again come face-to-face with his ancient enemy.

"Welcome home, Hawwah," he declares.

CHAPTER 29
THE TRAGEDY OF MAEVE TURNER

Before she leaves for Africa, Maeve teleports herself from the throne room to her bedroom. She picks up her TV remote from the stand next to the bed. She takes a deep breath, then lets out an exasperated sigh. She turns on the television.

The TV blinks to life, and multiple thumbnails appear, displaying news reports of "aliens" landing on Earth. Maeve squints her eyes to see if she can catch a glimpse of her face, the face of the queen of Planet Chaos. She was told that Hawwah would not return to Earth herself. Hawwah would certainly send surrogates who could be easily defeated, forcing the queen to negotiate for concessions. Hawwah, the irresistible force of nature that even the devil himself fears, would not be a factor in this scheme.

Maeve shakes her head. She clenches her fists so tightly that she crushes the remote. Seeing her TV remote explode into pieces, Maeve lets out a long scream that more than exemplifies her level of frustration.

Maeve teleports from her bedside to her closet. She pulls off her sweatshirt and slips on the body-armor-reinforced black dress she had specially made for encounters with enhanced Eshanashim. She shakes and shimmies until the dress lies on her body just the way she wants.

She then pulls off her sweatpants and slips into her reinforced, black, six-inch high-heeled pumps. She drapes the long, black cape over her back and secures it by locking the clasps on the dress's choker collar.

Maeve sighs again. Letting out an extended sigh, she walks over to the six-foot mirror in the corner of her closet. She reaches for her final accessory, a black, pointed hat with the point bent to the left. She places the hat atop her blazing red hair.

Maeve stands in front of the mirror, staring at herself for an instant. She takes a deep breath to steady herself.

"You never looked better, old girl!" Maeve says enthusiastically in her thick Irish accent.

Then, in a flash of light, she teleports herself across the Iberian Peninsula and directly to Northeast Africa. Maeve materializes, hovering high above Eritrea. She teleports to the ground just outside The Leader's campsite.

Born Maeve Riley Aisling in 1995, Maeve is the daughter of an Eshanashim father and an Irish mother. Her late father was a member of The Leader's cult who migrated to Earth to play a role in destabilizing the various governments of the nations around the globe. The objective of The Leader's movement, The Takeover, is to establish a global, Eshanashim-controlled oligarchy on Planet Earth.

Maeve's father was a Drākanashim whose human-lion-mixed DNA produced microscopic hairs covering his body that made him appear to be a man of European descent. Maeve's mother was born to Earth-bound Irish parents from Kinsale on the southwest coast of Ireland. Maeve's parents moved to Dublin shortly after she was born.

The Takeover tried relentlessly to indoctrinate Maeve and a host of other children like her, born to Eshanashim and Earth-bound parents, to conform to the ways of the cult. Throughout Maeve's teenage years, many of the leaders of the cult were engaged in sexual relationships with young ladies of Maeve's age. Maeve's mother did not want that life for her daughter, so she kept Maeve away from The Takeover as much as she possibly could.

When Maeve enrolled in university, she was introduced to G. Elon Lynch Jr., the man referred to as "The Heir" among the members of the cult. He was also the man who declared himself to be "the living embodiment of racism." Racism took a special interest in Maeve. He often praised her for her beauty and her wit. Maeve enjoyed the attention.

Maeve's mother, however, feared that racism was grooming Maeve to become one of his personal concubines. Despite her mother's best efforts, Maeve fell into the web of Racism's charm and extravagant lifestyle. Not only did he heap lavish gifts upon Maeve, but Racism also treated Maeve to unique experiences in incredibly beautiful and interesting places around the world.

Maeve would eventually surrender to Racism's sexual advances. But she would soon try to pull herself out of her relationship with Racism as she began to learn about his secret families with Earth-bound women. That was not the life Maeve wanted for herself. So she allowed Racism to connect her with a prestigious job opportunity back in Ireland and moved back home with her folks.

By the time Maeve turned thirty, she was thriving. She loved her job. She had even gotten her own place, but visited her parents once a week. She did her best to keep Racism at arm's length but found his intrusions into her life to be relentless.

After about three years of living on her own, Maeve received a call from her father. He pleaded with her to resume her relationship with Racism. He told Maeve that Racism missed her terribly and might actually be in love with her. Maeve refused to be involved with Racism any further.

Maeve's father gave her a warning to stay away from Racism if she truly did not want to be Racism's love interest. A few weeks later, her father was killed by a random stranger in a botched robbery during a business trip in Cork. Maeve was devastated.

At her father's memorial service, Maeve did everything she could to avoid Racism. Catching Maeve off guard at the gravesite, Racism was able to pull Maeve off to the side. Maeve did not want to cause a scene, so she walked with him.

"I can't imagine how you feel," Racism begins. "I feel so terribly for your mother, but my heart breaks for you. I want you to know that I miss you so much. I would do everything I could to take care of you and give you comfort, if you would only come back to me."

"I appreciate your offer, but I know me mum and I can manage," Maeve replies, without looking at Racism's face.

"I love you, Maeve. You must know that. Don't you?" Racism says insistently.

"You love me? Hrrrmmmph. How's that, then? D'ya love all of us? Your wife, your black girlfriend in America, Barbara, and the hot-blooded Latina you talk about so much?" Maeve asks sarcastically, folding her arms and only looking up at Racism sparingly.

"Not one of them is like you. You're special," Racism shoots back. "If it makes you happy, I'll get rid of the rest of them. I'll do whatever it takes to make you happy. That's how much you mean to me," he continues, desperately trying to sustain eye contact with her.

"Oh, bollix! You cannot get rid of the kids you have with these women. Some of them are younger than me! I'm sorry. I just don't want that life," Maeve replies.

Maeve wipes a tear welling up in her left eye, then looks back toward the ground. She looks around desperately for an exit to this conversation.

"Maeve!" her mother shouts. "The chauffeur's ready to go. Come, Love!"

"I'd better go," Maeve says insistently.

Before Racism can get out another word, Maeve waves goodbye and walks swiftly to the limo. She does not even look back to see Racism's reaction.

"This isn't over," Racism mutters to himself.

Over the next several months following her father's memorial service, Maeve started receiving cryptic text messages, alleging that her father's death was no accident and that her mother's safety may also be in question. Maeve decided to move her mother in with her.

Things began to settle again. Maeve, however, did not feel comfortable leaving her mother at home alone for too long. One day, as Maeve walked from the train platform to retrieve her bicycle, she literally bumped into a young African American man named LeVaughn Julius Turner.

"I'm so sorry," he says.

Time seemed to stand still for Maeve. She found the kindness in his eyes to be disarming. Looking down at the ground, she used her left hand to sweep the hair from her face.

"No worries. I'll be okay," Maeve replies softly.

Something inside her kept her from resuming her swift march to the bike rack. She looked up to see the young man staring at her with a huge smile on his face.

"My name is LeVaughn, but my friends call me LJ. I hope I've not delayed you or something," he says softly.

"No... no... no, no trouble. I'm good. I'll just be on me way, then," Maeve replies.

"It was nice meeting you..." he pauses, waiting for her reply.

"Oh, bollix." She laughs. "I'm Maeve," she says, extending her hand.

LeVaughn takes Maeve's hand and kisses it gently. Maeve's face turns bright red.

"I hope I run into you again, Maeve," LJ says smoothly.

Two days later, Maeve and LJ saw each other again on the same platform. They exchanged a few pleasantries and departed.

A day or two later, they connected again and engaged in a longer conversation. LJ explained that he was in Dublin on a two-year work assignment for his father's company.

By next week, LJ was walking Maeve home each evening. A month later, LeVaughn and Maeve went on their first date.

A month after that, they would begin to spend every available moment they could together. LJ and Maeve would spend Sunday afternoons at the park. LJ always brought his guitar and would serenade Maeve. His performances usually drew a crowd.

Maeve's mother raved about LJ to her friends, especially since LJ would regularly cook for Maeve and her mother.

On a Sunday night the following year, LJ proposed to Maeve while her mother was in the middle of setting out the dessert plates after dinner. Maeve enthusiastically accepted.

That night, Maeve and LJ made love for hours. They had not previously had sex with each other. In fact, Maeve had not been with anyone sexually since Racism.

Lying next to each other in a post-coital embrace, LeVaughn whispered that he had something to tell Maeve.

"I have a confession I need to make," he begins.

"Spit it out. You've gotten everything from me now," Maeve replies with a hearty laugh.

Chuckling, LJ rolls over onto his side and props himself up on his elbow.

"Us meeting that day wasn't by accident. I know that now. My father arranged for me to be here. He may have even orchestrated us connecting that day. I think he was hoping we would become friends so that he could lure you back to him," LJ opines.

"Who's your father? I'd remember hanging out with a Black guy," Maeve replies in total confusion.

"You misunderstand. My father is Elon Lynch Jr.," LeVaughn says gently, staring up at the ceiling to avoid Maeve's immediate reaction.

Shocked and angered, Maeve jumps up. She grabs a sheet and pulls it over her bare chest. Still in shock, Maeve delivers a firm slap across LJ's face.

"How dare ya?!" she shouts. "Bollix! I've had sex with your father, man!" she screams.

LJ laughs and pulls Maeve back toward him. Maeve puts her hands in front of her face in disgust.

"This is no laughin' matter," Maeve says sternly.

"Babe... babe, calm down. I know. He's creepy, but he doesn't control us," LJ replies, his face beaming.

Maeve settles a bit. Her shoulders drop. She lets out a loud, long scream. Her left hand still clutching the sheet, she continues to press it against her breasts.

"Can't I ever be rid of 'em?" she exclaims.

"Yes," LJ answers softly. "We're both free of him. I promise."

Maeve looks directly into LJ's eyes. She sees the same kindness that captured her gaze the first time she met him. She releases the sheet from her grip, grabs LeVaughn's face with both hands, and kisses him passionately. LJ responds by kicking the top sheet off the bed and lying back. Maeve lifts her left leg and settles herself onto LJ's throbbing erection. They continue to make love throughout the rest of the night.

The following year, LJ and Maeve got married in Detroit. LJ's older siblings, Jay and Deja, paid for the wedding and even funded the trip across the Atlantic for Maeve's mother, family, and close friends to attend the ceremony. Even Racism attended the small, intimate gathering. Racism told the couple that his gift was a lavish, all-expenses-paid Seychelles honeymoon.

However, when they returned from Africa, LJ was greeted with an eviction notice at his condo in Detroit. His brother Jay even called him into the office to let LJ know that he would no longer be a part of the company. LJ was devastated. Sensing this situation had everything to do with her rejection of Racism, Maeve convinced LJ to move back to Dublin with her. LJ agreed.

Over the next nine years, LJ and Maeve built a life in Ireland. Without Racism's influence or financial backing, they faced challenges in finding gainful employment. But no matter what they faced, they remained happy.

One day, Maeve told LJ and her mother that she had a big announcement after dinner. However, on her way home, a strange man pushed Maeve onto the train tracks. Other commuters came to her rescue. The fall caused Maeve to lose a lot of blood, so she was rushed to the hospital.

At the hospital, the ER physician delivered the devastating news that Maeve had previously been pregnant, but there was evidence that the baby had not survived the fall. Furious, LJ vowed to make his father pay. He ran out into the night.

Days passed without LJ returning home. A week later, the police stopped by their house to notify Maeve that LJ's body had been found. Maeve locked herself in her room and cried for three days straight.

Twenty-five years later, Maeve laid her mother to rest. Again, Racism attended the memorial service. Maeve ignored him altogether this time. She never remarried. She refused even to date. She did, however, notice that although she was in her early sixties, she had not aged at the same rate as the people around her.

Maeve began to make inquiries into her father's Eshanashim origins. Over the next forty years, Maeve studied Kemetic history and theology incessantly. She came across lost texts and obscure legends regarding the Waters of Kaos. Her investigation eventually led her to Dr. Gerald Butler, a little-known preacher and Kemetic scholar in New York City.

Maeve worked with Dr. Butler and his oldest daughter, eight-year-old Alpha, to uncover the location of the Waters of Chaos. Another ten years would pass while Maeve worked tirelessly to uncover the location of the lost pool of primordial water. Once she was convinced she and Dr. Butler had discovered the location, Maeve coerced LJ's siblings into financing an expedition to Africa.

By the time they reached the location somewhere in the Democratic Republic of the Congo, Maeve was 114 years old. But because of her Eshanashim heritage, she still appeared to be a young woman. After years of searching, Maeve and Dr. Butler had found the Waters of Chaos.

Maeve walked into the midst of the pool and submerged herself in the waters. When she emerged from the water, she began to laugh uncontrollably. She immediately propelled herself into the sky and continued to laugh.

Alpha ran into the midst of the water, but before she could submerge herself in the water, several winged men entered the chamber and pulled Alpha from the pool. Maeve was able to wrest Dr. Butler and Alpha free from the winged men and fly them to safety.

Alpha discovered she had gained superhuman strength in her legs from her brief exposure to the Waters of Chaos. Maeve, however, had become something more. In addition to superhuman strength and the ability to fly, Maeve could expel tremendous bolts of electromagnetic energy. She also would soon discover that she could teleport herself to points across the planet and even bridge any two points in the space-time continuum.

Dr. Butler tried his best to get Maeve to join the collective he was organizing. Maeve, however, declined his offer.

"I did all this for LJ. And I'ma take away the only thing his father wants. I'm going to take over this planet," she declares coldly. "In fact, I intend to be the biggest witch this world has ever seen!" Maeve says before vanishing in a flash of light.

CHAPTER 30
PRELUDE TO EPILOGUE

Just as the war parties depart for the cave, Maeve arrives at The Leader's campsite dressed in the accouterments of her nom de guerre, "Miss Witch." She strides confidently up to The Leader and slaps him in the face with the back of her hand. He stumbles backward several feet from the force of the blow.

The Leader's bodyguards immediately train their weapons on Maeve. Racism steps back and freezes as if paralyzed by shock. Each time he has seen Maeve throughout this process, he has not been able to determine whether she intends to kill him. And that is precisely the way Maeve wants it. While Maeve suspects that Racism had LJ killed, she cannot yet prove it. And she does not want to murder him unnecessarily.

Dozens of red dots appear on her chest, head, neck, and back. Maeve smirks defiantly.

"Tell your boys to put their toys away. I promise to play nicely. Besides, they cannot harm me anyway," Maeve says with a smile.

"Lower your weapons," The Leader commands, rubbing his face.

Curious to see her abilities, the Grand Reverend grabs a plasma rifle from one of the mercenaries and walks toward Maeve, discharging the weapon as he advances. The shots from the rifle spark as they collide with Maeve's chest. She does not budge an inch.

Maeve raises a force field around herself and rises several feet off the ground. As mercenaries, following GR's lead, let loose with their weapons, the shots spark harmlessly against Maeve's force field. She then unleashes a tremendous bolt of energy that completely decimates her assailants in a matter of seconds.

She slowly descends to the smoldering earth beneath her and walks slowly toward the GR, who throws his weapon down and raises his hands with a look of pure satisfaction on his face. Confused, Maeve turns back to The Leader.

"So, the queen made an appearance, didn't she? You assured me that she wouldn't come here," she says calmly.

Maeve's thick Irish accent almost makes her frustration seem pleasant. Energy begins to build around Maeve's clenched fists.

"Well, since you came here, you now stand with us! Now that the queen has arrived, the alternative becomes spending the rest of your life in a Chaosian prison," The Leader retorts gruffly.

"What d'ya expect me to do, then? Kill Hawwah?" Maeve asks sarcastically.

"No, leave that to my master. Your task will be much simpler. You only need to destroy the Seven Sons of Chaos," he replies.

* * * * * * *

Back at TGHQ, Sphinx convenes a meeting with her team to discuss the incident involving Director Mandrake. Though the missing children have been found, the question of how they were taken remains.

"Did you get anything from the conversation the director was having, Vix?" Sphinx asks.

"No, as soon as she knew I was in the room, she pretty much stopped talking," Vixen replies.

Sphinx lets out an exasperated sigh.

"Okay. From the reports we received, most of the children were taken from school. They were abducted from Planets Chaos, Memphis, Pen-Meroe, and Ikw-n-tA, plus Giza Moon Colony. But there is no indication that any of the children were abducted from any of the territories or settlements on remote moons or planets outside of the solar system," Sphinx declares, thinking through the available evidence out loud.

"That could mean all the children abducted meet the same demographic somehow," Nefertiti posits.

"Just from the planets in the solar system, we've got Drāks, Ants, and Pens. Same demographic? How so?" Mina asks skeptically.

"That's because we're not thinking broadly enough. The demo we need to include could be labeled 'kids from politically connected families.' My brother, President Djet Drone's children,

Monolith Ant's grandchildren, and my goodness, if you throw a rock at a group of random kids on the street on any planet, you might hit one of President Mandrake's grands," Sphinx says flippantly.

The Gatekeepers laugh boisterously while Sphinx tries holding back her laughter at first, then lets go.

"Now that I think about it, I resemble that comment. He's my paternal grandfather, too," Sphinx says, breaking into a hysterical laugh.

"You know what? You're not wrong, Sis! Do you remember that retreat we attended a few years ago?" Nefertiti asks, with a tone of excitement in her voice.

"Yeah, the... Get Together... the... no! The Gathering!" Sphinx exclaims, snapping her fingers and pointing at Nefertiti.

"Right! I would wager that if you cross-reference the guest list from that event against the list of the kidnapped kids, they would match up pretty well," Nefertiti adds.

"That's why none of the kids were taken from the remote areas. Their parents are not on the political or social radars yet," Sphinx concludes. "Is my dad still here? I need a favor," Sphinx asks.

"He's still in-house, Chief. I set him and the members of the PDFJC up in a conference room on Sublevel 3," Eman says.

"Hammer, get the Queen's Arrow ready on Alert 4. We're wheels up in forty-five minutes, people," Sphinx orders.

"Uh... where're we going?" Vixen asks, with a confused look on her face.

"We are going to go see the Convener, but first, we need to make a stop at Rhakotis Base," Sphinx replies, rushing out of the room.

"Okay!" Vixen says, hopping out of her chair and following Sphinx out of the room.

Sphinx and Vixen take the private elevator to Sublevel 3 while their teammates make preparations to get their starship underway. When they walk off the elevator, the king is there to greet them. He gives each of them a hug and a kiss on the cheek.

"Ladies? What may I do for you?" King Armacaust asks.

"Dad... I need a favor," Sphinx says cautiously.

"You know you could just call me Armacaust. You're, like, so much older than me. Like, sooooo much older," King Armacaust says with a chuckle.

"Ha ha. I know. But calling you 'Dad' makes me feel soooooo much better about myself," Sphinx says with a sly smile.

"Got it," King Armacaust replies with a huge smile.

"Okay. I need you to get us into the WSA," Sphinx says with an expression that suggests she is awaiting the king's objection.

"Ah, you want to investigate the director's involvement. Don't you think this is a matter for the Intergalactic Patrol?" King Armacaust asks.

"Yes, but I would like to go before they get there. I need to confirm a piece of evidence before following up on another lead. This thing seems to have tentacles we may not have yet considered. After I get what I need, I promise that the IGP can have it. And if we don't go now, I'll have to charm my way in later, and you know how much I hate being charming," Sphinx says with a smile.

"All right! You convinced me," King Armacaust begins. "But Sarah... I mean, Sphinx... try not to break anything."

Sphinx gives the king a half salute, followed by a kiss on the cheek. She then turns and heads back toward the elevator. Vixen hugs the king and follows Sphinx into the elevator.

"So, how much older are you than the king, really? I knew you were older than him, but, like, how much older?" Vixen asks as soon as the elevator doors close.

"I was born in 6863, and he was born in 8706. So, like... 1,800 years... give or take several decades," Sphinx says with a laugh.

"Oh, I was born in 6864. Wow! We're like his ancestors," Vixen says.

The two friends look at each other and break into a boisterous laugh. The elevator door opens to Sublevel 1. Sphinx and Vixen exit the elevator and board the SS Queen's Arrow.

****

In the cave, final preparations are being completed. Gad gives the Seven Sons their assignments.

"43 formation, east and west," he calls. "Bird, take Mantis and Crypto to the entrance of the cave. Step, you, Batmyte, and Rah are with me," Gad orders.

"But I'm always assigned to the twins," Dr. Step replies.

"There're scary monsters in here. You're with me today. The twins have Crypto," Gad responds with a smile.

"We have Crypto," BlackBird says to Mantis with a giggle.

The pair starts to laugh hysterically. Crypto rolls his eyes.

"Shut up," Crypto sighs. "It's not even that funny," he says dryly.

Mantis stops laughing abruptly. His ability to sense danger has set off alarms throughout his nervous system.

"Gad, they're coming!" Mantis declares.

"Seven Sons, it's go time!" Gad commands. "Princess," Gad says, gesturing for Princess Zilpha to open the first portal. "The time has come."

CHAPTER 31

IT ALL COMES TO THIS

BlackBird, Praying Mantis, and Crypto race to the entrance of the cave. Prince Armacaust accompanies them. Just as Prince Armacaust flies ahead and takes point, Mantis pushes him out of the way of a plasma bolt cutting through the darkness, causing a minor explosion of rock and debris as it strikes a wall.

"Thanks!" Armacaust says enthusiastically to Mantis.

Mantis nods. The two then proceed to dive toward the cavern floor, evading a barrage of plasma rifle fire being let loose by Seth Zomibi, Sphinx Genet, Abanoub Boateng, Ptah Mercury, Tewagi Negus, Gbeto Negus, and Mino Negus, along with a handful of mercenary soldiers.

An energy blast explodes from Mantis's eyes that completely obliterates the mercs. Armacaust flies straight into the Negus brothers, a group of winged Drākanashim brothers who serve on the pirate ship, the SS Dread Crescent, under the leadership of Captain LionMane.

The Negus brothers are each extremely strong and durable, as their physiology combines human genomes with both elephant and bird DNA. Though the Negus brothers have proven to be a "hard out" for most in a fight, they cannot stand against the power of the young prince of Planet Chaos.

Prince Armacaust knocks Gbeto and Mino unconscious with ease. He grabs Tewagi, carrying him into the rafters of the cave and disappearing into the darkness. But no sooner do the two disappear than Tewagi comes hurtling back down to the cavern floor, crashing with tremendous force.

Sphinx Genet fires precise shots into Crypto's chest that spark against his breastplate and shoulders. Genet then fires a shot directly at Crypto's head, only to have that shot blocked by BlackBird, flipping over his brother's head and using his shield to deflect the shot.

BlackBird locks eyes with Genet, who almost immediately crumples to his knees from a searing pain felt in almost every part of his brain, as BlackBird uses his mental abilities to fire every electrical pulse in Genet's brain all at once. The attack nearly kills Genet, who passes out from the shock.

Mina Seshperonch begins to join the fight when Set Aha grabs her by the arm.

"We should live to fight another day, my dear," Set whispers to Mina.

Mina looks back at him and snarls until she realizes that, aside from Circe Defiance and Rings, she and Set are the only ones left. And neither Circe nor Rings is in plain sight. Mina allows Set Aha to pull her into the cover of the shadows, where they can lie in wait until the next round of fighting.

****

In the confusion of the battle at the cave's entrance, Rings has made her way to the lower cavern where the Eshanashim children are making their way through the portal opened by Princess Zilpha. Rings causes another diversion to draw the teens' attention away from herself.

She begins to grab young ladies from the throngs of children waiting their turn to enter the portal. She binds their hands and feet, gagging their mouths each time. Seth Zomibi and Abanoub Boateng continue to cause distractions as Rings goes about collecting girls. Rings collects six young ladies until she draws the attention of Addis HD.

Addis leaves her brother to attempt to rescue the young lady she saw Rings snatch. Before she can even reach Rings, Seth Zomibi grabs Addis by her hair and lifts her off her feet. And even though Addis' Drakenashim physiology makes her stronger than the strongest human on Earth, she is no match for the mechanical grip of Zomibi's battle suit.

Rings binds Addis HD's hands and feet, then gags her mouth.

"Such a pretty one," Rings says excitedly.

Rings reaches her hand between Addis HD's legs and pulls down Addis' panties. Rings touches Addis HD thoroughly between her legs, examining her genitals.

"And pure," Rings declares delightedly.

Addis HD begins to sob uncontrollably as a multitude of thoughts flood her mind. She realizes that the strange woman who has bound her intends to enslave her in the sex trade or sell her as food to cannibals, or possibly both.

She struggles but cannot free herself from the bonds Rings has placed on her hands and feet. Zomibi lays Addis HD prone on the cavern floor. Addis HD immediately forces herself onto her back, fearing someone will violate her right there in the cave.

She cannot stop crying. She begins to pray earnestly for God to deliver her from this situation. She calms herself just enough to hear the other young ladies offering their own prayers through their sobbing.

Out of the corner of her eye, Addis HD sees a very young girl lying a few feet from her. The young lady has long black hair and is wearing a pretty blue dress that covers her down to her ankles. The dress has gold accents and a golden six-point star at the chest. Rings removed the younger girl's shoes, just as she did to Addis HD.

Addis HD inches her way closer to the younger girl and manages to get close enough that the younger girl is able to roll over and place her face on Addis' shoulder. Addis HD can feel her sleeve become wet from the girl's tears, which makes Addis cry even more.

****

A mile or more on the other side of the cave, Gad, Batmyte, RahStar, and Dr. Step reach the scene of the battle between the Wiles of the Devil and Asenat, Shaka, Sojourner, Solomon, and Seraphina.

Gad bends down to inspect the cavern floor when Despair and Animosity crash through the roof of the cave. RahStar teleports to Gad's side and teleports Gad away just before a massive rock crashes to the cavern floor where Gad was crouching.

Batmyte transforms into an African bull elephant and charges at the monstrous brothers. Despair swats Batmyte away with ease. Dr. Step creates a rock hand that extends from the cavern floor to catch Batmyte. Dr. Step immediately raises a column from the floor that lifts Despair high into the air and another column that drops from the ceiling onto Animosity.

Envy and Jealousy bounce in from the hole in the cave wall. They drop onto Batmyte, who is still in his elephant form, and stomp down with their feet as they land on his back and right side. Batmyte collapses and lies still.

Furious, Gad removes the pull of gravity from both Envy and Jealousy. They immediately begin to float helplessly off the ground.

Deacon El, a Drākanshim who walks on two legs but is still more elephant than human, drops from the ceiling and begins to swing wildly at Gad. Gad is able to evade El's attacks, but not well enough to muster a counter. Dr. Step rushes in and delivers a blow that launches El back through the roof of the cave.

"See, scary monsters. That's why you are here with me," Gad says to Dr. Step with a smirk.

"Understood, but this isn't over yet," Dr. Step replies.

Despair, who had jumped back down to the cavern floor, pushes the column extending from the floor onto Dr. Step. The column shatters harmlessly over Dr. Step's head and back. Again, Dr. Step does not flinch. Instead, Dr. Step turns his head in Despair's direction.

The earth opens under Despair's feet, and Despair falls into a deep cavern, as if a trapdoor opened underneath him. Despair can be heard screaming frantically as he falls. After several minutes, an unconscious Despair shoots out of the chasm as if the earth itself spat him out of its mouth.

He crashes violently on the cavern floor and lies still.

"Let's collect the Myte and get to the other side of the cave," Gad says somewhat anxiously.

"Copy!" Dr. Step and RahStar say in unison.

* * * * * * *

Prince Armacaust, BlackBird, Praying Mantis, and Crypto arrive back at the lower cavern just as the last contingent of Eshanashim children is preparing to enter the portal created by Princess Zilpha. Mantis suddenly pauses.

"Oh, no!" Mantis sighs loudly.

"What is it?" Prince Armacaust asks with a tone of great concern.

The Praying Mantis does not respond. Instead, he rockets toward the ceiling of the cave. The ceiling explodes just as Mantis reaches the rafters. Using his super speed, Mantis pulverizes, catches, or pushes the huge rocks starting to rain down on the lower cavern.

Prince Armacaust launches into action himself. BlackBird, too, flies high above the Eshanashim children, now running to cram into the portal. He uses his shield to generate a force field wide enough to shield the children from the falling debris that Mantis could not stop.

Apep bursts into the cavern in his Dragon form and immediately breathes a powerful blast of fire into Prince Armacaust. Again, the young prince remains unharmed and continues his charge toward the colossal beast. The attack has once again, however, left Prince Armacaust completely naked.

Seeing Apep distracted, Mantis unleashes a massive energy blast that staggers Apep, who turns his attention to Mantis. Prince Armacaust uses this opening to release a pulse of energy that serves as an EMP capable of disrupting paranatural abilities. Caught in the pulse, Mantis immediately plummets toward the cavern floor, dropping nearly a hundred feet in mere seconds.

Without thinking, Crypto runs toward the falling Mantis and leaps into the air, catching Mantis before Mantis can crash into the cavern floor. Shocked, Mantis looks up at the naked prince.

"That's what you were going to do to me earlier? You could have killed me!" Mantis yells.

"Stop whining. You're still alive," Prince Armacaust responds with a smirk.

Apep stops his attack for a moment. Something does not feel right. He cannot place it. He ignores the strange feeling and draws a breath, again blowing a blast of fire and lightning toward the fleeing Eshanashim children.

BlackBird's force field continues to hold, as his shield is unaffected by Armacaust's EMP. It also keeps BlackBird aloft in the air.

"Crypto, if our weapons still work, you and Mantis likely still have your physical strength," Bird yells, hanging from the handle straps of his shield.

"Right!" Crypto replies.

He swings Mantis around and launches Mantis straight at Apep the Dragon. Mantis always carries two swords, along with a plethora of other weapons. He reaches his right hand to his back and draws his flaming sword from its sheath.

Apep's heads snap furiously at Mantis as Mantis hurtles toward him. Using his superior agility, Mantis is able to evade being bitten in half by any one of Apep's heads, leaping, somersaulting, and slicing his way to Apep's chest.

Even without the benefit of his super speed, Mantis proves to be virtually untouchable, even to a being with Apep's reflexes. Mantis inflicts several severe wounds on Apep's heads and necks before finally reaching Apep's chest.

Mantis plunges the brilliantly burning blade into Apep's chest. Mantis then uses all of his might to cut a huge laceration in the beast's torso. Though in tremendous pain, Apep finally clamps the jaws from one of his heads onto Mantis's right leg.

Mantis feels his leg snap, yet without hesitation, he hurls his sword to his twin brother, who catches it and immediately hurls the sword into the head holding Mantis. Apep releases Mantis as the blade penetrates Apep's lower jaw.

Mantis again falls to the earth but is caught by Prince Armacaust. Mantis reaches into a pocket of his battle suit and presses a patch in the shape of an ankh against Prince Armacaust's chest. A battle suit identical to Mantis's begins to cover Armacaust's naked body.

"Nanite-powered battle suit," Armacaust says approvingly.

"Yup! It's about time you dressed appropriately for the occasion, Prince," Mantis replies.

Just then, Apep's heads corral and surround Prince Armacaust and Mantis.

"Well, this doesn't seem good," Mantis says sarcastically.

"No, this isn't good at all," Prince Armacaust says plainly.

Both Mantis and Prince Armacaust realize that, even though Apep is weaker, Apep's fiery and electrically charged breath will eventually prove extremely harmful to them both, especially to Mantis, who is now without the benefit of his abilities to absorb energy and heal quickly.

Each of the Dragon's heads inhales as if in preparation to fricassee the pair. Prince Armacaust raises a force field in preparation for the blast. Unfortunately, though the energy shield will protect them from the flames, sustained exposure to the tremendous heat from Apep's breath could eventually kill Mantis.

For now, their courage unshaken, the teenage boys await Apep's next move, looking for an opening to take further action, hoping for the best.

And almost inexplicably, the beast stops. All of his heads turn in unison toward the hole in the roof of the cave. Suddenly, the beast lurches upward as if an irresistible force has pulled him from the cave.

And in fact, that irresistible force is H.

The Queen has arrived.

CHAPTER 32

I WAS SENT HERE TO KILL YOU

H swings Apep around and hurls him high into the sky, then uses an energy blast to push Apep into the upper atmosphere. As Apep soars out of sight, Hawwah makes a quick scan of the cave, using focused beams of X-ray radiation to peer right through the various rock formations separating sections of the cavern. She is able to see the Eshanashim children making their escape through the warp gate created by Princess Zilpha. H smiles. She turns her attention to Prince Armacaust and the Praying Mantis.

"Hotep, boys! Sorry, I'm late," she says enthusiastically.

Prince Armacaust can only exhale in relief. Along with his mother floating above the cave, Prince Armacaust recognizes several familiar faces, including Dean Starlyte, Lady Photon, Senator Nova, Lady Twinkle, his older sister, Princess Libby, and Marshal Constellation.

Mantis can only stare in amazement at the queen. He has heard stories of the great queen of the Eshanashim, who has swum against currents of time and shaped human societies on two planets. In some ways, she has always sounded too good to be true. Now, he stands witness to her in the flesh.

The throbbing pain in his leg, however, brings him back to reality. Mantis collects himself after being in awe and notices a group of assailants advancing on his twin and Crypto, who remain powerless.

"How long will this effect continue to last?" Mantis asks Prince Armacaust intently.

"Should only be a few more minutes," Prince Armacaust replies.

"Well, looks like we have work to do," Mantis says matter-of-factly.

"Boys, you clean up in the cave. We will take care of Apep and crew," Hawwah directs with a smile.

"Yes, Mother!" Mantis exclaims.

He stretches out his arm and taps a quick sequence into his palm before clenching his fist. A cable explodes from the brace on his forearm. He then wiggles himself free from Prince Armacaust's embrace and swings back toward the cavern floor.

"He's intense," H says playfully.

"You've no idea," Prince Armacaust replies with a sigh.

H swoops down and hugs Prince Armacaust tightly. The prince buries his head into his mother's shoulder.

"I'm so proud of you, Son!" H whispers to Prince Armacaust, with tears pooling in her eyes. "Oh... and you look good in that suit. Now, go!" she commands before streaking back into the sky.

Prince Armacaust smiles and wipes his own tears from his face. He turns and dives back toward the cavern floor.

The Praying Mantis has already made his way to the cavern floor by disconnecting the cable and somersaulting into a perfect landing on his left foot, right next to BlackBird.

"How much longer?" BlackBird asks.

"Not long," Mantis replies.

The three brothers prepare to face Set Aha, Mina Seshperonch, Tewagi Negus, Gbeto Negus, Mino Negus, Adrian Dawit, Abanoub Boateng, Ptah Mercury, WarHorse, and his son, K'Estiti, without their paranatural abilities.

Mantis quickly taps a sequence onto his right thigh. His battle suit responds by forming a cast and walking boot around his right leg. Mina draws her sword. Mantis responds in kind by drawing his second sword.

"Go!" Bird commands.

Mantis and Crypto spring into action. Mina charges straight for Mantis and almost connects on a well-placed thrust that she follows with a flawless overhead strike. Mantis blocks the second attack with his blade, then uses his superior strength to cast Mina aside with little effort as their swords clash.

Mantis then hops on his left foot and leaps into the air, delivering a devastating spinning kick to the side of Ptah Mercury's head, rendering him unconscious. Abanoub Boateng tackles

Mantis before he can land. Pressing his advantage, Abanoub snatches Mantis's cape and swings Mantis into the cave wall.

Abanoub delivers a ferocious body shot into Mantis's midsection with his left hand and a powerful right hook to the side of Mantis's head. Mantis ducks Abanoub's ensuing left jab and plunges his sword into Abanoub's left arm.

Spinning around to Abanoub's back, Mantis releases his blade from his right hand, which he slides to Abanoub's chin. Mantis deftly pulls the sword from Abanoub's arm with his left hand while throwing Abanoub to the ground with his right hand.

Abanoub skips and rolls violently across the cavern floor. Before Abanoub can regain his bearings, Mantis leaps within a foot of Abanoub's back. Mantis delivers a strike to Abanoub's spine that nearly folds the mercenary in half. Abanoub's broken body flops listlessly to the ground, where Abanoub lies motionless.

Several feet away, Crypto and Adrian Dawit lock hands as if they are engaged in a contest of strength. Adrian Dawit is the Drākanashim son of renowned geneticist and Ant Planet oligarch Dr. Gyasi Dawit. Gyasi conducted the bioengineering required to splice both of his sons' DNA with that of animals. Neither Gyasi nor his sons' mother, Bennu, is Drākanashim. Gyasi is an Ant, and Bennu was born and raised on Planet Chaos by Chaosian parents.

Adrian's physiology represents the blending of human genomes with those of the great white shark. Standing at an impressive seven feet tall, Adrian is amazingly strong and durable. And though Adrian can deadlift more than two thousand pounds, his strength does not compare to Crypto's. Crypto can deadlift close to twenty-five tons.

Realizing that he is physically superior to the massive Drākanashim, Crypto crushes Adrian's hands. As Adrian drops to his knees, screaming in pain, Crypto delivers a front kick to

Adrian's chest that sends Adrian several feet across the cavern, rendering him unconscious.

Just as Crypto lifts his eyes, an arrow strikes his breastplate and falls harmlessly to the ground. Mantis uses his sword to deflect another arrow meant for Crypto's head. BlackBird uses his shield to generate a force field that blocks a barrage of arrows flying from various points around the cavern.

"How many of them are there?" BlackBird asks.

"Two!" Mantis declares. "They're just moving really fast."

Just then, Gad, RahStar, and Dr. Step, carrying a laboring elephant, arrive at the cave's entrance.

Set Aha emerges from the shadows and strikes at Gad with his spear. Gad evades the first blow, then increases his density as the second blow lands on his head. Gad shrugs it off.

Arrows ricochet off Dr. Step's helmet.

RahStar teleports himself within a few feet of K'Estiti. K'Estiti kicks RahStar before RahStar can react. RahStar falls to the floor and receives an arrow right in his right thigh, just above the knee. The arrow has pinned RahStar to the cavern floor.

However, RahStar teleports again before another arrow pierces the space that RahStar's head previously occupied.

RahStar again teleports close to K'Estiti, but this time, Rah grabs K'Estiti and teleports him into the sky, more than three miles above the cave.

K'Estiti swings his bow at RahStar, who disappears. K'Estiti plummets to Earth. Resigned to meet his end, K'Estiti closes his eyes and prepares for his transition.

RahStar reappears just before K'Estiti crashes to the ground and teleports them both back into the cave, where RahStar drops K'Estiti right in front of Dr. Step, who backhands K'Estiti unconscious.

Just then, BlackBird, Crypto, and Mantis realize their powers have returned.

"Power's back on!" BlackBird exclaims excitedly.

"Good!" a female voice yells out. "Whatever that means," Maeve says with a laugh.

Energy bursting from her hands sparks against the walls and floor as her stiletto heels click along the cavern floor. Terrified that she will be forced to defend herself against H, Maeve wants to get this encounter over as quickly as possible.

"I think I was sent here to kill ya," she says in a folksy tone.

Mantis taps a sequence on his right thigh. The cast and walking boot morph back into his regular footwear configuration. His right leg immediately reforms into its usual shape.

Gad raises a finger and, pausing, looks in Mantis's direction.

"Uh, Mantis, before we engage in another fight, please tend to Batmyte," Gad says.

Mantis nods and rushes to Batmyte's side. Prince Armacaust lands next to Gad.

"Allow me to fill in for the Praying Mantis," Prince Armacaust says.

"Fine with me," Maeve says.

Maeve raises her hands and unleashes a powerful bolt of energy that throws BlackBird into Prince Armacaust, forcing them both into Gad and ultimately knocking all three boys into Dr. Step. BlackBird was barely able to raise his shield before being struck by the tremendous bolt of electromagnetic energy.

"Why did I get out of bed today?" BlackBird asks jokingly.

"I wish I woke up in my bed today," Prince Armacaust shoots back.

Several feet away from the fighting, Mantis kneels next to the injured Batmyte, still in his elephant form. Mantis begins to call out telepathically to his flaming sword, which remains lodged in the chin of one of Apep's heads. It wiggles itself free of Apep's flesh and zips back toward the cave.

While he awaits the sword's arrival, Mantis examines Batmyte's vitals. Mantis's acute hearing can detect Batmyte's heartbeat and breathing patterns.

"Heart rate low and breathing impaired due, perhaps, to a partially collapsed lung," Mantis thinks out loud.

Mantis scans over Batmyte's body with focused beams of X-ray radiation from his eyes. He takes mental notes of what he sees.

"Hmmmm... broken ribs... large hematoma in the abdomen, which could be due to a lacerated liver, and swelling around the spinal cord. Yikes! Who did this to you?" Mantis says, verbalizing his inner monologue.

The Praying Mantis suddenly spins around to catch an arrow aimed perfectly at his head. Mantis immediately camouflages himself. By blending perfectly into the background of the cave, Mantis makes himself virtually invisible to WarHorse. Unbeknownst to the master assassin, Mantis begins to hunt him.

Suddenly, WarHorse sees Mantis's flaming sword fly into the cavern. The sword stops abruptly in a vertical position. The flaming blade shines brilliantly, illuminating the entire cavern. Mantis reveals himself, holding the sword.

After performing a whirling kata with the flaming blade, Mantis hurls the sword at WarHorse. WarHorse barely evades the attack, but the sword finds its other intended target, Mina Seshperonch. The blade pierces her shoulder. The force of the throw also lifts Mina off her feet and pins her to the cavern wall.

Mina screams as the flaming blade begins to burn her. To the surprise of all looking on, the sword returns to Mantis's waiting hand. WarHorse responds with lightning speed, drawing another arrow. That is when he realizes that Mantis was not aiming the sword at him, but rather at his bow. Mantis has cut the bowstring. Mantis stands ten feet from WarHorse with a smirk of satisfaction on his face.

Mantis sheathes the sword and opens his arms and hands wide as if to invite WarHorse to engage in a fistfight. WarHorse obliges, leaping at Mantis with frightening speed and deadly precision. Mantis evades the attack with ease, grabbing WarHorse's outstretched arm.

Mantis yanks WarHorse's arm while simultaneously delivering a roundhouse kick to WarHorse's rib cage. WarHorse hears the awful popping sound of his ribs breaking. Mantis does not release the assassin's arm, which is now dislocated as a result of the devastating kick.

Mantis follows up this assault by driving an uppercut into the bottom of WarHorse's chin. The assassin's jaw shatters in three places. Still holding on to WarHorse's dislocated arm, Mantis whirls WarHorse around and delivers a downward elbow strike to WarHorse's temple that sends the master assassin into a coma. WarHorse drops unconscious onto the cavern floor.

Mantis hurries back to his injured brother. Mantis removes a combat knife from his boot and begins making incisions over the areas of Batmyte's internal injuries. Mantis begins by working on draining the pools of blood collecting around Batmyte's injuries.

Mantis then takes the flaming sword from its sheath and cuts his own forearm. He proceeds to squeeze several drops of his blood onto Batmyte's injuries. The platelets in Mantis's blood begin to regenerate the tissues of Batmyte's injured internal organs. After several minutes, Batmyte opens his eyes and slowly returns to his human form.

"Ohhhhhhhh, this hurts," Batmyte says, exasperated, as if he is out of breath. "How long was I out?" he asks.

"I have no idea. All I know is that somebody kicked your can!" Mantis says with a laugh. "Hold still. You need a lot of silk," Mantis says playfully.

Once he completes patching Batmyte up, Mantis takes a seat next to Batmyte. Batmyte places his right hand on his left side and rubs his rib cage.

"It looks like you and I will be on the sidelines for a few more tics, Bro," Mantis says with a chuckle.

"Good. I feel like I got run over by a truck," Batmyte says.

"What did you guys encounter back there?" Mantis inquires.

"These three huge, red, monster-lookin' dudes. They were dropping from the ceiling," Batmyte declares.

"That's wild," Mantis replies.

"As soon as I heal up, we'll go finish this. You know the other five have a hard time surviving without the two of us," Batmyte states.

"No doubt!" Mantis exclaims.

The brothers share a fist bump and sit silently.

CHAPTER 33
SOME THINGS NEVER CHANGE

On the opposite side of the cave, away from the battle raging at the entrance of the cave and a mile or more away from the fleeing Eshanashim children, the Grand Reverend enters the cavern through the now large window, widened from the multiple conflicts that occurred in this section of the cave. The Grand Reverend surveys the area to find Envy and Jealousy still floating off the ground in a state of weightlessness. Using a cable to lower himself to the cavern floor, he sees that Despair, Hatred, and Animosity remain unconscious.

"Who could do this?" Grand Reverend wonders out loud.

He immediately examines the area for any lingering threats, then begins tethering his adopted sons together. He again scales the wall of the cave and pulls the Wiles of the Devil back down the side of the mountain. High above the roof of the cave, but still several klicks below the peak of Emba Soira, he sees H and the Eshanashim delegation gathered with her. The Grand Reverend does all he can to remain inconspicuous. He knows that H can probably sense his presence, but she has probably determined him not to be a threat worthy of her attention.

Still hurtling toward outer space, Apep finally regains his stability and is able to fly back to the cave. He lets out a bloodcurdling roar as he swoops into view. His ten heads snake in various directions, looking over the Eshanashim delegation assembled before him.

"Hmmm, not as scary as I remember," Z says dryly.

"I no longer sense the children in the cave," H says. "Starlyte, you, Z, and Libby collect Prince Armacaust and have him take you to the rest of the kids," she orders.

"Yes, Mother," Starlyte responds.

Z lingers until she sees her sister nod, then she follows her husband into the cave. H continues to dispatch the remaining Eshanashim assembled with her.

"Nova, you and Twinkle deal with the base camp and any contacts I am sure Apep has assembled for this little caper," H commands.

"Yes, Mother!" Nova replies before streaking off at supersonic speed toward the base camp. Twinkle follows close behind.

"And, Marshal, would you be so kind as to support the Seven Sons in their cleanup efforts, as Armacaust will be needed elsewhere?" H asks respectfully.

"My pleasure, Mother!" Constellation responds.

As the Eshanashim leaders disappear from view, H and The Dragan stare at each other. Neither of them intends to back down.

"Alone at last," H says sarcastically to her ancient enemy.

"For the last time, woman!" Apep snarls.

H shakes her head and chuckles under her breath. She clenches her fists and looks back up at Apep with fierce determination in her eyes.

"Have it your way!" she exclaims, catapulting herself at Apep.

The beast responds with a full-throated blast of fire and lightning from each of his ten heads. H flies straight through each blast effortlessly. She plows into Apep's chest with staggering force. Apep lurches backward. With blinding speed, H begins pummeling each head individually with blow after blow. Dazed and confused, Apep begins to realize that H means to destroy him.

"Wait!" he screams just as H unleashes a massive bolt of electromagnetic energy into his torso.

Apep crashes violently into the Great Rift Valley. His monstrous form dissolves to reveal Apep the Challenger.

"So nice of you to show your true face," H says sarcastically.

Apep the Challenger lets out a thunderous cry and rockets toward H. H stands firm, awaiting his attack.

"I will destroy you, witch!" Apep exclaims.

He tackles H in midair and begins to pummel her with blows to her head and chest, pushing her higher into the sky. Though each punch breaks or bruises H's skin, her wounds heal almost instantly. H fights back but quickly realizes that Apep's skills in hand-to-hand combat easily exceed her own. For the first time in thousands of years, she finds herself losing a fight to Apep.

"Imhotep isn't here to save you this time! And Mikael's not coming to your rescue! I'll be victorious!" Apep shouts as he continues his bloody assault.

"It's disturbing you actually believe Mikael has ever intervened in any conflict between the two of us to save me," H says dryly.

Infuriated by H's insolence, Apep grabs H by her hair and delivers a merciless blow to her midsection. Continuing to hold on to her hair, Apep begins to swing H around at a high velocity, throwing her violently to the ground. Her body causes a massive crater as she crashes to the Earth. H manages to struggle her way to her feet before Apep can stomp on her head.

"Okay. New strategy," H says intently, staring into her enemy's eyes.

****

Nova and Twinkle fly to the Leader's base camp. One hundred or so support staff and soldiers remain on the ground. Most of them seem to be packing equipment and salvaging weapons.

"Should we just fly down and start wrecking things?" Twinkle asks.

"No," Nova replies, surveying the adjacent mountain range.

"I have an idea. Get on the ground and use your speed to search every tent. Make sure none of our people are being held captive here. Once you give me the "all clear," I will take care of the camp. At that point, you and I can cover the skies, My Love," Nova says.

"How will I know to evac the camp?" Twinkle asks.

"Trust me. You'll know," Nova replies.

Nova flies closer to Twinkle and plants a passionate kiss on Twinkle's lips, then streaks off toward a towering mountain peak. Twinkle flies down to the camp. She uses her superspeed to check every tent and every vehicle on the ground.

As he gets closer to the mountain, Nova stretches out his hand and projects a focused beam of energy that slices through the mass of rock, snow, and trees. The severed peak begins to slide toward the valley below. Nova flies in and lifts the large section of rock off the mountain range.

The stone, roughly the same size as the villages lining the Great Rift Valley, engulfs the camp in shadow as Nova hovers over the camp, holding the stone aloft. Seeing the sunlight disappear, Twinkle looks up. She sees her husband holding the gargantuan rock aloft. She flies up next to him and smiles.

Nova stops at a point he believes to be the dead center of the camp. He flips the stone up ever so slightly. He and Twinkle fly at light speed to get from under the path of the falling rock. The massive stone falls to the Earth, crushing everything and everyone beneath it.

The Grand Reverend watches this entire scene unfold from the relative safety of the base of the mountain in amazement.

"I can only hope that Defiance was still in the camp when the rock fell," Grand Reverend says to himself.

"Father, how do we get home?" Envy shouts.

"I know someone who can help with that," Grand Reverend replies. "Let's just hope she doesn't get herself killed."

****

Maeve continues her onslaught against the Seven Sons and Prince Armacaust. Although Prince Armacaust and BlackBird move extremely fast, Maeve is able to teleport away from them just before their attacks can reach her. Similarly, Prince Armacaust and BlackBird are able to evade her energy blasts.

RahStar is able to teleport behind her, but Maeve uses a burst of light to blind him. RahStar is temporarily disoriented, giving Maeve an opening to blast him unconscious. Still, RahStar held Maeve's attention long enough for BlackBird to land a kick to her back.

Maeve tumbles across the floor, giving Prince Armacaust just enough time to fly up to her and grab her, pinning her arms to her torso. Though she is now genuinely worried that she may come to real physical harm, she wiggles her hands free and delivers a tremendous jolt of electromagnetic energy to Prince Armacaust's head, neck, and chest. Armacaust absorbs a significant amount of the energy but is quickly overwhelmed by Maeve's awesome power. He finally succumbs and drops toward the cavern floor. Dr. Step catches the rapidly falling prince.

"You boys fought well, but the time has come," Maeve says before her monologue is interrupted by a powerful blow from Princess Libby.

Constellation streaks past Libby and tackles Maeve in midair, pushing her into the cavern wall. Maeve attempts to block an incoming punch but is completely overwhelmed by Constellation's tremendous strength. The punch lands on the side of Maeve's face, throwing the back of her head into the cave wall.

Fighting to remain conscious, Maeve slides down the cavern wall toward the floor.

She teleports to the other side of the room before Constellation can connect with an energy blast of her own. Sensing another imminent attack, Maeve barely raises a force field in time before she gets plowed over by Z in her laser beam form. The beam splinters against Maeve's force field and reconstitutes on the other side of the cavern as Z regains her human form.

Suddenly, the ground beneath Maeve opens. Maeve maintains her position by catching herself in flight. A large stone hand reaches out of the ground and grabs her.

"Ugh … Criminy! Tenalach!" Maeve screams as she struggles to get herself free from the hand's grasp.

Maeve finally resolves that she is not strong enough to break the hand's grip. She teleports out of the hand just before Princess Libby can deliver another strike to her face. Maeve reappears on the opposite side of the cavern, but with her back to a wall. The Eshanashim contingent seems ready to pounce on her. And Maeve feels completely exhausted.

"I know when I'm beaten. To be continued!" Maeve shouts as she opens a gateway back to her castle.

The gateway closes, however, before she can enter it. Maeve looks up in astonishment.

"Unfortunately, young lady, you will not be going anywhere," Starlyte says dryly.

"In that case, I surrender," Maeve responds.

Maeve drops to her knees. She puts her hands up in the air. As Constellation and Gad walk toward her, Maeve teleports, but this time, she materializes back in her castle.

"Who was that?" Libby asks indignantly.

"Someone who will be hearing from us very soon," Gad says dryly.

*******High above Emba Soira, H soars miles into the sky and flies in the opposite direction from Apep. She streaks off so fast that he does not even hear the sonic boom until she reappears behind him, delivering a powerful strike to the back of his head. Apep tumbles several hundred feet through the air before he can gather himself. Again, before he can react, he is hammered by a blow from Hawwah.

This occurs several more times. Dazed and confused, Apep does his best to protect himself but realizes he cannot defend against what he cannot see. Then, it dawns on him: H is literally circling the globe and attacking him from various angles. His flesh explodes back into his monstrous form as Apep the Dragon, his ten heads scanning the horizon in all directions.

H finally slows herself enough for Apep to see her. She floats within a meter of him. They hover high above the Earth, staring at each other.

Each of the Dragon's heads begins to draw breath, but H is much quicker on the draw. She raises a hand and unleashes a massive bolt of electromagnetic energy that sends Apep tumbling across the entire continent of Africa and over the Atlantic Ocean.

H flies ahead of his listless body and grabs the beast's tail with both hands. She spins Apep around as if he were trapped in a super-powerful centrifuge and flings him toward the upper atmosphere. She streaks upward at incredible speed and delivers a punch to his midsection that launches the Dragon into low orbit above the Earth.

H again flies ahead of the Dragon's hurtling body. She draws ambient light to herself and fashions a giant collar connected to a chain. She uses her fantastic speed to bind all ten of Apep's heads in the collar and clamps it shut. She then uses the chain to pull Apep's heads so that he is forced to focus on her face.

The Dragon dissolves away. H disperses the chain.

"Well done," Apep says, rubbing his throat.

"Hmmm, I only have one thing to say to you," H says dryly.

In the blink of an eye, H flies close to The Challenger's head and whispers something in his ear. Apep's eyes grow dark. Although the seething rage becomes apparent in his face, Apep turns and streaks off into the void of space.

"Somehow, I don't feeeeeelllll like I won that fight," H thinks out loud.

CHAPTER 34
GATEWAYS AND GAMBITS

At the sports complex in Indianapolis, the Eshanashim children finally complete filing out of the gateway created by Princess Zilpha. Unbeknownst to them, the Leader, Racism, Circe, Rings, and Seth Zomibi were brought to the complex by Maeve before she engaged the Seven Sons.

Rings and Zomibi resume their operation of trapping young ladies. Circe causes a distraction within the massive assembly of kids by opening several canisters containing a powerful aerosolized sedative.

Merneith Grey engages Circe. Unfortunately for Merneith, Circe, an already formidable hand-to-hand combatant, benefits from the enhancements to her physical prowess that her battle suit provides. She easily overwhelms the young Merneith. And even though Merneith possesses the power of regeneration, Circe is still able to render her unconscious.

Circe continues her attack on the enhanced Eshanashim children. Circe charges Shaka and takes him down easily with a spinning sweep kick to the back of his feet. Solomon reacts swiftly but takes a punch to the face that knocks him unconscious.

Circe turns just in time to avoid being tackled by Sojourner but finds herself being bounced off a wall by one of Asenat's exploding orbs. Circe manages to fire a shot from her forearm blaster in Asenat's direction before she is forced to dodge Sojourner once again. Circe manages to roll out of the way before Sojourner crashes through the wall in front of which Circe was standing.

Circe stands to realize that her shot has not only struck Asenat, but that the young Eshanashim is lying still on the ground. Horrified that she actually hurt a child, Circe stops moving for a few seconds. This inaction proves costly.

A frustrated Sojourner finally connects with Circe on a lunge. Grabbing Circe around her waist, Sojourner flies through the wall on the other side of the corridor, using Circe as a shield. Sojourner wastes no time lifting Circe above her head and slamming her to the ground.

A rush of adrenaline allows Circe to stumble to her feet. Sojourner's onslaught becomes too fast for the now-injured Circe to defend against effectively. Sojourner is so strong that a simple shove throws Circe hundreds of feet across the room. Sojourner flies past Circe's body as it tumbles through the air and delivers a double-fisted blow into Circe's back that sends Circe through the floor.

With tears in her eyes, Sojourner begins to scream, "If you've hurt my sister—"

Sojourner is interrupted by Asenat's voice yelling, "Hey! SoJo! I'm all right. Come back over here. We need you!"

Sojourner flies to her sister's side. They lovingly bump foreheads and return to the main room. Asenat removes her right hand from her left shoulder to reveal where the laser shot by Circe struck her. The hole in Asenat's shoulder makes drawing a breath painful; nonetheless, she inhales and uses her vortex breath to blow the sedative cloud choking the Eshanashim children into an exhaust vent.

When the cloud clears, the teens realize several young ladies are missing from their group. On the lower level of the complex, the Leader and Racism collect the battered Circe.

****

Sphinx and The Gatekeepers arrive at Rhakotis Base, the headquarters of the Warp Star Authority.

Without revealing that she is holding Director Mandrake as a prisoner at The Gatekeepers HQ, Sphinx provides the access code delivered to her by King Armacaust. Seeing that Sphinx is the person requesting access, Senior Deputy Director Wubete Menewa does not even question or authenticate the access code provided.

"How may we help you, Princess?" she asks.

"My team and I need to review your logs, Director Menewa. May we land?" Sphinx responds.

The shield opens, and the SS Queen's Arrow proceeds to the landing zone. Once on the ground, the WSA security chief escorts Sphinx, Vixen, Gbeto, and Arisone to the main control room, where WSA Senior Deputy Director Wubete Menewa greets them. SDD Menewa walks straight up to Sphinx, looks at her rather sternly, then embraces her with a loving hug.

"It's been too long, Love!" she says with a smile.

"My apologies, Auntie," Sphinx responds with a warm smile. "We need to catch up, but right now, we have a situation."

SDD Menewa is the younger sister of King Armacaust's father, Khonsu. Their father, Abrax, was one of two physicians who worked tirelessly to save H during the journey from the Milky Way to Ant-Galaxo Devearous.

While Abrax was not on the bridge when Z, Starlyte, Monolith Ant, Aharon, Annipe Lassiterri Akhet, and Ahmose Pen-Nekhbet developed their paranatural abilities, others, like Abrax, Bastet filia Wepwawet, Baahir Callis Ankhesenamun, Aha Meketaten II, and Djoser Mandrake, all carry the genetic markers to produce enhanced offspring.

Sphinx fills the senior deputy director in on her suspicions that WSA Director Merneith Mandrake has been engaged in a conspiracy that led to the mass kidnappings of the missing Eshanashim children. Sphinx reveals that the children have been found on Planet Earth, but the extraction has been met with a lot of resistance.

SDD Menewa orders her team to provide The Gatekeepers with full access to WSA travel logs. Gbeto and Arisone work with Deputy Director Hannibal Seshperonch and his team to review the wormhole travel logs and structural analysis reports. Sphinx and Vixen interview the security team in an attempt to identify any anomalies in WSA operations.

After several hours, Arisone finds several inconsistencies in the logs. Dawit Menes, who leads the WSA cybersecurity operations, confirms the anomalies. Sphinx convenes a meeting between The Gatekeepers and the WSA leadership team to exchange information and bring everyone up to speed on what The Gatekeepers have found so far.

"If you're right, Princess, your investigation is leading you straight to the Convener's door," Deputy Director Eskender Meketaten offers.

Deputy Director Eskender Meketaten serves as a detective in the Intergalactic Patrol's investigative corps. He is permanently assigned to the WSA and acts as the WSA director of Security Services.

"Then it's time to call Mom," Sphinx replies. "But before I do, how would someone use the Warp Star to move so many children from different locations to one location in another galaxy?" Sphinx asks.

"They could use a 'clicker,'" Deputy Director Dr. Noah Saqqarah offers.

"What's a clicker?" Vixen asks.

"A clicker is a device that provides a location beacon for the warp gateway generator to lock onto a single article, person, group of items, or group of people, even if they are in different locations. The generator can then use the clicker's location to create a localized gateway to anywhere in the known universe. We use clickers in the field to conduct counterintelligence operations, especially when we need to bring a team conducting operations in separate locations back to base at the same time," Chief Biffu Ramses explains.

Chief Ramses leads the WSA Counterintelligence Team. She also serves as the second in command of all WSA security services personnel.

"But to move 33,300 people all at once would take a generator with a massive power source," Dr. Gelila Selamawit argues. "I mean, you could do that from here, obviously, pretty easily. But if you're not here, it would take someone with the power of Dean Starlyte to accomplish something like that. Plus, the likelihood of 33,000-plus devices all working properly at the same time is a marvelous engineering feat in and of itself."

Dr. Gelila Selamawit serves as the WSA Chief of Engineering. Dr. Selamawit is arguably the leading authority on warp generator technology. The university uses her papers as training material in its engineering course offerings. She is also the mother of the Memphisonian Envoy to the Giza Moon Colony, Waithe Selamawit.

Sphinx walks out of the conference, where The Gatekeepers continue to meet with the WSA leadership. She removes a device from a compartment on her belt. This special device emits a signal that can only be heard by Queen Hawwah, no matter where she may be in the Known Universe.

After a few minutes, H picks up on the alert. She focuses on the source of the signal and immediately puts herself in a meditative state. Once in deep meditation, H projects her astral form to Sphinx's location.

"Hotep, Daughter!" H says enthusiastically.

"Hotep, Mother!" Sphinx responds. "And remember, we talked about this. When I'm working, call me 'Sphinx.'"

"My apologies," the queen replies with a smile. "What do you have for me, Sphinx?" H asks in a more professional tone.

After listening intently to Sphinx recount how the structural integrity of several wormholes had been compromised over the last several days, H takes a moment to think.

"I only know of one person who could do that, and he's married to my sister. Besides, their youngest son happens to be one of the kids who was taken. Also, from what I have seen, I can confirm that most of these children were abducted from school. Plus, it certainly looks like the bad actors targeted children from the most prominent families across the solar system. The question becomes how they knew who to target," H responds.

Sphinx nods and tells H that is exactly where she is heading next. She just needed one final piece of info to confirm it. H tells Sphinx to keep digging and to call her back when she confirms what they both seem to be thinking.

Sphinx walks back into the conference room and pulls SDD Menewa to the side to tell her about Vixen's encounter with Director Mandrake.

"Where is she now?" SDD Menewa asks with concern in her voice.

"With your nephew and a special forces team from the PDFJC," Sphinx replies.

"Oh, God help her," the deputy director replies.

****

Back in the cave, H returns to her physical form. Prince Armacaust relates the evacuation plan to H and the Eshanashim delegation. Starlyte opens a warp gate back to the SS Long Arm. He invites the rest of the Eshanashim dignitaries who made the trip from Ant-Galaxo Devearous to be reunited with their children in Indianapolis.

With the rest of the Eshanashim dignitaries in tow, Starlyte opens a warp gate to the sports complex in Indianapolis. Once onsite, the Seven Sons begin conducting triage on the Eshanashim children. As a whole, the group is suffering from various minor injuries and a fairly significant dose of emotional trauma. Seeing his compatriots coughing and the structural damage caused by the battle between Sojourner and Circe, Prince Armacaust covers his mouth with both hands in disbelief.

"What happened here?" he asks.

"We were ambushed, Bro!" DwarfStar replies with a sigh.

Princess Zilpha begins to explain how they were attacked immediately upon arrival. Although their assailant was defeated, she apparently escaped. Zilpha further explained that several young ladies are also missing, including Addis Hor-Den.

"They took Addis HD?!?" Prince Armacaust exclaims.

The other teens begin to hang their heads remorsefully. Addis HK walks up to Prince Armacaust and takes his right hand, wrapping her other arm around his right arm. She buries her face in his shoulder and begins to cry.

Upon hearing that a trafficker has taken her daughter, Addis HD's mother, Professor Alpha Rho HorDen, drops to her knees and begins sobbing uncontrollably. Dr. Addisu Hor-Den kneels to try to comfort his wife. H walks over and wraps her arms around them both.

"Wait," Dr. Hor-Den shouts. "Where's our son?"

"I'm here, Dad!" Imhotep yells as he runs up to his parents.

H moves out of the way so that the Hor-Dens can receive their son. She looks up remorsefully at Z, who is wiping tears from her own eyes.

"Yes, they took her," Addis H says softly.

Prince Armacaust hangs his head and clutches Addis HK's hand tightly. A great sense of fear washes over the other Eshanashim dignitaries. H immediately takes the time to walk among the scores of children, hugging and kissing as many of them as she can.

Marshal Constellation rises into the air, frantically scanning the throngs of children. She finally hears a familiar voice shouting her name excitedly.

"Aunt Connie! Over here. Aunt Connie! We're over here!" Asenat, SoJo, Shaka, and Solomon yell in turn.

The intergalactic marshal streaks in the direction of the sound and finds Asenat, Sojourner, Solomon, and Shaka. Constellation hugs and kisses each of the four Menelik kids fervently.

"Oh, my God," Constellation exclaims, sobbing. "I'm so glad you're okay. I was so worried something had happened to you."

Seraphina stares at Constellation in disbelief. Shaka notices that Seraphina cannot take her eyes off the marshal.

"You okay?" he asks Seraphina.

"Marshal Constellation is your aunt?" she asks Shaka.

"I didn't mention that?" Shaka responds sarcastically.

Seraphina punches Shaka playfully in the shoulder as a response. They look at each other and laugh.

"She's only my idol," Seraphina says in a low voice.

"Let me introduce you," Shaka says, gently taking Seraphina by the hand.

Shaka and Seraphina look at each other and break into a blushing smile. Shaka introduces Seraphina to his aunt and proceeds to tell Constellation how brave Seraphina had been throughout the entire ordeal.

Seraphina blurts, "I'm like your biggest fan, Marshal!"

Constellation smiles with tears still in her eyes and grabs Seraphina in a huge hug.

"Thank you for helping to keep each other safe!" Constellation declares.

Seraphina closes her eyes and exhales. She hugs Constellation back. And for the first time in days, Seraphina feels safe.

Just when she releases Constellation, Seraphina sees her parents across the room. Seraphina can hardly contain herself. She runs as fast as she can toward her parents and leaps into her father's arms, almost knocking him over. Elder Shadd and Professor Kebede Hotep kiss and hug Seraphina as if they have not seen her in months.

Constellation and the Menelik kids walk over and introduce themselves to Elder Shadd and Professor Hotep. Elder Shadd gives each of the Menelik kids a big kiss on their foreheads.

"Thank you! Thank you! Thank you for taking care of each other!" Elder Shadd exclaims.

As soon as they see him, Nova and Twinkle run over to DwarfStar. Nova scoops DwarfStar up in a bear hug, squeezing him tightly. Twinkle wraps her arms around them both and nestles her face into DwarfStar's back.

"C'mon, guys. You're embarrassing me," DwarfStar says with a chuckle.

In reality, he does not want his parents to stop. Starlyte and Z locate Django. Z wraps her arms around his shoulders and begins to cry. Starlyte draws them both under his cape and kisses their heads repeatedly.

Kebret and Makeda Dawit locate Rajaa and Horo. They lovingly embrace them both. Makeda then bends down to ask Anippe if she can help Anippe find her parents. Anippe agrees. Makeda takes Anippe by the hand, and they begin to walk through the crowds. Kebret follows closely behind, holding both Rajaa and Horo tightly by the hand.

Ambassador Aberash Hotep and Lady Dani find President Sekhmet Djet Drone's children, Aster and Kebede. Lady Dani grabs them and hugs them so tight that Aster and Kebede begin to giggle.

"That tickles, Aunt Dani," Aster laughs.

"Well, I'm not letting go," Dani responds happily.

Senator Moses Garvey grabs Lady Fannie Lu's hand. They walk among the crowds of children, searching anxiously. Lady Fannie Lu cannot shake the fear that traffickers would take either of her children. She has lain awake for the past two nights, praying that she would see her precious daughter and son again.

"Moses, I just don't see them. I don't see them," she says in a worried tone.

"Don't worry, baby. Just keep lookin'," Moses replies calmly.

"Moses," Fannie Lu says, lips quivering.

"I know, baby. I know. We'll find them," Moses says.

"I know. Look," Fannie Lu responds, tears streaming from her eyes.

Moses looks up to see Brooklyn and Malcolm standing about fifty feet from them. He puts his free hand up to his face, covering his mouth. He and Fannie Lu begin to walk toward their children, slowly at first, then breaking out into a sprint.

Brooklyn and Malcolm see their parents running toward them and make up the rest of the distance, running toward their parents themselves. Moses drops to his knees and grabs both kids in a tight embrace. Fannie Lu folds herself over her husband's back and sobs uncontrollably.

"Oh, my God!" Moses shouts. "Thank you, God! Thank you!"

Moses' deep voice reverberates throughout the space. Brooklyn wraps her arms around her dad's neck. She cries loudly.

"Daddy, we were so scared," she cries.

"It's okay, baby. It's okay. We're here now," Moses reassures her.

Deputy Satellite increases her size so that she can get a better view and hopefully provide her children with a better opportunity to see her. Seeing her mother, Merneith zips through the air and wraps her arms around her mother's neck as if she were hugging a tree trunk. Satellite returns to her normal size. She kisses Merneith fervently and passes her to her father, RADM Torian Grey II.

Satellite rises back into the air and streaks toward the boys. She scoops them up and flies into the rafters of the sports complex. She twirls them around, laughing and kissing them. The twins giggle and squeeze their mom as tightly as they can.

"Daddy!" Addis H shouts.

Prince Bekele turns from his father, Prince Wepwawet. He would recognize that voice anywhere. He taps his wife, Captain Ayana PN Horus, on the shoulder. She looks up and sees their children standing not far off. Prince Bekele grabs Ayana's hand, and the couple sprints toward their children.

Addis H, Nekhbet, and Bekele II break out into an all-out run toward their parents. Bekele II arrives first. He is scooped up by his father, who squeezes him and kisses his forehead. Prince Bekele passes his son to Ayana. He stops. Addis H and Nekhbet stop in their tracks as well. Nekhbet breaks down in tears. Addis H begins to sob. Prince Bekele scoops his daughters up into his arms and holds them close.

"Oh, my darlings!" he cries. "I was so worried about you!"

Prince Montu and Prince Wepwawet fly over to Prince Bekele. Each places a hand on Prince Bekele's shoulders.

Captain Aha Jupiter finally locates the twins and his son. He runs excitedly back to Jenna.

"I found them, Love!" he declares.

For most of her life, Jenna has been lauded as one of the most beautiful women in the entire System. And many consider her to be the most beautiful woman in the System. Jenna does not mind the attention or the accolades. She married Aha mostly because she felt like he was one of the few men she had known in her life who genuinely loved her.

Jenna would much rather be known for her talents as a lawyer and her expertise as a legal scholar. But today, none of those things matter. She slips out of her shoes and follows Captain Jupiter through the throngs of people, holding her shoes in her hand.

Once she sees Aha II and the twins, Jenna drops her shoes and breaks into an all-out dash. She tackles Aha II. The twins leap on top of Jenna and their brother. The four of them roll around crying and laughing. Captain Jupiter removes his jacket and joins his family on the floor.

Seeing her cousin reunited with his parents, Fusion takes to the sky. She scans the crowd and sees her mother, the incomparable Admiral Dr. Ayana Powell Meketaten. Fusion flies back to her siblings, Ahmose and Den II. She wraps an arm around each of their backs and takes off again.

Fusion flies her siblings to their parents. Dr. Den Meketaten grabs the kids out of the air. He squeezes them lovingly. ADM Meketaten wraps her arms around her family and cries tears of joy. Dr. Meketaten pauses momentarily to ask about his younger sister, Abebe.

"Oh, no! I haven't seen her since we left the cave," Ahmose says, sounding worried.

"Let's go ask DwarfStar if he's seen her, Babe," ADM Meketaten says softly.

Den nods. He gives each of the kids another kiss on their foreheads before placing their feet back on the floor. The family begins to walk hand in hand over to Nova, Twinkle, and DwarfStar.

Prince Adisa and Elder Wells walk calmly through the throngs of children. Elder Wells stops suddenly, placing her hands over her mouth. Prince Adisa turns in the direction his wife is staring. Prince Imhotep and Princess Zilpha lock eyes with their father. Princess Zilpha immediately bursts into tears. Prince Imhotep runs to his father. Zilpha flies across the room straight into her mother's arms. The family stands huddled together in the middle of the large room.

Chief Justice Frederick Burghardt Shadd of the Chaosian Supreme Court and his wife, Carla Drone-Shadd, walked the entire floor of the sports complex without locating their son, Thurgood. Five-year-old Thurgood is somewhat small for his age. The Shadds are hoping they have simply missed him, as children are moving and shifting around in the crowd. Between other parents being reunited with their kids and the Seven Sons performing triage, the Shadds remain optimistic.

"Mommy," a tiny voice calls out.

Carla cannot contain herself. She melts into a puddle of tears. Chief Justice Shadd runs over and scoops Thurgood up into his arms. He rushes the boy back to his kneeling mother. Carla clutches Thurgood and holds him close.

"I'm not ever letting you go," she sighs.

After several hours, Mantis reports his preliminary medical findings to Gad, who sighs and shakes his head. H asks Gad to join her and Speaker Setepenre Djoser, leader of the Senate of Planet Memphis; Prince Montu of the Ant Planet; and Speaker JaneStar, leader of the Chaosian Senate, while the rest of the Seven Sons continue their triage efforts.

H apprises Gad and the planetary leaders that several young ladies remain missing, and she fears traffickers may have taken them. She further explains that Sphinx and the Gatekeepers were onsite at Rhakotis Base, searching for leads on the full list of co-conspirators behind this crime.

"And just where is this investigation leading?" Prince Montu asks assertively.

"Giza." H sighs. "Sphinx believes a connection exists between the children who were kidnapped and The Gathering, the private retreat hosted by the Convener a few years ago."

"What evidence does the princess have so far?" Speaker Djoser asks.

"She has determined that several anomalies exist in the Warp Star logs. And that none of the children taken live in any of the settlements or territories outside the solar system, which leads us to believe these children were targeted based on a single source, possibly a single database. Only one person owns a database that large and that specific," H explains.

"Well, my father should be apprised if Sebayt becomes a real suspect. He is going to want to know that," Prince Montu argues.

"Certainly," H replies. "We will also alert the IGP once we know more. For now, I want to make sure that all our governments are kept in the loop."

****

At a secondary base camp near Bahir Dar, Ethiopia, Rings catalogs the girls she captured from her work in the cave and at the sports complex. She has examined the genitalia of each of the girls to determine which of them may already be sexually active. Rings orders Zomibi to separate the sexually active girls from the virgins.

Of the thirty girls they captured, only three of them have had sex, according to Rings' examinations. Rings and Zomibi prepare each of the girls for transport by laying each of them supine on a mobile cot. They strap the girls to the cots and inject them with a liquid sedative.

"When you wake up, you will each be in your new home," Rings declares.

Zomibi laughs.

He continues preparing the girls by attaching a clicker to each of the mobile cots. Addis HD feels the sedative taking effect. She turns her head to take one last look at the young lady who cried on her shoulder back at the cave.

"Tell me your name. Tell me your name!" Addis shouts desperately through the gag.

"Abebe," the young lady cries back.

Addis's eyes shut slowly. The last thing she sees is Zomibi standing over Abebe with a delighted expression on his face.

****

After watching the Eshanashim delegation depart Emba Soira, the Grand Reverend returns to the cave. He walks through the entrance, surveying the battle damage. He would love to find genetic material he can use in his next experiment.

And he finds several mangled bodies, corpses still smoldering from being bathed in electromagnetic energy from one of the enhanced Eshanashim or engulfed in flames spewed by Apep the Dragon. The Grand Reverend removes a collection kit from his backpack. He takes out a scalpel, plus a box of cellophane bags, and begins collecting samples.

As he goes about his business, he hears faint groaning. He follows the sound and finds Abanoub Boateng lying face down on the cold cavern floor. Abanoub's upper body shakes violently as the severely injured mercenary struggles to move.

"Are you alive?" the Grand Reverend asks flippantly.

"I am," Abanoub answers. "I think my spinal cord has been severed. I cannot move my lower body, and I can only move my arms sporadically."

"Hmmmm, I think I can help you, my son. What would you be willing to do for my assistance?" the Grand Reverend inquires.

"Anything! Just get me out of here. I don't want to die here! Not like this," Abanoub cries.

"Very well," Grand Reverend replies. "If you pledge your soul to my master, the Morning Star, and your carnal body to me, I will not only get you out of here, but I will also help you claim your vengeance against those who did this to you. What do you say, my son?"

Abanoub manages to lift his head enough to look up at the Grand Reverend. Abanoub studies the expression on the Grand Reverend's face. He has heard rumors about a devil-worshipping scientist who develops genetically enhanced soldiers for parties throughout the System. Tears begin to stream from Abanoub's eyes as he realizes that the Grand Reverend is serious about the requirements of his offer.

"I hereby pledge my soul to your master. And I give my body to your service, from this moment and until I die," Abanoub mutters.

"Then, let us begin, my son!" the Grand Reverend declares.

****

Set Aha, Mina Seshperonch, and the Negus Brothers exit the cave on the opposite side from the entrance. The Negus Brothers take turns carrying Adrian Dawit, WarHorse, and K'Estiti. Ptah Mercury carried Sphinx Genet off under his own power and separated himself from Mina and Set's crew once outside the cave.

Descending the mountain, their party becomes instantly confused, as there seems to be a mountain where they expect to see the base camp.

"I'm telling you, that wasn't there before," Mina snaps.

"Unless it's a new volcano, that mountain didn't simply grow out of the ground, my dear," Set replies dryly.

"So, what do you suggest? How will we get home?" Mina inquires.

Set twirls his spear around in his hand and implants the tip into the ground. He removes his mask and walks over to Mina. Set grabs Mina around the waist with both arms. Mina reacts by attempting to break Set's grip.

"Release me!" Mina demands.

The Negus Brothers drop their loads and begin to advance on Set. Seeing that his arms won't budge, Mina stops resisting. She waves the Negus Brothers off. Set stares intently into Mina's eyes.

"What's the meaning of this?" Mina inquires.

"It's time we start our own crew," Set proposes.

"You and me?" Mina asks, laughing.

"Us and your men," Set replies.

Mina pauses. Observing her hesitation, Set lifts Mina so that their faces meet. Mina begins to breathe heavily. She stares into Set's eyes. She suddenly grabs Set's face and plants a passionate kiss on his mouth. Kissing him wildly, Mina begins to lick both sides of Set's face. Mina blinks. Her eyes change their shape and color.

"Just as I expected. A cannibal," Set declares delightedly.

Mina hisses. Her mouth remains open as she closes her eyes. She tilts her head back. Set can see fangs extend from both her top and bottom row of teeth. He lets out a loud laugh. He waits for a moment until Mina regains her composure. Both her eyes and teeth return to normal. Set sets Mina back on her feet and kisses her passionately. Mina reciprocates. They stop kissing after a few minutes and stare directly at each other.

"What gave me away?" Mina asks.

"Your body is cool to the touch. There is a Drāk named Kiram Hor-Khufu who is a human-snake hybrid like you. I'm sure you have heard of him by his other name, 'Hermes Love.' At any rate, sexual contact drives his cannibalistic inclinations. I only met Love once. My former employer was employed to clean up a mess he left. We watched the security recordings," Set explains.

"So, I take it that the kissing meant nothing to you?" Mina inquires.

"Quite the contrary, My Dear. I want you, all of you. I just had to make sure I knew what I was dealing with," Set explains.

Mina smiles. Set places his thumb tenderly on Mina's chin. He leans in and places his forehead against hers.

"Together, then?" Set asks.

"Together!" Mina declares.

"Gentlemen, what say you?" Set shouts without removing his head from Mina's.

"We'll follow where she goes," Tewagi responds.

"Then we have a crew, My Dear!" Set declares.

"How do we get off this rock, Darling?" Mina asks.

"I have an idea," Set replies. "It will involve trading the assassin and his son for passage back to the System."

Mina smiles. She then reaches up, grabs Set by his face with both hands, and kisses him passionately. Set wraps his arms around Mina, and the two continue to kiss for the next several minutes.

****

Just as H wraps up her briefing millions of miles away on Earth concerning The Gatekeepers' activities at Rhakotis Base, Arisone and Gbeto finally experience a breakthrough in their data mining efforts. They rush to Sphinx and tell her that someone at the WSA has been giving the kidnappers on Earth intel.

Sphinx and SDD Menewa review the logs together and discover that Deputy Director Hannibal Seshperonch has been deleting key evidence from the records. SDD Menewa orders

Deputy Director Meketaten to take Hannibal Seshperonch into custody.

Upon interrogation, Deputy Director Seshperonch reveals that he was coerced into working for the conspiracy by his nephew, Haile Seshperonch, the super assassin known as WarHorse. He relates that he does not know where the info on the families came from. Still, he does know that an Earth woman with red hair, calling herself "Miss Witch," was given access to the wormhole map, and that she is somehow able to tunnel into different wormholes and even predict where a new branch will open.

"This 'Miss Witch' sounds like a problem. Any idea where we can find her?" Sphinx asks Deputy Director Seshperonch.

"No, I don't know where she is, but she talks funny," Deputy Director Seshperonch replies.

"You can trace her wormhole activity, though, yes? Where did she start? You knew she was from Earth? How did you know that? Did she tell you, or did you track her movement through the wormhole network?" Sphinx asks in rapid succession.

"I don't know. I just figured she was from Earth because of the way she dressed and that accent," Deputy Director Seshperonch replies with a tone of stress in his voice.

"I'll be back. Don't go anywhere," Sphinx says sarcastically as she exits the interrogation room.

"Well, it looks like what we thought all along has been proven true. We only know one person with a database expansive enough and detailed enough to connect the dots for this scheme," Sphinx says to Vixen.

"The Convener!" Sphinx and Vixen say in unison.

Sphinx hails H again. Once H answers, Sphinx begins her update.

"Mother Dear, I think I found the branch we were seeking. But I will need a warrant to investigate further," Sphinx reports.

Sphinx goes on to explain that she needs to go to the Convener's compound to search for more evidence. Sphinx also provides a description of an Earth-bound woman with red hair, with powers similar to those of Dean Starlyte.

"Hmmm, I'm sending you a few boys who can help with this one. They call themselves the Seven Sons of Chaos," H responds. "And, Sphinx, no collateral damage. Sebayt is not likely to welcome this intrusion. Also, Monolith Ant's very angry with me. If he knows you are anywhere near his planet, he may try to test my resolve by being overly aggressive with you."

"When is he not angry with you, Mother?" Sphinx replies sarcastically.

H smiles and returns to her physical form in Indianapolis. H confers with Gad, who agrees that the Seven Sons will lend an assist to Sphinx and her team. H then gets Starlyte to warp the Seven Sons to Rhakotis Base.

Starlyte opens a warp gateway right into the WSA control room. The Seven Sons file through the gateway and enter the WSA control room, each of them looking around in wonderment at the advanced technology not available anywhere on Earth.

As she normally would, Sphinx takes inventory of the Seven Sons as they exit the gateway. However, for some reason, Sphinx locks eyes on Mantis as he enters. Sphinx's eyes glance over his twin brother but land squarely on Mantis. Her attention remains so captivated that she seemingly does not hear Gad introduce himself. Noticing Sphinx's stare, Vixen clears her throat.

"Welcome to Rhakotis Base," SDD Menewa says warmly to Gad, shaking his hand.

Vixen walks over to Sphinx. Noticing Vixen approaching her, Sphinx finally unmoors her gaze from the Praying Mantis.

"I know he's beautiful, but geeeeezzzz, Sis. Pull yourself together," Vixen says slyly.

"He is beautiful. Do you think anyone else noticed me staring?" Sphinx replies.

"Yes!" Vixen shoots back.

Unbeknownst to Sphinx and Vixen, Mantis can hear every word being spoken between them, but he does not give any indication that he has.

"Sounds like someone has a crush on you, Bro," Bird says to Mantis telepathically.

"You heard that?" Mantis inquires back telepathically.

"C'mon. Okay, no, I read their minds," Bird admits.

"STOP that!" Mantis shouts back telepathically to his twin.

Bird smiles slyly. Mantis walks over and stands next to Sphinx. Seeing that Sphinx cannot take her eyes off Mantis, Vixen begins to brief Gad, Batmyte, Dr. Step, and Crypto on the situation.

Crypto joins Gbeto and Arisone at the control panel. Arisone shows Crypto the signature of a wormhole with an origination point on Planet Earth.

"Step, get over here. Take a look at this," Crypto yells across the room.

Step walks quickly over to the monitor, takes a look at the screen, and turns to Crypto when he realizes the same thing Crypto has. The brothers shake their heads in unison.

"Ireland!" Dr. Step and Crypto shout together.

"That tracks, given her accent," Gad says dryly. "That's where we will find the lady who tried to kill us."

Gad, Batmyte, BlackBird, and Praying Mantis walk over to the monitor to view the wormhole analysis Arisone is working up for display. Coming back to her senses, Sphinx interrupts.

"Gentlemen, if you would be so kind as to accompany us on a little fact-finding mission first, we would be most appreciative," Sphinx declares.

"Yeah, I'm sure you will be very appreciative, Sis," Vixen whispers to Sphinx, giving Sphinx a playful bump with her elbow.

Sphinx notices Mantis chuckling at the comment. She smiles and pretends not to notice his reaction to Vixen's comment.

"He can hear you, Girl," Sphinx whispers back to Vixen.

Sphinx stands and walks away from Vixen to hide her embarrassment. Doubly embarrassed, Vixen radios Hammer aboard the Queen's Arrow.

"Uh … we're on our way back. Please make room for seven additional guests," Vixen orders.

"Copy that," Hammer replies.

Sphinx asks her great-aunt what will happen to Deputy Director Seshperonch. SDD Menewa explains that she and Deputy Director Meketaten will bring in the Intergalactic Patrol to investigate further. She wants to look into the situation further to determine if criminal charges are appropriate.

The venerable senior deputy director further explains that she has known Hannibal Seshperonch for more than a thousand years now and wants to offer him every opportunity to exonerate himself, especially since he was coerced into the conspiracy.

Sphinx agrees. Sphinx kisses SDD Menewa goodbye and leads The Gatekeepers and the Seven Sons to the SS Queen's Arrow.

****

As the Eshanashim children and their parents board one of the three starships that will transport them back to their home planet, Dr. Meketaten finally gets a chance to ask DwarfStar about the whereabouts of Abebe.

"You saw her, right? She was wearing a full-length blue dress. We couldn't locate her in the sports complex," Dr. Meketaten inquires.

A chill runs down DwarfStar's back. His face grows pale. He launches into the sky and rockets back to the sports complex. Memphisonian soldiers remain on the ground, collecting the remnants of their supplies and conversing with officials from Planet Earth.

"Abebe!" DwarfStar cries. "Abebe! Where are you?"

DwarfStar zips around the entire sports complex. He calls Abebe's name but receives no response. After several minutes of a fruitless search, DwarfStar streaks back to the SS Long Arm. He drops to his knees. Tears begin to stream from his eyes. Prince Armacaust runs over to his friend.

"What's wrong?" Prince Armacaust asks frantically.

"She's gone. They must have taken Abebe, too," DwarfStar mutters through his tears. "It's all my fault. I should have kept a better eye on her. How could I let this happen?" he sobs.

Dr. Meketaten walks over and kneels next to DwarfStar. Dr. Meketaten pulls DwarfStar close and hugs him tightly. DwarfStar continues to cry profusely. ADM Meketaten pulls

Ahmose, Fusion, and Den II close to her body. Dr. Meketaten and DwarfStar rock back and forth. Dr. Meketaten's own eyes erupt in tears.

"I'll get her back. I'll find her. And… I… will… get… her… back!" DwarfStar exclaims. "I promise!"

****

Having not found Anippe's parents among the crowd, the Dawits invite Anippe to join them on the SS Long Arm. They tell Anippe that they will take her home personally once they return to the System. Anippe looks sad but agrees. They board the starship and sojourn in a private cabin provided by CDR Ramses. Makeda begins to ask Anippe about her parents.

"Well, my mom is Kimboti Boateng," Anippe declares proudly. "And my granddad is Abrafo Boateng, the Leader of the Sea Tribe."

Overhearing the conversation, Kebret leans in and begins to listen intently.

"Hey, Sweetie, did I hear you say that your granddad is Abrafo Boateng?" Kebret asks.

"Sure is!" Anippe responds.

"Who's your father, Sweetie?" Kebret inquires.

"Well, I am not supposed to say anything, but he is an Ant Planet oligarch. His name is Abasi. He's a really big deal on his planet and on Giza," Anippe replies, her face beaming.

"Abasi?" Makeda asks with a tone of concern in her voice.

Makeda and Kebret look at each other, confused. Makeda shifts Horo and Rajaa to the other side of her body as she leans closer to Anippe.

"Is your father Monolith Ant, Dear?" Makeda asks.

"I'm not sure. I think I've heard Granddad call him that once or twice. Mom calls him Abasi. I have not met him yet. I wish I could. I hope he and I can meet real soon," Anippe declares.

"I hope so, too," Makeda replies.

Kebret and Makeda engage the kids until all three of them fall asleep. Once they are sure the kids cannot hear them, they recount what they heard Anippe tell them.

"Does this child belong to Monolith Ant?" Makeda asks her husband.

"I think so," Kebret replies.

"What do we do?" Makeda asks earnestly.

"We don't tell anybody. The last thing we want to do is get caught up in drama between the Edwesu Crime Family and the ruler of the Ant Planet," Kebret replies. "My goodness! This poor child has no idea who her family is," Kebret exclaims.

"For her sake, I hope she remains ignorant of that knowledge as long as she can," Makeda declares. "She's such a sweet little thing."

Makeda strokes Anippe's hair and kisses her on the top of her head. Kebret sighs and sits back in his seat. He reaches over and holds his wife's hand. He squeezes lightly to let her know that the two of them stand together in this. Makeda looks over to Kebret and smiles.

"This stays with us for now," she says softly.

Kebret smiles and nods his agreement. They both close their eyes and try to relax.

CHAPTER 35

CALL MONOLITH ANT

Many starship commanders across Ant-Galaxo Devearous believe the SS Queen's Arrow to be the fastest starship in the System. Its light-powered engines can achieve a maximum acceleration that exceeds the speed of light. The Queen's Arrow serves as the secondary transport for Queen Hawwah. On official diplomatic missions, the queen travels aboard one of the several luxury starships provided and crewed by the Planet Chaos Planetary Defense Forces Joint Command.

On her personal errands around the galaxy, H either flies herself or travels with The Gatekeepers aboard the Queen's Arrow. Its name derives from both the queen's aptitude for archery and its design. Sporting a "flying wing" design, the Queen's Arrow has a detachable saucer as its fuselage. It literally looks like an arrowhead. The Queen's Arrow features exceptionally strong blast shielding but carries very few weapons. And no other starship in the System can match the Queen's Arrow in maneuverability.

Taking off from Rhakotis Base on the Warp Star, Hammer pilots the Queen's Arrow into low orbit and awaits the signal to enter the warp gate that will take the ship to a location a mere ten thousand miles from the Giza Moon Colony, home to Professor Sebayt Loemba Menes, known to most as the Convener.

The Warp Star lies outside of the gravitational pull of the solar system's seven suns and is not actually a star at all. The Warp Star is a planet that lacks the size required to maintain the fusion that would otherwise allow it to become a star. The Warp Star does, however, lie at the mouth of a small nebula. Additionally, the Warp Star seems to be the nexus for billions of wormholes. Many Eshanashim scientists describe the Warp Star as the center of a spider web that reaches across the entirety of the Known Universe.

The planet is surrounded by several rings of warp gates that provide access to trillions of locations across the universe. Similarly, the surface of the Warp Star is littered with warp gates. A cluster of warp gates even lies just outside the orbit of the planet.

Rhakotis Base serves the dual purpose of research station and law enforcement outpost, monitoring and logging travel through the various wormholes connected to the warp gates on and around the Warp Star. Living conditions on the Warp Star are harsh, as the surface temperatures vacillate between too cold and too hot to support human life.

The twenty-seven thousand professionals who live and work at Rhakotis Base represent the three major planets in the System, having been appointed by their respective governments. The appointments to serve at Rhakotis Base are confirmed by the Galactic Security Council.

Hammer receives the signal, as well as the coordinates to the warp gate he needs to use. He directs the Queen's Arrow on that heading and begins the journey to Giza. Even at light speed, the flight time to reach Giza from the Warp Star would be seven hours. Traveling through the wormhole will save The Gatekeepers four and a half hours.

Aboard the SS Queen's Arrow, Mantis and Sphinx shyly exchange banter with each other as if they are on a first date. Sphinx touches Mantis's arm at one point during their conversation, but withdraws her hand when she realizes she might seem to be a bit too comfortable around him. Mantis touches Sphinx's hand to calm her. In doing so, his hypersensitive sense of touch detects the microscopic hair follicles that cover Sphinx's skin.

"Recombinant tiger DNA," Mantis thinks out loud as if reaching a moment of clarity.

"So, you're a geneticist?" Sphinx asks flippantly.

"Not exactly," Mantis says with a smile.

In an instant, Mantis transforms into his tiger form. Like Batmyte's apparel, the twins' nanotech battle suits conform to their bodily dimensions. While Batmyte can take the shape of any animal, insect, or microorganism, the twins' ability to shapeshift is limited to their singular animal form. The Praying Mantis can take the shape of a giant tiger with black fur and gold striping. BlackBird can take the shape of a giant Martial Eagle, which can further morph into a fire-breathing phoenix. Each of the twins grows stronger and more durable in their animal forms.

"I just recognize my own kind," Mantis growls.

Sphinx blushes at the gesture. She has gotten into the habit of avoiding men altogether. She rarely even pays any male who is not a member of her family much attention. But somehow, the

Praying Mantis has touched a part of her inner self that Sphinx thought she locked away decades ago.

"That's just about the sexiest thing she has ever seen," Vixen whispers to Gad with a smile.

"If you say so," Gad says, looking in the opposite direction and shaking his head with a devious smirk on his face.

"Wow! That's impressive. Now, I cannot do that. But I am a Drāk," Sphinx says with a tone of excitement in her voice. "Do you know this term, Drāk?" she asks, staring at Mantis, scanning for a reaction.

"Uhhhh … Drāk, short for Drakanashim, I take it? Other than that, I'm fuzzy on the concept," Mantis replies, returning to his human form.

"Ah, very good! You're not wrong," Sphinx begins. "My grandfather commissioned the first research program on combining human genomes with those of certain animal species. His name is Aharon Man-Drake." Sphinx emphasizes the ending syllable in her grandfather's surname. "So, people like Vixen and me are called Drāks," she declares with a nervous laugh. "Anyway, he's always been obsessed with replicating a certain … someone. His researchers found that the human-zebra hybrids can produce nearly cloned offspring."

While Sphinx delivers this explanation, both Dr. Step and Batmyte walk over to be educated on the details behind the origins of the Drākanashim. The two renowned scientists listen with engrossed attention as Sphinx continues her explanation.

"We are here, Chief," Hammer calls out to Sphinx.

"Comms on my location," Sphinx orders.

"Hotep, Princess! How may I help you?" the Convener asks.

"Convener, I need an audience. This is somewhat of a private conversation," Sphinx responds.

"Well, you can land about six klicks from the compound. I will send the boys to pick you up," the Convener responds.

Hammer directs Gbeto to follow the coordinates sent by the Convener and her staff. As the SS Queen's Arrow docks, Gad accompanies Sphinx to the airlock.

"Bird, you and Mantis stay here. Back us up if anything goes awry," Gad instructs.

"Sir," Bird responds, somewhat surprised.

"Step, stay with the twins. Myte, Rah, Crypto, you're with me," Gad orders.

Sphinx disembarks with Vixen, Mina, Hammer, Gad, Batmyte, RahStar, and Crypto in tow. Upon seeing the large landing party, Chacha Loemba, one of the Convener's personal bodyguards, snarls.

"We have orders only to retrieve the princess," Chacha snaps.

Chacha Loemba and his brother, Abuya, are two of the Convener's first cousins. Like the Convener, they are human-hippopotamus hybrids. Neither Chacha nor Abuya has much body fat, despite their hippo DNA. Both brothers can deadlift well over two thousand pounds. And Chacha stands at six feet, six inches tall, weighing in at a massive 375 pounds.

"Chacha," Sphinx replies somewhat seductively, "c'mon, you know how this works. Unfortunately, this is not a social call. My team comes with me. I promise. It will be like they are not even there," Sphinx coaxes.

Chacha's retort is cut short by the stern, gravelly voice of Lu Mabiala, the Convener's head of security.

"Let them in," Lu orders. "But only because it's you, Princess."

"Thank you, Lu," Sphinx sings.

Inside the compound, the Convener warmly welcomes her guests. Sebayt has made hospitality the chief component of her brand.

"Oh, this is a pleasant surprise, don't you know? Now, what's so pressing you had to come all the way here at this hour?" the Convener inquires.

Sebayt Loemba was born on the Giza Moon Colony to parents gripped by poverty under the oppressive regime of the Ant Planet Oligarchs. Settlers from the Ant Planet are allowed to claim homes or land owned and occupied by Drākanashim families, who are not afforded any recourse in the Ikwentashim courts. The interplanetary community looks on in horror as the Ant Planet settlement defense forces, known as the Giza Garrison, brutally enforce the segregation of the Drāks through fear, intimidation, starvation, and torture.

Neither Chaos nor Memphis intervenes out of concern for starting a war with the System's largest and most industrial planet. The Giza Authority Directorate, led by Neith Ramses, the WingDrake, provides some relief and protection to the Drākanashim living on Giza, but so much more needs to be done to ensure the freedom and security of the indigenous people of the Giza Moon Colony.

Although Sebayt faced such tumultuous conditions during her formative years, she rose through the Kemetic Mystery School System to earn the title of professor, the highest academic honor bestowed by the System's educational leadership upon those outside of the clergy. Sebayt is considered to be among the twenty-five most intelligent Eshanashim alive. She married her husband

and business partner, Dr. Baraki Hor-Aha Menes, right out of university and parlayed her intellectual prowess and academic achievements into establishing the largest data-mining operation in the System, amassing a huge fortune in the process. Her company also conducts the official census for each of the three major planets in the System. Sebayt is the third-wealthiest individual in the entire System.

Her Drākanashim physiology reflects a combination of human and hippopotamus DNA. Though her purplish-pink skin is made extremely soft by the abundance of fat cells her body naturally produces, Sebayt works very hard to control her weight. In fact, Sebayt's five-foot-six-inch frame presents as a very attractive, curvaceous woman. Sebayt is also notorious for disarming people with her genuinely pleasant demeanor.

She adopted the moniker "The Convener" as her company won the opportunity to organize and host The Conclave, the gathering of the most intellectually gifted Eshanashim from across the System. The Conclave sets academic standards for all Eshanashim learners in the System's version of the Kemetic Mystery School System, decides upon curriculum, and selects leaders to guide the educational system until the next Conclave convenes. However, the educational system is ultimately administered by the clergy, and the delegates to the Conclave act as independent arbitrators of truth and knowledge.

Sebayt used this success to develop "The Gathering," an invitation-only, twenty-one-day retreat to be held only once each century to allow the most influential families across the System to network and conduct a bit of matchmaking. The inaugural Gathering was held two years ago, in Year 9313, at the resort connected to the Convener's compound on Giza. Both Sphinx and her sister, Nefertiti, attended the retreat, Sphinx representing the Amun Family and Nefertiti representing the Djoser Family.

"Sebayt," Sphinx begins. "You know I'm a huge fan."

"So huge," Vixen chirps.

"I have to ask, though, has anyone hacked into your database recently?" Sphinx asks, shrugging her shoulders.

"Oh, no! That could not ever happen! We have the tightest cybersecurity protocols in the entire solar system. Maybe in the whole galaxy, don't you know," the Convener responds.

"Which is why it was so weird that several of the kidnapped children were tied so closely to families that attended The Gathering a few years ago," Sphinx says directly.

"Weird? Neith! Has someone hacked our database?" the Convener yells frantically.

The Convener's younger sister, Neith, walks closer from an adjoining corridor. Neith is three minutes and several seconds older than her twin sister, Hajera, who elects to remain out of sight during this exchange.

"That's impossible, Ma'am. Our system has no vulnerabilities," Neith responds.

"Would you mind if we tried to crack it?" Gad offers calmly.

"Yes, yes, I mind!" the Convener exclaims.

The Convener begins to pant as if she is having a heart attack. Sphinx walks over to the Convener and calmly places a hand on the Convener's shoulder. Lu steps in closer. His ever-present partner, Unatti Hor-Den, takes a position between Sphinx and her landing party. Gad begins to take inventory, as more of the Convener's security personnel continue to fill the room.

"We're not here to accuse you of anything, Sebayt. We need to know who assisted the kidnappers," Sphinx says softly.

"It was her," Bird exclaims, revealing himself and pointing at Neith.

He and Mantis were in the room for most of the conversation. The twins had stayed out of sight by using their invisibility and camouflage abilities.

"Whoa! Where did you come from?" the Convener exclaims.

"Everybody, calm down," Sphinx says gently but insistently, trying to regain control of the situation.

Neith takes a look at Bird, then turns and runs into the adjoining hallway. The Convener raises a hand as if to get Neith to stop. But before she can get out a word, the fight begins.

"Runner!" Mantis exclaims excitedly.

Before he decides to move, Mantis is grabbed by Unatti Hor-Den, the six-foot, seven-inch elephant-human hybrid Drākanashim. Unatti delivers a powerful overhand right to Mantis's jaw, sending him flying across the room and crashing through a wall.

"Oh!" the Convener exclaims.

Lu Mabiala, a six-foot, five-inch gorilla-human hybrid Drākanashim himself, immediately steps in front of the Convener and begins to discharge the two radiators he pulled from his back holsters. Shots from Lu's radiators, deflected by Bird's shield, shatter priceless artifacts and ruin pieces of art around the room.

"Not in the house, Lu!" the Convener screams frantically.

Sphinx and Vixen use acrobatic maneuvers to evade the ricochets with ease. RahStar teleports behind Lu and applies the Sphinxman's grip. Instead of falling unconscious, Lu leaps backward, slamming RahStar into an adjoining wall. RahStar holds on to Lu despite the large Drāk's continued attempts to dislodge him.

Gad calmly increases the pull of gravity on the Makaya brothers, who walked into the room behind him only moments earlier. The Makaya brothers drop onto their hands and knees, paralyzed by their increased weight. Absko Teke throws a punch at Batmyte. His wrist bends violently as Batmyte catches it and quickly applies a wrist lock. Batmyte leverages the wrist lock on the much larger Absko to throw him across the room. Absko tumbles awkwardly into the Makaya brothers.

Mina draws her swords and engages Unatti. The towering Unatti finds it difficult to land a blow on Mina, who manages to pierce Unatti's right leg with one of her blades. Unatti kneels in pain. Vixen delivers a kick to the back of Unatti's head that bows Unatti even more. Batmyte removes one of the acupuncture needles from his belt and inserts it into a spot on the back of Unatti's neck. Unatti freezes in place, her muscles paralyzed.

"Wow! That's impressive," Vixen exclaims.

In the next room, Mantis handsprings back to his feet. Abuya immediately attacks him. Mantis evades or blocks the bevy of punches and kicks delivered by Abuya. Mantis takes a step back and inhales briefly. He holds his breath, waiting for Abuya's next move. Seeing Mantis pause, Abuya advances. Mantis exhales, blowing a stream of wind that throws Abuya through the same hole Mantis's body made in the wall. Abuya crashes into his brother Chacha, who was contending with BlackBird.

Sphinx takes off after Neith and has no trouble running her down. Before Sphinx can immobilize Neith, she is kicked from behind by Zuri Teke, the Convener's head geisha. The geisha in the Convener's employ are not only highly trained in the art of pleasure, but they are also highly skilled martial artists and expert knife fighters.

Sphinx rolls across the floor and back to her feet. She stares angrily at the tall and beautiful Zuri, who grins deviously back at her. Sphinx surges forward but must immediately dodge a kick coming in from her left. The kick was delivered by Malaika Luba. Sphinx sniffs the air and turns quickly to block a punch thrown by Lerato Tshokwe, the third geisha working in the Convener's organization.

"Three against one, huh?" Sphinx mutters. "Lovely. Bring it, ladies!"

Zuri and Malaika advance.

Sphinx wraps her arm around Lerato's arm and swings her into the path of a left jab being thrown by Zuri. Sphinx releases Lerato as she drops and snatches Malaika off her feet.

Rocking onto her back, Sphinx places her feet into Malaika's midsection and forcefully extends her legs, launching Malaika down the hallway. Neith's head and eyes follow Malaika's body as she sails over Neith's head. Malaika crashes hard into the floor.

Zuri leaps at Sphinx, who handsprings herself over Zuri's outstretched body. Sphinx lands, then dives forward into a roll that takes her to the opposite side of the hallway. Zuri rolls backward and onto her feet.

Sphinx and Zuri stare at each other, standing in their fighting positions.

Zuri advances.

Sphinx hops onto the wall to evade Zuri and delivers an overhead right hand to the side of Zuri's head. Zuri slams into the wall on the opposite side of the hallway.

Sphinx notices Neith standing at the end of the hallway in front of her. Neith turns and runs.

Sphinx resumes the chase.

Zuri hurls a knife at Sphinx's back. As if she has eyes in the back of her head, Sphinx turns, plucks the blade from the air, and flips it into the back of Neith's left leg. Neith slides to the ground.

Malaika steps between Neith and Sphinx.

Sphinx slides underneath a punch thrown by Malaika and uses a leg bar to take Malaika down. Sphinx once again handsprings herself back onto her feet, blocking a kick by Zuri.

Sphinx uses a jumping knee strike to finally knock Zuri unconscious.

"Okay, Neith. Where were we?" Sphinx asks flippantly.

Sphinx grabs Neith by her collar and slaps one of the "Chokers of Truth" onto Neith's neck. Each Choker of Truth works like a slap bracelet powered by AI-enabled nanites that produce an electrical charge. Once applied to a subject, Sphinx controls both the tension and the amount of voltage via a dial on the back of the glove on her right hand. These chokers can also be detonated, should the need ever arise for this tool to be used as an explosive.

"Neith, tell me everything," Sphinx says with a wry smile.

"I will not," Neith is interrupted by the choker tightening and delivering tiny but nasty jolts of electricity.

"Let's try this again, shall we?" Sphinx replies, her hand holding steady on the choker dial.

Neith remains silent. Frustrated, Sphinx turns up the voltage. Neith begins foaming at the mouth. Batmyte walks over and raises a hand.

"Allow me," he says calmly.

Batmyte removes another acupuncture needle from his belt. He removes the choker and inserts the needle into Neith's shoulder. Neith's eyes open wide.

"Neith, did you supply data to someone seeking information regarding the System's most influential families?" Batmyte asks.

"Yes," Neith responds.

"Why would you do something like that?" Sphinx asks.

"Someone promised me a bunch of money if I just gave them the location of certain families and info on any children in their families under the age of nineteen. I didn't think anyone would get hurt," Neith answers.

"Who asked you for this information, Neith?" Sphinx asks.

"I don't know. He was tall and mysterious. He said he was connected to some powerful people," Neith answers.

Sphinx puts the chocker back into the compartment on her belt. She looks at Batmyte with a satisfied expression on her face. She gives Batmyte an enthusiastic high five. Batmyte removes the acupuncture needle and places it back into the holster on his belt.

"Hammer, please take Neith into custody," Sphinx orders.

Hammer immediately walks over and binds Neith's hands. Neith's twin sister, Hajera, bursts into the room in which a very confused Convener remains standing. She runs over to the Convener and begins pleading with her to prevent The Gatekeepers from taking Neith away.

"I am in on it, too, Sis," Hajera cries hysterically.

The Convener thinks for a moment. She looks around at the damage to her home, the ease with which The Gatekeepers and the Seven Sons defeated her security team. She wants to do the right thing, but she cannot stop thinking about the promise she made to her mother.

"Wait!" the Convener screams. "Oh, no, no, no, no, Princess, I can't let you take my sisters. I promised our mother I would look after them after she passed. I need to get them a solicitor! Please leave. Bring back a proper warrant, or you cannot take them anywhere!"

"Them?" Gad asks.

"Lu, call Abasi," the Convener shouts.

Seeing the confusion on Lu's face, the Convener repeats herself.

"Lord Monolith," the Convener declares.

Lu still does not react.

"Oh, for Pete's sake! Call Monolith Ant. Do it now!" the Convener screams at the top of her lungs.

"Alright!" Sphinx yells, throwing up her hands. "To avoid an interplanetary conflict, I will leave your sister, or it looks like both of them are involved, so sisters here under your watch. But you will be held accountable if they disappear, Sebayt," Sphinx says sternly. "Gatekeepers, Seven Sons, let's go!" Sphinx orders.

The Gatekeepers, along with the Seven Sons, begin to file out of the compound. Gad lingers behind momentarily, staring sternly at a sobbing Convener.

"Nice punch," Mantis shouts to the panting Unatti, still kneeling on her injured leg.

Batmyte walks over and calmly removes the needle from her neck. Unatti collapses to the ground.

Gad walks over to Sphinx and pulls her close to him by her arm. Gad glares into Sphinx's eyes. Sphinx indignantly returns his gaze.

"We're leaving?!?" he whispers gruffly to Sphinx.

"Yes," Sphinx replies, now looking away from Gad. "If we do not leave, Chaos and Ikw-n-tA could end up at war. It's better if we go. Mom can sort this later, either diplomatically or through the courts. Moreover, you should have told me that your brothers were going to be in the room, visible or not. You compromised this mission. And one more thing, Gad. Let go of me, please. I do not like to be pulled at."

Sphinx locks eyes with Gad after her final statement. Gad releases her arm and takes a step back. Back aboard the SS Queen's Arrow, Sphinx debriefs the queen on the incident at the Convener's compound.

"Oh my," H sighs. "Okay. It looks like this is only the beginning," H ponders.

Sphinx sinks into her chair and lets out an audible sigh.

"Lovely," Sphinx exhales.

Two hours later, the atmosphere aboard the SS Queen's Arrow remains tense since its crew and guests departed the Convener's compound on Giza.

Immediately following her conversation with the queen, Sphinx delivered a stern reprimand to the Seven Sons during the team's mission debrief. The Gatekeepers rarely experience Sphinx unleashing such vehement criticism.

Gad offered several apologies for his miscalculation. Hammer even offered his own defense for the Sons' actions. Nothing seemed to calm Sphinx.

Following the debrief, Vixen and Mina decided to remain in the rear cabin with the Seven Sons.

Sphinx returned to the bridge and remains slumped in her captain's chair while her feet, crossed at the ankles, rest on the console in front of her. She watches the myriad streaks of light pensively as the Queen's Arrow streaks through deep space at the speed of light.

Sphinx shakes her head every few minutes, as if she is engaged in a private debate with herself.

The trip back to Planet Chaos will take a few more hours to complete. And no one has made a sound for the last ninety minutes.

The Praying Mantis decides the time has come to break the silence. He stands and straightens his belt and cape. BlackBird reaches up and grabs Mantis's hand. The twins lock eyes. BlackBird shakes his head to signal "no." Mantis responds by returning a playful wink. The twins begin a telepathic conversation.

"Just give her some time," Bird suggests telepathically to Mantis.

"I got this," Mantis argues back.

"Okay. Don't get thrown out of the airlock," Bird laughs.

Mantis accidentally chuckles out loud at his brother's joke.

Sphinx twists her chair around and glares in Mantis's direction. Seeing the annoyed expression on her face causes Mantis to clear his throat nervously. He notices Vixen and Mina giggling quietly to themselves. Vixen shakes her head with a wide grin on her face.

Mantis waves playfully at Vixen as he walks toward the bridge.

Sphinx twists her chair around once again when she hears Mantis's footsteps. She sighs and turns her back to him.

Undeterred, Mantis continues his advance.

Sphinx puts her feet back on the floor. She taps a button on her console. The cabin blast doors begin to shut.

Using his superspeed, Mantis zips onto the bridge just before the doors shut.

"That was rude," Mantis says jokingly.

Sphinx turns her chair completely around to face Mantis. The expression on her face reveals her complete surprise.

"So, you're fast, too?" Sphinx says sarcastically.

"I don't know how to take that, so I guess, 'yes,'" Mantis replies.

Sphinx turns her back to Mantis and pretends to check instruments on her console. She wants to engage, but she cannot help feeling responsible for the debacle that occurred at the Convener's compound.

"What can I do for you, Mantis?" Sphinx asks coldly.

"I was thinking you might want to have coffee with me sometime in the nearish future," Mantis replies.

Sphinx freezes. She cocks her head to the side. Then, turning her chair completely around, she locks eyes with Mantis. Sphinx leans forward and presses her palms and fingertips together. Anticipating another epic tongue-lashing to be incoming, Hammer stands and walks away from the pilot's station. Sphinx watches Hammer exit the bridge through her peripheral vision before addressing the Praying Mantis.

"So, you want to ask me out on a date. Now? Like that makes sense to you in this moment?" Sphinx inquires dryly.

"I literally do not know how much longer this trip will take. So, yeah, I just figured no better time than the present," Mantis replies stoically.

"Ummm … I see," Sphinx responds, looking down at the floor. "How old are you?" she asks flippantly.

"Eighteen," Mantis replies confidently.

Sphinx lets out an exasperated laugh. She shakes her head in disbelief. Propping her elbows upon her knees, she leans forward to place her face against her interlaced fingers. She flashes the Praying Mantis a discerning look. Keeping her fingers interlaced, Sphinx slides her hands to the side of her face.

"What makes you think I would even consider going on a date with you?" Sphinx asks huffily.

"Well, you think I'm beautiful. That's, at least, a start. I think you'll find that I'm also funny," Mantis answers.

"Oh, you're hilarious. I can tell. Do you know that in my culture, I am what's referred to as an 'Ancient'? I was born before what you on Earth call the 'Common Era.' Yeah, I was alive before the birth of Christ," Sphinx replies flippantly.

Mantis takes a deep breath and smiles. He can sense that Sphinx enjoys his company. He can also sense her unresolved anger, which Mantis attributes to the possibly looming difficulty involving interplanetary politics between Planets Chaos and Ikw-n-tA. He attempts to tread lightly.

"Well, I think I understand your concern. But if my math is correct, you will likely live another fifteen hundred years or so. And your physiology allows you, and most Eshanashim women, to give birth to children at virtually any point during your lifetime. As a so-called 'enhanced' myself, my lifespan will likely match yours, so long as I don't manage to get myself killed. I mean, like you, I do have a fairly dangerous occupation. So, we seem to have a lot in common," Mantis argues.

"How do you know so much about us?" Sphinx inquires.

"Oh, I spent several hours talking to a group of lovely Eshanashim children and their parents at a stadium in Naptown," Mantis responds with a laugh.

"What's 'Naptown,' did you say?" Sphinx asks.

"It's a city on Earth in a place called Indiana. Anyway, the point is, I may not possess the same breadth of life experience as you, but you and I share something I surmise you have yet to find in the men you encounter on your planet," Mantis retorts.

"And you want to have children, do you?" Sphinx asks flippantly.

"Yeah, one day," Mantis answers earnestly.

Sphinx manages to contain her delight as she continues to banter. She loves it when a man in whom she is interested shows a genuine interest in her. She hates creeps, men who are overly aggressive or impatient, especially those who offer her things she can otherwise provide for herself. In fact, she would rather that men not offer her anything at all. For the most part, Sphinx would rather just be left alone. Still, she finds Mantis to be sincere in his attempt to connect with her. So, she decides to continue the conversation.

"How would we even do this? We live billions, that's 'billions' with a 'B,' miles apart?" Sphinx asks.

"See, you didn't say 'no.' I thought about that. I have a brother who can bridge any two points along the space-time continuum almost instantly. In fact, we are definitely using a gateway to get home. And you're a princess, a member of the royal family of Planet Chaos. I am sure you have access to a warp gate or two," Mantis argues.

Sphinx sighs. Though she tries to resist, a bright smile spreads across her face. She swivels her chair back to her console.

"I'll think about it," Sphinx says with her back turned to the Praying Mantis.

"Outstanding! I'll take that," Mantis responds excitedly.

Sphinx presses the button on her console that controls the cabin doors. The blast doors open. Mantis smiles and begins to saunter back to the rear cabin. Hearing her chair move, Mantis stops and turns his head back toward the bridge.

"Tell you what. If you can make it back here next week, I'll meet you for tea. I don't drink coffee," Sphinx says.

"It's a date, then," Mantis replies confidently.

"Hmmm …" Sphinx retorts.

She swivels her chair back to face her console.

Mantis walks past Vixen, giving her a playful wink, and retakes his seat next to BlackBird.

Vixen leaps out of her seat and runs to the bridge. She cautiously approaches Sphinx, who remains facing forward. Sphinx has her left elbow propped upon the console while she bites on her left thumb.

Vixen takes a seat at the station next to Sphinx.

The two friends look at each other.

Sphinx, again, closes the blast doors.

As soon as the doors shut, Vixen and Sphinx erupt into uncontrollable laughter.

"Did I hear correctly? You're actually going on a date with an actual human person?" Vixen entreats.

"We'll see. He has to make his way back here next week," Sphinx replies with a giggle.

"OMG! You like him!" Vixen exclaims.

"Sadly … I think I do," Sphinx replies.

"Sadly?" Vixen retorts.

"For him. You know how possessive I can get," Sphinx responds with a laugh.

Fin.

EPILOGUE

As the Eshanashim delegation continues their preparations to depart Planet Earth, H introduces Minister Chaos to Gen. Mohammed Sobhi. The minister arrived mere hours ago and has been engaged with Lt. Insp. Menes and his crew aboard the SS Long Arm since landing in Egypt. Minister Chaos smiles warmly at his counterpart.

"Minister Chaos, it's a pleasure to meet you," Gen. Sobhi says in English. "There are some who say you're a myth. Others suggest you're a dangerous terrorist."

"And you, Minister? What do you say?" Minister Chaos inquires.

"Me? I think you're like me. You fight for the freedom and safety of your people. Things inevitably get messy from time to time in our business," Gen. Sobhi replies.

"I'm glad we understand each other. And it's an absolute pleasure to make your acquaintance," Minister Chaos replies.

The two men exchange a hearty handshake.

H smiles. She watches as the Long Arm shuttle lifts off the ground.

"Well, gentlemen, that's my cue," H declares.

"I will leave you in the more than capable hands of Minister Chaos, whom I hereby appoint as my representative on Planet Earth," H says to Gen. Sobhi.

H places her right hand over her heart and bows slightly before Gen. Sobhi. The general nods his acknowledgment. H turns to Minister Chaos, smiling warmly.

"It's so good to meet you finally. Your boys are headed to my place, by the way. I will send them back to you soon. I promise," H says.

"Understood, Mother. And they're your boys, anyway. We all are," Minister Chaos replies, smiling.

H wraps her arms around Minister Chaos and hugs him tightly. Minister Chaos closes his eyes and hugs H back.

"Take care, My Son," H says, her face beaming.

H releases Minister Chaos and gives him a playful wink. She rises into the air and ascends rapidly into the open shuttle bay on the SS Long Arm. The shuttle bay closes, and the SS Long Arm begins to advance skyward. The other Memphis and Ant Planet starships follow the Long Arm's lead.

Military and media aircraft follow closely behind the three Eshanashim starships as they climb swiftly into the upper atmosphere, eventually disappearing. Gen. Sobhi watches in astonishment as the starships depart, his left hand shielding his eyes from the glaring sun. He shakes his head in disbelief.

He turns to Minister Chaos and places his right hand on Minister Chaos's left shoulder. The two men begin to walk to a caravan of military vehicles barricading a crowd of reporters shouting questions and taking pictures. Gen. Sobhi stops walking and turns to Minister Chaos. A very serious expression spreads across his face.

"Her representative on Earth?" Gen. Sobhi inquires in his thick Egyptian accent. "I just have one question, then. Who or what is this Queen Hawwah Menewa?"

Minister Chaos takes a deep breath and exhales. A smile creeps over his face as he looks skyward in the opposite direction of the sun and explains, "However Hawwah came to exist, whether by an explosion caused by colliding particles or a voice calling out into the darkness, she was, at one time, the canvas upon that which we understand to be the 'Known Universe' was painted. Then, she became human. She became human, but she retained her access to the energy, the very power, that brought her into being and allowed her to give birth to all things. She is the one whom ancient Greeks called 'Kaos,' the same one whom people in this part of the world referred to as 'The Great Khairunnisa.' In fact, throughout human history, she has been known by many names: Eve, Neithhotep, Renpetneferet, Hatshepsut, Ruth, Marie-Cessette Dumas, and Huru-Nala Powell. Who is she? She is Hawwah, the 'Bearer of Life,' the 'mother of all living'!"

ABOUT THE AUTHOR

Amir Clayton "AC" Powell loves God, family, the law, and politics. He connects with people across cultural, generational, political, and socioeconomic barriers. In fact, AC became a dynamic organizational development guru by heeding his mother's advice to always listen more and talk less.

Infusing this philosophy into his leadership style guided AC's success in various senior management roles in nonprofit organizations, as well as in his entrepreneurial endeavors. He has provided executive direction and compliance leadership to nonprofit organizations and start-ups for more than twenty years.

AC speaks with passion, depth, and a bit of humor about issues concerning African American males, climate change and mitigation, criminal justice, leadership, small business and nonprofit management, voting rights, spirituality, workforce development, and the pivotal position of the Hip Hop Generation in the American sociopolitical landscape.

This Hoosier turned Washingtonian and self-described wannabe New Yorker lives on the Northern Virginia side of the DMV. Follow AC on Instagram at @aclaytonpowell or Bluesky at @amirclaytonpowell.bsky.social.

www.ingramcontent.com/pod-product-compliance
Lightning Source LLC
LaVergne TN
LVHW010050110826
845155LV00028B/280

* 9 7 9 8 9 9 6 4 1 5 2 0 5 *